Daring men, tempestuous women, they roamed Australia's wild open spaces in search of glory . . . and gold

BIG MICHAEL CADOGAN—Betrayal made him a prisoner in Tasmania's cruelest prison. Escape made him a rogue hero, forced to keep running or die.

KITTY CADOGAN—The search for her brother sent the raven-haired heiress from Ireland to the outback, where secrets swept her from a new love's arms into a crossfire of crime and shame.

JOHNNY BROOME—Burning passion drove the young journalist into dangerous territory where a shocking, hidden truth threatened his career and his life.

JENNY BROOME—Blind trust in her new husband, Colonel William De Lancey, carried her to an exotic land to face the ultimate test of her commitment to her country, her courage, her heart.

NANA SAHIB—A cunning smile hid an insatiable bloodlust as he lured the unsuspecting British into a deadly snare.

THE GALLANT

VOLUME VIII OF THE AUSTRALIANS

William Stuart Long

A DELL BOOK

Created by the producers of
The Kent Family Chronicles,
Wagons West, and Stagecoach.

Chairman of the Board: Lyle Kenyon Engel

Published by
Dell Publishing
a division of
Bantam Doubleday Dell Publishing Group, Inc.
666 Fifth Avenue
New York, New York 10103

Produced by Book Creations, Inc.
Chairman of the Board: Lyle Kenyon Engel

ISBN: 0-440-12785-8

Printed in Canada

July 1986

10 9 8 7 6 5 4 3 2

WFH

This book is dedicated to the memory of a young Australian, known most deservedly as "Brave Charlie," who, very sadly, lost a gallant battle against cancer.

To me, Charlie was the epitome of gallantry; I felt privileged to know him, and I shall never forget him for the courage he displayed in that long struggle, which, in the end, took his young life.

Acknowledgments and Notes

AS ALWAYS, I acknowledge very gratefully the guidance received from Lyle Kenyon Engel in the creation of this book, as well as the cooperation and help of the editorial, research, and publicity staffs at Book Creations, Inc., of Canaan, New York, and in particular that of my editors, Philip D. Rich and Glenn Novak. I also greatly appreciate the friendship and encouragement so generously given by Marla and George Engel, Carol Krach, Jean Sepanski-Guarda, and Mary Ann McNally.

I should like also to put on record my appreciation of the help given me by my British publisher, Aidan Ellis of Aidan Ellis Publishing Ltd., by Dell USA and Macdonald Futura UK, the paperback publishers, and by the distributors of the Australian editions, Doubleday Australia Pty. and Hodder & Stoughton Australia. On my recent visit to Sydney I had reason to be most grateful to Ian Parry-Okeden of Radio 2 UE, to the Sydney booksellers in general and to Selwa Anthony in particular, and to the staff of Doubleday Australia for their hospitality and support. It is my hope that I shall be able to join the bicentennial celebrations in Sydney in 1988, reliving the story of the characters, both real-life and fictional, that I wrote of in the first book in *The Australians* series, *The Exiles,* while being reunited with my much-loved Australian family in Hunters Hill and my good friend and invaluable Australian-based researcher, Vera Koenigswarter.

The main books consulted included: *The Australian Encyclopaedia:* Angus & Robertson, 1927; *The History of Tasmania:* J.

West, Dowling, 1852; *Transported:* Christopher Sweeney, Macmillan, 1981; *History of Australia:* Marjorie Barnard, Angus & Robertson, 1962; *The Gold Seekers:* Norman Bartlett, Readers Book Club, 1965; *New Zealand:* Richard Horsley, T.C. & E.C. Jack, 1912; *Australian Historical Monographs* (various titles): edited by George Mackaness, Ford, Sydney, 1956; *Notes of a Gold Digger:* J. Bonwick, 1852, reprint; *The Indian Mutiny in Perspective:* Sir George MacMunn, Bell & Sons, 1931; *Government State Papers* (Lucknow and Cawnpore): edited by G.W. Forrest, Military Department Press, Calcutta, 1902; *The Sepoy War:* Sir Hope Grant and Henry Knollys, Blackwood, 1873. I have also taken the liberty of adapting, from one of my earlier works, material pertaining to the Sepoy Mutiny of 1857-8.

With the author's generous permission, I made extensive use of *Punishment Short of Death* by Margaret Hazzard, Hyland House Publishing, Melbourne, 1984. This meticulously researched history of the penal settlements of Norfolk Island gives a view of the last commandant, John Price, that is not perhaps shared by everyone, but which my own research has led me to conclude is correct. Commandant Price emerges as one given the power of life and death over the "incorrigible" convicts and committed to "punishment [only] short of death," which he exercised to the full. By the standards of the period and granted the character of the convicts sentenced to penal servitude on Norfolk Island, a harsh regime had to be maintained; nevertheless, from the evidence available—including that of some of the convicts themselves and of the island's one-time chaplain—Price *does* appear to have erred on the side of severity.

I have fictionalized some of the diaries kept and books later written by Norfolk Island convicts, including that of Mark Jeffrey, and condensed these into a single record, which nonetheless is based on fact. For a factual account of the Norfolk Island penal settlement from beginning to end, however, I warmly recommend Mrs. Hazzard's book.

My book, like the others in *The Australians* series, is written as a novel, with fictional characters superimposed on the historical narrative. The adventures and misadventures of the real-life characters are based on fact, and I have not embroidered or exaggerated the actions of any of them, save where it was expedient to dramatize these a little to avoid writing "dull" history. For the background information pertaining to the Port Arthur

Penitentiary I am indebted to Vera Koenigswarter; the account of the escape by steamer is, however, fictional.

Finally, my thanks to my book supplier, Conrad Bailey of Sandringham, Victoria; to Ian Cottam for the loan of books; to Kenneth Wrightson also for books supplied; and to Ada Broadley for her unfailing help and support in the domestic field.

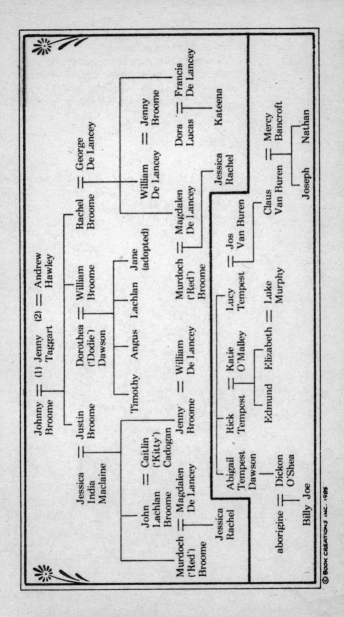

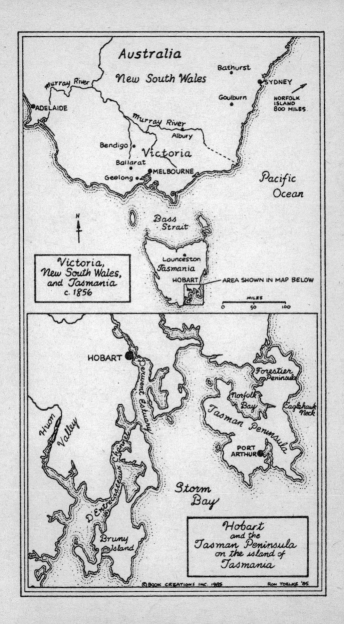

Australia

New South Wales

Murray River

Bathurst

Goulburn

SYDNEY

NORFOLK ISLAND 800 MILES

ADELAIDE

Murray River

Albury

Bendigo

Victoria

Ballarat

Geelong

MELBOURNE

Pacific Ocean

N

Bass Strait

Victoria,
New South Wales,
and Tasmania
c. 1856

Launceston

Tasmania

HOBART

AREA SHOWN IN MAP BELOW

MILES
0   50   100

HOBART

Huon Valley

Derwent Estuary

Forestier Peninsula

Norfolk Bay

Eaglehawk Neck

Tasman Peninsula

PORT ARTHUR

D'Entrecasteaux Channel

Bruny Island

Storm Bay

Hobart
and the
Tasman Peninsula
on the island of
Tasmania

© BOOK CREATIONS INC. 1985

RON TOELKE '85

Prologue

September 1828

The *S.S. Pyramus*, bound from the port of Liverpool to Sydney, New South Wales, wallowed sluggishly in mountainous seas, the howling, gale-force winds driving her remorselessly off course to the Irish coast.

Securely battened down though she was, and with only storm canvas set, she seemed, to the only passenger who had ventured on deck, to be in imminent danger of foundering. Henry Osborne clung with numb fingers to the rail on the weather side of the upper deck, regretting the impulse that had led him to leave the warmth and comparative safety of the cuddy. But its smoke-filled airlessness and the pungent fumes of the alcohol some of his fellow passengers had been consuming had induced such queasiness in his stomach that, fearing this might overcome him, he had decided to go in search of fresh air.

Certainly it had cured his seasickness. But now, he reflected ruefully, he would have to remain where he was until wind and sea abated—or until the infernal ship capsized—for to cross the deck to the companionway from which he had emerged would be to risk life and limb to no avail.

The *Pyramus*, he had been assured when he had booked his passage, was a sturdy, seaworthy brigantine of close on five hundred tons burden, well found and under the command of an experienced master, and until the storm had struck, he had had no reason to doubt that she was everything the shipping agent had claimed. Indeed, he— Henry braced himself, clutching at

his precarious handhold as the ship heeled suddenly, to plunge
into the trough of a towering wave, her bluff bows and most of
her fo'c'sle vanishing momentarily into its depth.

Tons of icy water cascaded across the deck, soaking him to
the skin and threatening to sweep him off his feet. As the water
drained slowly away, he heard the master bellow an order
through his speaking trumpet to the two men at the helm. The
wind seemed to Henry to bear the words soundlessly away, but
evidently both helmsmen understood the import, for, between
them, they spun the wheel and brought the ship's head to the
wind. Her bows rose, shuddering, and he felt the deck lift beneath his feet as, with an ominous creaking of her straining
timbers, she gained the crest of the following wave and plunged
on.

God in heaven, Henry thought, his stomach heaving anew,
why had he embarked on this voyage halfway across the world?
What mad, ambitious dream had led him to sell his farm at
Dromore, in Ireland's County Tyrone, in order to go out to
Australia as a settler? True, his two elder brothers, Alick and
John, had gone out there as naval surgeons and had urged him
to follow them, stressing in glowing terms the prospects the
colony offered to young men with the will to work and some
capital behind them.

They had taken land grants—John at Garden Hill, sixty
miles south of Sydney, with Alick nearby, at a place he called
Daisy Bank—and he had the required capital with which to set
himself up. He had a thousand pounds, raised by the sale of his
farm, but— The *Pyramus* heeled over once again, flung almost
onto her beam ends, and it seemed to Henry an interminable
time before she righted herself and, pitching heavily, struggled
on.

He groaned aloud, not caring who heard him. Worst of all, he
reminded himself miserably, he had been compelled to leave
behind his betrothed, the lovely Sarah Marshall, because of her
parents' objections to his decision to emigrate.

"Your future is too uncertain, Henry my dear boy," the old
rector of Dromore had told him, when he had endeavored to
plead his case. "Our daughter has been gently reared, in a safe,
secure home background. Sarah is not suited to the rough life of

a pioneer, in the wilds of an unknown land, such as she would be called upon to face were she to become your wife. It is out of the question, and I must forbid it."

"But we love each other, sir," Henry had protested. He had added, although to no avail, that he would never have considered leaving his native Ulster had he for one moment supposed that Sarah would be forbidden to accompany him.

"You should have thought of that possibility," the Reverend Benjamin Marshall had answered uncompromisingly, "before you sold your land, my dear young man—and before you had advanced your plan to emigrate to the point of no return."

He had been every sort of a fool, Henry told himself bitterly, remembering Sarah's tears and her stricken face when he had paid his final visit to the rectory to bid her farewell. They had clung together, both of them too heartbroken for any words, and finally, when he had had to tear himself away in order to catch the Liverpool packet, she had whispered brokenly that she would wait for him. He heard her voice now, above the roar of the wind.

"Send for me, dearest Henry, when you are settled and have made your way in New South Wales. I will come, I swear it— whatever my parents say, or however long it may be!"

He wanted to believe her, but . . . Sarah Marshall was a beautiful, appealing girl. There would be suitors aplenty after he had gone—young men with better prospects than his had ever been. There was the lawyer, Patrick Hare, and a brace of well-off farmers, once his friends—Damien Hamilton, who was kin to Sarah's mother, and, devil take him, Guy O'Regan, who would have a clear field now that his closest rival had left Dromore, with scant prospect of a speedy return or—

A rending crash from somewhere above his head interrupted his thoughts, bringing his attention abruptly back to the present. Henry watched with horror as, silhouetted starkly against the gray, scudding storm clouds, the foremast lost the single sail it had borne and, split off at the cap, came hurtling down to the forward part of the deck in a welter of torn rigging and shattered spars.

The crew reacted with swift courage in response to the master's shouted urging, and Henry found himself caught up in the

rush of men. Someone thrust an ax into his hand, and he
hacked and tore at the wreckage with the rest of them, blind
instinct guiding him, as the ship swung dangerously, broadside
on to the pounding waves, the whole deck awash.

Their frantic efforts succeeded at last. The shattered topmast
went by the board, and, relieved of its weight, the *Pyramus*
answered to her helm, the pumps slowly ridding her of the
water she had shipped.

Henry stood back, exhausted, aching in every limb, his hands
blistered and bleeding. The master paused briefly beside him,
his lined, weather-beaten face creased into a mirthless but approving smile.

"Good work, mister," he said. "Thanks for your help." He
added, the smile fading, "We're going to put in to Belfast to
have that topmast replaced. It'll add a week or ten days to your
journey, I'm afraid . . . but then, we ain't none of us in that
much of a hurry, are we?"

He stumped on, the speaking trumpet again raised to his lips
as he bellowed a succession of incomprehensible orders. Henry
stared after him, unable at first to take in the meaning of what
he had been told; and then, suddenly, his heart was singing.

A week in Belfast—ten days, perhaps . . . time enough,
God willing, for him to ride back to Dromore and renew his
pleas to Sarah's parents. Time enough, even if they again refused, to wed her without their consent.

The hand of God had surely brought him back, and the Reverend Benjamin Marshall could scarcely deny that it had been
the hand of God that had preserved him, with the *Pyramus* and
her passengers and crew, from the fury of the storm.

The Irish coast was in sight and the wind had abated when
Henry Osborne limped back to his cabin in search of dry
clothes and a much-needed glass of brandy in the cuddy.

It was another sixteen hours before the *Pyramus* entered Belfast Lough and he saw again the familiar gray buildings of the
city. He wasted no time in going ashore and, on a hired horse,
set off on the long road to Dromore. Through Lisburn and
Lurgan, skirting Lough Neagh, he rode, urging his jaded hire-
ling with voice and heels to a furious pace. The animal was
incapable of further effort when he reached Dungannon, and it

was raining steadily when, wet and tired, he pulled up in darkness outside a hostelry on the outskirts of the town.

The landlord, a cheerful, hospitable fellow, made him welcome, supplied him with an excellent meal and a comfortable room, and, for the first time since leaving the ship, Henry was able to relax. His clothes were again soaked, but he had had the forethought to bring a valise with him, and he handed over his outer garments to be dried, satisfied that—provided the morrow did not bring more rain—he could present himself, respectably clad, at the rectory the next day.

As good fortune would have it, the following morning dawned bright and clear. He donned his best suit and, fortified by a substantial breakfast, set off eagerly on the last twenty miles of his journey, mounted on a more willing horse and leaving his still-sodden cape and jacket steaming before the inn's kitchen fire, on the landlord's promise that he could redeem them on his return to Belfast.

Henry reached Dromore in the early afternoon, and after stabling his borrowed horse, he presented himself at the rectory. To his joy, the doorbell brought his adored Sarah in person to admit him, and when she went, half swooning, into his arms, his joy knew no bounds.

"Oh, Henry—dearest Henry, you have come back!" Sarah cried, as he held her tenderly to him. "I am so happy, I scarcely know what to say."

Henry, too, was momentarily bereft of words to express his feelings, but when Sarah led him by the hand into the withdrawing room, where both her parents were seated, he was dismayed when—as Sarah had done—they took it for granted that he had returned for good.

"So you have thought better of the foolhardy notion of emigrating to New South Wales," the old rector said, beaming his approval. "My dear boy, I am more than pleased."

Henry faced him unsmilingly. "No, sir," he denied, "I have not. The voyage is delayed and my ship is in Belfast to effect repairs to damage inflicted in a terrible storm in the Irish Sea. It is only by God's grace that I am here, Mr. Marshall, and—" He hesitated and then plunged in. "Sir, I swear that the hand of God brought me back to Ireland to—to plead with you once more to permit your daughter Sarah to wed me. I love her, sir, more than life itself."

The rector eyed him from beneath furrowed brows. He exchanged a questioning glance with his wife, as Henry stammered out a breathless description of the storm and the loss of the *Pyramus*'s foretopmast.

"Then it is your intention to continue the voyage, when the ship—when the *Pyramus* has completed her repairs?"

Henry inclined his head, jaw jutting obstinately.

"Yes, that is so, sir. She will sail within the next ten days, and I—Mr. Marshall, I beg you to allow me to take Sarah with me as my wife."

"Ten days, you say?" Again the Reverend Benjamin Marshall glanced across at his wife, receiving an almost imperceptible nod in response. He sighed heavily. "That does not give us much time to arrange your wedding, does it, my boy? But . . ." He repeated his sigh, and Henry, realizing suddenly that his plea had been successful, put his arm round Sarah's slim, muslin-clad shoulders.

"I suppose," the rector said resignedly, "that it can be done and that, in these—ah—circumstances, one reading of your banns will be sufficient. I shall have to inquire, I—" His expression relaxed and he held out his hand.

Henry took it thankfully, his heart full. "Thank you, Mr. Marshall—thank you. I will not be unworthy of your trust, sir —Mrs. Marshall—I give you my word."

Judith Marshall smiled at him, tears in her eyes.

"It will not be the lovely wedding we had hoped for our daughter, Henry," she reminded him. "But if, as it would seem to be, it is God's will, then so be it. Certainly it is nothing short of a miracle that brought you back here." She rose from her chair and embraced both Henry and her daughter in turn, the tears now flowing freely.

Henry was deeply moved. Over luncheon, which he took with the family, he talked at length of his plans.

"I have the money from the sale of my smallholding—a thousand pounds, which Alick and John assure me will be an adequate sum with which to set up as a farmer in the colony. I shall be given a grant of land and convict labor to work it. The money will amply suffice for the building of a homestead and the purchase of stock. It is in the form of a draft, cashable in Sydney and—" Intending to display the draft, in proof of his words, Henry felt in the pocket of his coat and found it empty. Horror-stricken, he recalled that he had been carrying the precious document in the pocket not of the jacket he was wearing, but in the heavy outer cloak, which . . . He drew in his breath sharply. Which, thrice-damned, careless fool that he was, he had left with the landlord of the inn in Dungannon!

His bright, happy dream abruptly faded. Without capital, what future could there be for Sarah and him in New South Wales? He would be a virtual pauper, dependent on his brothers. He . . . Somehow he contrived to talk on as if nothing had happened, keeping his anxiety hidden. Plans for the wedding were proposed, discussed, and agreed upon. It would take place at the Dromore parish church on September 11—two days before the *Pyramus* was expected to sail—provided the question of the banns could be cleared up; and Sarah and her mother would work day and night to make her wedding dress, calling in her sisters, if need be, to help them with their task.

The meal at long last over, Henry excused himself. He took lingering leave of his affianced wife, and, giving the impression that he intended to go to his own parents' house in nearby Dernaseer to acquaint them with the news of his forthcoming nuptials, he mounted his horse again and rode, as fast as the animal would take him, back to Dungannon.

Darkness had long since fallen when, stiff and weary, he dismounted outside the inn. As before, the landlord greeted him with cheerful warmth, inviting him into the taproom and pouring him a glass of whiskey laced with spices, a wide grin on his homely face. Then, before Henry could state the reason for his return, he laid the crumpled bank draft on the counter between them.

"Well, now, would it be this that brought you back so swiftly, young sir?" he questioned. "Sure you had no call to worry—we are honest folk here. 'Tis a mite damp, I'll grant you, yet it's quite legible. But—" His grin widened, as Henry put out a visibly trembling hand to pick up the precious draft. "I'd not carry a valuable paper such as this on my person, by the faith I would not! And you just about to set sail for Botany Bay, if I remember rightly. 'Tis asking for trouble, so it is."

Chastened, Henry gulped down his drink, relief loosening his tongue. "I have been foolish," he confessed. "I . . . but how else can I carry it? It is my capital, it's what I need to set myself up—to set my wife and myself up on a farm out there."

The landlord refilled his glass, then poured himself a generous tot of the same warming mixture, a thoughtful expression on his face. "You could use it to buy trade goods, sir," he suggested practically. "Before you leave Ireland. From what I hear, the folk in Botany Bay are in sore need o' such goods—of silks and satins and woven cloth—aye, and of fine Irish linen, too. It has all to be imported, a seafaring man was after telling me a few weeks ago, and it sells for three or four times its cost, if it's shipped out to Sydney Town. I doubt the master o' your ship would ask you a large sum for carrying bales o' linen, and it travels well."

Henry stared at him, impressed by what he had said. It was an excellent suggestion, he recognized, and a thousand pounds would buy a fair quantity, but . . .

"It's short notice . . . and I should have to get it to the ship," he began. "She's due to leave port in just over a week."

"The mill here would supply you, sir," the landlord assured him. "And they would attend to the loading, too, I fancy, if you were to explain the circumstances. The mill manager's a friend o' mine. I'd gladly give you an introduction to him in the mornin', and you could fix things up in a couple of hours."

He was as good as his word, and the next day, the mill manager, pleased by so large a sale, readily agreed to arrange for Henry's purchase to be sent to Belfast and loaded aboard the *Pyramus.*

"You need concern yourself no further with the matter, Mr. Osborne," he asserted. "The bales will be packed up, and they'll be stowed on board your vessel by the time you rejoin her. The mill will pay transport costs, as a discount for your prompt cash settlement, if that is satisfactory to you."

Elated, Henry agreed that it was eminently satisfactory. He signed over his draft and, with the landlord's good wishes ringing in his ears, set off once again for Dromore and the family home he had never expected to see again.

The wedding, for all the haste with which, of necessity, it had been arranged, was the happiest day of his life. Virtually all the inhabitants of the little town attended the service, together with his and Sarah's families and friends, and as he watched his bride walk up the aisle toward him on the arm of her eldest brother, Henry's heart swelled with pride.

Sarah, he thought, had never looked more beautiful or more desirable, and her wedding dress, with its billowing skirts and its daintily ruched sleeves, set off her loveliness to perfection. From behind the veil that covered her face, she was looking up at him with a shy smile curving her lips and her dark eyes aglow, and he put out his hand to take hers as the rector started to read the wedding service.

"Dearly beloved, we are gathered together in the sight of God and in the face of this congregation, to join this man and this woman in holy matrimony, which is an honorable estate, instituted of God in the time of man's innocency, signifying unto us the mystical union that is betwixt Christ and His Church. . . ."

Henry Osborne bowed his head, and, as the old rector's deep, resonant voice woke echoes from the stone walls of the little church in which he had worshiped since his boyhood, he breathed a silent prayer of his own.

"Merciful Father in heaven, of Thy compassion my life was preserved and I returned here to claim my beloved Sarah to wife . . . let me not fail her in the far-off land to which we must journey. Grant us fields to sow and reap and cattle to breed, that we may by our toil enrich the land and render it prosperous for our children to inherit in the fullness of time. Bless our going, O Lord, and bring us safely to our destination—" The rector's voice broke into his consciousness.

"Henry Archibald, wilt thou have this woman to thy wedded wife, to live together after God's ordinance in the holy estate of matrimony? Wilt thou love her, comfort her, honor and keep her in sickness and in health and, forsaking all other keep thee only unto her, so long as ye both shall live?"

Henry lifted his head. In a firm, strong voice he answered, "I will!" and the answer came from his heart.

Forty-eight hours later, entered in the ship's books as Mr. and Mrs. Henry Osborne, he and his bride boarded the *Pyramus,* the brigantine hove up her anchor, and with both their families and many of their friends waving from the wharfside, they stood together on deck, waving too, as the sails filled and the long voyage began.

Spring, 1856

The three-masted White Star Line clipper *S.S. Spartan,* under charter to the Government Emigration Department and bound for Melbourne and Sydney, lay alongside Liverpool's Water Street wharf, a long line of steerage passengers patiently waiting permission to board her.

The first feverish rush to the Australian goldfields had passed its zenith, but more than half those picking their way, with varying degrees of difficulty, through the dimly lit warehouse leading to the dock were bound for the diggings in Victoria. The rest were poor Irish emigrants, whole families of them, delivered—in some cases weeks ago—by the steam packet from Dublin and driven, by the continuing effects of the potato famine, to seek indentured employment on the sheep and cattle stations of the now-thriving colony.

They bore their worldly goods with them, men, women, and children, stumbling blindly over the mass of cordage and the heaped-up cargo that filled the warehouse. Bent under the heavy bundles with which virtually all were burdened, they were hard put to it to dodge the incoming and outgoing cargo slings that swung constantly above their heads, and they were roundly cursed by the stevedores if they tripped or strayed out of line.

But their ship was in sight, and they gazed at her in awe. The *Spartan* was the newest vessel of the Pilkington and Wilson White Star fleet, built only the previous year to an American design by the Hood yard in Aberdeen. Seen through the thin haze of a Mersey drizzle, with the distinctive swallow-tailed house flag of a white star on a red ground flying from her mainmast head, she made a splendid sight. Her sides were painted green, with much gilded scrollwork and a gilt streak running their length, and her sharply raked bow was adorned with a magnificent figurehead, depicting a Spartan warrior, helmeted and armed with a spear.

Emerging at last onto the dock, those at the head of the line exclaimed in admiration, oblivious of the increasing downpour, which, now that they were no longer protected by the roof of the warehouse, threatened to soak them.

"They do say as one o' these 'ere clipper ships made the passage to Melbourne in just over sixty days," a black-bearded Cockney observed, to no one in particular. "But they're Yankee built, seemingly—pity we can't build the like o' them over 'ere, ain't it?"

"We can and do," an elderly man in clerkly garb, standing nearby with his wife and a bevy of small children, hastened to correct him. "This one's home built, and so's the *Runnymede* and the *James Baines*—aye, and the *Marco Polo* likewise. They all made runs around seventy days, and the *Marco Polo* held the record for a long while. We started building clippers later than the Yankees, but 'twas a Scotsman living in Nova Scotia, name of McKay, that first designed them. But he had to build his ships in Boston—I reckon because the British government wouldn't give him the backing or the money he needed. That's typical, of course."

"Too bloomin' true," the black-bearded man agreed. "But how come as you knows so much about clippers? You a seaman or what?"

His informant smiled wryly. "No, I'm a shipping clerk—worked in Water Street all my life, for the Black Ball Line and Mr. Baines till a couple of years ago. Then I went to Pilkington and Wilson, the owners of this ship." He gestured to the *Spartan.* "Though truth to tell, I always had a notion to go to sea."

"Well, you're goin' now an' no mistake, ain't you?" the Cockney suggested. He glanced at his new acquaintance and then, a trifle uncertainly, at the older man's wife and children. "But, if you'll pardon me for sayin' so, with a family like yours I'd have supposed as you'd have thought twice about quittin' a good job to go gold seekin'. No offense intended," he added quickly. "It just seems a mite strange to me."

The shipping clerk sighed. "No offense taken," he answered, smiling. "I'm going to better myself . . . and that doesn't mean I'm aiming to become a gold digger, sir."

"You ain't?"

The little man shook his head emphatically. "No. I'm going out to work for one of the biggest landowners in the state of New South Wales. A Mr. Henry Osborne of Mount Marshall— a fine gentleman, who went out about . . . oh, it must be nearly thirty years ago. It's a long story, but, to cut it short, my father kept an inn in Dungannon, County Tyrone. He did Mr. Osborne a service all those years ago, and he kept in touch. When I was taken on by the Black Ball Line, he—Mr. Osborne, that is—entrusted me with filling his shipping orders. And I must have carried out his commissions to the gentleman's satisfaction, for he offered me employment. I never took up his offer, but—" His smile widened. "We sent our two eldest boys out, and they've been urging us to follow them ever since. Such tales as they tell about Mr. Osborne's property—his fine house, his cattle and sheep, and his family, too. So one day, the wife and I —well, we decided that we would take the plunge before we're too old. You don't get rich on a clerk's wages, and we—"

He was interrupted by the arrival of a dray, laden with luggage, which was followed a few minutes later by a small procession of carriages. Bringing up the rear was a barouche, bearing the crest of the Adelphi Hotel on its doors, with a liveried coachman on the box and two porters, in hotel livery, perched on the jump seats.

"The cabin passengers," the erstwhile shipping clerk informed his neighbor, who retorted sourly.

"Aye, so I see. Let's hope they'll let us on board out o' this pesky rain when the gentry's bin disposed of."

One of the ship's officers descended the stern gangway to receive the new arrivals with due ceremony, a pair of stewards at his heels, carrying folded umbrellas.

"Don't mean for *them* to get a duckin'," the black-bearded young Cockney added, still sour. "Well, when *I* make me strike at Ballarat, *I'll* hire a couple o' flunkies to follow me around

wiv' sunshades!" His tone changed and he pursed his lips in a
silent whistle as, from the hotel's barouche, a slim, elegantly
dressed young woman descended, gracefully accepting the arm
of the ship's officer, who hastened forward to assist her.

Even from that distance, she was startlingly beautiful. A wisp
of a flower-decked bonnet barely concealed a mass of curling
dark hair, and, from beneath it, the girl's small, piquant face,
exquisitely oval shaped, was turned in the direction of the waiting line of steerage passengers, clearly reflecting concern. Her
voice, raised to question the *Spartan*'s young mate, did not
carry to the watchers on the dockside, but its musical quality
did, and the bearded Cockney lost the last remnants of his sour-
ness.

"Gawd's truth!" he exclaimed. "That's what I call quality—
that's what I call a lady! *She* can have all the ruddy umbrellas
she wants, far as I'm concerned. I wonder who the devil she is?"

For once, the knowledgeable shipping clerk could offer him
no help, but, overhearing his query, a plump woman with a
woolen shawl wrapped tightly about her ample frame supplied
the answer. Stepping to his side, she said scornfully, " 'Tis no
use the loikes av you casting sheep's eyes in dat direction, mister—no use at all. Sure, dat is Lady Kitty Cadogan of Castle
Kilclare—Castle Kilclare in County Wexford," she added impatiently, as the Englishman appeared not to understand. "In
Oireland! And I should know, for amn't I coming from the
selfsame place?"

"*What* did you say her name was?" He was still puzzled, the
bearded lips agape.

Obligingly, the woman repeated it, giving the name four syl-
lables. "Cad-o-*gow*-an, mister. C-a-d-o-g-a-n. And her brother
will be wid her—the Honorable Patrick Cadogan. He's her twin
brother, so he is, and dey are never apart. As loike as two peas
dey are, the pair av dem. There, see for yourself!" She pointed
as a tall, dark-haired young man—as striking in appearance as
his sister—descended from the barouche and strolled unhur-
riedly to join her at the foot of the gangway.

The stout Irishwoman was about to say more when a gasp
went up from the waiting crowd as Lady Kitty Cadogan, scorn-
ing the umbrella a steward sought to hold over her, came run-

ning across the wet dockside toward them. Both small, white-
gloved hands outheld, she greeted the now-beaming woman
warmly.

"Why, Mary O'Hara, I do declare! Where in the world did
you vanish to? I've searched Liverpool for you ever since we
arrived here. You've not forgotten our bargain, have you?"

Thus addressed, Mary O'Hara reddened in embarrassment
and dropped a clumsy curtsy. "No, me lady, indeed I swear I
have not. But I was biding wid relations here and—well, one o'
me kin died, God rest his soul, and dere was a wake and—"

Lady Kitty Cadogan cut her short. "Very well, Mary—we'll
let it pass. Suffice it that you are here. Come on now—let us go
on board. They are waiting for us, you know, so that these folk
can board, and we don't want to keep them standing in the rain
any longer than they must." The charm of her smile encom-
passed the rain-drenched line, and many of the glum faces lit up
in instinctive response. Lady Kitty put out a hand to aid Mary
O'Hara with her cumbersome bundle, but the black-bearded
Londoner was before her. Sweeping off his cap, he grabbed the
bundle and hefted it onto his shoulder.

"Permit me, ma'am—me lady. You lead on and I'll follow."

She thanked him prettily, seemingly deaf to the hissed reproach of the shipping clerk's wife when he, too, attempted to
volunteer his services.

"Keep your place, Benjamin Doakes. They'll not let *him* on
board ahead of us, you'll see."

She proved to be right. One of the *Spartan*'s stewards relieved
the enterprising young upstart of the woman's bundle, and,
with the officer from the gangway holding an umbrella over her
bonneted head, Lady Kitty Cadogan permitted herself to be
escorted back to the foot of the gangway, the stout Irishwoman
trotting meekly at her heels.

They went on board, vanishing from sight at the entryport.
After a brief delay, while the last of the cabin passengers' baggage was winched up on deck, the drayman turned his horses,
and his vehicle lumbered off in the wake of the Adelphi Hotel's
barouche. Then the officer moved to the forward gangway and,
with a raised arm and a stentorian bellow, indicated that the
steerage passengers' long wait was at an end. Thankfully the

ragged line surged forward, soaked to the skin but jubilant, humping their rolled blankets and their cooking utensils, their awkward bundles of clothing and their sacks of provisions with cheerful lack of complaint.

They, too, vanished, directed to the dimly lamp-lit orlop deck in the bowels of the ship and to the tiers of wooden bunks that awaited them, women and children on the starboard side, men to larboard.

Two decks above them, in well-furnished adjoining cabins, Lady Kitty Cadogan and her brother Patrick looked about them with mutual approval.

"If she's as fast a sailer as they claim she is," Patrick observed, seating himself on his sister's cot with a smile, "we'll not fare badly, Kit. Not badly at all."

"Better than poor Michael did," Kitty reminded him, a bitter note in her voice. "Imagine what it must have been like going out in chains! And in those days the convict transports took six or seven months to reach Hobart."

Her brother's smile faded. "I've not forgotten. But—Kit, I'm a mite worried about Mary O'Hara. If she talks—"

"She won't. She gave us her solemn word, Pat. She's a good soul and as loyal as they are made—you know she is. Besides," Kitty spoke with conviction, "she's coming as my maid, which means that she will have a cabin to herself on the 'tween-deck. She will not mix with the others—she'll not want to."

"Well, let us hope your faith in her is not misplaced. Because if anyone were to suspect . . ." Patrick did not complete his sentence, and Kitty did so for him.

"We might find ourselves in serious trouble. But we've always known that, haven't we? We know we're taking a risk. But—oh, Pat, English memories are short, particularly where happenings in Ireland are concerned. They neither remember nor care! And since all else, including the appeal, has failed, what choice is left to us?"

"Not a great deal," Patrick conceded. "Damme, I don't mind risking my neck. I owe it to Michael—that and much more. But it's you I'm worried about. I wish you hadn't insisted on coming with me, Kit. I wish you'd go back now. There's still time, and you—"

"We've always done everything together," Kitty returned, her tone calculated to put an end to her brother's lingering doubts. "The Cadogans stick together, and when it's a question of a cruel injustice visited on one, the others are in honor bound to use their best endeavors to set matters right. And remember—" She took off the tiny flowered bonnet and tossed her dark head at him in a show of bravado. "I may not be a man, but, faith, I wasn't known as Madcap Kitty for nothing! There's not much you can do that I can't do as well or better. We—" A knock on the cabin door caused her to break off. "Yes," she acknowledged. "Who is it?"

A gray-haired steward entered diffidently.

"Your pardon, sir—m'lady. The master has instructed me to present his compliments and to say that he will be honored if you would both join him in a glass of punch in the saloon, so that he may make your acquaintance, before we cast off."

"Now?" Patrick questioned.

"If it is convenient, sir."

Brother and sister exchanged a swift glance, and Patrick inclined his head. "My compliments to Captain Bruce, steward, and be so good as to tell him that her ladyship and I will be pleased to join him."

The steward departed, and they looked at each other with barely suppressed amusement.

"If he only knew why we are here!" Kitty exclaimed, her merriment suddenly bubbling over.

"It's amazing what respectability a title confers," Patrick said dryly. "Well, I suppose we had best make the acquaintance of the master and our fellow passengers, since we shall be seeing rather a lot of them during the next two or three months. Do you intend to put on that absurd bonnet again?"

Kitty shook her head, and her brother put an affectionate arm about her slim shoulders.

"Then come on, little sister, and let us get it over with. It will afford us the opportunity to feign respectability, and I'm sure the practice will serve us in good stead when we disembark in Sydney."

"I hope it will," Kitty echoed dubiously, but she assumed a demure expression, belied only by the sparkle in her dark, expressive eyes, and linked her arm in that of her brother. "If the captain offers us a drink of—what was it?—of punch, we'll make it a toast to Michael, shall we? A silent toast."

"That we will," Patrick asserted. His hand closed about hers, and they left the cabin together.

PART ONE

The Searchers

Chapter I

LUKE MURPHY REINED in his horse and, a hand raised to the brim of his hat to shade his eyes, looked out across the paddock to the cluster of distant buildings that made up the homestead of his father-in-law's property of Pengallon.

It was, in fact, a small, self-contained village, built up over the years to serve the growing needs of one of the largest sheep and cattle stations in the Macquarie River Valley of New South Wales. The homestead itself had been added to considerably since Rick Tempest had taken possession of the original land grant during General Lachlan Macquarie's governorship. Now the pleasant, white-painted house consisted of two stories, with wide verandas at front and rear. There were cottages for the laborers and their families, sheep and cattle pens, stables, a large, shingle-roofed shearing shed with pens and sluices surrounding it, and a wool store, a blacksmith's shop, and a lumberyard adjoining. There was his own cottage—Luke's gaze went to the familiar stone-and-weatherboard building, half hidden behind its screening gum trees—which, for the past fourteen months, he had shared with his young wife, Elizabeth, Rick Tempest's only daughter, and . . . He found himself smiling. Those fourteen months, following his return from the Victoria goldfields, had been the happiest of his life.

Elizabeth—beautiful, golden-haired Elizabeth of the soft voice and the shy, gentle charm—was all he had ever dreamed of in a woman. He worshiped her, and now— He felt a sudden tightening of the throat. Now, to make their marriage complete, Elizabeth was about to give birth to their first child. She was no longer in their cottage; a week ago, at her mother's insistence, she had moved into the homestead to await the birth, cosseted and fussed over by her family—although, according to the midwife's calculations, she was not due to be brought to bed for at least another week or ten days.

Luke's smile faded. He had gone on with his work, as an antidote to the anxiety he felt. The station was still short-handed, although three of the older men, disillusioned in their search for gold, had returned a couple of months ago to take up their former employment. Even so, there never seemed to be enough of them to cope with the demands of the vast acreage and the livestock Pengallon supported. This year had seen the largest wool crop the station had ever produced; and when the shearing was completed, the fleeces had to be sorted, graded, and baled, ready for transport to Sydney—a long, hot, back-breaking task that had engaged virtually all his time for the past six weeks.

Grading wool was a skilled job; he was not yet as expert as his brother-in-law, Edmund, or even, come to that, as his wife, and the recent drought had caused dust to be collected in the fleeces after the sheep had been washed, with detriment to the wool's quality. But at last it was over; the wool crop had been loaded onto the ox-wagons in tightly packed bales, ready to be shipped out to England in Claus Van Buren's new clipper ship . . . in time, it was hoped, to reach London before the first sale lists closed.

Missing that list, Luke had learned, could spell disaster, since it would entail months with the entire cargo warehoused, at great expense, and a possible fall in wool prices before the next sale was scheduled. Even so, he was thankful to be free of the oppressive heat and stench of the sorting shed. It was still hot enough, in all conscience, and his ride out and back from the far paddocks had taken all day, but . . . he had been in the open air, alone and without the need to keep up the pretense of being carefree in front of the other men.

Once again Luke felt his throat tighten. He was anxious on Elizabeth's account, for her pregnancy had put a severe strain on her, and the doctor—the experienced Dr. Morecombe, of Bathurst—had warned him that certain complications were a possibility, when her time came. He had not fully understood Morecombe's guarded explanation, but evidently Elizabeth's mother had, for it had been she who had issued what amounted almost to an ultimatum, when he had wanted the birth to take place under their own cottage roof.

"You want what is best for her, Luke," Katie Tempest had said unanswerably. "And *I* want her under my eye. I had a difficult time when both she and Edmund were born, and I lost two babies, you know. We don't want that to happen with Elizabeth, and God forbid that it should."

"Oh, no!" he had echoed, shocked and robbed of argument. "Of course not. God help me, I did not realize."

He wanted the child—they both wanted the child, to set the seal on their loving, happy union, but . . . Luke swore under his breath as, with the swift approach of dusk, a horde of stinging insects appeared, seemingly from nowhere, to lay siege to his face and arms. Irritably, he brushed them away and dug his heels into his horse's sides. There was a line of fencing he had intended to inspect, but it was half a mile away, and both he and his mount were bone weary. The fence would have to wait until tomorrow; he would check the water trough in the brood mares' paddock—there was time to do that—and then call it a day.

Elizabeth would be in bed when he got back to the homestead, but they would have an hour together, while she ate her evening meal and before her mother banished him from her room, on the plea that she needed all the rest she could get to prepare her for her coming ordeal.

He wanted to be with her, heaven knew; he wanted to sustain and reassure her, to hold her in his arms while she slept. He loved her so deeply, he— The thud of hooves brought his head round, to see the rider coming toward him at a brisk canter, emerging from the paddock to which he had been making his way. The huge figure with the heavy beard was unmistakable— Luke raised his arm to wave, knowing that Dickon O'Shea, who was deaf and dumb, would not hear his shout. The approaching horseman changed direction at once and gave an answering wave.

Conscious of a warm glow of affection, Luke quickened his pace. Dickon O'Shea was Rick Tempest's nephew, an oddly childlike giant of a man, who, since his boyhood, had made his home at Pengallon. There was, despite his handicap, nothing that Dickon could not do; a superb horseman, he was also an expert stockman and shepherd and a first-rate shot, as much at home with the local aborigine tribe as he was with his own kind. He had taken an aboriginal girl to wife but had never brought her to the homestead or revealed the fact that he had formed any sort of tie until, to everyone's surprise, he had come in one day with a small, half-caste boy, who had addressed him solemnly, in English, as "Papa" and added that his name was Billy Joe. Thereafter, father and son had taken up residence in Dickon's quarters at Pengallon, and the boy—now, as nearly as anyone could judge, aged about ten—was in a fair way of becoming as useful a farmhand as the man who had bred him.

But Dickon was alone now, Luke saw, and he appeared to be in some haste. Elizabeth, he thought, with a sudden twinge of panic—Elizabeth had been brought to bed, and Mrs. Tempest had sent Dickon to find him. Or perhaps it was over—perhaps all his anxiety had been needless, and Dr. Morecombe's glum warnings without foundation.

"Dickon," he managed, as the big man pulled up beside him. Keeping his face toward the newcomer, to enable him to lip-read, Luke asked, forcing himself to speak calmly, "Is it Elizabeth? Has her time come?"

Dickon nodded. Forestalling the second question, he grasped Luke's rein and jerked his head in the direction of the homestead.

So it was not all over, Luke decided, with a sinking heart. And if Dickon was urging him to hurry, there must still, alas, be cause for anxiety. He kneed his tired horse into motion and, with Dickon beside him, rode at a headlong gallop for the station buildings.

In the living room of the homestead, he found his father-in-law and Edmund awaiting him. Rick Tempest, tall and white-haired, greeted him with a reassuring smile and the news that Elizabeth had gone into labor at about midday.

"Her mother and the midwife are with her," he added. "It'll be best if you stay here, Luke. It takes time, you know, when it's the first one. But I thought I ought to send Dickon to fetch you—I knew you would want to be here." He splashed brandy into a bulbous glass and, ignoring Luke's headshake, thrust the glass into his hand. "Drink it, lad—there may be a long night before us."

Luke obediently gulped down the neat spirit, and his father-in-law resumed his seat, his own half-finished drink in his hand. Addressing his son, he continued what had evidently been an earlier topic of conversation.

"I had a long talk with Henry Osborne of Marshall Mount—we dined together, after the Legislative Council meeting."

"Osborne?" Edmund's interest quickened. "Was he not the enterprising fellow who drove the mob of cattle to Adelaide a few years back, when the settlers there were hard put to it to feed themselves?"

Rick Tempest nodded. "Indeed he was . . . and it was an incredible journey, which took him over four months. I'd never heard the full story before, and, I confess, after hearing Osborne's account of the hardships they endured and the difficulties they encountered, my admiration for him knew no bounds. It was in December of thirty-nine that they set off—Osborne, with his foreman, three convicts, and three abo stockmen. They gathered a mob of nearly nine hundred cattle and about the same number of fat wethers, and, of course, when they finally reached Adelaide he was able to ask his own price for them."

"He must have lost some," Edmund demurred, frowning. "For God's sake, Father, it's—what? Close on a thousand miles from Lake Illawarra to Adelaide, and in thirty-nine there were no roads—just wild bush. And I don't imagine that all the black-fellows he met were friendly."

"Quite the reverse," his father confirmed. "And at one point, Osborne told me, he came pretty near giving up, abandoning the herd and making tracks for home as best he could. They had been ten days without finding water, but then—miraculously, Osborne said—the wind veered and the cattle suddenly picked up the scent of water and made for it. He lost a few head, but he delivered the bulk of both sheep and cattle in good condition . . . and made his fortune." Rick Tempest smiled. "By heaven, he deserved to! It beats gold digging."

"That's debatable," Edmund retorted, echoing his father's smile. "And coming from you—" He turned his gaze on Luke, anxious to draw him into the conversation, but the younger man was sunk in his own thoughts and appeared not to hear him. Edmund shrugged. "You said you met Mr. Osborne at the Legislative Council. He's a member, I take it?"

"An elected member, yes. But now that the new constitution is about to give us a Legislative Assembly and fully responsible government, thanks to William Charles Wentworth's efforts, Osborne intends to stand down. His eldest son is to take his place and stand for election in one of the Illawarra seats. As—" Rick Tempest paused and laid heavy emphasis on his next words. "As I wish *my* son would!"

Edmund's explosive reaction had the effect of disrupting Luke's reverie, and he looked up, startled, as Edmund exclaimed, "Oh, for God's sake, Father! Perish the thought!"

"Why, Edmund?"

Edmund spread his big, work-scarred hands in a gesture of disgust. "Why, sir? Well, for a start because I'm not cut out to be a politician. I'm a pastoralist, a squatter, and I love the land. If I were to serve in the Assembly it would mean that I'd have to spend half my time in Sydney, socializing and attending a lot of their infernal dinners and routs, as well as trying to make speeches and dressing as a blasted dandy. You carry on, sir, and let me take care of the property with Luke and Dickon, as I always have during your necessary absences on government affairs. You've nothing to complain of on that score, have you?"

"No," his father conceded readily. "Nothing at all, my dear boy. But I'm past my threescore years and ten, you know, and I'm beginning to feel my age. Henry Osborne is in his early fifties. He owns more land than I do, and more stock, it's true, and he has a large family—thirteen children, I think he told me, though they have not all survived. But . . ." Again he paused, eyeing Edmund a trifle reproachfully. "He has heirs, Edmund. Your mother and I have long hoped that you would marry and give us grandchildren, but you've left it to Elizabeth and Luke, haven't you?"

Edmund reddened. "There's time enough, Father. I'm not in my dotage. I—" Dickon came in, and, as if he welcomed the temporary distraction, Edmund got to his feet and went to pour a drink for the new arrival, taking the opportunity to top off his own glass. "Luke?" he invited. "Just the thing for one who is about to beget an heir."

Luke shook his head. He seldom drank spirits, and already the brandy he had been given had made his senses swim. "No, thanks," he said. "I'm fine."

Edmund returned to his seat, still looking disgruntled. "Do you suppose that getting myself elected to the new Assembly would enhance my chances of finding a bride, Father?" he asked aggressively.

"I imagine anything that took you to Sydney and forced you to—how did you express it?—socialize and attend dinners and routs might do just that," his father answered, a slight edge to his voice. "Burying yourself up here lost you the lovely little Jenny Broome, did it not?" He sighed, reaching for his pipe. "I attended her wedding while I was in Sydney, Edmund. You know, of course, that she married William De Lancey?"

"Indeed I know!" Edmund, to Luke's shocked surprise, appeared perilously near to losing his temper. "Devil take it, Father, if I *had* wasted my time at balls and garden parties and picnics, which is how folk in Sydney amuse themselves, what chance would I have had against a hero of the Light Cavalry Brigade's charge at Balaclava? And one, furthermore, who returned here with an empty sleeve and the exalted rank of lieutenant colonel! Jenny had no eyes for me when Will De Lancey came on leave from India, for the Lord's sake!"

Luke, fully distracted now, stared at his brother-in-law in frank bewilderment. The names meant nothing to him, and he said, in an attempt to stem Edmund's unaccustomed anger, "Who is William De Lancey, Edmund? I suppose he's a relation of Francis De Lancey, the one I met on the Turon River. But—"

Edmund controlled himself with a visible effort.

"They're brothers, the sons of Judge De Lancey. Here—" He

rose again and, crossing to the table on the far side of the room,
selected a copy of one of the newspapers his father had brought
back with him from Sydney. "You can read all about Will's
exploits in this. Or I'll read it for you." He picked up an oil
lamp and, setting it by the arm of his chair, spread out the
paper on his knee and commenced to read in a flat, expressionless voice.

"Eulogies have been written, by this newspaper and others, lauding the heroism and the superb discipline of the
British Light Cavalry Brigade in the recent Russian War.
The fact that the charge was made as the result of a misunderstanding of the late General Lord Raglan's order in no
way detracts from the glory with which the gallant participants covered themselves—or the terrible price exacted from
them by the guns of their enemies.

"Out of a total strength of just over six hundred of all
ranks, half that number were killed, wounded, or taken prisoner, and subsequent deaths from wounds brought the number of casualties to well over three hundred.

"It is fitting, therefore, that this colony should extend a
hero's welcome to Lieutenant Colonel William De Lancey,
late of Her Majesty's Eleventh Hussars and the elder son of
His Honor Justice George and Mrs. De Lancey of Sydney.

"It is understood that Colonel De Lancey, who was
awarded brevet rank, has been recommended by Lord
George Paget, second in command to the Earl of Cardigan,
for the new medal for gallantry, which, at Her Majesty's
express wish, is to be known as the Victoria Cross. Although
this gallant officer was reluctant to discuss the deed which
led to Lord Paget's recommendation, it seems that, despite
being himself severely wounded, he risked his life in an, alas,
abortive attempt to save his servant from death or capture at
the hands of a party of Cossacks.

"The colonel did, however, tell our correspondent that he
had intended to sell his commission and return to Australia
as a settler, but he was offered command of a Bengal native
cavalry regiment by the directors of the Honorable East India Company, which offer he has accepted.

"He and his bride, the former Miss Jennifer Broome—
only daughter of Captain Justin Broome, Royal Navy retired, of Elizabeth Bay, and the late Mrs. Broome—will be
taking passage to India following their honeymoon, which,
we understand, is being spent in this country.

"A description of their wedding at Sydney's garrison
church was published in our last edition, before the above
facts became known to us. But doubtless our readers will
forgive us if we conclude this report by quoting from the
poem, recently written by Lord Tennyson, the poet laureate,
to commemorate the epic charge."

Edmund paused, an oddly tense expression on his tanned,
good-looking face. But his tone, Luke noticed, as he continued
his recital, was still resentful.

> *"Half a league, half a league,*
> *Half a league onward,*
> *All in the valley of Death*
> *Rode the six hundred . . .*

> *"Cannon to the right of them,*
> *Cannon to the left of them,*
> *Cannon in front of them,*
> *Volley'd and thunder'd . . .*
> *Into the jaws of Death,*
> *Into the mouth of hell*
> *Rode the six hundred—"*

His voice broke and he seemed to lose his place, but recovering himself, he went on:

> *"Not tho' the soldier knew*
> *Some one had blunder'd.*
> *Theirs not to make reply,*
> *Theirs not to reason why,*
> *Theirs but to do and die. . . .*

"And they did that, by God!" Edmund rose, still with the unfolded newspaper in his hand, and, pacing the room from fireside to window, went on reading the poem seemingly at random. He concluded:

> *"When can their glory fade?*
> *O the wild charge they made . . .*
> *Noble six hundred!*

"Honest to God, Father, what chance did I have when entering the lists with Will De Lancey?"

His father did not answer him. Instead he declared flatly, "Well, I'm not contesting my seat at the election for the new Assembly, and that's final. I think you owe it to us—to your mother and me, Edmund—to stand in my place. Think about it, boy." He added, with a faint smile, "You will be in no danger of meeting Jenny and her husband at any of the garden parties or routs in Sydney, if that is what is worrying you. They've gone to Marshall Mount, to the Osbornes'. Will told me that one of Henry Osborne's nephews was a surgeon in the Crimea, to whom he was indebted for his recovery—which, I gather, was for some considerable time in doubt. The poor fellow—the surgeon, that is—contracted cholera afterward and died, and Will, it seems, promised that he would deliver his effects to the family. After which, of course, he and Jenny will be off to Calcutta."

Edmund said nothing, and an awkward silence fell, which was broken by a loud knock at the door and the entry of the midwife. Luke sprang to his feet.

"Is it over, Mrs. Lee?" he asked eagerly, praying that it was.

The woman shook her head. "You'll need to ride to Bathurst for the doctor, Mr. Murphy," she told him, tight-lipped. "I'm not able to do any more for your wife. The poor young soul is exhausted, and . . . it's a breach presentation, you see. It needs the doctor's skill now."

Luke's heart sank. All his earlier fears returned full force to torment him. He bit back the reproaches he had been about to utter and made for the door, but Dickon was before him, indicating that he would go. No one, Luke knew, could match

Dickon's horsemanship; the big man would cover the intervening distance faster than he himself could, but . . . nevertheless he hesitated.

"It's my place to go, Dickon," he began. "I . . . Elizabeth's my wife, and—"

The midwife put in quickly, "She's asking for you, Mr. Murphy, and Mrs. Tempest thinks it may calm her if you go up and sit with her for a while."

"I can see her?" Luke felt Dickon's strong brown hand close about his in wordless sympathy, and then the big man was gone, the door swinging shut behind his retreating back. Rick Tempest exchanged a few whispered words with the midwife, then turned to Luke.

"I'll write a note for Dickon to take with him—you go to her, Luke boy. And tell her—tell her we're thinking of her."

Luke waited to hear no more. He ascended the narrow wooden staircase to the upper floor, taking the steps two at a time, sick with apprehension, the elderly midwife following breathlessly at his heels.

"Quietly, Mr. Murphy!" she called after him. "You'll scare her if you go rushing in hell for leather like that. The poor young thing's scared enough as it is."

Luke slackened his pace, cursing himself for a witless fool. He entered his wife's room on tiptoe, his stomach churning, fearful of what harm her long labor might have wrought. But she lay very calmly in the big bed, her small face flushed and damp with perspiration and her eyes closed. Her mother, seated in a chair beside her, bent forward to wipe the beads of moisture from her daughter's brow before yielding her place to Luke.

"Elizabeth, my dear," she said softly. "He's here—Luke's here."

Elizabeth opened her eyes, and Luke was appalled by the pain he read in them. But she managed a brave little smile and held out a hand to him, the smile momentarily lighting her face into a semblance of pleasure at the sight of him.

"It's . . . it's taking a very long time, Luke. I don't know why. Mrs. Lee says . . . she says the doctor will help me when he comes." Her voice was faint and the smile faded, as a spasm of pain wrung a cry from her. "I . . ." Her strong white teeth closed over her lower lip, stilling its trembling and stifling the cry. "I hope it . . . will be over soon."

"So do I, my dearest love." Luke ignored the chair and dropped to his knees beside the bed, clasping her hand in both his own. He loved her so deeply, but—for all he would have given his right arm to help her—there was nothing he could do. "Dickon's gone for the doctor—he'll be here soon, Elizabeth."

He longed to hold her to him, but a warning glance from Katie Tempest banished the thought. Instead he leaned forward to plant a kiss on her cheek, shocked anew to feel how feverishly hot her skin had become.

"I love you, darling," he told her huskily and, recalling her father's message, added wretchedly, "We're all thinking of you —your pa and Edmund and Dickon, of course."

But Elizabeth seemed not to hear him. Her heavy lids fell, and from behind him her mother whispered, "Let her sleep, Luke dear. If she can sleep until the doctor gets here, perhaps she will recover her strength."

"Yes, I—if you say so." Luke clambered awkwardly to his feet, gently disengaging his hand from hers. For a long moment he stood looking down at her, sick with pity, unable to reconcile the frail little figure on the bed with the lively, happy girl who had been his wife. Elizabeth had always been so strong and full of spirit, he reflected glumly, putting him to shame often by her effortless skill on horseback, her knowledge of the stock, her boundless energy and enthusiasm. And they had wanted a child, but . . . He drew in his breath sharply. Not at this price, not at this cost to its mother.

"She'll be all right, won't she?" he asked, lowering his voice. "Mrs. Tempest, Elizabeth will be all right?"

Katie Tempest led him to the door. "She will be all right in Dr. Morecombe's hands, Luke. But it is a—well, a difficult birth, you see. Mrs. Lee's done her best, she—leave her to us now, Luke. As I said, it will help if Elizabeth can sleep."

"Yes, I know, I—" Luke choked, unable to give voice to all he wanted to say. "It's Elizabeth who—who matters. Even if the baby is—" He could not go on, but, with swift understanding, Katie Tempest inclined her white, neatly braided head.

"She matters to me, too, Luke. Try not to worry, my dear

lad." Before closing the door, she added practically, "It's supper-time. You should try to eat. Tell my husband to see that you do."

The door closed softly but firmly behind her. Left alone, Luke stood leaning against the stair rail, listening tensely for any sound coming from the room he had just left. But there was none. He had wasted so much time, he thought—time that he and Elizabeth might have spent together. They had had only a little over a year together, but he had wasted much longer than that in his futile pursuit of the man, Jasper Morgan, who had murdered his brother Dan. He had followed Morgan's trail from the Turon River to the Victoria goldfields, obsessed with the longing for revenge. The hunt had ended at the Eureka Stockade at Ballarat, and Morgan had met his end there, it was true, but not at *his* hands. A stranger had fired the shot that killed him, while he himself . . . Luke felt bile rise in his throat. He himself had kept his lovely Elizabeth waiting, and only on his belated return to Pengallon had he claimed her as his wife. He—

"Luke!" It was Edmund's voice, and his brother-in-law came up the staircase to his side. "The meal's ready. Father says you're to join us."

"Yes, all right." Numbly Luke followed him to the dining room, lamp-lit now, as the darkness closed in. "The doctor—Dickon's not back yet?"

"No." Rick Tempest's tone was gruff. He plied his carving knife with the skill of long practice, deftly cutting slices from the leg of lamb on the table in front of him. "Even Dickon couldn't make it this fast, and Morecombe will come in his trap. They'll be another hour at least." He held out a piled plate. "How is Elizabeth?"

Luke took the plate, scarcely conscious of what he did. He bit back a sigh. "I don't know, sir. She seemed—oh, God, poor little girl, she seemed very tired. Mrs. Tempest said she would sleep until Dr. Morecombe arrives. I—I hope she can."

"Yes, let us hope so." Rick Tempest finished his carving in silence, and, when he seated himself at the table, he changed the subject with considered deliberation. His talk, addressed mainly to Edmund, was of the recently appointed governor general, Sir

William Denison, whose record in Tasmania—where he had previously filled the office of lieutenant governor—had made him almost universally unpopular.

"He's a dry sort of fellow," Rick Tempest opined thoughtfully. "And he seems to be convinced of his own rightness, whatever the verdict of the citizens of Tasmania. He opposed the cessation of convict transportation, for one thing . . . and he waxes very eloquent on the question, given half a chance! I had to listen to him for a solid hour the other day, when he gave me chapter and verse on the reasons why he fell out with the Hobart judiciary. But—" He shrugged his broad shoulders. "I fancy what really made so many people dislike him was the support he gave to that sadistic swine John Price, the late commandant of Norfolk Island. He and Bishop Willson were in a state of open warfare on the subject of Price, but then the British government stepped in and ordered Norfolk Island to be closed down as a penal settlement and the convicts transferred to Port Arthur."

"Which no doubt pleased the bishop," Edmund suggested. "And the Catholics of Hobart."

"Indeed it did," his father confirmed. "Norfolk is to be handed over to the Pitcairn Islanders when the evacuation is completed. The Pitcairners, as you probably know, are the descendants of the *Bounty* mutineers, who fled there from Tahiti. Worthy folk, I am given to understand, despite their origins, whose refuge has become too small for them." He rose, gesturing to the sideboard. "More lamb? What about you, Luke?"

Luke shook his head. The food he had attempted to eat had come near to choking him, and it took all his composure to remain at the table while both Edmund and his father took second helpings. But he restrained himself, and Rick went on, "However, Governor Denison had the last word where Price was concerned. No sooner was his Norfolk Island appointment terminated than Denison gave him the post of inspector general of penal establishments in Victoria. With the connivance"— Rick's tone was faintly sarcastic—"of the acting governor, Colonel Edward Macarthur." He pushed his plate away and, in an attempt to draw Luke into the conversation, went on, "You've heard of his father, John Macarthur, haven't you, Luke?"

Luke attempted to collect his scattered thoughts, aware that his father-in-law was trying to distract him from the anxiety that, on Elizabeth's account, kept him in silent torment.

"Yes," he admitted uncertainly. "He was an officer in the old New South Wales Corps, wasn't he, and led them in a rebellion against Governor Bligh?"

Edmund gave vent to an amused laugh. "Well, that's putting it in a nutshell, Luke old son! Apart from leading the Rum Corps' rebellion, Macarthur introduced purebred merinos into the colony—the first man with the wit and forethought to visualize the benefit that would accrue from the venture. At one time he owned more land and more sheep than the rest put together. He . . ."

But Luke was not listening. He caught the sound of hoofbeats and, thrusting his untouched plate aside, said in a cracked voice he scarcely recognized as his own, "They're here, sir—Dickon and Dr. Morecombe." He was at the window, peering out into the darkness. "Yes, that's the doctor's buggy, thank God!" Relief flooded over him, and, without waiting for the other two to join him, he picked up a lamp and went stumbling to the front door. "I'll let him in."

Dr. Morecombe, a portly, red-faced man in shirtsleeves and breeches, greeted Luke with brisk cheerfulness.

"Not doing too well, our little Elizabeth, eh? Well, don't you worry, lad—I'll soon put things to rights. I anticipated that the birth wouldn't be easy. I warned you, didn't I?" He yielded up his shabby medical bags and, with maddening deliberation, paused to don his jacket before following Luke into the house and, at the door, again halted to wave to Dickon, who was leading his horse away.

"She needs you sorely, Doctor," Luke urged. "She—"

"There, now," the doctor reproved him. "Don't rush me, boy. I came as soon as I could, and it's a long drive in this heat. You cut along and tell the good Mrs. Lee that I'm here, and then tell them in the kitchen that I'm going to need boiling water, lots of it, you understand?" He stumped into the dining room and, to Luke's dismay, was still there ten minutes later when he returned, his own errands completed.

But at last, when Luke's self-control was near to deserting

him, the plump doctor set down the glass of brandy Rick had poured for him and announced that he was ready to do battle.

"Compose yourself, boy," he advised, not unkindly. "I know fatherhood's a strain the first time. When it's your third or fourth, you'll have learned better. But I've brought hundreds of young Australians into the world, so you just sit back and leave Elizabeth to me, eh? Take a drink—Mr. Tempest keeps an excellent brandy."

Shamefacedly, Luke took his advice. As he was sipping the lavish tot his father-in-law had given him, Dickon came in and, with more understanding than the doctor had shown, put a big, muscular arm about his shoulders in wordless sympathy, before seating himself at the table to eat his belated meal.

After that, time passed on leaden wings. As before, Rick and Edmund talked of the colony's affairs, but now Luke gave up all pretense of listening. The brandy glass still unemptied, he sat slumped in his chair, a prey to nameless fears and ever-growing despair, straining his ears for the sound of a baby's cries—the sound that would signify Elizabeth's ordeal was ended.

But that sound did not come. After what seemed several hours—but, according to the clock on the mantel, was barely one—Katie Tempest came down, to snatch a brief respite from the vigil in the sickroom.

"It's going slowly, Luke," she confessed, unable, for all she tried, to keep the anxiety from her voice. "Dr. Morecombe is doing everything he can. We must just be patient." A maid brought her tea, but she hardly touched it, jumping up suddenly and, with a whispered "I expect Mrs. Lee could do with a cup," returning upstairs with the tea tray, her visit adding to Luke's despair.

An uneasy silence fell, and after a while Luke slept, a silent, inarticulate prayer on his lips as sheer weariness overcame him. He wakened with a start to the sound of voices and, struggling back to consciousness, realized that it was daylight outside and that Dr. Morecombe had come into the room.

The portly little physician had lost all his former jaunty cheerfulness; he looked wan and exhausted, and his voice was hoarse as he said, "I deeply regret to tell you that the child was stillborn and that, despite all I could do, I have now to say that only a miracle can save little Elizabeth's life. Miracles do happen, but . . ." He broke off, shaking his balding head sadly.

Luke stared at him in stunned dismay, unable at first to take in the news he had brought. That his firstborn child had died he could accept, but not, dear God, not Elizabeth! For a moment he could not speak, the words strangled in his throat, but then, sick with bitterness, he asked, "Can I go to her?"

"Luke?" The doctor stared back at him with red-rimmed eyes, seemingly without recognition. Then, recovering himself, he nodded jerkily in assent. "You're her husband, of course, you —yes, go to her by all means. You, too, Mr. Tempest . . . all of you. But I fear she will not know you. She—the poor young soul is not conscious."

Rick Tempest put an arm about Luke's shoulders and together they climbed the narrow staircase to the upper floor.

As before, Elizabeth was lying very quietly in the curtained bed, which had been set to rights, its curtains half drawn to cut out the light from the nearby window, and, as before, her eyes were closed. But this time she did not rouse herself when he knelt beside the bed, and Luke knew, with bleak, instinctive certainty, that the miracle of which Dr. Morecombe had spoken was not to be. Her mother, unable any longer to hide her grief, was weeping openly, and Rick Tempest, after bending to drop a light kiss on his daughter's brow, muttered something Luke did not hear and led his wife away, to stand by the window, holding her in his arms.

Edmund and Dickon came in briefly and left together, Dickon, his bearded face taut with pity, pausing, as he had done earlier, to touch Luke's shoulder with a big, gentle hand. Silence fell, broken only by Katie Tempest's stifled sobs, and Luke went on kneeling at the bedside, numb with grief. He held one of Elizabeth's hands to his lips, pouring out his love for her in a choked voice and praying desperately to the God he had worshiped in the boyhood that now seemed infinitely far away.

"Save her, Father in Heaven—I beg you to save her! Of your infinite goodness and mercy, let her live. Take my life, not hers —I would gladly die for her! Elizabeth, my dearest, sweetest love, try to speak to me—try to rouse yourself! I love you so. . . ."

But his frantic pleas elicited no response; Elizabeth's small, work-roughened hand was limp, her face shuttered and remote, and her eyes remained tightly closed. Luke did not know for how long he knelt there as her life ebbed away, but after a while Dr. Morecombe bade him get to his feet and stand aside, and after a brief examination he said flatly, "She has gone, boy, God rest her soul. You'd better go downstairs."

The next two days were a nightmare, during which Luke managed somehow to do what was required of him and keep his emotions under iron control. The funeral of his wife and still-born child took place at Pengallon, conducted by a curate from Bathurst, who was a stranger to him, and attended by a host of people, most of whom were the Tempests' friends and also strangers to him. He accepted their expressions of sympathy in a state of frozen acquiescence, locked in his own grief as if it were a cage, and even Elizabeth's family, try as they might, could not reconcile him to his loss.

It was as if they, too, had become strangers, and the day following the funeral, Luke made up his mind to leave Pengallon. The place held too many memories; wherever he went, to the paddocks, to the stables, to the shearing shed, or to his own cottage, the memories of Elizabeth came flooding into his mind, haunting him like some small, beloved ghost that was never absent and was yet unreal.

Rick Tempest, to whom he made known his decision, proved sympathetic and understanding and did not attempt to dissuade him.

"Take time off by all means, Luke. I realize, indeed we all do, how hard this has hit you. But come back to us, lad, when you feel you can. Elizabeth's inheritance will be yours, and Pengallon is your home—remember that."

Luke thanked him, his heart full. "I reckon I'll go to sea again, sir," he added. "Maybe go back to the States for a while, if I can find a ship bound for 'Frisco. But if I can't—well, just about any ship will do, wherever she's bound. I'll ask Claus Van Buren if he can give me a berth in one of his traders."

He took his departure soon after talking to Rick. Edmund, when the time came to bid him farewell, urged him to stay. "Or at least," he suggested, wringing Luke's hand, "don't make it too long an absence this time. Because I've thought about what my father said, and . . . I owe it to him to do as he asked. I'm going to stand for the Assembly in his place, Luke, and do my share of electioneering, if that's what he wants. So you'll be needed here, to run the station and help the old man out when I can't. That gives you a year's freedom. It should be long enough, shouldn't it?"

Would it? Luke wondered dully—would he be able to recover from Elizabeth's loss in twelve short months? But he did not argue, and with Dickon and the boy, Billy Joe, he rode to Bathurst, gave his horse into their care, and took the Crane and Roberts coach to Sydney. Dickon's woebegone face and the little boy's tearful waving, as the coach pulled out of the staging-post yard, were a measure of their disappointment at his departure, but Luke steeled himself against the impulse that bade him stay on their account. He waved once and then settled back on the roof of the lurching coach, resolutely refusing to look back.

He was stiff and cold when the coach decanted its passengers at the depot in Sydney, having covered the 140-mile journey in sixteen hours, with brief halts at changing stations to hitch up fresh teams of horses and enable the passengers to stretch their legs and refresh themselves. Luke had not eaten; the mere thought of food was abhorrent to him, and he did not take advantage of the meal that was on offer at the coach depot. Instead, unshaven and in crumpled clothes, he set off on foot for the Van Burens' residence in Bridge Street, his few possessions contained in a cloth-bound bundle slung over his shoulder.

The servant who answered the door peered at him uncertainly in the dim light of a distant streetlamp and brusquely directed him to the tradesman's entrance, at the rear of the opulent house.

"But if you've come begging for charity," the man added dismissively, "you'd best go elsewhere. The master's at sea, and the mistress won't receive you."

Becoming belatedly aware of the spectacle he presented, Luke sighed but held his ground.

"Tell your mistress that Luke Murphy would like to see her," he requested, and, ignoring the fellow's attempt to impede him, he strode into the hall. Mercy Van Buren saved him from further embarrassment; evidently hearing and recognizing his voice, she came hurrying down the wide, curving staircase to fling herself into his arms with a glad cry of welcome.

It was over a year since he had seen the girl who had joined his pursuit of Jasper Morgan and traveled with him from San Francisco in Claus Van Buren's clipper *Dolphin,* and Luke's flagging spirits lifted at the sight of her. He started to stammer out an explanation for his sudden appearance at her front door, but Mercy waved him to silence.

"Luke dear, it does not matter why you are here—it's enough that you've come! And clearly you need shaving water and a bath and—goodness, a change of clothing and, I feel sure, a meal. Then you can tell me why you've come." Turning, she issued brisk instructions to the manservant who had been so reluctant to admit him, and, when the man had gone to carry them out, she added, laughing, "And you may come and bid good-night to my sons when you are looking less like a scarecrow. I was putting them to bed when I heard your voice, and they won't sleep until they've seen you."

An hour later, freshly shaven and clad in a borrowed suit, Luke was introduced briefly to Mercy's small, sleepy twin sons, Joseph and Nathan, and then, as if sensing his distress, she led him to the dining room.

"You must eat," she insisted. "Then we can talk. I wish Claus were here, but he's at sea, on his way to Batavia in the *Dolphin.* He will not be home for six or eight weeks at the earliest, but I'm thankful he did not go to England with the wool crop this year. I'd have lost him for much longer."

There was a wealth of affection in her voice, and Luke, forcing himself to sample the food she placed in front of him, reflected, without envy, that Mercy's marriage was as happy as his own had been. They had come a long way together, he and she—the Mormon farm boy from the California valley and the waif from the wagon train who had lost her parents and her friends in the long, perilous overland journey to the American goldfields.

The meal over, a servant brought him pipe and tobacco, and then and only then did Mercy permit him to explain the reason for his presence. He told her in a clipped, controlled voice, and there were tears in her eyes as she listened.

"Oh, Luke, I'm deeply sorry, sorrier than I can find words to tell you. But you—you've left Pengallon?"

"Yes," Luke confirmed, tight-lipped. "I could not bring myself to stay. It's—oh, the whole place is full of Elizabeth. I'd see her at every turn, Mercy. I hadn't the heart to stay there."

"Then what will you do?"

"I want to go back to sea. I—well, I'd hoped that Claus might be willing to sign me on as one of his hands. But if he's on passage to Batavia, then I'll just have to look elsewhere, find another ship—work my passage back to the States, maybe. But—"

"There are no American ships in port here at present," Mercy told him. "They mostly berth at Port Phillip or Geelong, carrying Americans to the Victoria diggings. There is—" She hesitated, eyeing him uncertainly. "There is the *Mercedes* brig, one of Claus's traders. She's due to sail for New Zealand in the next few days, and Silas Deacon, who was mate of the *Dolphin,* if you remember, is in command of her. He is a very good man —Claus has always thought highly of him. But New Zealand . . . perhaps you—"

"No," Luke put in quickly. "I don't care where I go. I simply want to get away, to work till I drop, Mercy. I'm at the end of my tether, you see. I . . . do you suppose Silas Deacon would be willing to sign me on?"

"Yes, I'm quite sure he would. I can write him a note, if you wish, but—oh, he'll remember you, Luke. And all our ships are short of hands these days, particularly experienced hands."

Luke got to his feet. "Where can I find him?"

"He'll be on the Van Buren wharf," Mercy said. "But it's late, Luke—after eight o'clock. Stay here for the night, have a good night's sleep, and—"

He shook his head. "I can't sleep. I'll go now, get it settled, if Silas is there. I . . . thanks for your hospitality and for offering to let me stay. But I'm not fit company for anyone, least of all for you and those boys of yours. I—" He gestured to the suit he was wearing. "I'll send these garments back before we sail."

Mercy studied his face for a long moment and then rose too, making no attempt to argue or to detain him. At the door, she kissed him on the cheek and stood there, watching him out of sight.

Silas Deacon was in the small office on the wharf, a pile of cargo manifests in front of him. To Luke's relief, the onetime mate remembered him. He asked no questions and, after hearing his request in silence, readily agreed to sign him on.

"You can go aboard right away, if you want to," he said. "I've done as much as I can with these blasted papers tonight, so I might as well come with you." He grinned and laid a friendly hand on Luke's, as he set down his pen. "It's good to see you again, young Luke, though I have to say I didn't expect to. Reckoned you were one who'd swallowed the anchor . . . but if you didn't, then I'll be glad to have you." His grin widened. "You'll find an old friend of yours on board the *Mercedes,* name o' Yates—Simon Yates, my second mate he is now. Went gold digging with him and his brother, didn't you, a few years back?"

Luke's spirits lifted. "Yes," he answered. "Yes, I did, Captain. On the Turon River. When I left, he and Rob were still hoping to strike it rich."

"Well, they didn't," the master of the *Mercedes* stated with finality. " 'Tis a fool's game, this gold seeking. For every man that makes his fortune, there's a thousand that never do. But you can't tell 'em, and they keep on coming, packing in good jobs, running from their ships, deserting their wives and kids. But some learn sense, like the Yates lads—and like you, seemingly."

"Yes," Luke agreed flatly.

"All right, lad, I'm not bothered as to why you're signing on with me. You proved yourself useful enough on the passage from 'Frisco, so I reckon I can rate you A.B. this voyage. That's it, then, unless—" Deacon hesitated, his white brows knit as a thought occurred to him. "Well, just so long as you ain't running from the law for any reason. You ain't, are you?"

"No," Luke assured him. "I'm not, Captain Deacon."

But, he reflected unhappily as he followed old Silas Deacon across the wharf to his waiting boat, he was running harder than he had ever run in his life, running he knew not where, from the memory of Elizabeth's dead face, just as he had run from the memory of Dan's—and it felt suddenly as if the devil himself were after him.

"I heard tell," Deacon said, coming unexpectedly to a halt, "as you were mixed up in the Eureka Stockade affair at Ballarat. I don't rightly recall who told me, but—were you there, Luke?"

Luke made an effort to remember. It seemed a long time ago, part of another life. "I was there," he admitted. "But I was a police trooper then, not a digger. Don't worry, there's no price on my head."

"And did you find the feller you were after, the one you left America to hunt for?" Deacon persisted.

"Yes, Captain," Luke answered. "I found him. He was killed at the Stockade."

"Ah, then that's all right, then," the old man said, relieved. "I was just a mite afraid of what you might have done when you found him." He gestured to the boat. "Least said, soonest mended, eh? I'll ask no more questions. Into the boat with you, lad—and you can pull an oar, if you ain't forgotten how. You'll have to earn your rate, you know."

"I'll earn it, Captain," Luke promised. "I'll earn it, never fear."

Chapter II

It was the habit of Henry Osborne and his family to attend morning service every Sunday at the parish church at Dapto, six miles from Marshall Mount, Henry's prosperous sheep and cattle station near Lake Illawarra.

The male churchgoers went on horseback, forming a sizable cavalcade to escort the two big drays in which Sarah Osborne and her younger daughters traveled, with the female members of the establishment, who included stockmen's wives and children and domestics.

Jenny De Lancey, invited by her hostess to take a seat in the family dray, accepted with relief. She and her husband had ridden, in admittedly easy stages, from Sydney to the Illawarra, but, unaccustomed to such strenuous exercise, she was saddlesore and stiff, and the dray was comfortably cushioned, its occupants shielded by an awning from the glare of the sun.

William, for all he had been convalescent on his arrival from England two months earlier, had very swiftly recovered from the toll the Crimean campaign had taken of him, and Jenny's gaze was proud as she watched him ride past at Henry Osborne's side. True, he was still painfully thin, and his empty right sleeve bore witness to the ordeal he had endured, but, if anything, his loss of weight had enhanced his good looks, and the flecks of gray in his hair and his immaculately trimmed cavalry mustache and side-whiskers added to his air of distinction. Although in civilian dress, he still contrived to maintain his soldierly bearing, adding credence to the reasons he had given for his decision to accept the appointment he had been offered in the East India Company's Army of Bengal.

"I'm a soldier," he had insisted, when both Henry Osborne and his wife had urged him to stay in Australia and settle on the land. "Soldiering is all I'm fitted for, and, deuce take it, the fact is I know India a great deal better than I know the land of my birth! I'm utterly ignorant of farming—unlike you, Henry, it's not in my blood. And besides, my sweet wife is willing to come with me to India, aren't you, Jenny my love?"

She had, of course, assured him of her willingness, Jenny reflected a trifle ruefully. She was deeply in love with her husband of a month, reluctant to refuse him anything he might ask of her, but . . . She sighed. It would be a wrench to leave Australia, to part—perhaps for years—from her family and friends, and to begin life anew in a strange land, with which William was familiar and she was not. A land, moreover, that was peopled by the seething multitudes of a dark and warlike race, whose language she did not speak and whose religions and customs were alien to her.

"You will live like a queen, my darling," William had asserted, when she had ventured to express her doubts. "With a score of excellent servants to wait on you, a fine house, and a social life that has its equal nowhere else . . . and certainly not in Sydney, believe me."

She did believe him; indeed, she trusted him implicitly. Yet for all that, Jenny found herself wishing that he had paid more attention to the Osbornes' persuasive arguments, instead of shutting his mind to them.

She bit back another regretful sigh. This was such a lovely place, a place in which she would have been happy to stay for much longer than the scant few days William had allowed for their visit. In the distance, as the wagon wound its way slowly along a well-worn cart track through the bush, she glimpsed the lake—Lake Illawarra—gleaming silver in the bright sunlight, behind its screen of trees and flowering shrubs. Nearer at hand, but also hidden by the close-growing gums, a stream flowed placidly by, and all around it were great tracts of lush green pasture, with cattle grazing and, on the gentle slope of hillside to the east, the white dots that her hostess had told her were sheep.

As far as the eye could see was, she knew, Osborne land—a vast acreage, sustaining countless flocks of sheep and the herds of prime beef and dairy cattle that the family now owned. And their holding was not confined to this station, Henry Osborne had said, in no spirit of boastfulness but with simple pride. His eldest son, Harry, had leased from him the Narrow Plains station at Colombo, across the Dividing Range, and—a month or so before she and William had arrived to pay their promised visit—his second boy, Patrick, had set off to establish a new sheep run on land at Lake Urana, between the Murrumbidgee and Murray rivers.

It had taken years—a lifetime, in truth—to build up to their state of prosperity. Henry and Sarah had talked of the early, pioneering days, of the initial hardships they had endured, of the cares of a young and growing family reared in a primitive cabin, many miles from any other human habitation, always with the risk of drought or bushfires, of aboriginal raids or the predatory attention of convict escapers on the run. But shrewdness, enterprise, and skillful planning, as well as prodigious hard work on both their parts, had brought success and a happy, united family.

Henry Osborne smilingly described himself as a squatter now, his tone when he claimed the title at once deprecating and oddly defensive.

"Where my livestock spread out in search of new pasture, I took possession of the land, as did many others. The land was empty, unexplored and unsurveyed, certainly unsettled. But we had no security of tenure. At first we could only take out annual licenses—pastoral licenses, they were called—with the risk of being dispossessed. It took ten years of struggle with the government, but finally, by banding together, we won the right to purchase at a favorable price the freehold of the land we leased. It took an Order in Council from the British government to gain us that right, and the public, as well as successive governors of the colony, opposed us at every turn."

Perhaps, Jenny thought, if William had stayed in Australia and become a pastoralist five years ago, when he had come on leave from India, the challenge would have had its appeal—a stronger appeal than fighting his country's battles in the Punjab or the Crimea had offered. But as it was . . . She was conscious of a sudden feeling of intense sadness. It was too late to cherish even the smallest hope that her husband would change his mind or that anything the Osbornes might show him would deflect him from his chosen path; yet—against all reason—the hope persisted, and she felt tears well into her eyes.

William was like her brother Red, she told herself—for had not Red put his naval career before the ties of home and family? Besides, if she herself had really wanted to settle on the land, she would have married Edmund Tempest—as everyone had supposed she would—instead of choosing to wed the man in the bemedaled British cavalry uniform, who was now about to take her away from the world she had always known to one that, however secretly, she feared.

As if sensing her unvoiced distress, Sarah Osborne touched her arm and pointed to a line of low stone buildings that came into view just ahead. Most of the buildings appeared to be of utilitarian origin—store sheds and stables or the like—but in the center stood a white-painted cottage, with an overhanging shingle roof. The cottage was picturesque, its walls and the veranda that fronted it covered by a vividly flowering creeper, and its garden, behind a low picket fence, was ablaze with color. Vines, fruit trees, and flowers grew in healthy profusion in well-cared-for plots to the sides and rear of the flower beds, and the path to the front door was paved, with white-painted stones placed at intervals to mark its course.

The cottage appeared to be unoccupied, despite the neatness of its garden; no smoke rose from its single cookhouse chimney, and a flock of brilliantly colored parakeets, disturbed by the approaching cavalcade, took wing with shrill cries of alarm, to seek refuge in a nearby apple tree.

"That was our first home—Pumpkin Cottage, Jenny," Sarah Osborne said. "And the first garden I stole from the bush and planted with flowers and trees that reminded me of home. The vines and the vegetables came later—even the potatoes had to take second place to my flowers! Originally it was a bark cabin. It's been added to, of course—as our family grew, so did our dwelling place. But then we couldn't add to it any more, and Henry built our present homestead, Marshall Mount, and planted the Moreton Bay fig tree you admired—goodness, it must be almost ten years ago that we moved! I still love this little house though, and the homestead garden has never quite matched this one. Dear Pumpkin Cottage!"

She smiled reminiscently, and, studying her serene, still-beautiful face, Jenny thought how much she liked and admired Sarah Osborne.

The years and the strain of childbearing had robbed her of her once slim and elegant figure; her hair was graying, brow and cheeks were deeply lined, but she had retained in full measure all her charm and her zest for life.

And her husband and those of her children still living under the paternal roof made no secret of the fact that they adored her. . . . Jenny echoed her smile.

"It's lovely, Mrs. Osborne," she said, referring to the cottage and its surroundings. "But is there no one living here now?"

"There will be very soon," her hostess assured her. "The family of our two young stockmen from the old country, Tom and Joseph, will be coming out within the next few weeks." Her smile widened. "It's quite a romantic story, really. Henry had always maintained that he owes his start out here to the proprietor of an inn called the Gillespie Arms, in Dungannon, County Tyrone."

Sarah launched into the story, smiling the while, as she described her husband's eagerness to reach her father's rectory in Dromore, which had led to his forgetting the draft for a thousand pounds—his entire capital—in the pocket of the cloak he had left in the inn to be dried.

"Old Mr. Doakes preserved the draft for him," she concluded. "And it was on his advice that Henry invested the money in a cargo of Irish linen, which he sold for three times its cost in Sydney when we arrived. And on the proceeds he was able to stock the land grant he was given as a new settler."

It was, indeed, a romantic story, Jenny thought. And evidently, being the kind of man he was, Henry Osborne had not forgotten the debt he owed to the proprietor of the Gillespie

Arms in far-off Ireland. The two young men, Tom and Joseph, must be the innkeeper's sons, and . . .

"The boys are his grandsons." Sarah Osborne answered her unvoiced question. "The old man died several years ago, but his son Benjamin—the boys' father—was a shipping clerk in Liverpool. Henry entrusted him with the arrangements for the trade goods and livestock he has imported ever since we came out to Australia—a trust he fulfilled most admirably. He sent Tom and Joseph out under indentures, and they—as well as Henry himself—have long urged Benjamin and the rest of the family to emigrate, too. Well, now they are coming here, and Pumpkin Cottage is ready and waiting to receive them." Sarah spread her small hands in a gesture of finality. "Benjamin Doakes, thanks be, will relieve me, at long last, of the bookkeeping. He is trained to it—he worked for the Black Ball and the White Star shipping lines all his adult life, whereas I . . ." She smiled wryly. "Well, I had to pick up the rudiments as best I could, Jenny. And with all the land Henry now owns—and the new sheep runs across the range—it's become too much for me."

Which was scarcely surprising, Jenny conceded, her admiration for her charming, gray-haired hostess growing. Sarah Osborne had, as a young girl—younger, by several years, than she herself was now—abandoned home and family and friends to follow her husband to an unknown land, just as she was being called upon to follow William, in a few short weeks, to India. And Sarah had not hesitated. She had followed her heart and the man she loved, on a journey that had taken her halfway round the world.

Again, uncannily, as if she had read her guest's unspoken thoughts, Sarah's hand closed about hers, and Jenny sensed both understanding and sympathy as the older woman said softly, "Your husband is a fine man—and a brave one, Jenny. Henry's nephew, poor young surgeon Alec Osborne—the one whose effects William brought here—wrote to us of the gallantry the Light Cavalry Brigade displayed. And your William has been chosen from amongst those gallant souls to receive the highest award Her Majesty the Queen can bestow . . . the new medal, the one that is to be known as the Victoria Cross. He is worth any sacrifice, Jenny."

"Yes," Jenny agreed, her voice choked. "I know he is, Mrs. Osborne."

"And you will not change him, child. He's not cut out to be a farmer, whatever Henry says. Soldiering is in his blood. Perhaps, in his own good time, he may come to it—he may want to come back to the colony. But I doubt whether that will be for a very long while yet."

She doubted it, too, Jenny thought resignedly, but she looked back at the beautiful cottage the Doakes family were to occupy and then, her eyes misted, to the tall figure of her husband, riding at Henry Osborne's side, his handsome dark head thrown back in laughter at some jest his companion had made.

They reached the little township of Dapto half an hour later, and the Osborne cavalcade wound its way along the single main street, to join a procession of other worshipers on foot, on horseback, and in traps or drays like their own, all heading toward the church.

Greetings came from all sides, friendly and respectful—the Osbornes, Jenny swiftly realized, were universally popular and known to everyone. A gray-bearded stockman, his face deeply tanned and his smile warm, came to meet the dray, gallantly sweeping off his wide-brimmed hat as he assisted Sarah Osborne to alight.

"This is Noah Wrightson," Sarah said, when Jenny joined her. "He was with Henry when he drove the first mob of cattle from here to Adelaide in—when was it, Noah? Thirty-nine?"

The old man's smile widened. "Aye, 'twas in the December o' thirty-nine we set off," he confirmed. "Eight of us, there was, ma'am—me an' Mr. Henry, three convict lads, an' three abos. An' we hadn't no maps nor roads to follow in them days. Took us four months, it did, but we got 'em to Adelaide. Over eight hundred head o' cattle an' a flock o' nigh on the same number o' fat wethers, an' they all was in good condition when we drove 'em into the township!"

"And he's never tired of boasting about it, are you, Noah?" Sarah accused indulgently.

"Course not, Mrs. Osborne, ma'am," the old stockman answered, unabashed. "No more'n Mr. Henry, when there's new folk to listen." He eyed Jenny curiously, and then, as William finished tethering his horse and came striding over to them, his faded blue eyes lit up. "Ain't that the gentleman they was writin' about in the Sydney newspapers? Him that rode in the cavalry charge in the Crimea an' lost his arm?"

Sarah Osborne performed the introductions with easy grace, and, when the old man shambled off to greet her husband, she said, lowering her voice, "He's a great character, old Noah. Like Henry, that daring drive to South Australia was the foundation of his fortune, and at one time he owned as much land as we did. Sad to say, however, he has only a few acres left now. . . . Sunday is the only day when the poor old fellow is sober. Well, I can hear the organ. We had better go in. Girls—" She turned to call to the two pretty daughters who had accompanied them in the dray, both of whom were chatting to friends. "It's time we went in . . . your aunt Marshall is playing the organ voluntary, and she's always upset if we're late for it. Put Benjy's hat straight, would you please, Judy dear? And make sure he has his collection money."

"I do have it, Mama," her youngest son protested indignantly, displaying a bright new penny in his small, grubby paw. "And why do I have to wear my hat when I only have to take it off in the church?"

"Because it is seemly," Sarah told him. "Your papa is wearing his, isn't he? And so is Colonel De Lancey. Be a good boy and do as I bid you."

With her family mustered into an orderly procession, servants bringing up the rear, Sarah Osborne took her husband's arm and led the way into the small, stone-built church. It was cool and dark inside, the wooden pews and rush-matted upright chairs swiftly filling, and, directed to a seat at William's side, Jenny smiled at him before dropping to her knees in brief and silent prayer. The organist—a thin, gray-haired woman in sober black, evidently a relative of Sarah's—turned in her seat to acknowledge the arrival of the Osborne party with a brisk, approving nod and then launched into a spirited rendering of the Old Hundredth, which brought the congregation to their feet.

The rector of Dapto, also black-robed and gray-haired, made his entrance as the organ recital came to an end and, in a pleasantly accented Scottish voice, began the familiar service of

Morning Prayer with an exhortation to the assembled worshipers to seek forgiveness for their sins.

"Dearly beloved brethren, the Scripture moveth us in sundry places to acknowledge and confess our manifold sins and wickedness and that we should not dissemble nor cloak them before the face of Almighty God our Heavenly Father . . . but confess them with an humble, lowly, penitent, and obedient heart, to the end that we may obtain forgiveness of the same by His infinite goodness and mercy. . . ."

My heart is obedient, Jenny thought. *For all I dread the prospect of leaving Australia and going to India, I will go, because that is what William my husband asks of me. Yet I am afraid, and with each day that passes I am more reluctant and my fears grow.*

She sank again to her knees, very conscious of William's tall, imposing person at her side, as the rector declaimed, "We have erred and strayed from thy ways like lost sheep. We have followed too much the devices and desires of our own hearts. We have offended against Thy holy laws . . . and there is no health in us. But Thou, O Lord, have mercy upon us miserable offenders. . . ."

Jenny whispered the words after him, her eyes tightly closed. "Spare Thou them, O God, which confess their faults. Restore Thou them that are penitent. According to Thy promises declared unto mankind in Christ Jesu our Lord. And grant, O most merciful Father, for His sake, that we may hereafter live a godly, righteous, and sober life, to the glory of Thy holy name. . . . And give me the courage, O dear Lord," she added earnestly, "to say, as Ruth said, 'Whither thou goest, I will go' and to mean it, with all my heart."

Throughout the service, Jenny found herself silently repeating her prayer for courage, and the rector's lengthy sermon fell, so far as she was concerned, on deaf ears; but the act of prayer, performed in such surroundings, gave her consolation and fresh hope. She joined, happily enough, in the Osborne family's belated luncheon, and later, after riding round the sheep paddocks with William and their host, took part in a lively game of charades that the younger members of the family enthusiastically organized following dinner.

That night, as she lay in the sanctuary of William's embrace, after his tender lovemaking, she began to believe that her prayer had been answered, since her fears for the future seemed, at last, to have faded. But then, to her bitter dismay, with sleep came a nightmare so hideous that she wakened, sobbing uncontrollably, her body drenched in perspiration. Like the dream she had had when William had been in the Crimea, on the eve of his regiment's fatal charge on the Russian guns, every detail was so clear that she felt she had been present in reality, and it took all the resolution she possessed to refrain from waking her sleeping husband in order to describe the vision that still filled both mind and senses.

Jenny drew a long, shuddering breath and somehow managed to stifle her sobs, as William slept on, undisturbed and seemingly as deaf as she had been to the rector of Dapto's sermon earlier that day.

In the dream, she had been crouching beneath the shade of a great, gnarled tree—of a species she had never seen before—and there had been a wide, fast-flowing river some distance below her. Boats, their brown lateen sails in flames, were aground on what had appeared to be a sandbar. The boats, rough, cumbersome wooden craft, were filled with dead and wounded people —soldiers in red coats, and women and children, too crying their agony aloud, as volleys of musketry and the boom of cannon rent the sultry air.

She had huddled, petrified, beneath the tree, Jenny recalled, stunned and powerless to move, as the ghastly slaughter went on and screams and cries of the wounded in the boats gradually faded into silence. There were men all about her hiding place— men with dark faces, some in blue-and-scarlet uniforms, others in flowing white garments, with turbans on their heads, and . . . as the firing ceased, she had watched them run to the river's edge and wade across to the sandbank, to complete the killing at close quarters with spears and sabers or, in some cases, with their bare brown hands.

Then the terrible scene had vanished, cloaked by darkness, but . . . just before the nightmare ended and she had awakened, she had seen the dawning of a new day, and—almost more horrifying than what had gone before—heralded by the loud beat of wings, a vast flock of obscene, bald-headed birds had descended from a blood-red sky to waddle, squawking and quarreling, on the boats with their lifeless cargoes.

Surely, Jenny thought, seeking desperately for consolation as she relived her nightmare—surely such horror was not possible? India, William had told her repeatedly, was at peace, a well-governed, orderly country now that the Sikhs had accepted British domination by right of military conquest. Warriors from the Punjab now served in the East India Company's armies. There were strong garrisons of British troops throughout all three presidencies, and with them native regiments, both Moslem and Hindu, of long and proven loyalty, devoted to the British officers who commanded them.

"They fought with us in the Sutlej and Punjab campaigns, Jenny," her husband had said. "They fought and died with us, just as so many did in Clive's day. And whilst some of the native princes may not like yielding up their autocratic powers, they have been well compensated. And their people have every reason to be grateful, because they are spared from tyranny and misrule and now enjoy the Company's protection."

William must know, Jenny told herself. All his adult life, from the age of sixteen, had been spent in India, in the Company's service. His opinion was based on firsthand experience, and he was nobody's fool. Her own baseless, panic fears had conjured up the nightmare, and . . . despite the similar dream she had had two years ago, about the Light Cavalry Brigade's charge and William's part in it—a dream that had proved so unaccountably accurate—she had never supposed that she possessed the gift of . . . what was it called? Second sight. Indeed, until tonight, she had had no other similar dreams or visions of the future, and the one she had just endured was . . . merciful heaven, it was too hideous, too farfetched to be worthy of serious consideration, least of all William's.

For all this reasoning, during the days that followed, Jenny was tempted to tell William of the dream; but each time she was on the point of doing so, she uneasily decided against it, fearing that he might misunderstand and attribute it to her reluctance to go with him to India. She did not suffer the nightmare again, and by the time they took leave of the Osbornes and returned to

Sydney, the memory of it had faded, at least to the extent that she was able to dismiss it as a figment of her imagination.

Benjamin Doakes and his wife and family arrived at Marshall Mount the day before her and William's departure, and Jenny enjoyed the celebrations that marked their arrival and their installation in the refurbished Pumpkin Cottage, with which, clearly, they were delighted.

They had made a very fast passage, the onetime shipping clerk announced with pride, on board the White Star clipper ship *Spartan,* reaching Sydney in eighty-five days.

"She is a beautiful vessel, ma'am," he told Jenny. "Built in Aberdeen by the Hood yard, with no expense spared. You'll see her when you go back to Sydney. And no doubt you'll meet the titled lady and gentleman from Ireland—Lady Kitty Cadogan and her brother, the Honorable Patrick, from Castle Kilclare in County Wexford, who took passage with us from Liverpool. A handsomer, livelier pair it's never been my good fortune to meet, ma'am . . . and not a bit of swagger to either of them. I'm sure the society folk in Sydney will be eager to make them welcome."

The names of the two young Irish aristocrats who had incurred Benjamin Doakes's admiration meant nothing to either William or herself, Jenny reflected, but—since titled immigrants were rare in colonial circles—she did not doubt that Sydney society would indeed be eager to make them welcome, particularly if, in addition to being titled, they were also wealthy and socially inclined.

The long ride back to Sydney was less fatiguing than the outward journey had been, partly because William—as if he, too, were regretting their imminent departure from their homeland—set a more leisurely pace, savoring the beauty of the countryside and the miles of wide, untamed bush through which their way led them.

Having spent much of her time at Marshall Mount on horseback, Jenny found that her initial saddlesoreness had ceased to trouble her, but . . . She sighed. Apart from infrequent visits to the Tempests' property near Bathurst, she had become a typical city dweller, she thought wryly, venturing forth on social occasions more often by chaise or carriage than astride a horse. And no doubt in India it would be the same, since the climate precluded the indulgence by women—white women—in strenuous exercise, or prolonged exposure to the monsoon rains or, during the hot weather months, the fierce glare of the sun. Officers' ladies, William had told her, remained for the most part in their cool, well-staffed bungalows, where they entertained in lavish style and occupied their spare time in such gentle pursuits as needlework, knitting for charity, and meeting each other over afternoon tea or at exclusively female luncheon parties. Visits and calls were made in covered chairs, known as *doolies,* borne on the shoulders of native servants, or, if the occasion called for formality and the weather permitted it, by carriage, again with numerous native servants in attendance . . . and always in the cool of evening.

Looking out over Sydney's beautiful, sunlit harbor as they neared her father's house in Elizabeth Bay, Jenny repeated her sigh. There was a ship, evidently newly arrived from overseas, making for Circular Quay under head and topsails, with one of the port's steam tugboats preparing to take her in tow. She was a three-master with white-painted ports, broad of beam and with an elaborate gilded figurehead, a crimson house flag fluttering from her lofty masthead, and a number of passengers crowding her upper deck.

William stifled an exclamation, studied her in pensive silence for several minutes, and then, with a jerk of his bridle-hand, he drew Jenny's attention to the vessel, a slow, pleased smile spreading across his face.

"I fancy that is our ship, my love—*La Hogue,* from Calcutta, unless I'm much mistaken. If it is, she's made port ahead of time . . . which means that we shall not have much longer here, so we had best start making our farewells."

He sounded so pleased and eager that Jenny could find no words to answer him. Her throat tight, she nodded, and then, fearful that she might betray herself, she kicked her tired horse into a trot and hurried ahead of him, down the hill to her father's house.

Unbidden, the memory of her dream returned and tears stung her eyes, but when her father came from the house to meet her, she resolutely blinked them back, and as William drew rein beside her, she managed a smile and slipped from her saddle and into Justin Broome's warm and comforting embrace.

If William was right, she told herself, and if the newly arrived vessel was indeed *La Hogue* from Calcutta, then there would be no time for tears. . . .

Chapter III

"I WONDER," KITTY Cadogan observed thoughtfully, leaning back against the cushioned seat of the carriage and smoothing the folds of her shimmering taffeta skirt demurely about her knees, "what he is like, this Crimean hero. Does he, do you suppose, Pat, have the arrogant redcoat mentality we've always hated and rebelled against?"

"I presume you are referring to Colonel William De Lancey?" her brother Patrick responded. He settled himself beside her and nodded to the coachman to move off, a slim hand tugging irritably at his immaculate white tie. "Infernally uncomfortable form of dress, this! I'd no idea that colonials went in for such formality."

Kitty ignored the digression. "Yes, of course," she confirmed, in answer to his question. "According to the invitation from Their Excellencies Sir William and Lady Denison, is it not to bid farewell to Colonel De Lancey and his wife, on their departure for India, that we are privileged to attend a soiree at Government House?" She added, her tone faintly derisive, "If Michael were here, would Their Excellencies have invited *him* to join in the farewells, do you imagine?"

"You would be wise to temper your rebel notions with discretion," Patrick warned her wryly. "And to keep a guard on your tongue, Kit! Don't forget, this evening's celebrations are to mark the victory of Great Britain and her allies in the Crimea and the signing of a peace treaty with Russia. Which is an occasion for rejoicing that no one can deny, not even the Irish, whose soldiers were there too. The Inniskilling Dragoons, the Connaught Rangers, the Green Horse . . . and that light cavalry charge was a damned fine thing, you know. Don't decry it."

"I'm not decrying it," Kitty denied. "It's only that . . ." She did not complete her sentence, but, with intuitive understanding, her brother put out his hand to clasp hers.

"Just be your own charming self," he advised her gently. "And win their hearts and their cooperation. I must contrive to get to Norfolk Island somehow, Kit, and I've heard it rumored that one of the naval frigates is under orders to proceed there within the next week or two, to assist in the evacuation of the convicts. I told you that, didn't I?"

"Yes, you told me. You said you thought it was Her Majesty's ship *Galah,* whose commander is a certain Captain Broome— whom everyone calls Red Broome, from which I presume he must have red hair. Well, provided I am able to recognize him and obtain an introduction, I will do all in my power to win his cooperation." Kitty smiled at him, her normal good humor at least partially restored. "But it is taking so *long* to find out anything, Pat!"

"We must be cautious, little sister. You know as well as I do that we cannot afford to take risks," Patrick reminded her.

"Oh, yes, I know," Kitty conceded unhappily. The long, idle weeks of their voyage out had tried her patience sorely, and it troubled her conscience that almost another three weeks had passed since they had disembarked in Sydney, with virtually nothing achieved.

They had rented a pleasant house some distance from the center of the city, on the South Head Road overlooking Double Bay; they had hired this carriage and, after some difficulty, engaged two indifferent house servants, but . . . Kitty glanced at her brother and then away, an anxious frown creasing her brow. Until they were able to ascertain Michael's exact whereabouts, there was little they could do to aid him, and such inquiries as they were able to make had, so far, revealed only the fact that he had attempted to escape and, on being recaptured, had been sentenced to penal servitude on the dreaded

Norfolk Island. The people of Sydney called it Island of the Damned, a terrible place of exile where . . . Kitty's lower lip trembled. Where punishment was said to be only just short of death. And because she and Patrick dared not admit their relationship to him, they did not know whether their brother Michael was alive or dead. Or, if he had survived the appallingly harsh treatment meted out to the Norfolk Island prisoners, he might have been evacuated to one of the mainland jails.

"There's the diary," Patrick said, seeming to read her thoughts. "The diary the man O'Brien told us of—the one he hid in his cell and which is still there, in all probability, unless they've pulled down the prison buildings. I *have* to get to Norfolk Island, Kit, before the evacuation is completed. Someone there must know where Michael is."

"Or if he's dead," Kitty put in bitterly. "The letter O'Brien gave us was written two years ago. *Two years!* I—" She broke off, her voice choked. "If we had only known sooner—if we had known that he was going to be sent to Norfolk Island! Instead of believing Michael when he wrote that he was engaged as tutor to a wealthy landowner's children and living in luxury!"

"We had no means of knowing, Kit. And we've been into this a hundred times. It will do no good to blame ourselves, truly it will not. We came out here as soon as we could after O'Brien brought us Michael's last letter." Patrick's strong fingers tightened about hers. "God willing, we'll not have come in vain. But you must not lose heart."

"No," Kitty agreed, her lower lip still visibly trembling. But she managed to give him a shaky, uncertain smile and, freeing her hand from his, tossed her dark head defiantly. "No, I'll not lose heart. It is my patience that is wearing thin. And having to leave most of our inquiries to Mary O'Hara. She is a good, loyal soul, heaven knows, but she is not blessed with very much intelligence."

"She does her best," Patrick defended.

Their carriage joined a small procession of other vehicles heading in the same direction, and the coachman reined back his horses to the more leisurely pace of the phaeton immediately in front of them, as it turned into Macquarie Street.

Patrick leaned forward to take stock of its occupants and,

resuming his seat, flashed his sister a mischievous grin. "Why, Kit, look, will you—a captain of the Royal Navy with red hair, who, I take leave to surmise, is Red Broome, commander of the *Galah,* with a beautiful wife beside him! And a fine-looking fellow with a beard, who appears to be unaccompanied . . . and who is feasting his eyes on *you,* unless I'm much mistaken."

"You are mistaken," Kitty asserted. But she found herself peering round their coachman's broad back and met the undoubtedly interested gaze of the man her brother had described as a fine-looking fellow. He was in civilian dress—a tall, broad-shouldered man with a neatly trimmed beard, who was seated with his back to the coachman's box, facing his two companions. She quickly averted her gaze, conscious of her own heightened color, and Patrick's grin widened in affectionate mockery.

"He'll seek you out, Kit," he prophesied. "You see if he doesn't. And that might well be the stroke of luck that's been eluding us. If the *Galah* is about to sail for Norfolk Island, what better than the chance to make the acquaintance of her captain without appearing to have any motive for doing so? Don't be riding on your high horse now . . . if there's to be dancing, you'll want a better partner than myself, in any case."

Perhaps she would, Kitty was forced to concede. Her twin was accomplished in virtually every social grace save dancing, for which, as she knew to her cost, he appeared temperamentally unsuited, moving clumsily and possessing no ear for music.

"That is the plain truth, Pat my dear," she agreed. "But all the same, it will be for the bearded gentleman to make the first move, for I shall not."

Joined by others from neighboring streets, the procession of carriages slowed to walking pace, and when, some twenty minutes later, Kitty and her brother alighted in front of the ornate Gothic pile that was the official residence of the governor of the state of New South Wales, the occupants of the phaeton were nowhere in sight. Having deposited her cloak, Kitty took her brother's proffered arm and they mounted a short flight of richly carpeted stairs, leading to what she deduced was the ballroom, at the entrance to which Sir William and Lady Denison were waiting to receive their guests.

Immediately ahead of them in the slowly advancing line were two scarlet-robed prelates of the Catholic Church, flanked by their chaplains, and beside her Kitty felt Patrick suddenly stiffen and draw in his breath sharply as a liveried footman, positioned by the balustrade, announced the churchmen's names in stentorian tones.

"The Most Reverend Dr. Polding, archbishop of Sydney, Your Excellencies, and the Right Reverend Robert Willson, bishop of Hobart, with the Reverend Father John Joseph Therry and—"

Patrick whispered excitedly, "Now that *is* a stroke of luck, Kit—Bishop Willson is largely responsible for the British government's decision to close Norfolk Island as a penal settlement! You remember what Captain Thomas told us about the treatment meted out to—what was his name? The man who was dismissed from the Anglican chaplaincy . . . the Reverend Rogers?"

Kitty remembered and her lovely mouth tightened. Chaplain Rogers had been summarily dismissed from the prison service because he had made repeated reports of the excessive severity of the commandant of Norfolk Island, and the only man who had listened to him had been, ironically, one not of his Anglican persuasion but the Roman Catholic Bishop Willson, who . . . Kitty caught her brother's excitement. Who was standing only a few paces from them at this moment, being received with unconcealed coldness by the governor, who bowed but did not shake the aging bishop's hand.

Captain Wilfred Thomas, of the 40th Regiment, whom they had met during the *Spartan*'s brief stay in the port of Melbourne, had told them, with a certain wry amusement, that Sir William Denison—at that time governor of Tasmania—had engaged in numerous acrimonious exchanges with Bishop Willson on the subject of Norfolk Island. Wilfred Thomas had not known, of course, the reason for her and Patrick's interest in the penal settlement, and they had been at pains to disguise it, so they had not learned as much as they might otherwise have done. But, Kitty reflected, they had learned enough concerning Commandant Price to cause them renewed anxiety on Michael's behalf. The civil commandant had ruled the convicts with a rod of iron, and Governor Denison, ignoring the strictures of both Bishop Willson and Chaplain Rogers, had given his support and approval to Price's administration. He—

The viceregal footman was looking at them inquiringly, and Patrick gave their names.

"Lady Kitty Cadogan—the Honorable Patrick Cadogan!" the man announced, and as they moved forward, Patrick said softly, "I'm going to have a word with Bishop Willson, Kit. Carry on without me, will you?"

Kitty nodded her assent. Governor Denison, a stiff, solemn-faced man in an immaculate full-dress uniform, unbent sufficiently to give her a wintry smile and bid her welcome to the colony of New South Wales. His hand, when she shook it, felt cold and unexpectedly limp, but his greeting seemed friendly enough, and Lady Denison's was even more so. Both, as nearly as she could judge, were in their fifties, the governor a few years older than his wife.

"You have only recently arrived here, I believe," Lady Denison observed. "You and your brother . . . so you will not yet be acquainted with Colonel and Mrs. William De Lancey, to whom, sadly, we are bidding farewell this evening, on their departure for India. Come, Lady Kitty, and let me make you known to them."

The De Lanceys were a good-looking couple, Kitty saw as, her hostess's hand on her arm, she was led up to them. Colonel De Lancey, contrary to her preconceived notion of him, was tall and darkly handsome, a man in the prime of life, with intelligent brown eyes and a humorous smile, his hand clasp—in contrast to the governor's—firm and warm, for all it was made with his left hand. His wife was young and slim, her beautiful auburn hair unfashionably dressed in a simple knot at the nape of her neck, which somehow became her better than any sort of elaborate coiffure would have done. Her gown, too, was plain, but in an exquisite shade of greenish blue, reflecting the color of her deep-set, smiling eyes and emphasizing the slim shapeliness of her figure.

Despite her earlier prejudices, Kitty found herself taking an instant and purely instinctive liking to them both. Conscious of a feeling of regret that there would be no chance to further an acquaintance with them, she turned, seeking to draw Patrick into their conversation, and then realized that he was not behind her.

"Your brother," Colonel De Lancey said, gesturing to the center of the room, "is with the Catholic archbishop and his brother bishop from Hobart, Lady Kitty. Not," he added, lowering his voice, "the best way to win the approbation of His Excellency, I fear, supposing that to be his desire. Sir William and Bishop Willson have crossed swords rather frequently in the past, I'm told, when Sir William was governor of Tasmania. The bishop has long been opposed to convict transportation, whereas His Excellency holds the opposite view—a somewhat unpopular one these days, particularly in New South Wales, as no doubt you will have gathered. Isn't that so, Jenny my dear?"

Thus appealed to, his wife inclined her head a trifle reluctantly. "We must not give the impression to new arrivals like Lady Kitty that we are quarrelsome colonials, Will," she reproved him gently.

"No, indeed," De Lancey conceded. "But I thought that a— well, a word of warning might be in order, if Lady Kitty and her brother are planning to settle here. Are you, if I may ask, Lady Kitty?" He frowned, glancing across to study Patrick's half-turned face uncertainly. "Or is your brother aiming to join the gold seekers?"

Such an intention was easy to deny, and Kitty relaxed, shaking her head emphatically. "Oh, no, certainly not, Colonel. If we do settle here, it will be on the land. We have an estate at home in Ireland, and Patrick is interested in bloodstock breeding. We—" She was saved from the necessity of offering a more detailed explanation by the arrival of a frail, white-haired lady in a black lace gown, leaning on the arm of a young ensign of the garrison regiment. Both the De Lanceys greeted her with warm affection as "Aunt Abigail."

Kitty slipped away, intending to merge with the crowd of guests now gathering in the ballroom. Patrick, she saw, was still talking to Bishop Willson, but the archbishop and his elderly, black-robed companion, Father Therry, had moved away, and she hesitated, wondering whether or not to join her brother. As she stood undecided, the military orchestra on a dais at the far end of the room struck up a lively waltz, and a hand touched her lightly on the arm. She turned, to find herself looking into the bearded face of the man she had seen earlier, seated in the phaeton that had been ahead of their carriage in Macquarie Street—the man whom Patrick had confidently predicted would seek her out.

At close quarters, he was taller and better-looking than she had supposed, and—like the naval officer who had been seated opposite him in the open phaeton, whom Patrick had guessed was "Red" Broome—his hair and beard could only be described as red. Admiring blue eyes met hers as she confronted him; he bowed, a trifle awkwardly, and then lifted his head, smiling.

"Permit me to introduce myself, ma'am—John Broome, at your service, requesting the pleasure of this waltz."

It was done with an odd mixture of diffidence and effrontery, and before Kitty could answer his request, he swept her into his arms and onto the dance floor, holding her closer than current fashion decreed. But he was an excellent dancer, moving for all his height and broad, muscular body with easy lightness and, a little to her surprise, in silence. Not until the dance came to an end and the polite applause died down did he speak, and then it was only to thank her, with grave formality, for permitting him to partner her.

"I enjoyed it," Kitty told him truthfully. "You are a very good dancer, Mr. Broome."

"And so are you, Lady Kitty," he assured her.

"You know my name?"

"It's my business to know the names of new arrivals, ma'am." He smiled, the smile, as before, lighting his face. "I'm a journalist—a newspaper correspondent. But . . . there are new arrivals and new arrivals. Some who arouse no curiosity, and some who make me very curious indeed. You come into the latter category."

"Do I?" Kitty's pleasure evaporated. She looked round for Patrick but could see no sign of him. Despite this, she made to excuse herself, but John Broome laid a detaining hand on her arm. "Please don't desert me," he begged, swiftly contrite. "I'd no intention of offending you, believe me. It's just that . . .

well, most new arrivals in this colony come here for obvious reasons. There are the officials, civil and military, the settlers, and of course the fortune hunters, drawn here by the lure of gold. They come from every walk of life and in every nationality. But . . . it's very seldom that members of the aristocracy come out to Australia, you know . . . unless they're in the services. The idle rich don't."

"The Irish aristocracy," Kitty pointed out, with a touch of asperity, "should not be confused with the English, Mr. Broome. My brother and I are Irish, and we are neither idle nor rich."

"Nor particularly lovers of the English?" John Broome suggested shrewdly.

Kitty reddened under his scrutiny. "We are patriots, sir," she returned, with a sudden flash of temper that she instantly regretted. But her partner did not take advantage of her momentary lapse; the orchestra struck up again, and he smiled and held out his arms to her. "Shall we continue? Your brother is still deeply engaged in conversation with Bishop Willson."

He was observant, Kitty thought, and clearly well informed; a man to be wary of, because he would not easily be deceived, but . . . he was truly an excellent dancer, and so long as she remembered to keep a guard on her tongue, there would be no harm in waltzing with him. Besides, as Patrick had remarked, an introduction to Captain Red Broome of Her Majesty's frigate *Galah* might result and afford the opportunity for one—or even both of them—to request passage to Norfolk Island. Royal Navy warships did, on occasion, carry civilian passengers. . . . She echoed John Broome's smile and went gracefully into his arms.

As they danced, she asked innocently, "Is not your brother in command of the *Galah,* Mr. Broome? And was he not with you in the carriage that brought you here, just ahead of us?"

"That's so," her partner confirmed readily. "With his wife, my beautiful sister-in-law Magdalen, who is the daughter of Judge De Lancey and, of course, the sister of tonight's guest of honor, Will De Lancey—to whom, I believe, you were introduced?" His smile widened. "We are all related—Will's wife is *my* sister, Jenny. A mite confusing, I fear. We colonials tend to intermarry." He came to a halt, gesturing to a tall, distinguished-looking gentleman who had just then entered the ballroom. "The judge himself, Lady Kitty—a veteran of the Peninsular campaign and Waterloo but born in an erstwhile colony, America."

"Then not a rebel?" Kitty suggested.

"Far from it, Lady Kitty. The De Lanceys are all of the kind once called colonial Loyalists, whose loyalty, perhaps needless to tell you, earned them scant reward from the British government." John Broome resumed the dance, swinging her effortlessly round the floor in time to the lively beat of the music. "But," he added, when the waltz came to an end, "they have all made good out here. Australia is a land of opportunity, even for those who came out in chains . . . as my forebears did."

Taken by surprise at this admission, Kitty stared at him. "Did they, Mr. Broome? That seems hard to credit."

"It's the truth," he assured her. "My grandmother—the one from whom we've inherited our red hair—came out in Governor Phillip's first fleet. She was sixteen years old and had been sentenced to death—the sentence commuted to transportation for life . . . her crime the theft of a few shillings! But, fortunately for us, she came of farming stock and eventually became the emancipist owner of a sizable sheep run on the Nepean River. Even more fortunately for us, Grandfather Broome—one of the few who ever made a successful escape from here—subsequently had a not undistinguished career in the Royal Navy during the French wars."

"And your brother also? He has made a distinguished career in the Royal Navy, hasn't he?" Kitty suggested. "I mean," she added, seeing his hesitation, "command of one of Her Majesty's frigates is no small achievement."

"Indeed not. I . . . would you like to meet him, Lady Kitty? I'm sure that he and Magdalen would be more than delighted to make your acquaintance—although in Red's case it will not be for long. The *Galah* is under orders to sail during the next day or so, to assist in the final evacuation of the convicts from Norfolk Island." John Broome offered his arm. "If you'd care to follow me—"

Kitty gave her assent, careful not to sound too eager. It had been easier than she had anticipated, but . . . Again she looked round for Patrick. *"My* brother would very much like to meet yours, I know, Mr. Broome. He is hoping for a chance to visit Norfolk Island, you see, and . . ." She glimpsed Patrick's dark head and waved to him urgently, conscious that John Broome was eyeing her in some surprise. Perhaps, she thought, it had been a mistake to mention Patrick's desire to visit the penal settlement. Perhaps—since she could offer no valid reason for such a desire—her disclosure had been premature and might arouse suspicion. She fell back on the explanation they had agreed upon, purposely making it sound vague: "Patrick is deeply interested in prison reform, and he intends to write a book on the subject. The prison on Norfolk Island is one he is particularly anxious to see in person."

To her relief, her companion appeared to accept her explanation at its face value. "I see," he said. "Well, I don't imagine there will be much difficulty where Norfolk Island is concerned. The evacuation is almost complete—only the few good-conduct prisoners and staff detailed to put the place in order remain there now. It's to be given to the descendants of the *Bounty* mutineers from Pitcairn Island as their permanent home, as possibly you may have heard. And"—he sounded unexpectedly vehement—"I say thank God for that! It's a beautiful island, which for too long has been hell on earth for the poor devils of convicts condemned to serve their sentences there. They—" He broke off as Patrick joined them, acknowledging Kitty's introduction politely.

He looked pale and tense, however, as if what he had learned from his lengthy conversation with Bishop Willson had shocked and disconcerted him. Fearing an impulsive outburst, Kitty put in quickly, a plea for restraint in her eyes, "Pat dear, Mr. Broome will present us to his brother, the captain of H.M.S. *Galah*—you know, the frigate that is shortly to sail to Norfolk Island. You know how much you wanted to make contact with him, in the hope of asking him to give you passage to the island."

To her relief, Patrick's expression relaxed, and he summoned a smile. "Yes, indeed. I'll be greatly obliged to you, Broome, if you'll present us to the captain. I—" He glanced with sudden uneasiness at Kitty. "I don't know what my sister has told you, but we—that is, I—"

Kitty interrupted, with deliberate lightness. "I told Mr. Broome about your book and your interest in prison reform, Pat, and he does not think there will be much difficulty in obtaining permission to visit the Norfolk Island prison, since—" She turned her gaze on John Broome, still speaking with seeming casualness. "Since most of the convicts have been evacuated now."

"Yes," her brother said, with bitterness he could not hide. "Evacuated to an even more hellish prison in Tasmania—Port Arthur, the bishop informed me."

"They are all what we term capital respites, Cadogan," John Broome reminded him. "That is to say, men sentenced to death for crimes committed since their arrival here and whose sentences were commuted. Or incorrigibles, serving long sentences for bushranging and the like. Please—" He held up a hand, forestalling Patrick's indignant protest. "I'm no defender of our prison system, I assure you—rather the reverse, and my paper has long campaigned for reform and an end to all transportation. But men sent to Norfolk Island or the Tasmanian penitentiaries are hardened criminals, you must understand, considered to be beyond reform or redemption, the majority of them. They—"

The band struck up again, and as people crowded onto the floor, the rest of his words were lost in the beat of the music and the soft thud of dancing feet. Kitty grasped her brother's arm in mute warning, and once again his expression relaxed.

"I'll watch my tongue, Kit, don't worry," he whispered. "Let's go, shall we?"

John Broome led the way to the far side of the ballroom, skirting the milling couples on the dance floor, and Kitty and Patrick followed him to where a small group had gathered beneath the portrait of a former governor in military scarlet.

The De Lanceys were there, and the frail, white-haired lady in the black lace gown occupied a chair, talking animatedly to those seated on either side of her, one of whom Kitty recognized as the judge who had fought at Waterloo. The other had been a passenger in the Broomes' phaeton—a lovely young

woman, with dark hair and deep-set blue eyes, whose fashion-
ably cut magenta silk ballgown was draped to conceal but did
not entirely hide the fact that she was in an advanced state of
pregnancy.

Behind her, a hand resting affectionately on her shoulder,
was the red-headed Captain Broome, as pleasant looking if not
quite as tall as his brother John, who performed the introductions with faultless courtesy.

"May I present the latest arrivals in the colony—Lady Kitty
and Mr. Patrick Cadogan. Mrs. Dawson, to whom we all lay
claim as our aunt Abigail. Justice De Lancey, Will and Jenny
De Lancey I think you've met—Mrs. George De Lancey, who
is my aunt Rachel. My father, Captain Justin Broome, late of
the Royal Navy. My brother Red—Captain Broome, Royal
Navy, and his wife, Magdalen. Alexander Dawson, of Her
Majesty's Fortieth Foot . . ." The names tripped off his
tongue, and even as she acknowledged them, Kitty became confused.

As John Broome had confided to her, it seemed that they
were all related, close-knit families, descended from both convict and free settlers but with little social difference between
them now, since they had intermarried and—yes, as the uniforms bore out—many of them held commissioned rank in the
armed forces of the British Crown. Doubtless the rest were
landowners, with vast sheep runs and palatial houses, whereas
poor Michael—how had John Broome described the wretched
prisoners now being evacuated from Norfolk Island to continue
their living death sentences in Tasmania?

He had said they were capital respites, hardened criminals,
considered to be beyond reform or redemption . . . *Michael,*
her beloved elder brother, whose only crime had been defiance
of an unjust system that deprived the Irish people of their freedom! But they had termed it treason and branded him a traitor,
for whom there could be neither forgiveness nor mercy.

Magdalen Broome was speaking to her, inviting her to seat
herself, and Kitty swallowed her momentary resentment, recalled to the role she must play. But the talk passed over her
head; she managed to smile, to murmur polite and meaningless
rejoinders, even to reply to questions with the right degree of

evasive reticence. Let them think her shy or even gauche, so
long as she did not betray herself. . . . Patrick, she observed
thankfully, had attached himself to the group surrounding Captain Red Broome and, with his accustomed easy charm, was
seemingly quite at ease.

A tanned, white-haired man in civilian evening dress—evidently a late arrival—joined the party. Magdalen told her his
name, which was Tempest, adding the information that he was
a member of the Legislative Council and the owner of a sheep
and cattle station near Bathurst, and Kitty listened, without
any particular interest, until she heard him say, in a voice harsh
with pain, "It was bad enough, losing our dearest Elizabeth and
the child—but now we've lost Luke as well."

"You've lost him, Rick?" Judge De Lancey exclaimed,
clearly startled. "You don't mean the boy's dead, do you?"

Rick Tempest shook his head. "No, no—he simply walked
out on us, said he could not bear to stay at Pengallon, which I
suppose is understandable. He had no plans, poor lad, but nothing I could say would induce him to change his mind. I've been
worried about him, as you can image, but . . . I learnt today
that he shipped out in one of Claus Van Buren's traders, bound
for New Zealand—as a deckhand." He shrugged his broad
shoulders, and Kitty's heart went out to him as she heard him
sigh, the pain he was enduring somehow reaching across to her
as if it were a living thing.

"Luke's heartbroken," he added flatly. "And so are we all.
Given time, though, the lad will get over it and come back to
Pengallon, God willing. Well—" He braced himself and then
bent to drop a kiss on Abigail Dawson's lined cheek. "Forgive
me if I don't stay. I had to put in an appearance here, but I
won't wait for the toasts—I'm aiming to make an early start for
Pengallon in the morning. We're short of labor, as always, and
the Chinese I've taken on are pretty useless, though they claim
to be shepherds." He turned to shake Judge De Lancey's hand
and then that of Captain Justin Broome. "I'm resigning from
the Council—in fact, I informed the governor today. Edmund is
going to stand for election to the Assembly in my place."

"I'll walk you to the door," the older Broome said, and took
his arm. Watching them go, Magdalen Broome said sadly,

"Poor soul, his only daughter died in childbirth a few weeks ago, Lady Kitty. Her husband, the one he was talking about— Luke Murphy—is such a fine young man. An American, he came over here from the California goldfields, and the whole family are devoted to him. It's a tragedy—they were so happy, he and little Elizabeth. I . . . ." She flushed, looking down at her distended stomach and then at Kitty. "It makes me a little afraid, you know. Childbirth can be risky, and Elizabeth was so *young.*"

Kitty's diffident attempt to console her was cut short by the announcement that a buffet supper had been prepared for the viceregal guests and was now ready. They wended their way slowly into the adjoining anteroom, and seeing that Patrick was engaged in earnest conversation with Captain Red Broome and his father and brother, she did not go to join him but remained in the pleasant, feminine company of Magdalen and the two ladies John Broome had claimed as his aunts Abigail and Rachel.

The laden tables occupied their attention, and when they had again found seats, the servants brought round glasses of wine, and Governor Denison rose to make a short speech. Kitty gave it only cursory attention; the governor's delivery was slow and a trifle pedantic, but when he raised his glass to propose the first toast, she heard him say, with a wealth of pride and feeling, "Ladies and gentlemen, may I ask you to charge your glasses and be upstanding? Let us drink to the heroic victory of Great Britain and her allies in the Crimea, and to pray for peace henceforth with Russia and all other aggressors. As you will have read in your newspapers, a peace treaty was signed in Paris on March the thirtieth, and our troops and ships will, by this time, be on their way home."

The toast was drunk to loud acclamation, and the governor, still on his feet, held out his glass to be replenished and again raised it high above his head.

"This reception, as you will also know, my friends, is being given in order that we may bid farewell to Colonel and Mrs. William De Lancey, who are about to depart this colony for service in India. William De Lancey was one of that immortal band which, in obedience to an order from their commander in chief that was most tragically misunderstood, yet obeyed and charged the Russian guns at the far end of the valley that has come to be known as the Valley of Death. Few survived the charge unscathed, and Colonel De Lancey, in a selfless endeavor to save the life of one of his troopers, suffered most grievous wounds. His heroism is, we have been given to understand, to be rewarded with Her Majesty's highest honor—the medal of the Victoria Cross. I regret that I shall not have the privilege of investing the colonel with it—that privilege will, in due course, be given to the governor general of India, since Colonel De Lancey will be unable to attend the investiture in London by Her Majesty the Queen in person."

The governor paused, an erect, soldierly figure in his full-dress uniform. He lifted his glass to William De Lancey, a warm smile lighting his austere, high-boned face.

"Ladies and gentlemen, I invite you to drink to the health and future prosperity of Colonel and Mrs. De Lancey, to wish them Godspeed and, let us hope, a safe return to these shores when, in the fullness of time, the colonel's service with the Honorable East India Company comes to an end and both are free to come home to Sydney!"

The applause was thunderous, and Magdalen turned with tears in her eyes to clasp Kitty's hand before resuming her seat.

"They are both such fine people," she said huskily. "And we shall miss them sorely—my husband more than most, for he worships Jenny. I just hope and pray that *he* will be permitted to remain on this station. There are alarming rumors of trouble in China, but—" She blinked back her tears. "At least whilst his ship is engaged in the evacuation of the Norfolk Island convicts, Their Lordships cannot order him there. And Red does not anticipate such an order. The *Huntsman* was sent to join the China Fleet a few weeks ago, so that the *Galah* is the only frigate left here now. Red says that it is unlikely in the extreme that the Admiralty will contemplate denuding Australia and New Zealand of all save a few small sloops and colonial steam vessels. I hope, with all my heart, that he is right!"

It was natural, Kitty thought with ready sympathy, for her to want her husband at least nearby when their child was born, but, with newfound cynicism, she wondered whether the British

Admiralty would set as much store by the evacuation of a far-off colonial penal settlement as they would over the protection of commercial interests in China. But she refrained from saying so, and Magdalen went on, in a more optimistic tone, "It was a stroke of good fortune, really, that the colonial vessel *Lady Franklin* was found to be unseaworthy and had to be taken out of service. For the past six months the *Lady Franklin* had been employed in the evacuation, you see, and Red's ship was the only vessel large enough to take her place. Otherwise, I feel sure, the *Galah*, too, would have been on her way to Hong Kong. But—" She broke off, with an apologetic exclamation. "I don't know what I'm doing, telling you all this, Lady Kitty, since you cannot possibly be interested in the navy's comings and goings. Or, come to that, in Norfolk Island."

"Oh, but I'm very interested, Mrs. Broome," Kitty began impulsively. "You see, my brother is—" She had been about to embark once more on a description of Patrick's proposed book, but there was a call for silence, and Colonel De Lancey rose to reply to the governor's toast.

He spoke briefly and modestly, expressing his regret and that of his wife that they must leave the colony, and then, bowing to Governor Denison, invited the assembled company to join him in drinking to Their Excellencies' health.

The toast was drunk, and, as the applause died down, Kitty saw Patrick making his way through the crush of people toward her. He looked elated, and her heart quickened its beat when he reached her side and whispered triumphantly, "It's all arranged, Kit—we sail for Norfolk Island on board the *Galah* in two days' time."

"We?" Kitty echoed, unable to hide her surprise. "Do you mean that I—"

"That's precisely what I mean, little sister," Patrick confirmed excitedly. "But we can't talk now. I'll tell you all about it on the way back to the house."

It was another hour before they were able to take their leave, and as their hired carriage bore them away from the congested streets of the city, Patrick launched into his promised explanation.

"I had a long talk with Bishop Willson, and he gave me

chapter and verse concerning the inhuman treatment meted out to the Norfolk Island convicts by the civilian commandant, a certain John Price. I won't go into the details, Kit, because they would break your heart, truly they would. Suffice it to say that Price must be the most brutal, sadistic human being I've ever heard of! But he married the daughter of a former lieutenant governor of Tasmania, owed his appointment to Norfolk Island to another, and was supported throughout by Governor Denison, despite the evidence of his extreme cruelty put forward by a onetime Anglican chaplain named Rogers—whom he had dismissed—and the bishop himself. There were others, too, quite a number of them, but Price got rid of them, and their protests were ignored. It seems there was a mutiny on the island, due to laxness on the part of a previous commandant, and Price was charged with the task of restoring order and discipline. He did that all right—with torture and the lash!"

Kitty caught her breath on a sob. "Oh, poor Michael," she whispered, her throat tight. "Poor, poor Michael!"

"Yes, poor Michael," her brother echoed grimly. "But—" He brightened. "There's hope for him, Kit—we're going to the island, both of us, as I told you. It was lucky, really, that I had the chance to speak with Bishop Willson and that the governor saw me speaking with him, for it seems they are on very bad terms, and he was only invited to this evening's reception because he was a guest of the archbishop. Well, to cut a long story short, I made a point of staying close to Captain Red Broome. He mentioned that he was shortly sailing for Norfolk Island, and I took my courage in both hands and, after giving him a much exaggerated account of the book I'm supposed to be writing, asked him point-blank to give me passage in his ship. And I asked him if I could bring you with me." Patrick smiled widely. "He was on the point of refusing—I could see it coming. He started to say that, provided I obtained official permission to visit the island, he might consider taking me, but women on board ships of war were a distracting influence, and it was a practice frowned upon by the British Admiralty. But then—" He threw back his head and laughed aloud. "Oh, Kit, it was a wonderful stroke of luck! His Excellency was passing, and he overheard us—I suppose he took in what I'd been saying about the book. Anyway, he intervened. 'By all means give them both passage, Captain Broome,' he said. 'Let Mr. Cadogan see for himself what manner of men are imprisoned as capital respites in our penal settlements. Once he has done so, I do not doubt that he will be less inclined to give credence to Bishop Willson's carping criticism, and his book might then be unbiased.' "

"Oh, Pat!" Relief flooded over her, and Kitty hugged him. "It's wonderful—it's—it's little short of a miracle! And . . . we *might* find Michael still there. Captain Broome's brother told me that the—the good-conduct prisoners had been retained, with some of the overseers and warders, to prepare the island for its new inhabitants—the families from Pitcairn. I feel sure that Michael must have conducted himself well and—"

In the dim light, she saw her brother's face cloud over. "Don't be too sure of that, Kit," he warned.

"Why, Pat?" Kitty questioned, her bright hopes abruptly fading. "Why should I not? Michael was once a lawyer. He always had respect for the law."

"But he always fought against injustice, little sister. And," Patrick added, a harsh note in his voice, "under Commandant Price, there *was* injustice, if Bishop Willson is to be believed—and I'd stake my life that he is." He took Kitty's small hand in his and said, more gently, "Let's pray that we find him, shall we?"

Kitty closed her eyes. Her prayer, silent and swiftly improvised, yet came from her heart.

Chapter IV

HER MAJESTY'S CORVETTE of war *Galah* lay at anchor in Norfolk Island's Sydney Bay, and from her quarterdeck, glass to his eye, her captain, Commander Red Broome, watched the approach of his returning gig through the perilously narrow channel in the reef that guarded the landing jetty of the Kingston penal settlement.

Putting ashore by oared boat at Kingston had always been hazardous, Red recalled. He remembered his father's complaints on that score, when he had been sent in command of the government sloop *Elizabeth* to conduct a survey of the abandoned prison buildings, prior to the reopening of the island for penal occupation in 1825. Indeed, he reflected, since Governor King's day there had been repeated suggestions that the channel should be widened by blowing up part of the half-submerged, weed-grown reef to permit an easier passage between ships and the shore, but little if anything had ever been done.

Successive commandants had, no doubt, preferred to retain the hazard as a deterrent to would-be escapers from the infamous jail, but perhaps now that the Pitcairn islanders were to be given the place as their permanent home, Governor King's long-forgotten advice would be acted upon.

Red sighed, his glass still trained on the gig as the coxswain carefully steered his frail craft through the cauldron of white, hissing water and into the calmer blue-green depths of the bay beyond. His brother Johnny, he saw, was seated alone in the sternsheets, shoulders hunched in an attitude suggestive of despondency, his hat pulled down over his eyes.

Evidently, Red's mind registered, the young Cadogans had elected, once again, to remain on shore. The *Galah* had been there for just over a week, and Lady Kitty and her brother had not returned to the ship since their arrival, seeming to prefer the hospitality of the acting commandant, Captain Henry Day of Her Majesty's 99th Regiment, to that which the *Galah* could offer.

True, Henry Day was a pleasant, friendly fellow, possessed of a pretty wife and several lively children, but . . . Red trained his glass on his brother's half-hidden face as the gig came nearer. There was no doubt about it, he thought—Johnny had permitted himself to become deeply enamored of the lovely, vivacious Lady Kitty, and her sudden rejection of his company rankled as much as anything ever had. And the more so because, during their passage from Sydney, she had appeared to offer a considerable measure of encouragement, walking the deck with him, seeking his opinion and advice, laughing with him in her charmingly irrepressible way, and gently teasing him for what she called his colonial view of life.

And Johnny had taken the teasing in good spirit, more amused than offended when she had nicknamed him "Boy" Broome, implying a certain lack of sophistication, which—had anyone but Kitty Cadogan implied it—would have had him up in arms, hotly defending himself. But as it was, he answered to the absurd name—Johnny, whose easy conquests of any woman who took his fancy had, in the past, evoked the envy of his rivals!

Red smiled a trifle wryly to himself as he took in his brother's woebegone expression and then lowered his glass. Old Johnny had fallen hard, from the moment he had first set eyes on Kitty Cadogan on the way to the Government House reception. Good Lord, no sooner had he realized that she was to be permitted to take passage to Norfolk Island on board the *Galah* than he himself had petitioned for a berth, claiming that his newspaper had commissioned him to report on the Pitcairners' future home!

Well, perhaps his editor *had* asked for such a report, but, Red told himself, the idea must have come initially from "Boy" Broome and been very persuasively put forward, for time had, to say the least, been extremely short.

The midshipman of the watch hailed the approaching boat as naval custom decreed, the gig tied up alongside, and, a few minutes later, Johnny came on deck and strode across to join him, himself subscribing to custom by removing his hat.

"By your leave, Captain?" he inquired formally.

Red clapped him affectionately on the shoulder.

"I'll recruit you for my ship's company yet, brother—you're shaping up well!"

"I'd be rated a landsman, and that's all I'd ever be, Red, so you can look elsewhere for your seagoing volunteer!" Johnny protested, laughing. But his laugh was forced, and Red gestured to the distant shore, with its cluster of deserted buildings.

"You're back early—how's your report coming along?"

"Remarkably well, as it happens. In fact, I've just made something of a discovery. I found this—" Johnny held up a package, wrapped in a dingy sailcloth covering and loosely tied with twine. "It was in one of the cells where they used to put poor devils of convicts sentenced to solitary confinement. Someone had hidden it in the brickwork, and I only stumbled on it by chance, but—" Now there was a note of excitement in his voice. "I haven't had time to examine it closely, but I think it's a diary. Certainly there are references to the late commandant, John Price. Can we go to your cabin and look at it properly?"

"Yes, of course," Red agreed readily. "The sun's over the yardarm—we can have a drink whilst we're examining it." He nodded to the officer of the watch, young acting-lieutenant Dixon. "The first lieutenant's still ashore. Keep your eyes peeled for his signal, Mr. Dixon, and send the whaleboat to pick him up. He'll be bringing fresh provisions and some baggage to be loaded, so you had better rig a winch to get it inboard. I'll be in my day cabin if I'm needed."

"Aye, aye, sir," Dixon acknowledged. "How about the passengers, sir—the Cadogans? Are they coming aboard this evening?"

Red glanced at his brother, brows raised in question, and Johnny shook his head. "No," he answered, an edge to his voice. "They're staying ashore till the last minute, as far as I can ascertain. The Days are giving a farewell party at Orange Grove. I—" He broke off, but went on when Lieutenant Dixon was out of earshot. "I was invited, but I declined, since it would seem that Kitty is intent on avoiding me, God knows why! If I only knew why, it would be easier, perhaps—but I don't. Damme, Red, they were poking about in the old prison hospital this morning when I was there, but they scarcely said two words to me! And then later, when Patrick was with one of the convict trustees, we ran into each other in the solitary-confinement block—where I found this package—and he lit out as if I had the blasted plague!"

Red did not reply. He ushered his brother into his day cabin and, dismissing his steward, poured brandy into two glasses and set one down at Johnny's elbow.

"Drown your sorrows, Johnny," he advised.

Moodily Johnny gulped down the contents of his glass. "She means a great deal to me, you know, Red," he confessed. "Everything in the world, from the first moment I met her. She— oh, God, Kitty Cadogan is the most beautiful, charming, desirable woman I've ever known! I wasn't even thinking of taking a wife—I'd decided I preferred my freedom to marriage, until Kitty came into my ken. But since then, devil take it, I've thought of little else . . . and I was starting to hope that my feelings for her might be reciprocated, even though I'm a dyed-in-the-wool colonial and she's a member of the aristocracy." He smiled thinly. "The *Irish* aristocracy, as Kitty herself constantly points out."

Once again, Red remained prudently silent, contenting himself by replenishing his brother's glass. Johnny made no move to open the canvas-wrapped package he had found; it was almost as if, despite his earlier elation at its discovery, he had forgotten it. Instead he asked unexpectedly, "Red, do you believe that Patrick Cadogan really intends to write a book, as he claims?"

Red frowned. He had doubted the claim initially, and he admitted, with some reluctance, "Well, since you ask, the answer must be no. He's not the type, is he? I've thought about it, Johnny, and come to the conclusion that—well, that he's made it an excuse for coming here, a justification for his undoubted interest in Norfolk Island. And in the penal settlements as a whole. During the passage, he asked me a great many questions about the Port Arthur prison and Pentridge, in Victoria. I couldn't tell him much about either, of course. The extent of my knowledge of penal settlements stops here, at Norfolk Island."

Johnny eyed him thoughtfully over the rim of his glass. "You were here before, weren't you, Red? During Price's time?"

"Yes, indeed I was," Red confirmed. "When it was truly hell on earth." His mouth hardened. "I met and talked to the Reverend Adam Rogers, the unfortunate chaplain whom Price had dismissed because he reported to Bishop Willson what was being done here."

Memory returned and he saw again the pale, unhappy face of the onetime prison chaplain. They had met after he had attended divine service on the island, and he had watched as the convict worshipers had shuffled in, all but a handful wearing leg-irons, their faces blank masks of suffering and their voices never raised above a whisper, even when hymns were sung by the rest of the congregation. Later, Adam Rogers had told him of the sickening punishments, the brutal floggings and the confinement in cells too small to permit the occupants to stand upright, and of men spread-eagled in the sun until they screamed for mercy . . . and all this for the most trivial of offenses.

"Mr. Price was sent here to restore order after the convicts mutinied under the previous commandant, Major Childs," Rogers had said with bleak resignation. "He has done that, with greater brutality than any of his predecessors ever indulged in. There is order, without a doubt, for the convicts are too cowed and frightened to rebel. But Mr. Price is hated more bitterly than ever Major Childs was, believe me." And he had turned away, Red recalled, to hide his tears, adding in a low, harsh voice, "I am soon to be dismissed from my post because I am, according to Mr. Price, 'too easily disturbed and lacking in discretion.' But judge for yourself, Captain Broome—you have seen the faces of cruelly tortured men in my church this morning. But it is Mr. Price the lieutenant governor believes and not myself. . . ."

And as for John Price, that tall, handsome man, with his monocle and his deceptively genial air . . . Red turned his gaze on his brother, about to repeat the details of his previous visit to the settlement, but Johnny, he saw, was not disposed to listen.

"I *like* young Patrick, Red," he asserted. "I like him very much, but—oh, for God's sake, I think he's playing a part, that he has some other, far more personal reason for wanting to come here than simply to collect material for a book."

"If he has, then so has your lovely Lady Kitty," Red reminded him dryly. "Have you considered that?"

Johnny shrugged. "I've tried to, but—you're right, of course. Kitty has to be involved." He leaned forward to pick up his glass, and his hand brushed against the discarded package. "We might as well look at this, Red. I don't imagine it will tell us much that you don't already know, but if it *is* a diary kept by some poor devil of a convict, I might offer it to Patrick as material for his book! At least it would force his hand, would it not?"

With impatient fingers, he started to remove the mildewed wrapping, to reveal some twenty or thirty sheets of coarse paper. The paper was ruled in columns—purloined, in all probability, from a convict or military roster book, Red decided, picking up a sheet to study it. The writing was small and cramped, but it was in an educated hand, and as Johnny had surmised, it appeared to be a diary, for each entry bore a date.

"Some of the pages are damaged," Johnny warned. "The damp permeated one whole section, in spite of the canvas wrapping, and, as you can see, the ink has run badly in places. But quite a number of pages are legible, I think, in a good light." He shuffled through a batch of the stained papers, blowing on them gently to remove a green powdering of mildew. "There's no clue, as far as I can see, that would tell us who kept the diary, but—let's spread the whole lot out on your chart table, shall we, and see how many of the undamaged pages we can sort out?"

Red nodded his assent and, handling the musty papers carefully, helped Johnny assemble the find in more or less chronological order.

"I wonder why the writer went to so much trouble to hide this?" Red said. "You say you found it in one of the solitary-confinement cells?"

"Yes, that's so. As I told you, it was hidden in the brickwork. A couple of the bricks had worked loose and—" Johnny glanced up, smiling. "I stumbled as I went in, and dislodged them. I—" His smile faded, and he picked up one of the pages and started to read from it. "Here's your answer, Red. Listen . . . this seems to be the last page he wrote, or one of the last. And the date's clear—fifteen January, 1853:

"In three days' time, God be praised, I shall quit this accursed island for Hobart Town on board the *Lady Franklin*. So also will the civil commandant—that archfiend in human form, Mr. John Price, with his wife and family, of whose sadistic cruelty this diary is, in part, a record.

"I have served my sentence and, by a miracle, I have survived. When I land in Hobart, it will be as a free man, but Overseer Bolton told me that we shall all be searched before we are permitted to board the ship. I dare not attempt to take this journal with me, for if it were to be found on my person, Mr. Price would see to it that my release was indefinitely suspended—if he did not flay me alive.

"Therefore I must hide it, before Bolton comes back to strike off my fetters. I can only pray to the good Lord that one day it will be found and the awful truth concerning John Giles Price revealed."

His hand not quite steady, Johnny passed across the table the yellowing page from which he had been reading.

"See for yourself, Red," he invited grimly. "It's a pretty damning indictment of Price, by heaven it is!"

Red glanced at the cramped scrawl and frowned. This had been written hurriedly, words and lines running into each other, but it was clear enough, the writer evidently taken by surprise at the overseer's announcement and fearful of discovery—a more than adequate reason for his having hidden the diary, even though Commandant Price's rule on Norfolk Island had come to an end.

"Let us see what the fellow has revealed, Johnny," he suggested. "Look, this is one of the earlier pages—it's dated two years earlier, March fifteenth, 1851." In a flat, controlled voice, Red went on:

"Big Michael is again in Mr. Price's black books. He had scarce served his three weeks in solitary, and for all he was weak as a kitten from the bread-and-water diet, the commandant ordered him to the quarry gang, to work in irons. During inspection, he complained that his overseer—a brute named Silas Jones—was giving him only corncracker and water, and that the water was filthy and contaminated with slime. Price had the water changed but ordered Big Michael fifty lashes for making his complaint insolently, and doubled the sentence when Michael laughed at him.

"They flogged him, with a dozen others, this evening. He took the flogging without making a sound, and then spat at Price's feet when they cut him down. Price put his damned eyeglass in his eye and shouted, 'Give him the gag!' And then put him back in solitary for ten days. The constables hauled him off and beat him with their clubs, in the commandant's plain view, but he did not reprimand them."

Red drew a deep, angry breath. "God, Price was a sadist all right! You would never think so to meet him, though. I supposed him to be something of a martinet but no worse, until Chaplain Rogers opened my eyes."

Johnny swore under his breath, continuing to search among the pages of the diary. "This is barely legible," he observed, selecting one at random. "It is dated thirteen October, 1846:

"Twelve of the fourteen prisoners condemned to death as ringleaders of the mutiny in July, when Major Childs was in command, were today hanged. We watched them led from the cells in the Old Gaol, six at a time, with Chaplain Rogers and Father Bond attending them to the foot of the gallows. Thank God, it was swiftly done. Each man was pinioned, the noose put around his neck, and the bolt pulled. They protested their innocence right up to the last—Kenyon and

Kavanagh shouting it as they were turned off. There were the usual awful struggles, but not a man among the watchers broke silence. There was a strong guard of soldiers, of course, in case of trouble and—

"There are two lines I can't read," Johnny put in, "but it goes on:

"The bodies were piled into wooden coffins and hauled off in a bullock cart to the old sawpit outside the cemetery, where on Price's orders a communal grave had been prepared. The Reverend Rogers had gone to change into his vestments, ready to read the burial service, but when he reached the sawpit, the bodies had already been interred.

"He told me himself, a few days afterward, when he visited me in the hospital, that it was on Commandant Price's instructions that Christian burial was denied the condemned mutineers. Murderers and mutineers, in the civil commandant's book, are seemingly beyond even heavenly forgiveness and should be treated like carrion. Whilst it is true that the men they hanged were all what we call Old Hands of the Ring—the gang leaders and capital respites—only two took part in the killings and three in the initial attack on the two constables. Jacky-Jackey Westwood bludgeoned Constables Quion and Saxton, and he led the attack on Overseer Smith, but most of the others were condemned because it was claimed they had blood on their clothing. They were members of the Ring, however, and Commandant Price was determined to break the Ring, and he did not care how he did it."

"It was a pretty bloody affair, the mutiny," Red offered. "From all acounts."

"But that doesn't justify the denial of Christian burial, when the wretched men had paid the penalty for what they did," Johnny objected. "They hanged them, didn't they? And they were men—human beings, not animals."

"Perhaps our diarist is prejudiced," Red returned, with faint sarcasm. "Though I suppose he has reason to be."

"I think he undoubtedly has. Listen to this—it's dated April 1847:

"The civil commandant seems determined to rid himself of every official who shows pity for the unfortunates imprisoned here. He has abolished the office of stipendiary magistrate and Mr. Barrow is to go. Mr. Gilbert Robertson, the agricultural superintendent, has been dismissed for showing indulgence to his assigned servants, and the Reverend Rogers was packed off to Hobart last month. We are left with those who dance to Price's tune, with convict informers made overseers and constables.

"And the punishments grow more merciless and barbarously inhumane. Compassion is not permitted. Men are brutally flogged and sent back to their labor gangs next day, with no dressing for their lacerated backs save a wet cloth or a banana leaf. Each day, at least a score are sentenced to the lash, and the ground on which the last few stand at the triangles is saturated with blood.

"But there are worse punishments than the lash. Solitary confinement for six to fourteen days; imprisonment in a cell called the Nunnery, which measures six feet by twelve and sometimes houses a dozen men, with neither light nor adequate ventilation, whatever the outside temperature. The bridle and bit, used as a gag; the spread-eagle torture, with the unhappy prisoner secured to ring-bolts by hand and foot and placed against a wall. Even in the hospital, men are frequently strapped to the beds, unable to move and gagged to prevent them from crying out.

"These penalties for such trivial breaches of discipline—a few minutes late at muster, for example—can earn a prisoner fourteen days in solitary. An attempt to abscond could mean three *months* and a hundred lashes in addition. I know this to be exactly true, for I have suffered it, and my taste of freedom in the bush was a scant two days and nights!"

From the deck above came the faint sound of a boat being hailed, and Red started to get to his feet.

"I must go, Johnny," he apologized. "That will be the whale-boat, with our fresh provisions and—"

"Cannot your officer of the watch deal with it?" Johnny said impatiently. "This is important, Red. For the Lord's sake, your Mr. Dixon is efficient, isn't he?"

"He is very efficient. But Francis will be bringing instructions for the embarkation tomorrow, and it's always a tricky job ne-gotiating the reef with fully laden boats, as you must realize by this time." Red turned to peer through the stern window. The whaleboat, with Francis De Lancey, his first lieutenant, at the tiller, had come through the narrow channel without mishap, and the oarsmen were pulling clear of the pounding surf. The boat, however, was exceedingly low in the water; Francis must have crammed more than he should have into her, the young idiot, but . . . He turned back to his brother. "All right, Johnny, what have you found?"

"More about the fellow whom the diarist mentioned before, Big Michael. The poor devil who seems to have been the object of Commandant Price's particular venom. And it's given me—well, let's say an idea. Listen, will you?"

Red resumed his seat at the chart table. "Very well, I'm lis-tening. But make it short, will you please? I have to have a word with Francis about receiving the convicts. We have to accommodate fifty of them, in addition to Henry Day and his family and ten of his redcoats—not to mention the Cadogans. I shall have to give up my night cabin to Mrs. Day and her children, so my gear will have to be shifted this evening. And I may have to ask your Lady Kitty to double up with them."

Johnny smiled thinly but offered no comment. He spread out two sheets of the diary in front of him, so that the faded hand-writing caught the light from the stern window.

"It's a mite hard to make out, but I'll do my best, Red. The entry is dated November fourteenth, 1850:

"Arrived the *Lady Franklin* from Hobart with an ensign and twenty men of the Ninety-ninth Foot and sixty-seven convicts, classed as capital respites and incorrigibles. One of these caused quite a stir, so much so that Commandant Price had him brought ashore ahead of the rest and heavily ironed. I chanced to see him, as I was with the unloading gang on the jetty. He is a big, striking-looking fellow, with the manner and appearance of a gentleman—and he is taller, by several inches, than Price, who boasts that he stands all of six feet in height himself.

"I was reliably informed that the new addition to our thrice-damned ranks is a special-category prisoner, condemned to transportation for life for high treason. He goes by the name of Michael Wexford, which is not his real name, and rumor has it that he is titled and once served in the Royal Navy as a midshipman. Needless, perhaps, to add that he is Irish and that he hails from rebel country in the South.

"The commandant has singled him out for special treatment—that is to say that, although he has committed no breach of discipline since disembarking from the *Franklin,* he has been put into the gaol gang, to work in chains. They say that his colonial conviction and present sentence to this godforsaken island was for bushranging, after absconding from his assigned place of work."

Johnny paused, glancing across the table expectantly. "Well?" he challenged. "What does all that put you in mind of, Red?"

Red returned his stare, brows knit in a pensive furrow as he took in the significance of the extract his brother had just read to him. The young Cadogans hailed from County Wexford—the surname the man known as Big Michael had adopted—they, too, were titled, and their home was in what the unknown diarist had called the "rebel country in the South." And Michael had been condemned for high treason, a charge all too often leveled against those of Irish birth when they rose in revolt against British rule.

"We cannot be sure, Johnny," he began. "Not on this evidence, for God's sake!"

Johnny did not pretend to misunderstand him.

"I reckon we can," he said firmly. "It all fits, doesn't it? The Cadogans came here hoping perhaps that Big Michael was still on the island—or, God help them, to find out from the records whether or not he is still alive. They don't know and they dare not risk asking too many questions. But here, with Patrick's supposed book as their excuse and Henry Day on terms of friendship, they could easily find out what they're searching for, could they not?"

"I suppose they could. *If* that is what they are after. But—"

Johnny's clenched fist came down on the chart table with a thud, scattering the flimsy pages of the diary. He retrieved them, murmuring an apology.

"Probably they were looking for this," he suggested.

"The diary? But how could they know of its existence?"

Johnny considered the question. "I don't know. Except that —Red, whoever kept this diary had served his sentence. He says so, on the first page, doesn't he?" He searched among the scattered sheets and, finding the one he wanted, read aloud: "'When I land in Hobart, it will be as a free man, but Overseer Bolton told me that we shall all be searched before we are permitted to board the ship. I dare not attempt to take this journal with me. . . .' He says he hid it, but it's evident that he hopes it will be found and . . . 'the awful truth concerning John Giles Price revealed.' Well, he could have left Australia and gone back to England. Or . . . damn it, Ireland! Why should he not have sought out Michael's family, told them about the diabolical treatment Price meted out to him, and—yes, told them about the diary, too! Red, this fellow's diary could be the material for Patrick's book . . . and, if it were published, it would do Price's reputation no good. It might ruin him. Perhaps that is what Michael wants, and Kitty and Patrick are trying to bring it about."

"That is rather a farfetched notion, Johnny," Red argued. "You've really nothing on which to base such a supposition, have you? I grant you that the poor devil the diarist refers to as Big Michael *might* be related to the Cadogans, but I'm not convinced of it, not by a long chalk. You—" There was a knock on the cabin door, and he broke off. "Yes? Who is it?"

"Midshipman of the watch, sir." Cap correctly tucked under his arm, the boy entered. "First lieutenant's respects, sir," he added breathlessly. "And I'm to tell you that he has the lists of passengers and convicts ready for your attention when—that is, when it's convenient, sir."

"Very good, Mr. Appleby," Red acknowledged. "Tell the first lieutenant I'll be with him right away." When the youngster had gone, Red turned to his brother with a wry smile. "Take the bull by the horns, Johnny," he advised. "Show the diary to the Cadogans."

"Yes, but—"

"You can assure them that they've nothing to fear from us, even if Michael Wexford turns out to be a member of their family. Quite probably, Johnny old man"—Red's smile widened—"the reason why the beautiful Lady Kitty has been avoiding you and staying away from this ship may well be because she is afraid to trust us. I'm an officer in Her Majesty's Navy, and you're a newspaperman . . . and it's possible that you asked her too many questions. Or else you answered the questions she asked *you* in the wrong way! At all events, her reaction to the diary should settle the matter, one way or another, don't you agree?" Red rose to his feet. "*My* sympathies are one hundred percent with Big Michael, as I'm sure yours are, so you can tell her that, for a start. And if Patrick decides to have the diary published, I'll do nothing to impede him. If the accusations against John Price are true, then on his head be it! He deserves no better."

Johnny jumped up, to clap him approvingly on the shoulder. "Well spoken, Red! I'll do precisely what you suggest. And if I'm wrong and the Cadogans have no connection whatsoever with Big Michael, I'll give this diary to my editor. Or to Bishop Willson perhaps, to use as he sees fit. In view of Sir William Denison's widely known support for Price, my paper might be reluctant to touch it."

"The *Hobart Chronicle* would have no such inhibitions," Red observed cynically. "In fact, they would jump at it." He picked up his cap and moved toward the door. "Dine with me, if you care to, Johnny. We'll have fresh pork, I expect, and maybe that will make up for the feast you are missing at the Orange Grove —even if the company's not all you want!"

"Thank you, Captain," Johnny acknowledged, with mock formality. "I'll make do with the company."

He started to gather up the scattered pages of the diary, and having replaced them in their proper order, he continued to read them from the beginning, a sick anger growing at the pitiless cruelty they revealed.

While it was true that the majority of those sentenced to penal servitude on Norfolk Island had been men sunk in depravity—murderers, thieves, and rapists—John Price had not attempted to reform them, but simply and solely to punish, until many sought escape from their torment in death. Sodomy, on the diarist's own admission, was rife throughout the prison settlement; the so-called Old Hands of the Ring were, he conceded, villains of the first water, evil men who preyed on their fellows for their own gain, but . . . they were men, human beings like himself, who might have reformed, had they been shown even a modicum of compassion.

Alexander Maconochie had offered proof of it during his administration, but he had been left in charge of the island for only four years and replaced by a succession of officers of the Price stamp—though none, Johnny thought, turning another page, his throat tight, none who had displayed John Price's sadistic enjoyment of the power he wielded.

Even the author of the journal he was reading—a quiet, self-effacing fellow who had accepted the harsh discipline without rebelling and, in consequence, earned his release—even he had suffered flogging and solitary confinement, once for sharing his own meager food ration with one of the chain gang and once, when smitten with dysentery, for being in the privy when the muster bell had rung. That crime had led to fourteen days in solitary and another fourteen in chains. . . .

The light was fading. Unbidden, the steward brought a lamp and set it at Johnny's elbow, but his eyes were tired, even, at times, filled with unmanly tears, and he stopped reading. It would not be advisable to let Kitty Cadogan see the diary as it stood, he decided. Patrick could read it in full, if he wished, but Kitty should be shown only those pages in which mention of Big Michael was made.

By the flickering light of the oil lamp, Johnny selected the requisite pages and, laying them on top of the rest, returned the diary to its canvas wrapping.

Was it possible, he wondered dully, that so gay and beautiful a young woman as Kitty Cadogan, whose laughter during the passage from Sydney had been music in his heart—was it, *could* it be possible that her gaiety had been only a cloak for the secret she was hiding? And had she, as Red had suggested, feared to trust him with it? God knew, even if she did not, that he would gladly lay down his life for her.

But at least it explained her sudden reluctance to be with him, her apparent distaste for his company. And tomorrow, when he showed her the diary, he would know the truth.

More cheerfully, Johnny left his brother's cabin and, with a spring in his step, made for the hatchway and the open deck.

Chapter V

"WE'VE FAILED, PAT," Kitty Cadogan said disconsolately. "For all our searching, we've failed, haven't we? There's simply no trace of Marcus O'Brien's journal."

Her brother Patrick, standing beside her at the foot of the jetty, turned from his anxious contemplation of the heavily laden whaleboat's progress through the reef, giving vent to a sigh of relief as it drew clear of the surf and headed toward the *Galah*. One of Henry Day's young sons, seated on his father's knee in the bow, waved triumphantly, and the convict rescue party, stationed at the far end of the jetty with their cork floats and lifelines, permitted themselves to relax, the danger past.

"It will be our turn next," Patrick observed ruefully, responding to the child's wave without enthusiasm. "What an infernal way to have to load human cargo!" Then, recalling Kitty's question, he shrugged. "In all honesty, Kit, I'd not say we'd failed. We may not have found the diary—obviously someone must have been here before us and he probably destroyed it. Or it's disintegrated in the damp. But we know, thanks be to God, that Michael is still alive. We know that he left this island for Tasmania last May—in reasonably good health, according to Henry Day—and that he was to be transferred to the prison at Port Arthur, after reaching Hobart."

"He has gone from one hell to another that is little better," Kitty reminded him.

"Yes, perhaps," her brother conceded. "But the *Galah* is going to Hobart, and Henry and his wife are now our friends. Henry has promised to give us an introduction to the new governor, who, praise be, is not Denison! We have achieved as much, or even a little more than we hoped to, and as to the diary . . . well, we've only O'Brien's word for it that the evidence it contains against the late civil commandant—what's his name? Price—could win a pardon for Michael. O'Brien was himself here as a convict, don't forget, and even though he served his sentence and was emancipated, would his evidence be believed? Especially since he's not here to swear to it, and nothing on God's earth would induce him to return!"

Kitty sighed, having no answer to his question.

"I still wish we had found the diary, Pat. It might have helped."

"We tried hard enough, Lord knows! Either O'Brien's directions or his memory must have been at fault. I went through every one of those cells, and yesterday, when I thought I was at last on the right track, who should I run into head on but John Broome! I had to beat a very hasty retreat, for fear of arousing his suspicions."

"I fear we *have* aroused them," Kitty said, a catch in her voice. "I think I did, before we came ashore. He's not convinced that you intend to write a book, and he thinks that I—oh, goodness knows what he thinks!"

"He is an extremely decent fellow," Patrick defended. "And he's fallen for you, little sister—hook, line, and sinker!"

It was true, Kitty thought unhappily. Johnny Broome had made no secret of his feelings, and . . . he was a very attractive man, one to whom it would have been easy to respond, had the circumstances been different, or had she been free. But she was not free; she had no right to think of herself when her duty was to Michael. That was why she was here, in this dreadful place to which they had brought poor Michael in chains, to suffer torment that, even now—in spite of what Marcus O'Brien had told her, in spite of what she had seen of the prison and its mounds of unmarked graves—was too hideous to think about or even quite believe.

And Patrick had been shown more than Henry Day had deemed it prudent for her to see. . . . Kitty felt a wave of

nausea sweep over her, as she glanced back at the towering
walls and the barred windows of what had been the prison
hospital. They had shown her *that*, and the memory still
haunted her, in sharp contrast to her recollection of the pleasant house built for the commandant, in which she had stayed
with Henry Day and his family, where flowers and fruit trees
flourished in a well-kept garden and the happy voices of children echoed throughout the sunlit rooms.

The hospital had been dank and dark, filled with the stench
of death, still lingering there, although it was now deserted.
Would it be pulled down, she wondered, before the Pitcairners
came to make their home on the island? The chapel would be
retained, of course, for all it opened onto the prison yard; and
so would the stone-built officers' quarters, the gardens, and the
livestock. And the cemetery, with its divisions . . . headstones
and well-tended graves for officers and free men and their families who had died there, but mounds of unmarked earth for
those confined as prisoners—graves destitute even of a wooden
cross or other tangible signs that those buried there had once
been men, known by names and not numbers. They—

"The boat is coming back," Patrick announced, breaking into
her thoughts. "You know—" He hesitated, eyeing Kitty uncertainly, and then, as if coming to a sudden decision, he caught
her arm, turning her to face him. "We might do worse than
confide in your Boy Broome, Kit. I've a strong feeling that he
would be sympathetic, if we told him the whole story."

"But he's a journalist," Kitty objected. "That's why I've kept
a guard on my tongue and why I've kept out of his way since we
landed here. He would want to print the story, and if he did, we
—oh, Pat, don't you see? It would destroy any chance we have
of helping Michael."

"Of helping him to escape, perhaps," Patrick countered.
"But it could help an appeal—an appeal for clemency, if not a
pardon."

"Well, yes, I suppose it might. Only—" Kitty gazed over the
water toward the whaleboat, which was returning from the *Galah*. "It would be taking a risk."

"Not if we only told him that we are hoping to organize an
appeal. And as you say, Broome is a journalist, so he has con-

nections—he could help us." Patrick warmed to his theme. "The more I think about the situation, the more I realize that we *need* help, Kit. We are strangers here, in no position to ask favors from the authorities. A newspaper campaign, if John Broome were willing to assist us to launch one, might gain Michael's freedom—or at least his release from the Port Arthur prison. Surely it is worth trying?"

Kitty was still conscious of a nagging doubt. They had kept their secret for so long, she told herself, confided in no one save the loyal, devoted Mary O'Hara, who had known them all their lives . . . and known Michael, too. It would be taking a risk to attempt to enlist John Broome's aid, and . . . She stifled a sigh. If, as Patrick insisted, he had fallen in love with her, would it not be the height of perfidy to take advantage of the feelings he had for her . . . and the more so, if she did not wholly reciprocate them?

She started to express her doubts to Patrick, but the whale-boat had come alongside the jetty, and young Ensign Mablon—Henry Day's son-in-law—whose men had been assisting with the embarkation, came up to them with a beaming smile.

"Time to leave this accursed place, Lady Kitty. If you and Mr. Cadogan are ready, we can brave the reef for the last time!"

"We're ready, Joe," Patrick assured him. He offered Kitty his arm. "Come on, Kit—you don't want to stay here, do you?"

She did not, Kitty thought, and shivered. The commissariat storekeeper, Mr. Stewart—who, with six trusted convict servants, was to remain in charge of the island pending the arrival of the families from Pitcairn—stood, hat in hand, to bid them farewell. She answered his good wishes automatically and took her place in the stern, courteously assisted by Francis De Lancey, the *Galah*'s first lieutenant, who was at the tiller.

The pull back to the ship was accomplished without mishap, and Captain Broome was waiting at the entryport to offer a greeting and apologize for the fact that she would have to share a cabin with Caroline Day and her children for the passage to Hobart.

"Our accommodation is stretched to its limit, I'm afraid, but the weather augurs well. We should have a smooth passage, I think, so it is to be hoped that you will not be too uncomfortable."

He was, as always, friendly but a trifle formal, yet for no reason that she could have explained, Kitty sensed a subtle change in his manner toward her and—yes, a warmth he had never previously displayed. A trifle mystified, she assured him that the loss of her cabin was of no account and followed the steward with her valise below.

Of John Broome there was no sign, but—having assisted Caroline Day as best she could to settle her three youngest children into the now-cramped accommodation afforded by the captain's night cabin—she went on deck and was just in time to see the arrival of the last boat from the shore. It was the gig, under the command of the captain himself, with his tall, bearded brother seated beside him. The boat was winched inboard, and a short while later the deck was swarming with seamen, as the order came to weigh anchor and the topmen went surging aloft in seeming confusion. Kitty sought sanctuary in the gunroom below, and there, as if he had been waiting for her, she found John Broome.

He said, without preamble, gesturing her to take a seat at the long mess table, "Lady Kitty, I believe I may inadvertently have stumbled on something for which you have been searching. Indeed, it may even have been the reason why you and your brother came to Norfolk Island."

Kitty stared at him in shocked surprise, and her heart missed a beat and then started to pound furiously as she watched him unwind the canvas wrapping of a bundle of papers that, instinct told her, could only be the diary Marcus O'Brien had kept during his imprisonment.

"I . . . I . . ." Taken completely off her guard, she sought vainly for words, forgetful of Patrick's advice. "I don't know what you mean, Mr. Broome," she managed at last.

"Do you not?" John Broome countered, his tone reproachful. "You can trust me, I promise you. I would never do anything to hurt you or cause you trouble."

Kitty made an effort to recover her composure. The gunroom was deserted, and they were quite alone, the rest of the Galah's company, judging by the thud of feet on the deck above and the shouted orders, fully occupied in taking the ship to sea.

"I'm sure you would not," she conceded unhappily. "But you don't know, you cannot know what—what is involved."

"I can hazard a guess, Lady Kitty, and a pretty accurate one." He gestured to the little pile of papers in front of him, offering two at the top of the pile for her perusal. "This is a record, in the form of a diary, kept by one of the convicts imprisoned here. I went ashore just before we were due to sail in the hope of finding out who the diarist was. And the storekeeper, Stewart—the man who is remaining as caretaker—gave me a name. Perhaps you already know it?"

Prevarication was of little use, Kitty recognized. She bowed her head. "Yes—it's O'Brien, Marcus O'Brien."

John Broome nodded in satisfaction. "That was the name Stewart gave me. O'Brien was released, having served his sentence, in January 1853." His big brown hand gestured to the first page of the diary. "Read this, if you will—it explains why he did not take the diary with him."

She did as he bade her, conscious of a feeling of impotence. "I knew why he left it hidden—he told us. He . . . that is, he came to see us when he returned to Ireland. He had been a seaman, and he worked his passage home from Hobart. The ships were losing men—they were deserting to the goldfields— and the masters did not ask questions. O'Brien returned illegally."

"Yes, I see." John Broome's expression changed, and Kitty read compassion in his eyes as he said, very gently, "On the next page he mentions a man he calls Big Michael. Perhaps you should read it, or—" He saw that she was in tears and offered quickly, "I'll read it for you, shall I? The ink has faded, and it's not easy to decipher."

Kitty put out a hand to take the yellowing sheet of paper from him, but her hand was trembling and he ignored the gesture, commencing to read in a low, expressionless voice.

"November fourteen, 1850. Arrived the *Lady Franklin* from Hobart, with an ensign and twenty men of the Ninety-ninth Foot and sixty-seven convicts. One of these caused quite a stir, so much so that Commandant Price had him brought ashore ahead of the rest and heavily ironed. I chanced to see him, as I was with the unloading gang on the jetty. He is a big, striking-looking fellow, with the manner and appearance of a gentleman—and he is taller, by several inches, than Price, who—"

Kitty was unable to suppress a sob, and John Broome broke off. "I'm sorry—if it pains you, I'll stop. Your brother can read it, and—"

"No." She shook her head, teeth closing fiercely about her lower lip. "Please go on."

He picked up the page again, holding it to the light.

"I was reliably informed that the new addition to our thrice-damned ranks is a special-category prisoner, condemned to transportation for life for high treason. He goes by the name of Michael Wexford, which is not his real name, and rumor has it that he is titled and once served in the Royal Navy as a midshipman. Needless, perhaps, to add that he is Irish and that he hails from rebel country in the South.

"The commandant—"

Kitty interrupted him, unable to stop herself.

"That was how you guessed, was it not?" she asked bitterly. "The name Wexford and the—the rebel South?"

"Yes," John Broome admitted. He smiled faintly. "I was puzzled, you see—and curious as to why you and Patrick were so anxious to come to Norfolk Island. And when I read that . . . well, it all became clear. Michael Wexford is your brother, isn't he?"

"My half-brother," Kitty said, a catch in her voice. She had a swift vision of Michael's face, the last time she had seen him, standing in court, deathly pale as he heard the red-robed judge pronounce his sentence, but proud—Michael had always been proud—and he had made no plea for mercy. He had lifted his handsome head a little higher and flashed a smile to Patrick and herself in the public gallery, refusing to be intimidated by the savage sentence or by the sour old judge's censure.

But she had been intimidated by it, Kitty recalled. She had clung to Patrick, weeping her heart out, hiding her face against his chest; and then, sobbing too, the old aunt who had brought them up after their parents' death—Aunt Dorcas—had led them out into the dark, rain-wet Dublin street. They had not been allowed to bid Michael farewell, for there had been a convict transport waiting to receive him and the other so-called traitors who had been condemned with him, and he had been taken aboard that very night.

"He escaped—absconded, did he not?" she asked huskily. "That was why he was sent to Norfolk Island?"

"Yes," John Broome confirmed. "According to O'Brien, he did."

He started to replace the pages of the diary in their wrapping, and Kitty, mindful of what Patrick had suggested to her earlier, as they waited on the jetty, added uncertainly, "We—Patrick and I—want to appeal for clemency on Michael's behalf. The diary—Marcus O'Brien said if we could recover it that it would —well, it would provide grounds for an appeal. He told us that Commandant Price singled poor Michael out for particularly brutal treatment and that he exceeded his authority, because Michael was guilty of no crime whilst he was here."

"It is possible," John Broome said. "A pardon, of course, can be granted only by the Crown. Clemency, a remission of sentence, might be granted out here." He hesitated, and Kitty guessed that he was anxious not to dash her hopes of such an outcome. Finally he offered, his tone encouraging, "I'd like to show the diary to Patrick and discuss it with him before we reach Hobart. Parts of it are . . . Lady Kitty, truly, they are not for your eyes."

Kitty did not attempt to argue. It was best that Patrick should deal with details of an appeal, she told herself; she had done as much as she could without overstepping the bounds she had imposed on herself. But—she had to ensure that John Broome, who was a journalist, would respect her confidence and not betray the secret he had uncovered.

"Mr. Broome," she began, "you—"

As if he had read her thoughts, he put in quickly, "I gave you my word that you could trust me, and I offer it again, so you need have no fear on my account. Or on Red's. He—"

"He knows? You told him?"

"Yes. But he too is, I assure you, fully to be trusted. He's read this diary, and that is guarantee enough. The treatment meted out to your brother by the former commandant was—well, suffice it to say that it turned Red's stomach, as it turned mine. Price undoubtedly *did* exceed his authority."

Kitty was silent for a long moment, endeavoring to banish the images his words had conjured up, tears aching in her throat. Poor Michael, she thought miserably. Poor, poor Michael—as a fifteen-year old midshipman on board the flagship *Princess Charlotte,* he had earned Admiral Sir Robert Stopford's commendation for gallantry in action against the Viceroy of Egypt, and only eight years later he had been found guilty on a charge of high treason. . . .

She said, in a choked voice, "My brother Michael has been transferred to the Port Arthur prison, Mr. Broome. Captain Day told us so."

"Yes," John Broome answered. "I learned that from Mr. Stewart." He reached for her hand. "I thought I was Boy Broome, not Mr. Broome, Kitty."

Kitty felt the warm, embarrassed color rising to flood her cheeks. The touch of his strong brown hand was oddly comforting, and she did not withdraw her own from its clasp. Yet, feeling ashamed because of the underlying reason for the nickname she had given him, she felt constrained to apologize.

"I . . . I'm sorry. I should not have called you that. It was arrogant of me."

"I probably deserved it," he asserted.

"No, you didn't. You—"

"Let's call a truce, shall we?" He was smiling broadly, refusing to take offense. "My given name is John Angus. You may take your pick, but . . . most people, most of my friends call me Johnny."

"Yes—yes, I know. Johnny it will be, from now on," Kitty promised. "You—" The sound of approaching footsteps heralded the appearance of Henry and Caroline Day and their eldest daughter, Catherine Mablon, and Johnny freed her hand.

He rose, gathering up the loosely wrapped pages of the diary, and said, lowering his voice, "I'll go and find your brother and show him this. And—you can count on me to give you all the help I can when we reach Hobart. It is just possible that I might be able to arrange a visit to Port Arthur, in my professional capacity, and perhaps even for Patrick also. I intend to try."

He did not wait for her reply but, with a smiling greeting to the Day family, left her with them.

Kitty felt renewed hope rising in her heart as she watched him go.

"We're under way," Henry Day announced cheerfully. "Which, in my book, is cause for celebration. Even the convicts are singing—can you hear them? I think we should drink to the demise of the Norfolk Island penal settlement and good luck to the Pitcairners! Steward!"

The steward brought the drinks asked for, and Day solemnly raised his glass.

Kitty drank with him, echoing the toast, and from the orlop deck below came the muted sound of men's voices raised in song. They were, she realized after a moment or two, singing a hymn . . . and singing it joyfully.

In the stone-built church at Port Arthur Penitentiary, close on six hundred convicts joined lustily in the closing hymn. It was not that they were seized by religious fervor; but because hymn singing in church was the only occasion when they were permitted to raise their voices, to a man they took advantage of the official approval to bellow the words as loudly as their lungs would allow.

From the boxlike stall in which he stood, the prisoner known as Number 9467, Michael Wexford, could see only the pulpit and the two rows of seats occupied by the military guard. Like the other fifty or so occupants of the wooden stalls, he was locked in and would not be able to leave until, at the conclusion of the service, the iron rod that secured each stall door was removed by one of the overseers or a constable.

It was as if he were a dangerous animal, he thought bitterly, only allowed the privilege of Sunday worship provided he was safely caged. The civil commandant, James Boyd, together with the superintendent of convicts, the prison surgeon, and the military officers with their families, sat in pews to the right of the altar, screened from the convicts' view by curtains, so that even those trusted to occupy the second-story galleries were unable to see them.

It was a curious arrangement, Michael reflected, and one that an all-seeing God might well have viewed with sadness, if not disapproval. Nevertheless, he raised his powerful tenor voice with those about him and sang as lustily as they, enjoying the sound, as the choir led into the last verse and the harmonium pealed forth its slightly off-key accompaniment. After seven long days of silence in the confines of a punishment cell, the noise and the human contact came as a pleasurable change.

"Jesu! Jesu!" he sang. "Advocate for sinners pleading, with the Father interceding; We beseech Thee, we beseech Thee, from every ill defend us! Thy grace and mercy send us . . . Amen!"

It was a singularly appropriately chosen hymn, Michael told himself cynically, and he repeated "From every ill defend us" before closing his hymn book, and—because the chaplin's gaze was ranging round the open fronts of the stalls, he bowed his head dutifully in readiness to receive the blessing.

It was strange, he thought, head still submissively lowered, how much he had come to look forward to the Sunday church services. They were Anglican, and he had been brought up in the Roman Catholic faith, but the priest appointed by John Price—or rather, the priest Price had caused to be appointed during his final year on Norfolk Island—had been a man of similar kidney to the commandant, wont to threaten with hell-fire and damnation any poor wretch who dared show even a spark of defiance. And he, of course—Michael's cracked lips curved into a wry smile—*he* had shown more than a spark. He had defied Price to break him and, on arrival at Port Arthur, had stated firmly that his religion was Anglican. And, since he had already suffered the torments of hell at Price's sadistic hands, the threat of continuation in the hereafter held no terrors for him.

Indeed, he would have sought escape and oblivion in death a long while ago were it not for the stubborn determination to avenge himself on the former commandant of Norfolk Island. That determination had become an obsession now, which he recognized for what it was—the sole reason for his survival and for his recently taken decision firstly to be accepted as a reformed and model prisoner at Port Arthur and secondly to abscond therefrom.

The iron bolt on his stall was withdrawn, and the overseer bawled at him to march back to his cell. Michael did as the man bade him and emerged, cap in hand, and the chain attached to his ankle fetters and running to his belt held in the prescribed manner, to enable him to walk without undue metallic clanking. He was clad in the yellow-and-black broad-arrowed livery of the convict "lifer," with the word *felon* printed on the jacket —a garb he hated. But . . . He fell into step with the line of men ahead of him, his tanned and bony face devoid of expression. Educated prisoners and those classed as gentlemen offenders were permitted to wear gray uniforms, and they were given tasks suited to their intellect, such as school teaching, gardening, or light work on the farms. Many sang in the church choir and earned privileges in consequence; but because John Price had given him a bad record, his own plea for a change of category had been rejected by Commandant Boyd.

"Prove yourself, Wexford," James Boyd had urged him. "Earn privileges by good behavior—that is the only way here. You've come from Norfolk Island classed as incorrigible, so that six months in the chain gang is mandatory. But I shall watch you, and if you can show a willingness to cooperate and reform, I shall see to it that you are rewarded."

Commandant Boyd was a fair man, Michael reflected; stern but never harsh or sadistic, as Price had been, and the convicts respected and, to a large extent, trusted him, for it was said that if he gave his word, he always kept it.

In his own case, however, the process of reformation had been fraught with difficulty. To the overseers—once convicts themselves—and the superintendents he was a marked man, regarded as dangerous because of his physical size and strength, and seen as the incorrigible Price had claimed him to be because of the scars on his back, with their outward and visible signs of past punishment with the lash.

Work as he might in quarry or timber yard, his zeal went unrecorded; let there be any breach of discipline in his gang and he was blamed for it. The Port Arthur commandant seldom resorted to flogging; the punishments he ordered were periods in solitary confinement and prolongation of the time to be served in one of the chain gangs. He himself had passed almost a year now, laboring in heavy irons, and had only today completed a week in solitary because an overseer had charged him with failing to obey an order. . . . Michael drew a long, sighing breath, as he waited, without impatience, for the door of his cell to be opened.

He was back in his own cell, on the ground floor of the penitentiary, but was still required to eat his meals there, instead of in the dining hall with the rest. He entered, in obedience to the turnkey's jerked head, and stood looking about him as the key rasped in the lock. The cell was small—four and a half by nine feet—with a small window in the front wall that admitted a little light. The door had a peephole in it, to enable the patrolling constables to observe the cell's interior, plus a trapdoor, through which food could be passed. It was limewashed and scrupulously clean and, like all the other cells in this wing, was furnished with a stool and three shelves, which accommodated a water cask, eating utensils, and a rolled hammock. Only when the bell rang for lights out was it permitted to sling and occupy the hammock, and even in the coldest weather the two blankets with which each prisoner was supplied had to remain, during the hours of daylight, neatly folded on the allotted shelf.

But at least, Michael thought, there were books—a luxury he had not enjoyed on Norfolk Island. The Port Arthur Penitentiary had a large and well-stocked library, and prisoners were encouraged to make use of it. Apart from the obligatory Bible, with which each cell was supplied, he had half a dozen bound volumes whose pages, until he had taken them out, had never been opened. Which was scarcely surprising, since one, by Charles Darwin, was entitled *Journal of Researches into the Geology and Natural History of the Various Countries Visited by H.M.S. Beagle 1832–36,* and the remainder were wordy legal tomes that no one but a lawyer would comprehend.

Michael's smile returned. He had read law at the University of Dublin after quitting the Royal Navy, and the law—or the practice of it—had never quite lost its appeal, although, he reminded himself sourly, the fact that he was a qualified attorney had been of singularly little help to him at his parody of a trial. Mr. Justice Lurgan had, from the start, been strongly prejudiced against him and had preferred the evidence of partisan and perjured witnesses to that which he had offered in his own defense.

In particular, the hatchet-faced old judge had given undue weight to the claims made by Captain Septimus Leonard of Her Majesty's Wicklow Rifles, without seemingly being aware that the captain had lost a considerable sum of money to him at the gaming tables. The charges themselves had been outrageous, and the suggestion that he had been one of the leaders of a rebel Ribbonist sect—made only by Leonard—had never been investigated, much less proven. He—

An eye appeared at the peephole in his cell door, and Michael stiffened.

"Your grub," the turnkey told him, and a wooden plate containing two hunks of bread and—because it was Sunday and the last day of his spell of solitary—a bowl of soup were pushed through the hatch at the foot of the door with such force that soup slopped over the lip of the bowl. "It's back to the jetty gang tomorrow for you, Nine-four-six-seven," the warder added, with a certain malice. "Seems as Superintendent Delaney's asked for you special 'cause they're loadin' timber at Cascades an' he wants an ox to do a bit o' heavin' for 'im. See you're ready to set off in an hour."

Michael offered no acknowledgment, but his spirits lifted. He knew the geography of the penal settlement on the Tasman Peninsula very well by now, having tramped the length and breadth of it in the course of his work with various chain gangs. Cascades, which took its name from a spectacular waterfall nearby, was the main timber-felling convict outstation, with a steam-driven mill and a jetty from which ships were loaded with the mill's produce. The station employed upward of three hundred men, but the hardest toil fell to the chain gang, who carried the heavy tree trunks from forest to mill, without any form of mechanical aid since the closing of the single-track railway, five or six years ago, on economic grounds and at the instigation of Governor Denison.

Michael pulled over his stool, picked up the meager meal the turnkey had brought him, sat down, and proceeded to demolish it. The soup was tepid, but it contained potatoes and some stringy scraps of meat, and he ate hungrily, dipping the dry hunks of bread in the greasy liquid to render it more palatable. He would need all his strength, he told himself, if the escape he had been planning for so long were to succeed.

His plan required that the attempt be made from some point near the narrow strip of land known as Eaglehawk Neck, which formed the only land access to Forestier Peninsula and East Bay Neck and thence to the mainland. Cascades, an inlet from Norfolk Bay, would be near enough for his purpose. It lay to the westward of Eaglehawk, but the going, following the line of the disused railroad, would be comparatively easy, even in darkness.

Eaglehawk Neck, however, presented an almost insuperable obstacle to any would-be absconder. It was a flat, 450-yard-wide strip of sand and rock, which was closely guarded, since it was the only way out of the prison settlement, and Michael was well aware that many had attempted to cross it to freedom but very few had ever done so successfully. In addition to a guardhouse and armed military sentries, there were kerosene lamps positioned at intervals and lit at dusk, and savage watchdogs were chained in front of the lamps, to give warning of the approach of any intruder. Each animal, as he had seen for himself, was housed in a kennel constructed from a disused wooden barrel and remained there day and night, with three more on platforms built out into the sea, to cut off any attempt to wade round the line.

Yet for all that . . . He sighed and, his scanty meal finished, pushed plate and bowl out through the trapdoor. After pausing for a moment to listen, he took one of the books from the shelf. Concealed inside it was a metal file. He had made it himself in secret, and in secret had painstakingly filed away at his leg-irons so that, when the time came, a few blows with a heavy stone would shatter the weakened metal—a very necessary prelude to his attempt at escape, since if anything went wrong and the guards or the dogs discovered him, he would have to swim to elude them.

He was a strong swimmer. Since his childhood, he had enjoyed the sport, and there had been two occasions, during his naval service, when his prowess as a swimmer had been the means of saving life—his own, on the second occasion. There was talk of sharks in Eaglehawk Bay and in the open sea on the eastern side of the neck, but . . . Michael's lips compressed into a thin, hard line. If all else failed, he would have to risk the sharks, just as Cash had. Better that than to submit to arrest and the inevitable punishment that would follow. And all else might *not* fail, if God had mercy on him and the plan to which he had given so much thought were to succeed.

True, he had not anticipated being assigned to the Cascades again quite so soon, but it made no difference—he was as ready now to put his plan into operation as he would ever be. In any event, it would be a lone escape; he wanted no companions when he made his bid for freedom, for there would be a long distance to cover if—*when*—he contrived to cross the Eaglehawk Neck and the isthmus beyond, which was known as East Bay Neck. The Forestier Peninsula lay between the two and was an area of wild bush country hemmed in by precipitous cliffs, in which the pounding sea had worn treacherous inroads and deep caverns. But once its perils had been overcome, the rest would be comparatively easy, for the East Bay Neck was said to be lightly guarded, and beyond was the mainland—sparsely settled, according to rumor among the convicts. Sparse settlements meant sheep runs and shepherds' isolated huts. . . . Michael finished his careful work with the file. He slipped the precious length of metal into the top of his heavy boot and stood up, easing it round his sock to prevent it from chafing.

Food—and more important, water—undoubtedly presented a problem, but he had made plans to solve that, too, based on what Cash had told him. He smiled, remembering. Martin Cash was a fellow countryman, born at Enniscorthy in County Wexford, and when he had been sent to Norfolk Island, he had talked freely of his exploits as absconder and bushranger, taking great pride in both.

Some eight or nine years before, he had made a successful escape from the Port Arthur prison with two companions—both members of the Ring and participants in the mutiny in Major Child's day—Lawrence O'Reilly and George James. The escape was still talked about for its daring and for the fact that the three of them had evaded capture for months by robbing shepherds' huts and holding settlers to ransom.

"We had a rare fine time while it lasted," Cash had said, laughing with genuine amusement. "The small settlements are far apart, and often 'tis only a man and his wife and children with a few sheep, and maybe a cow or two. Robbing them is child's play, so it is, for they're easily scared and offer no resistance. And the shepherds are ticket-of-leave men, who'll not lift a finger, as a rule. But—" His laughter had faded, Michael recalled, and he had added wryly, "Sure, I might have been bushranging yet but for the one fellow who proved an exception to the rule. He loosed off two charges of buckshot into me and then another brace into poor old Lawrie. We were hurt so sorely that we'd no choice save to give ourselves up, and that was the end of it. The dastardly rogue earned himself a fifty-pound reward . . . and for us 'twas life sentences on this infernal island, from where it truly *is* impossible to escape. But if it had been Port Arthur now, I swear I could have done it again, for I tell you there are no sharks in Eaglehawk Bay, and I'm the living proof of it!"

Curiously enough, on Norfolk Island the formidable Cash had become a model prisoner. Approaching his middle forties and sobered by the hanging of Lawrence O'Reilly following the mutiny, he had ceased to defy authority. Commandant Price had first broken him and had then shown him favors. When the commandant had left Norfolk early in '53, Cash had left with him, granted a conditional pardon and the promise of employment in Hobart as a free man. It was said that he was working in Hobart's botanical gardens, but in convict circles at Port Arthur his name was still a legend, spoken with awe.

Booted footsteps woke echoes from the long corridor outside, and anticipating the summons, Michael was standing by the door of his cell when it was jerked open and a stout, blue-uniformed prison officer put his head inside.

"Ready to take a walk, Wexford?" he asked briskly. "Gear packed up?"

Michael indicated his rolled blanket and, at a nod from the gray-haired officer, hefted it onto his shoulder. John Staveley was one of the more popular of the prison staff, an ex-sergeant wounded in the war between settlers and Maoris in New Zealand ten years earlier. He was known and respected for his fairness, and although a punctilious disciplinarian, he was one who, when out of the hearing of his superiors, was often willing to permit the prisoners to converse with him.

Cheered by the realization that Staveley was to be his escort on the journey to the Cascades station, Michael followed him with something approaching alacrity. But his momentary elation faded when, in the yard outside, he saw that half a dozen men, in chains like himself, were being mustered preparatory to departure. Four were strangers—newly arrived, judging by their apprehensive expressions and the awkward manner in which they handled their leg-irons—but the other two were well known to him.

Will Haines and Joshua Simmons had been on Norfolk Island during his time there, both capital respites, Michael remembered, and he remembered also, with disgust, their reputation as sodomists and the fact that Haines had been convicted for the brutal murder of a child in the Victoria goldfields.

He said nothing, but evidently his expression betrayed him, for Staveley observed in a low voice, "Not the company you'd have chosen, Big Michael, eh? Not the best of fellows to share a hut with, are they, those two?"

"No. Not those two, certainly, Mr. Staveley," Michael admitted, tight-lipped.

"Well, you'll have to put up with 'em, I fear," Staveley told him. "The commandant gave the pair of them three months, in heavy irons, for stealing tobacco and using threatening language. They got off lightly, in my view—the poor bugger they robbed is in hospital! All right, lad—into line with you and answer to your name, and then we can set off. I want to get back to my quarters before dark—my little lass Julie is ailing."

Michael crammed on his cap and obeyed.

Five minutes later, with two soldiers, sweating in their thick scarlet tunics, marching on either side of them, the prisoners shuffled through the gates of the muster yard and, chains clinking, breasted the slight hill in front of the guardhouse. The semaphore on its roof was in operation, its arms rising and falling rapidly and a checkered pennant flying halfway up the mast.

A system of signals, Michael knew from prison gossip, had once enabled communication with Hobart Town to be maintained. Numerically encoded messages were relayed by a series of signal stations, situated at regular intervals on high ground, throughout the intervening wastes of bush and sea, and a message sent from Battery Point, in Hobart Town, would be received in Port Arthur within less than half an hour. A previous governor, however, had closed the system down, on grounds of economy, and now only the local stations were manned.

Even so, attempted escapes from anywhere on the Tasman Peninsula could very rapidly be notified to the authorities, with search parties of troops alerted and guard boats standing by . . . and the signal station overlooking Eaglehawk Neck was manned night and day.

As Michael looked up at the rotating arms of the guardhouse semaphore, Warder Staveley, striding briskly at his side, followed the direction of his gaze and volunteered gruffly, "There's been a suicide at Safety Cove, seemingly. Some of the lads at the Juvenile Establishment are being released—they'll be taken to Hobart in the *Hastings* when she's finished loading. A boy who's *not* due for release threw himself off the cliff-top yesterday evening, poor young fool." He jerked his grizzled head in the direction of the semaphore. "Now they're arranging for his corpse to be taken to the Isle of the Dead yonder for burial. God rest his soul! By all accounts, he wasn't a bad lad."

But, bad lad or good, Michael thought with sudden revulsion, he would be interred in quicklime in that part of the cemetery reserved for convict dead, and there would be no headstone to mark his resting place. The strange old Irish lifer Barron—no one knew his Christian name—who lived alone on the small island facing the penitentiary, would dig his grave, as he had dug so many others, and then return to his primitive wooden hut to await the next call for his services.

And who knew, Michael told himself bitterly—the next call might be for *his* lifeless body, if his bid for freedom failed and the aim of one of the soldiers guarding Eaglehawk Neck should prove straight and true.

As if guessing the nature of his thoughts, Warder Staveley slowed his pace, a hand on Michael's arm holding him back. They were at the rear of the shuffling procession of fettered men, and the old prison officer seemed in a talkative mood.

He said, when they were out of earshot of the rest, "Why do you go on fighting, Big Michael? You've been over a year in the labor gang now. You could earn probation, if you set your mind to it. And you were born a gentleman, everyone knows that."

"I've forgotten it!" Michael retorted.

"Aye, you may have, but others haven't. With the education you've been blessed with, you could have a soft life, teaching school, for instance. Or tutoring the officers' children."

He had done that once, Michael recalled. Even on Norfolk Island, for a few short weeks after Commandant Price had left and Captain Deering of the 99th had been in temporary command, he had been taken from the prison to become mentor to the captain's children, and against all reason, hope had been born again. He had responded to the trust reposed in him and to the children's growing affection, but . . . Deering had asked to be relieved, Captain Day had replaced him, and one of Price's toadies—a convict constable named Baldock—had laid charges against him to the new commandant. Day had had no reason to accept his word against that of a constable, and since Commandant Price had officially entered him as incorrigible in the records, there had been no more tutoring but a return to solitary confinement, followed by hard labor.

And so it had been here. Not the arbitrary six months in the chain gang the Port Arthur commandant had initially told him he might expect but . . . over a year. Always Price's verdict was hung, like a millstone, about his neck. Yet Price had not broken him; he had defied the civil commandant to the last, disputed and disproved his boast that there was no convict rogue he could not bring to submission. And . . . Michael's big, callused hands clenched fiercely into fists at his side, letting the chain attached to his belt slip from his grasp.

John Price, the convict grapevine had asserted, had won government approval and promotion. He was now inspector general of penal establishments in the state of Victoria, in charge of its principal prison at Pentridge, while he himself . . . He stumbled, cursing aloud, and instantly regretted his loss of control. Any officer but Staveley would have put him on a charge, he knew; instead, the old warder told him gruffly to have a care, and as he gathered up his chain, the onetime army sergeant added mildly, "I'd put in a good word for you, Michael, if I thought you would make a real attempt to merit probation. Commandant Boyd does take heed of what I say."

Ashamed, Michael mumbled his thanks. But it was too late, he knew. He could not face year after endless year in this place, after all he had endured at Price's hands. Even if he earned probation and what the good old Staveley had called a soft life, it would still take years before the probationary period became conditional freedom. And there was Price, lording it in Victoria, indulging his sadistic pleasure in Pentridge Gaol. . . .

Staveley regarded him for a long moment, an odd sadness in his eyes, then Michael quickened his stride, aiming to catch up with the gang of prisoners.

"You'll not listen, will you, Michael Wexford?" he accused. "Well, no one can say I didn't try. There's something driving you, isn't there? Something evil, if the truth were known. You would do well to pray that you overcome it, for no good will come out of evil, lad. Not now, not ever." His tone changed, becoming stern as they drew level with the file of chained convicts. "God help you, Big Michael . . . All right, you men! Pick those feet up and march in step!"

He made no further attempt at conversation until the cluster of buildings that made up the Cascades outstation came in sight at a bend in the road. Beyond, a dazzling blue vista of sea and sky stretched the wide expanse of Norfolk Bay, and moored alongside the Cascades Bay jetty, the black-funneled paddle-steamer *Hastings* moved sluggishly in the slight, incoming swell, her hatches open, ready for the next day's loading.

The station had grown since its opening almost twenty years earlier, and, Michael reflected sourly, it looked a pleasant enough place at this distance. The timber mill was the largest building, but in addition there were a dozen single-story officers' cottages, a convict barracks with accommodation for more than four hundred men, the usual block of solitary cells, two messrooms, a chapel, a cookhouse, and a large bakery. The chapel, which doubled as a school, was little better than a wooden shed, but all the residential quarters were solidly built, with stone foundations from the local quarries, whitewashed brickwork, and picturesque shingle roofs. Well-tended gardens, growing fruit trees and vegetables in abundance, added to the deceptive air of rural peace and plenty—the more so because, it being Sunday, no work was in progress.

"Tell me," Warder Staveley invited, breaking his silence at last but still keeping his voice low, "has Mr. Delaney fixed up a match for you, Michael? Is that why he wants you back here?"

Michael shrugged. Superintendent Delaney was in the oddly contradictory habit of arranging pugilistic contests at the station—an enterprise that did not have official approval but to which authority turned a blind eye, in the belief that it boosted the general morale of both staff and prisoners. Indeed, according to Delaney, it also provided an outlet for prisoners of violent temperament, who might otherwise cause trouble.

He himself had displayed no violence and given little trouble, Michael thought cynically, but as always, his physical strength had singled him out, and Delaney—who was by no means the worst of the Port Arthur station superintendents—had selected him when he had first been sent to Cascades and induced him to play a regular part in the contests ever since. Inevitably bets were cast on the results; the prison staff and the soldiers wagered considerable sums from their pay, and whether or not the commandant was aware of it, Superintendent Delaney did well out of the practice.

"Well?" Staveley prompted. "Has he?"

"I suppose he must have," Michael returned reluctantly. "But I'm just out of solitary. A week on bread and water isn't the best preparation for a fight."

"Then I'd best not risk a wager on you, had I?"

"A couple of shillings, maybe. Not more, Mr. Staveley."

"If you say so." Staveley laughed, with ready good humor. "I'll have a word with the sergeant of the guard before I set off back. Lord, though, you're a rum one, Big Michael, and no mistake. For a gentleman born, I mean. You're just not like any gentleman I ever met—in Her Majesty's forces or here."

Perhaps, Michael thought, he had always been a rum one—a misfit in the role for which life had cast him. But until he had encountered John Giles Price, who had also been born a gentleman, he had at least subscribed to the code of honor of his class and kind. Perhaps if he had called Captain Septimus Leonard out and shot him with a dueling pistol, the damned old English judge who had sentenced him to transportation as a traitor would have imposed a lesser penalty and held that his action had been that of a gentleman.

He managed a mirthless smile in old Staveley's direction and followed the other prisoners into the barracks yard, where Delaney was waiting, two of his overseers at his side.

"I've a match for you tonight, Big Michael," the superintendent greeted him, a gleam in his dark eyes. "And you'll be well matched this time—I've found a fellow your size."

It was of little use to argue or to protest that his big body had been debilitated by the week in solitary, and Michael offered no objection. He drew himself up to attention and, as the rules demanded, doffed his cap.

"Very good, sir," he acknowledged woodenly.

It occurred to him suddenly, as he waited for his dismissal, that neither his sister Kitty nor his brother Patrick would recognize him if, by some miracle, they were able to see him now. From the window of the superintendent's office nearby, his reflection mocked him. It revealed a tall, stooping figure in ill-fitting convict garb—a man with a gaunt, bony face that was deeply lined and tanned almost to the color of mahogany, its expression one of sullen resignation. The lines, the sunken eyes, and the closely shaven head aged him far beyond the thirty years through which he had lived, and Michael turned away, sickened by the realization of what he had become.

But praise be to God, he thought, sweet little madcap Kitty would never have occasion to look at him thus, and young Patrick would retain the illusions he had always had concerning his elder brother. Even if O'Brien had contrived to keep his promise to deliver the letter to them at Kilclare, all he had asked of them had been that they engage a good lawyer to file an appeal on his behalf. That, Michael told himself, they would surely have done—*if* O'Brien had found them—and perhaps, God willing, the appeal would succeed before his spirit was broken and his courage finally failed him.

One of the overseers shouted out the number of the barracks room he was to occupy. Relieved that Haines and Simmons had been sent elsewhere, Michael lifted the chain to hold his ankle fetters clear of the ground and, moving with the ease of long familiarity with the impediment they offered, started across the yard. The gang from the timber mill stood in line outside the barracks, two overseers at their head. One of them—an ex-convict sub-overseer named Burke, whose report had earned him the week's solitary confinement—grinned in pleased recognition.

"So you're back, Big Michael!" he observed derisively. "Well, it's to be hoped you're in good trim for a fight. There's your match, standin' over yonder." He gestured to a man at the rear of the waiting line, and Michael stared in stunned disbelief. His opponent was a veritable giant, black-browed and powerful— one who clearly could give him not only four or five inches in height but at least a stone in weight.

He looked fit, in addition, a new arrival, evidently, who had not yet been worn down by long hours of toil in a chain gang or nauseated by the monotonous prison diet to a point where he could no longer stomach it.

"Meet Tobias Train," Sub-overseer Burke added, his tone tinged with conscious malice. "Big Toby to you! And I tell you this, Nine-four-six-seven Wexford—I ain't puttin' my money on *you* tonight. No soddin' fear I ain't! All right, take a good look, and then get on your way."

Michael did not reply to the taunt. If the fight went against him and he was badly hurt, his escape would, he knew, have to be postponed. But— He raised a hand in salute to the opponent Delaney had chosen for him and strode into the barracks with head held high, conscious that Train's gaze had followed him and that, for all his splendid physique, the giant was, of the two of them, the more afraid.

Chapter VI

"SO MUCH HAS been said—and written—concerning Mr. John Price's administration of the Norfolk Island penal settlement that, in all honesty, John, a true judgment is hard to arrive at."

Damien Hayes nodded his white head judiciously and glanced from Johnny Broome to his son Dominic, his brows raised in question. Dominic had succeeded his father some years ago as editor and proprietor of the Hobart *Chronicle* and was, Johnny was beginning to think, more radical in his views than was good for his paper's circulation or his own reputation. Certainly he was not afraid of confrontation, and he had admitted, almost with pride, that successive governors and the present Legislative Council had made strenuous efforts to close the paper down.

"We're to have an elected parliament this year," he had added, "which is what the *Chronicle* has long campaigned for. But of course the late Sir John Edarley-Wilmot and Sir William Denison were rigidly opposed to such a notion. By the same token, they both wanted convict transportation to continue, and we gave our support to John West and his Anti-transportation League. Incidentally, John, Mr. West is now editor of the Sydney *Morning Herald*—your chief, in fact—so I don't imagine you need me to tell you about our battles. I'm sure he will not have forgotten them!"

He had not, Johnny had been able to confirm. Dominic said now, a thoughtful frown creasing his brow, "Mr. Price was given the appointment as commandant of Norfolk Island following a serious mutiny, you know. To be fair to him, official policy as formulated by Governor Denison required him to restore order and put a stop to the vices and crimes that had been perpetrated there prior to his assuming command. And was it not Darling, when he was governor of New South Wales, who stated categorically that Norfolk Island was to be 'a place of the extremest punishment, only short of death'? In my view, John, Price did not exceed the instructions he was given."

"In spite of what's written in this journal?" Johnny countered, gesturing to the diary kept by Marcus O'Brien, which both Dominic and his father had read. "You can still say that? Was his treatment of the man called Big Michael in accordance with his instructions? And what of Bishop Willson's opinion and—more tellingly, perhaps—that of the Reverend Adam Rogers? Damn it, Dominic, Rogers was chaplain during Price's time! He saw what was going on, day after day."

"Price was no worse than some—no, many of his predecessors." Dominic appealed to his father. "Dad, you wrote leaders in the *Chronicle* about Colonel Foveaux and Major Morisset and Anderson—Major Joseph Anderson—that were critical of their harshness, didn't you?"

"Yes," his father confirmed, "I did. I also filled the pages of the *Chronicle* with praise of Alexander Maconochie and his system of reform, with equally negative results. I fear, John my boy, that when upward of nine hundred men of the worst character—murderers, bushrangers, and other, twice-convicted villains—are herded together on a small island, the severest discipline has to be imposed. If it were not, the place would be in a state of anarchy. And bear in mind the fact that the punishments Commandant Price ordered were those instituted by the majority of his predecessors—the lash, solitary confinement, hard labor in chains, even hanging. Price did not devise them—he simply followed precedent, and sentences were, in the severest cases, pronounced by magistrates, after a proper trial."

"Yes, but—" Johnny began. "Surely Mr. Maconochie's system met with some measure of success? Surely he—"

Damien Hayes shrugged his slim, elegantly jacketed shoulders. "Maconochie succeeded with quite a number of the Norfolk Island prisoners, it's true—but not with all of them. And his system led to leniency and abuse. Major Childs reaped what Maconochie had sown, and I believe Price did also, to a large extent. Perhaps—" He sighed. "Perhaps if Maconochie had been given longer, the need for harsh treatment might no longer have existed. It is possible that the capital respites and the incorrigibles *might* have seen the light. They might have responded and been reformed. Sadly, though, I doubt it. The men sent to Norfolk Island were the worst elements of a criminal society—degenerates, persistent absconders, and—"

"Mr. Hayes, sir," Johnny interrupted forcefully, "the prisoner known as Big Michael—Michael Wexford—was no degenerate, I do assure you!"

"Is he—was he known to you personally?"

Johnny was compelled to shake his head. "No. But his brother and sister are known to me—in fact, sir, they were both passengers on board the *Galah.* We disembarked together, after the *Galah* discharged the convicts from Norfolk Island and sailed for Sydney, under my brother Red's command. They—" He hesitated, looking from Damien Hayes's face to that of his son. "They have put up at the Customs House Hotel, and—well, it is on their behalf that I have come in the hope of enlisting your aid. As one of my father's oldest friends, sir, I thought that—"

"Of course, my dear young man, I shall do what I can to assist you and—er—your friends," Damien Hayes assured him. "We both will, Dominic and myself. I have great respect and affection for your father, and I always had the pleasure of entertaining him when his ship called here. For a start, this house is virtually empty, since the death of my beloved wife. My children are married and, like Dominic, have their own establishments. So—" His smile was warm and friendly. "You must bring your friends—er—the Wexfords here, and you must all be my guests."

"Their name is Cadogan, sir," Johnny said. He reddened, aware that his father's old friend had misunderstood the reason for his visit and wondering how best to explain precisely the help he was seeking. Frankness, he thought—particularly in Dominic's case—was called for, rather than any attempt to evade the issue or to pretend that it was other than it was. Kitty and Patrick would, he knew, appreciate the offer of hospitality, but they would not want to accept it unless their position were first made clear.

"Lady Kitty and the Honorable Patrick Cadogan," he added. "They—"

Dominic cut him short. He had picked up the diary and was leafing through it. Finding the page he was searching for, he read aloud: " 'I was reliably informed that the new addition to our thrice-damned ranks is a special-category prisoner, condemned to transportation for life for high treason. He goes by the name of Michael Wexford, which is not his real name, and rumor has it that he is titled—' That's true, then? He's titled, this Big Michael of yours?"

"Yes," Johnny confirmed. "His real name is Michael Fitzgerald Cadogan, seventh Earl of Kilclare."

Dominic's eyes narrowed. "And he's an Irish rebel, convicted of high treason?"

Recalling what Patrick had told him, Johnny's tone was brusque. "Both charge and conviction are highly suspect," he returned. "The charge was instigated by an English militia officer who had lost a considerable sum of money to Michael at the gaming tables." He went into the details of the case and ended, his tone still brusque, "The scandal killed his father, the sixth Earl. As I understand it, Michael never used the title—he inherited it only after his conviction. Indeed, he may not be aware of his father's death."

"And he did not appeal against his conviction?" Dominic persisted. "Surely he must have had grounds for an appeal, in the circumstances you've described?"

"According to his brother, he was given no time. He was put on board a transport within twenty-four hours of being sentenced. *They* have put in an appeal, Kitty and Patrick, I understand—but only recently, before coming out here, so the outcome is not yet known." Johnny gestured to the diary. "Marcus O'Brien, the convict who kept that journal, went back to Ireland after serving his time. . . ." Again he went into the details Kitty and her brother had supplied.

Dominic, he saw, was frowning. "Why," he asked, "was he

sent to Norfolk Island, John? Presumably he must have committed some crime after his arrival here?"

"Yes—he absconded, as far as we know."

"And took to the bush?" Dominic suggested shrewdly.

"I believe so, yes."

"But he was not on Norfolk Island when you went there?"

"No. He was transferred to the Port Arthur Penitentiary," Johnny supplied. "All we found in Kingston was O'Brien's journal."

"And the Cadogans have enlisted your aid?" Dominic pursued. He ignored a warning glance from his father. "You are in Hobart to play the knight errant, is that it, John?"

Johnny reddened furiously, but he controlled himself and bit back an angry retort. "I have promised to do all in my power to help them, Dominic, yes."

"To what end? An appeal to the governor for clemency, perhaps? That should not be difficult, should it, Father? An introduction can be arranged."

Damien, clearly disapproving of his son's interrogation of their guest, inclined his head at once.

"Of course it can—and I shall be more than happy to arrange for your young friends to meet His Excellency, John my dear boy, at the first opportunity. Sir Henry Young is a fine gentleman, who is making himself very popular here. He was governor of South Australia before he took up this appointment, as you probably know." He talked on about the governor, but Johnny scarcely listened.

His thoughts went back to the last night he had spent on board the *Galah*. In the frigate's overcrowded state, there had been few opportunities to seek out Kitty Cadogan or to be alone with her; indeed, he had seen more of her brother Patrick and talked with him exhaustively in the cabin they had shared. But, on the last night of the passage, he had contrived a brief meeting with Kitty, and . . . Johnny was conscious that Dominic Hayes was watching him with oddly searching eyes.

"You are in Hobart to play the knight errant, is that it, John?" he had suggested, and of course it was true. His decision to stay in Hobart, instead of returning to Sydney with Red, had been an impulsive one, dictated more by his heart than his head. Not

that Kitty had asked it of him or even, it seemed, expected him to stay . . . and the formidable Mr. West would not take kindly to his prolonged absence from the *Herald* office.

But he did not regret his decision. Kitty had thanked him, with tears in her eyes, when he had offered to stay and, standing on tiptoe, had kissed him on the cheek in swift gratitude, setting his heart beating wildly. He was in love with her, he thought— deeply, irrevocably in love with her, for all she had offered him little encouragement. Even if it were to cost him his job on the *Herald,* he could not have left her, and Red's skeptical "Well, I suppose you know what you are doing" had left him unmoved, when he had told his brother of his intention.

Dominic Hayes was saying something to him, and Johnny turned to him, reddening. "I'm sorry—you said?"

"I said that it crossed my mind that you might be contemplating a visit to the Port Arthur Penitentiary and that's really what you are hoping we can arrange for you."

"I . . ." Taken by surprise, Johnny hesitated. Dominic, he decided, was mistrustful, if not suspicious, seeking some motive behind his call that he had not revealed. He answered truthfully, "If it were possible, then yes, Dominic, I'd jump at the chance. But *is* it possible?"

"For you, as a journalist, it would be. The convicts are not permitted visitors or letters, if they are special-category men— as your Big Michael appears to be. But—" Dominic's expression relaxed, and he smiled. "Dr. John Stephen Hampton, the comptroller general of convicts—to give him his full title—is very proud of the so-called model prison at Port Arthur. I can give you an introduction to him, and if you make your request in the right way, I'm sure that he will authorize a visit. For yourself and, perhaps, also the Honorable Patrick."

Genuinely appreciative, Johnny thanked him.

"That would be excellent, Dominic. I'd be most grateful if you would put me in touch with Mr. Hampton."

"There would have to be no attempt to meet or speak to Michael Cadogan," Dominic warned. "I'd want your word on that."

"Well, I suppose I must give it," Johnny agreed, with some reluctance. "But I take it that you would raise no objection to my seeking an interview with the commandant, in order to make inquiries concerning the poor fellow?"

Dominic Hayes was still smiling. "Certainly not, my dear fellow. Commandant Boyd is generally held to be a humane man. He might, in the circumstances, allow you or Michael's brother to see him. But please understand," he added, his smile fading, "that I have to live here and run a newspaper, which in the past has been critical of the administration. So . . . as far as officialdom is concerned, I know nothing of a convict named Michael Wexford. Furthermore, I have never set eyes on—what is the man's name? O'Brien's Norfolk Island journal."

"I understand," Johnny asserted stiffly.

"And I have voiced no criticism of John Price, who—leaving aside the views of Bishop Willson and the Reverend Rogers—is well thought of here and who is presently holding an important administrative post in the prison service of Victoria." Dominic took out his pocket watch, clicked his tongue in apparent annoyance, and rose, holding out his hand. "Lord, I'd no idea what time it was! I must go, John. But I'll prepare a letter of introduction to Mr. Hampton for you, and you can pick it up at the office tomorrow. We'll keep in touch. I confess I'm curious to meet your Lady Kitty Cadogan and her brother—very curious. However—" He glanced across at his father. "If my revered parent has his way, all three of you will be staying under this roof whilst you are here—is that not so, Papa?"

"Indeed, yes. I will arrange a dinner party," Damien Hayes promised. "A family affair—and you and Marion must join us, if you can fit it in."

"We'll fit it in, you may be sure." His hand on the door, Dominic halted, frowning as if a sudden thought had struck him. "By George!" he exclaimed. "I fancy I must have seen Lady Kitty Cadogan on my way here this afternoon . . . on horseback, riding down Campbell Street, accompanied by a young gentleman of about the same age. Her brother, presumably. Tell me, John—is she a most exceptionally beautiful young lady, with dark hair, who sits a horse as if she were born to it?"

It was an apt description of Kitty Cadogan, Johnny recognized, and he nodded. She and Patrick had hired horses, he recalled—or they had talked of doing so—with the intention of sightseeing, while awaiting the outcome of his call on Damien Hayes. He had never seen Kitty on horseback, but, like everything else she did, almost certainly she would do it well.

"Yes," he admitted. "I think it must have been the Cadogans you saw."

Dominic flashed him an unexpectedly boyish smile.

"Then I understand your knight errantry, my friend! And I shall greatly look forward to your dinner party, Father." He bowed and was gone, leaving Johnny conscious of unreasoned resentment and, he was forced to concede, a twinge of jealousy.

He took his own leave shortly afterward, promising to convey Mr. Damien Hayes's invitation to the Cadogans.

To his disappointment, though not entirely to his surprise, they elected to remain in their hotel, Kitty charmingly excusing their decision on the grounds that they were very comfortably accommodated and, as complete strangers, did not wish to be beholden to Mr. Hayes or his son.

"They are doing enough for us, Johnny," she pointed out, "with the promise of an introduction to Dr. Hampton and, of course, to the governor. We shall be delighted to dine with Mr. Hayes and to meet his family, since they are such old friends of *your* family, but—staying at the Customs House will leave Patrick and myself free. You accept old Mr. Hayes's hospitality by all means—it will save you expense and ease my conscience on that account—and we'll keep in touch."

The dinner party was arranged for the end of the week. Johnny duly took up temporary abode in Damien Hayes's commodious house in Harrington Street, overlooking Saint David's Park and with a distant vista of Parliament House through the trees. He was most hospitably treated; Damien Hayes, he soon realized, was a lonely man, fretting since his retirement and, since the recent loss of his wife, often at a loose end with little to occupy his time. He seized gratefully on the presence of a guest and set himself assiduously to entertain the son of one of his oldest friends, talking to him freely and, to Johnny's embarrassment, revealing that he and his own son did not see eye to eye concerning the *Chronicle*'s editorial policies or the campaigns on which the paper was now embarked.

"After my beloved Sarah passed away, I lost heart," he confided. "Dominic wanted to take over sole direction of the paper, and—well, I permitted him to do so. Looking back now, I fear it was a grave mistake. I should have hung on, kept control, and seen to it that he exercised restraint. As it was, the former governor, Sir William Denison, very nearly succeeded in closing the *Chronicle* down. All that saved us was the fact that Denison became increasingly unpopular here and public opinion was united in the desire for responsible government and an elected parliament—which, of course, Dominic had campaigned for with every weapon at his command. If," he added dryly, "not with caution! Doubtless he will learn in time, but it is taking longer than I had hoped or anticipated."

The old man talked a great deal on this subject. Johnny listened with sympathy and what patience he could muster, having a genuine liking for him and admiration for all that he had achieved. As a virtually penniless young man, Damien Hayes had come to Hobart and launched the *Chronicle,* with himself as editor, reporter, printer, and at times even delivery boy, his sole source of income the articles he wrote and mailed to the London *Chronicle*—articles that, he explained ruefully, often took more than six months to reach their destination, with payment from the London office subject to equally lengthy delays.

At any other time, Johnny knew, he would have enjoyed his host's company and derived immense benefit from old Mr. Hayes's revelations, but . . . he was anxious on the Cadogans' behalf. And, far from keeping in touch, as she had promised, Kitty seemed once again to be intent on avoiding him. She and Patrick were away all day on some errands of their own, the nature of which they seemed unwilling to divulge to him. Their evenings were taken up in a social whirl from which he was excluded; Captain Day had introduced them in military circles, and Hobart society—impressed, Johnny could only suppose, by their aristocratic titles and Kitty's beauty and charm—plied them with invitations to routs and dinner parties and picnics. They rode with the Hobart Hunt, attended a Government House garden party, and appeared, to his growing disillusionment, to have forgotten the reason for their presence in Tasmania.

Even the dinner party Mr. Hayes gave for them served only to widen the rift; Johnny found himself partnered by Dominic's friendly but somewhat frumpish young wife, while Dominic, seated at Kitty's side, paid unabashed court to her and appeared, to Johnny's frustrated eyes, to meet with more than a modicum of laughing encouragement. When she and Patrick left at midnight, it was in Dominic's carriage, and he himself had barely managed to exchange half a dozen words with them.

The comptroller general of convicts, Dr. John Hampton, was out of town, and to Johnny's disappointment it was almost a fortnight before he returned and agreed to grant an interview. But this, at least, exceeded his expectations. He went, perforce, alone to Hampton's office, since Patrick, whom he had hoped would accompany him, was not at the hotel when he called there.

The comptroller proved to be a precise, somewhat aloof man in his middle or late forties. He was a qualified surgeon who, Mr. Hayes explained, had come out to Tasmania initially in medical charge of a convict transport a dozen or so years earlier. He made it clear, in the first few words he addressed to Johnny, that he fully supported Price's method of administration, and he poured scorn on the efforts Alexander Maconochie had made to reform Norfolk Island's capital respites and other long-term prisoners.

"When I took office as comptroller of convicts ten years ago, the situation was chaotic, Mr. Broome," he went on. "We had close on thirty thousand convicts here, and another four to five thousand were being sent out each year to add to their number. The countryside was flooded with unemployed ticket-of-leave men, and there were over ten thousand serving in the probation gangs, for whom there was little work and most inadequate supervision. Bushranging was revived on an unprecedented scale, so were crimes of violence, and men absconded almost at will. The gold rush to Victoria rid us of quite a number of undesirables, but we also lost most of our police force, and the crews of ships deserted wholesale, in a wild dash to Bendigo and Ballarat. We were in a state close to anarchy, and strong measures were called for to stem the rot. We took those measures, Mr. Broome, but inevitably they led to overcrowding in our penal settlements." He sighed audibly. "When Her Majesty's government, in its wisdom, elected to close down the establishment at Norfolk Island, we were faced with the necessity of expanding the prison accommodation at Port Arthur, in order to take the men transferred here."

Dr. Hampton paused, eyeing Johnny from beneath frowning brows. "There were over nine hundred of them, who had been gainfully employed under Mr. Price's excellent supervision; and they were not only self-supporting—they were able to export agricultural produce and meat to this colony. And the state of discipline which prevailed I can only describe as exemplary. But . . . when one is subjected to interference by the Church, what can one do?" He repeated his sigh, his frown deepening. "You have recently paid a visit to the island, haven't you, Mr. Broome?"

"Yes, sir," Johnny agreed, careful to refrain from comment, and, warming to his theme, Dr. Hampton talked on.

"However, good does sometimes result from—well, I cannot describe it as evil. Rather let us say from errors of judgment. The Port Arthur Penitentiary has, of sheer necessity, been expanded. The new model prison, which Mr. Hayes says you are anxious to see at first hand, Mr. Broome, is built on the design of Pentonville Prison, which I studied when I was last in England. The concept on which it is based was evolved by the Quakers—admirable folk, the Quakers. They called it the 'separate system,' in which, ideally, each prisoner occupies a separate cell. . . ." He went into somewhat pedantic detail, and Johnny listened, curbing his impatience. His role—that of a journalist studying prison reform—which he had assumed as a means of obtaining permission to visit Port Arthur, required him to appear interested, and he did not interrupt.

Only when, coming at last to the end of his recital on the merits of the Quaker system, Dr. Hampton looked at him inquiringly did he venture a question.

"Does it mean, sir," he asked, "that the chain gangs have been abolished?"

For a moment the doctor appeared disconcerted, but finally he shook his head.

"No, Mr. Broome," he conceded. "That has not yet been

possible. Special-category prisoners—capital respites, life sentence men, and persistent absconders—cannot be included in the separate system, unless and until they have served a probationary period in one of the work gangs. Escape from the Tasman Peninsula is virtually impossible and is seldom attempted —when you pay your visit to Port Arthur you will be shown why this is so. A strong guard of soldiers, augmented by watchdogs, is maintained on what is known as Eaglehawk Neck, which is the only way the mainland can be reached, except by ship. Let me show you. . . ." He opened a drawer in his desk and took out a map, which he spread out in front of Johnny. "See—here is the penitentiary, with the church, the commandant's and officers' quarters, and the hospital. And here—" The doctor's long forefinger pointed to the map. "Here is Eaglehawk Neck, and here another narrow isthmus, East Bay Neck, which connects with the mainland and is also guarded. Between the two lies the impenetrable bush country of the Forestier Peninsula. Few convicts escape, Mr. Broome, but human nature being what it is, a number do make the attempt. When they are caught or they give themselves up, retribution is swift and severe."

He continued to elaborate on this claim, and Johnny, studying the map with interest, was ready to concede that there was no reason to doubt its veracity. Only a desperate or a very brave man would dare to try. Was Big Michael a brave and desperate man, he wondered, or had even his spirit at last been broken, if not by Commandant Price on Norfolk Island, then by Port Arthur's "separate system," of which Dr. Hampton was so proud?

The interview came finally to a close. Hampton put away his map and readily gave permission for Johnny to visit the Tasman Peninsula, traveling to the penitentiary by the government steam-sloop *Opossum* in three days' time. However, to Johnny's chagrin, an unexpected objection was raised to the request that Patrick Cadogan might accompany him.

"You are an accredited journalist, Mr. Broome," the comptroller told him sententiously. "But Mr. Cadogan—the *Honorable* Mr. Cadogan is, I understand, a wealthy young gentleman traveling with his sister on some variety of grand tour. His interest in our penal establishments can only be superficial, in my view, and the book you say he intends to write on the subject . . . well, it can scarcely be expected to make a serious contribution to prison reform, can it? It might even be harmful, by creating a false impression of what we are trying to do here. Therefore, with regret, I must refuse to issue him with the required authority."

He was adamant, waving Johnny's pleas aside, and, fearing that to persist might lead to his own permit being withdrawn, Johnny thanked him politely and took his leave. Both Cadogans were still absent when he called at the Customs House Hotel to acquaint them with the result of his interview with Dr. Hampton.

"They went out with Seth Thompson in his sealer *Mary Ann,*" the proprietor volunteered. "Sightseeing, her ladyship said, and I reckon they'll be gone all day, sir. They had the kitchen pack them up food for the day."

Why, Johnny asked himself uneasily, would they go sightseeing in a dirty, malodorous seal-hunting vessel, unless . . . A sudden, unwelcome suspicion flashed into his mind, and try as he might, he could not dismiss it.

Over a late luncheon with old Mr. Hayes, he was offered a commission to write a report on Port Arthur's model prison. Pleased by the sum the old gentleman promised in payment for what, at most, would be only a day's work, he asked innocently, "Do you want a report for the *Chronicle,* sir? And will Dominic welcome it? I mean—"

"I know what you mean, my dear boy," Dominic's father returned with asperity. "And since you ask—no, Dominic almost certainly will *not* welcome it. But—" He spread his hands in an odd little gesture, his eyes bright as they focused on Johnny's face. "I have had it in mind for quite a while now, John, that I might start another daily newspaper. It would occupy my time and represent a challenge."

"A challenge, sir?" Johnny stared back at him in astonishment. "A challenge to the *Chronicle?*"

"Yes, precisely that," the old man confirmed. "My son Dominic has changed the paper radically since I entrusted him with its sole running, and he refuses to listen to my objections or heed my advice. So . . . I've thought about it, as I said, for a while—a long while. But I took no action, mainly because there was no one here in Hobart that I deemed suitable to assist me with the news gathering. And then *you* arrived here, out of the blue, and I had my answer. You're an experienced journalist—you've cut your teeth professionally and worked under an editor for whom I have great respect." Damien Hayes paused, eyeing Johnny expectantly. "What do you say, John—would you be willing to work for me? I could promise you a better salary than you're on with the *Herald,* and my new paper would be adequately capitalized—I'm a rich man. And I believe we should work well together . . . we see eye to eye on most matters."

"I—sir, I—" Taken completely by surprise, Johnny found himself lost for words. Damien Hayes was offering him a splendid opportunity, no denying that, and it was one he could not hope for if he stayed with the *Herald,* which, if anything, was overstaffed with men at least as competent as himself. Dominic would be furious, of course—not that he would permit Dominic's reaction to influence him—but . . . there were the Cadogans, there was Kitty. He swallowed hard. He had given Kitty and Patrick his word, had promised to help them in any way he could; and if his newly formed suspicions concerning their intentions were to prove correct, then . . . dear heaven, he might well find himself in a most invidious position! He . . .

Sensing his indecision, Damien Hayes said quietly, "Take time to think about it, John. There is no immediate hurry and much to do before I could hope to put a new paper on the street. I have a printer in mind, but an office would have to be found and government regulations studied and complied with—that will all take time. And I realize that you have a commitment to the young friends who accompanied you here—Lady Kitty and young Patrick Cadogan. And their unfortunate brother."

"Yes, sir," Johnny admitted, reddening. "I have. But I—" Kitty, he thought resentfully, had scorned his aid and, as she had done at Norfolk Island, had chosen to avoid him and seek other company. For all that, however, he knew that were she to ask him to keep his promise, he would not refuse. Whatever the cost, and even if it were to mean his refusing old Mr. Hayes's offer.

"I imagine," Mr. Hayes put in shrewdly, "that when you pay your visit to the Port Arthur Penitentiary, you will—notwithstanding any assurances my son Dominic extracted from you when the visit was first suggested—you will try to see the prisoner called Big Michael?"

Johnny replied to the question honestly. "I shall endeavor to do so, sir, yes. But if it is possible, with the commandant's permission. Or—depending on circumstances, sir—I would seek his consent to a visit from the Cadogans."

Seemingly satisfied, Damien Hayes inclined his white head. "Very well, my dear boy. I shall take it that, following your visit to Port Arthur, you will know more where you stand as regards your obligations to Lady Kitty and her brother . . . and I may then expect a decision from you concerning my offer?"

"Yes, sir. And I—" Johnny rose with him, extending his hand. "I'm honored by the offer, Mr. Hayes—deeply honored and grateful. There's no one I'd sooner work for, sir, believe me. But I gave my word to Lady Kitty, and—"

"And also, if I'm not mistaken, your heart, did you not?" Mr. Hayes's hand grasped his warmly. He smiled. "That question requires no answer, my dear boy. But if you will heed an old man's advice—which I fear you will not—you will think long and earnestly concerning any future—er—commitment of a permanent nature. The young lady is exceptionally beautiful, and she possesses great charm, to which, it will not have escaped your notice, my son Dominic is not immune." He released Johnny's hand and waved him to silence, anticipating his indignant protest. "I will say no more, John, save to tell you that women like my daughter-in-law Marion may not possess the same measure of beauty or charm, but . . . as wives you cannot fault them."

Johnny remained obediently silent, but he was still seething with indignation when, just before sunset, he went again to the Customs House Hotel in search of the young Cadogans. From the vantage point of the wharf, he watched for the return of the sealer *Mary Ann*, but it was dusk before a helpful passerby pointed the vessel out to him.

"That's her, that's the old *Mary Ann,* sir," his informant volunteered. "Her master's a feller name o' Seth Thompson. Bit o' a rogue, they reckon—served time at Port Macquarie a good while back for liquor smugglin'. But—" He broke off, lips pursed in a silent whistle, as he studied the figures standing on the sealer's dimly lit deck. "Well, I'll be damned! Fancy seein' *him* on board! And the quality. Wonders never cease, do they, sir? An' I'd heard as he'd got religion!"

Johnny drew in his breath sharply, his lingering suspicions concerning the Cadogans flooding back.

"Who," he asked tensely, "do you mean, if I may ask?"

The passerby—a seaman, by his garb—gave vent to a chuckle. "Why, Martin Cash, sir—that's who I mean. The only feller that succeeded in abscondin' from Port Arthur. Some years back, it was—I don't rightly recall 'ow many. Got 'is ticket-o'-leave in the end, Cash did—from Norfolk Island, I believe. They say as 'e's workin' here now, in the botanical gardens."

Still chuckling, the man went on his way, and Johnny watched apprehensively as he saw an oared boat lowered from the *Mary Ann*'s deck and splash into the water. Kitty and Patrick climbed down into it, followed by the man named Martin Cash. The boat pulled toward the wharf, but Johnny did not wait for it to come alongside. Instead, he walked briskly back to the hotel, and he was standing in the entrance when Kitty and Patrick made their appearance, talking excitedly to each other. They broke off at the sight of him, and after a moment's awkward silence, Kitty came running to his side. Martin Cash had vanished.

"Johnny—I'm *so* glad to see you!" Her greeting was eager, her smile radiant, echoing her words. It was, Johnny thought bitterly, as if it had been he who had eschewed her company, rather than she who had so persistently stayed beyond his reach. But, as always, he found it impossible to resist her charm, and taking the small, gloved hand she extended to him, he bore it to his lips.

"And I," he began, "am glad to—"

Patrick interrupted him. "I received your note, telling me of the appointment with Dr. Hampton, Johnny. I'm so sorry that I was unable to join you, but we had arranged a boating trip and a picnic with friends, you see, so I could not."

A boating trip and a picnic, Johnny thought, in the *Mary Ann,* with her rascally skipper and a *friend* named Martin Cash, notorious because he had made a successful escape from the Tasman Peninsula. . . . Surely they must think him naive, if they expected him to believe such a tale! He started to say so, but Patrick again cut him short.

"Were you able to obtain permission for a visit to Port Arthur?" he demanded. "Was Mr. Hampton agreeable?"

"He was agreeable," Johnny answered, unable to keep the resentment from sounding in his voice. "And he granted permission—but only for myself, Patrick. He refused on your account, I'm sorry to say."

Both the Cadogans looked crestfallen, and Patrick said angrily, "Oh, the devil! I was depending on you, I—did you tell him that I intend to write a book on prison reform? And that I had been to Norfolk Island with Sir William Denison's consent, with that end in view?"

"I told him all that. He simply wasn't impressed, Patrick. He—"

"But what reason did the infernal fellow give? He must have given a reason for refusing me?"

"Yes, he did." His voice devoid of expression, Johnny repeated what the comptroller of convicts had said. He added, looking at Kitty, "You *have* given the impression that you are lighthearted travelers, simply here to enjoy Hobart's social life. I imagine Dr. Hampton heard talk about it."

Patrick swore under his breath, but Kitty silenced him with a warning glance. "We cannot talk here, Pat. Let's go to our room. Please, Johnny, dear friend, come with us—we have a sitting room here, and we can order drinks or a meal."

She linked her arm in his, and Johnny, the warm, lovely scent of her hair strong in his nostrils, let her lead him into the hotel, conscious that once again he was falling victim to her charm.

Their sitting room was large, comfortably furnished, and with a fine view of the river from its windows. Patrick ordered refreshments, which were promptly served, and when the hotel servant had gone, he poured lavish measures of brandy for each of them and waved Johnny to a chair.

"When are you exercising your official permission to visit the penitentiary, Johnny?" he asked, his tone peremptory.

"In three days' time—that's on Thursday," Johnny told him with restraint. "I'm to be given passage in the government steamer *Opossum.*"

"And you'll stay for how long?"

"Dr. Hampton did not specify any limit, but—" Johnny shrugged, determined not to allow his annoyance at Patrick's brusque questioning to get the better of him. "I presume the ship will be there for two or three days. She delivers mail and supplies, which have to be unloaded."

"I suppose"—again Patrick ignored a warning glance from his sister—"you made no mention of Michael, when you talked to Mr.—that is Dr. Hampton, did you?"

Johnny shook his head. "I considered it best not to, especially since the doctor told me that special-category prisoners were not included in what he called the 'separate system' at the penitentiary. But I—"

Patrick leaned forward, almost overturning his glass. "But Johnny, you will try to see the poor devil, won't you?"

"Certainly I will try," Johnny promised. "It may not be possible. There are over nine hundred men in the model prison alone, as far as I could gather, and then there are outstations—a big timber yard at the Cascades, an invalid establishment at the Saltwater River, and an agricultural station at a place I think is called Impression Bay. Hampton showed me a map, but I'm speaking from memory. And—" He hesitated, looking from Patrick's flushed face to Kitty's pale one. "He showed me the map in order to demonstrate the impossibility of escape from Port Arthur. And I believe it *is* impossible, Patrick. You see—" He started to repeat what Dr. Hampton had told him, but Patrick put in, an edge to his voice.

"Johnny, we know the only way out is by an isthmus known as Eaglehawk Neck and that is strongly guarded, by troops and dogs. We—"

Kitty cut him short. She pleaded tearfully, "Oh, Pat, you

promised that Johnny should not be involved. He has to live here, whereas we—we can go back to Ireland."

But Patrick was not to be distracted. "Three men *did* escape, Johnny. They got past the dogs and the guards at that infernal neck. And I've talked to one of them. He told me how he did it. He—"

"I take it you mean Martin Cash?" Losing patience with him at last, Johnny abandoned pretense. "You had him with you on board the sealer—the *Mary Ann*—today, didn't you? Oh, for God's sake, man, don't trouble to deny it! I saw you come in. I was on the wharf."

"The devil take you!" Patrick reproached him furiously. "I had supposed you to be our friend, but you were spying on us, damn your eyes! Kit was so determined that we must not involve you by—by dragging you into our affairs that I did everything I could to keep you in the dark. Evidently I failed."

"Yes," Johnny retorted, restraining himself. "You failed. And since you did, why don't you quit trying to pull the wool over my eyes and tell me what you're up to? Or shall I hazard a guess? You're going to attempt to organize your brother's escape—that's about the size of it, isn't it? Or can't you trust me sufficiently to admit it?"

It was Kitty who answered him. She leapt to her feet and, setting down her virtually untouched brandy glass, dropped to her knees in front of his chair, her hands clasped as if in prayer as she looked up at him.

"Dear Johnny," she whispered, her voice taut with strain, "don't you understand it's because I truly care for you that I tried not to involve you? Not that Patrick and I don't trust you —we do, I promise you we do! And we need your help, if you can find it in your heart to help us."

"My help, Kitty?" Only a man of stone could have resisted her appeal, and Johnny's brief anger faded. He took her small, trembling hands in his, wishing that he could draw her into his arms—but prevented by Patrick's presence from attempting to do so. "How can I help you?"

"By delivering a letter to Michael," Kitty said softly. "Patrick would have delivered it, but . . . you said that Dr. Hampton has refused to allow him to visit the prison, so—there's no

one else, no other way, is there? We have to tell him that we are
here, haven't we, Pat? And that we will have a—a vessel waiting to pick him up, if he can make his escape from the prison.
We—"

It was madness, Johnny thought—a madness that carried
with it the most terrible risks, but . . . He looked into Kitty's
lovely, tear-filled eyes, his heart thudding.

"Why not try to obtain clemency for him? Why not appeal to
the governor to review Michael's case?" he questioned, desperately seeking an alternative.

"We have tried," Patrick told him harshly. "But to no avail.
Michael is a political prisoner—he was convicted of high treason, Johnny. That requires a royal pardon. Oh, we arranged for
our lawyers to lodge an appeal in the English courts before we
came out here, as Michael asked, but—even if it should be successful, it could be months before it will reach here. The governor here promised to look into Michael's case, but he held out
little hope that anything can be done at this end. Michael's
serving a life sentence, he . . . We have no choice, Johnny. We
have to help him to escape, bring him here to Hobart, and then
—" He smiled, suddenly eager and full of confidence. "Once
here, we have made plans to ship him to New Zealand. Martin
Cash is going there—there's a vessel ready and waiting."

"I see." Johnny was silent, his thoughts racing through his
head, now accepting what Patrick had said, now rejecting it.

Kitty's fingers closed about his in a convulsive clasp. "Will
you deliver our letter, Johnny?" she begged him. "Please, if you
care anything for me, will you try to make sure that Michael
receives it? It—it will be carefully worded. If it should fall into
the wrong hands, no one will be wiser. I—I know it's a great
deal to ask of you, but I—oh, Johnny, I *am* asking! Will you?"

Suddenly bereft of words, Johnny hesitated for a moment and
then reluctantly inclined his head.

And, as she had on the deck of the *Galah*, Kitty pressed close
to him, her soft lips brushing his cheek in gratitude.

Chapter VII

TALK IN THE messroom, as the men of the chain gangs ate their evening meal, was of the coming fight, with opinion sharply divided as to the chances of the two contestants.

"Train claims 'e went eighteen rounds with Jim Kelly," one of the lumberyard gang asserted. "For a purse o' an 'undred guineas at Ballarat."

"Well, I reckon 'e's big enough," another said, cramming his mouth full of the unappetizing potato broth in front of him. "An 'ole lot bigger'n Michael. Taller too, near as I could judge." He waved his spoon at Michael. "What do you think of 'im, Michael? *Can* you lick 'im?"

Michael affected not to hear the question. He had heard of the Kelly brothers—James, Thomas, and Charles—famous for their pugilistic prowess and, at various times, champions of Victoria at their different weights, commanding big purses in the goldfields as well as in Melbourne. And, even if he had heard nothing of them, the men about him were eager to fill any gaps in his knowledge.

"Jim Kelly was the one who fought Jonathan Smith at Fiery Creek for six an' a 'arf hours an' drew wiv' 'im."

"Aye, that's a fact. An' Charlie—'e was the youngest of 'em —'e fought Black Perry once an' licked 'im. But Perry was past it then—drinkin' 'imself to death, 'e was. 'Cause no one couldn't match 'im, after 'e beat Georgie Hough."

"I know who Delaney will be puttin' his money on tonight,"

Will Haines observed spitefully. "An' it won't be Big Michael this time, that's for sure!" He grinned at the man beside him, the thin little scarecrow who was his constant companion. "Eh, Josh?"

Thus encouraged, Joshua Simmons added his taunt.

"Naw—an' I'd not risk a ha'penny bettin' agin' a feller that stood up to one o' them Kelly boys, Will," he declared waspishly. "That's if I 'ad a ha'penny ter wager, which I don't. You won't be champion much longer, *Mister* Wexford—Train'll murder you! An' not afore time, in my 'umble opinion. Lose ter 'im an' Delaney'll send you back to the bleedin' quarry gang."

That was in the cards, Michael knew. Superintendent Delaney liked winners. He went on eating, refusing to be drawn or provoked by Simmons's spite, and one of his own gang, Jemmy Roberts, came to his defense.

"Train may be all you sods say he is, but there's one thing you've forgotten—and it'll weigh in Michael's favor."

"And what's that, Jemmy?" Haines demanded with a sneer. "You reckon 'e's lost weight, on account o' spendin' seven days in solitary?"

"No, that ain't it," Roberts countered. "But Train ain't never fought in leg-irons, has 'e? Michael has."

That was true, Michael thought, his flagging spirits lifting. By some odd quirk in his reasoning, Superintendent Delaney—although, by permitting fights to take place, he was breaking the rules—had always insisted that men sentenced to work in chains must also fight in them, because he had no authority to order the removal of their fetters. As a result, the fights were slugging matches, since evasive footwork was all but impossible, and retreat, impeded by the leg-irons, was fraught with danger of a stumble or, worse still, a fall.

Someone, no doubt, had told Toby Train this, and . . . Michael smiled, as he mopped up the dregs of his soup. That would explain the big man's apprehension and his uncertainty, despite his formidable record as a prizefighter. To defeat him would be not only possible but likely, if he were given no time to accustom himself to the restricted movement, which was all the chains allowed.

Evidently coming to the same conclusion, Jemmy Roberts slid along the bench to Michael's side.

"Go in fighting, Big Michael," he advised in a hoarse whisper. "He'll be used to long fights an' skillful punchin', like as not, so don't give 'im time ter settle. Hit 'im with all you've got, right from the start, an' you'll have the big sod beat!"

"Yes," Michael agreed. "That's what I'll aim to do, Jem."

The meal break ended and with it the freedom to talk. The men from both messrooms shuffled out, to form up in the yard and occupy three sides of the square, which had been paced out by two of the overseers, who were now engaged in placing kerosene lamps in position at its extremities. A work party brought out chairs for the superintendent and his officers and stools for the two contestants and the timekeeper, setting each meticulously in place. Despite the ban on talking, a low hum of voices rose from the convicts' ranks, to which officialdom turned a deaf ear, aware that to attempt to silence it would be futile. The soldiers detailed for guard duty marched up and were stood at ease; their off-duty comrades sauntered over, in twos and threes, leather stocks loosened and headgear discarded, to cluster about the table at which three of Delaney's clerks were recording wagers.

To Michael, the scene was all too familiar; apart from a glance through the messroom window to ascertain what stage the preparations had reached, he did not trouble to observe it. He had fought a score of times and won more often than not, but he gained no profit from the wagers and, in consequence, took little interest in the procedure, beyond an indifferent inquiry as to the odds being offered.

A sub-overseer named Wittington—like old John Staveley a pleasant-enough fellow when no senior officers were present—had been chosen to act as one of his seconds, and Jemmy Roberts was also fulfilling the same role. Michael submitted to their ministrations in silence, his mind elsewhere, scarcely taking in the advice both men were eager to offer him, since, as he was all too well aware, his opponent was a recent arrival at Cascades and no better known to them than to himself.

"He's mean, Michael," Wittington volunteered, "from what I've heard. Lie down on the table and let Jemmy and me give you a rubdown, why don't you? There's time enough—they ain't through taking the wagers yet." Michael obediently hoisted himself onto the scrubbed wooden table and, lying full length, forced himself to relax, as George Wittington started to knead the scarred flesh of his back and shoulders, exclaiming as he did so. "Lord, man, how many times have you been flogged? There's hardly an inch o' skin that ain't puckered up, right across your back!"

Michael glanced at Jemmy, who, unbidden, was pummeling the muscles of his legs, and ignored the question.

"What odds are they giving, George?" he asked.

The young overseer laughed. "Last I heard it was three to one on Train an' five to one on you. They ain't sure, see— Train's only bin here a week. No one knows if he's got guts. But like I told you, Michael, he's mean. His gang don't like him— they reckon he's a surly devil, and he don't pull his weight in the yard. But Mr. Delaney fancies his chances. Put a mint on him, according to one of the clerks."

So Delaney would be best pleased were he to lose, Michael thought, but—devil take Delaney! This would be his last fight, God willing; provided he was not too badly knocked about by Train, he would make his bid for freedom within the next forty-eight hours. If he succeeded, Superintendent Delaney would have to look elsewhere for his blasted gladiator, and if he failed —well, as far as he could foresee the future, he would be dead and Delaney's reaction of no further interest to him. But at least tonight he would have the chance to lose the superintendent his stake and write his name—the name that was not his—in the inglorious annals of Port Arthur's history.

"Train's gone out there," Jemmy warned, interpreting the shouts and catcalls from the square. "Yeah, he's there." He crossed to the barred window and peered through it, giving a running commentary on the challenger's movements and his appearance. "Looks good stripped, Michael—big chest on 'im, an' not an ounce o' fat. But 'e ain't handling his leg-irons too good, by Gawd 'e ain't! I see 'e's got that bastard Haines in 'is corner, talkin' nineteen to the dozen, but Train ain't listenin'. Lookin' about, 'e is, wonderin' where you've got to!" He grinned. "You ready to go out?"

"Let him wonder," Michael retorted. "And let him sweat for a little. I'll go out when I'm ready. Put some more grease on my waist-chain, will you, Jem? And, here—give me some to rub round those infernal leg-irons."

Movement was easier with the fetters greased, and Jemmy, still grinning, did as he had asked.

"Better go now, Michael," young Wittington advised. "The superintendent's moved over to his seat, and Lieutenant Murless has just come over, with that new young ensign—what's his name?"

"Bernard," Michael supplied. "Horace Bernard." He swung himself lightly from the table, flexing the muscles of his arms and shoulders.

It had been Ensign Horace Bernard, he recalled with grim amusement, who had first led him to hope that his escape attempt might succeed. Bernard was—or rather had been, until a few short weeks ago—the proud possessor of a six-chambered Adams handgun, a beautiful, handmade weapon that had probably been a gift from indulgent parents, for such pistols were both expensive and hard to come by. The young officer, lacking military experience and ignorant of the ways of convicted felons, had left the Adams on a table in his quarters, in full view from the window, and . . . Michael's lips curved into a wry little smile, as he remembered the impulse that had led him to purloin it and the ease with which he had managed to do so. The Adams was hidden now, in the lumberyard, and Ensign Bernard, evidently fearing a dressing down from his superiors if he reported its loss, had made no mention of it to anyone.

With such a weapon, Michael reflected, the watchdogs on Eaglehawk Neck would present less of an obstacle; and the sentries, however alert they might be, would not expect that a convict absconder was likely to be armed. They—

"Come on, Michael," George Wittington urged. "The superintendent's getting impatient." He gripped Michael's arm. "Go in and show 'em what's what, eh? You can do it!"

Michael shrugged in answer. He led the way to the lamp-lit ring, making no acknowledgment of the roars that greeted his appearance and, without even glancing at his opponent, seated himself on his stool, his two seconds ranged behind him.

The hubbub instantly subsided when Superintendent Delaney rose ponderously to his feet, his hand raised for silence. Stout and red-faced, with a heavy black beard, he was perspiring freely in his thick blue serge uniform and stiffly starched white collar, and he paused to mop his face before making the anticipated announcement.

"This will be a contest over twenty rounds between Michael Wexford in the red corner and Tobias Train in the blue. Three-minute rounds, with one minute between each round, and no punching after the bell has sounded. The winner to be decided by a knockout or when his seconds throw in the towel. All right, men . . . shake hands and then stand to your marks. Commence fighting at the bell."

The first two rounds were fought with caution, each man taking the measure of the other. Train had been warned of the dangers of fighting in leg-irons, Michael concluded, since he made no attempt to indulge in any of the fancy footwork Jem Roberts had expected he might try. He stood to his mark, guarding his face and chest with muscular forearms and occasionally essaying a jab with his right. With his superior reach, he could have landed his punches more often, but he seemed unwilling to risk the relaxation of his guard or, indeed, to do much more than spar, even when, just before the bell signaled the end of the second round, Michael contrived to score with a swift left and right to the big man's face. Train followed the same tactics in the next round, continuing to block punches while failing to respond with any aggression, and when the round ended, a bleeding lower lip and a swelling eye bore witness to Michael's skill.

"He's scared, Michael," Jemmy Roberts asserted, flapping his towel vigorously as Michael returned to his corner and resumed his seat on the stool. "It don't look to me as if he's even tryin'. You could take him, boy, if you go in fast, before 'e's expectin' it."

Perhaps he could, Michael thought, not entirely convinced, although Train's hitherto vociferous supporters had gone oddly silent and their champion was slumped forward in his corner, his head between his hands. The fellow was a trained, professional prizefighter by all accounts, but certainly, so far, he had not exhibited any of the superiority his past experience should have conferred on him. He was taller, heavier, and presumably fitter, and his seconds would have told him that Superintendent Delaney's money was on him, yet . . . Puzzled, Michael rose as the bell rang, to stand alone in the center of the ring for what seemed a long time before his opponent shuffled forward to face him.

He realized his mistake an instant later. Train suddenly erupted like a fury, taking him momentarily off guard. The man's hard knuckles pounded his ribs, driving him back onto his heels, temporarily off balance, and a savage right caught him low in the groin, leaving him gasping and sick with pain.

God in heaven, he thought, he could not afford to let this swine of a fellow maim him! He had been mad to allow him the chance. Ensign Bernard's pistol would not remain safely hidden forever, and even if the weapon had eluded discovery, if he lost this fight, Delaney might well transfer him to the quarry gang or, worse still, to the road gang in Port Arthur itself, from where Eaglehawk Neck would be all but inaccessible.

A second low blow, delivered deliberately, almost floored him, but somehow Michael kept his feet, both arms locked about Train's massive shoulders to hold himself upright. Saliva trickled down his cheek as his opponent spat at him, but he avoided the big man's lifted knee as Superintendent Delaney roared at them to break. The bell sounded before they could obey, and Train sneered, as Michael relinquished his hold. "I'll take you next round! And by Gawd I'll finish you!"

Jemmy said reproachfully, when Michael shakily regained his corner, "You let 'im trick you, Michael! George Wittington told you 'e was mean. You should've watched the swine."

"He hit me low twice, Jem." Michael gasped. His head back, he attempted to draw air into his lungs, waves of nausea sweeping over him. "What's he in for, do you know?"

Wittington answered him. "Robbery with violence, Michael. They say as he just about killed a settler and his wife. They couldn't prove rape 'cause the poor woman wasn't able to give evidence against him, but he got life, all the same. Don't let him lick you, lad, for Lord's sake—we don't want his kind lording it here." He held a water bottle to Michael's parched lips. "Just try and hold him off next round, till you get your strength back."

But Michael was in no mood for delay. A slow anger was building up inside him, fueled by the tactics Train had employed. In none of his previous fights had he felt animosity toward an opponent; he had fought because he had been ordered to fight and, confident in his own physical strength and skill, had never done more than was necessary to win, without inflicting serious injury. Suddenly he was conscious of a savage determination to make Tobias Train pay, not only for the low blows and the spittle drying on his cheek, but also for what the lumbering giant had done to a nameless settler's wife, who had been too sorely injured to testify against him.

He let the cool water trickle from his mouth and drew a long, deep breath, no longer caring what victory might cost him. Joshua Simmons's high-pitched voice, screeching a derisive "Come on, Big Toby—let 'im have it!" still further fired his smoldering rage. Let them find Ensign Bernard's hidden pistol; even if Train's fists were to cripple him and force him to postpone his escape attempt for days or even weeks, he did not care. Nothing mattered, save that he must beat the black-browed rapist into cowed, humiliating submission.

As he had done before, Train delayed his entry into the ring for several seconds after the bell had sounded, an ugly, contemptuous leer on his face and his great fists lowered in mocking invitation.

"Bloody Irish *gentleman* they say you are!" he taunted. "Bloody Irish traitor! Come on, Yer soddin' Honor—I'm goin' to take you apart!"

Michael ignored the taunt and the invitation. He stepped back and then sideways, knowing instinctively how much leeway his ankle chain allowed him and affecting a reluctance to come to grips. Another backward step had Train yelling at him. "Yellow, are you? Stand an' fight, damn your eyes!"

Michael laughed and deftly sidestepped again. His opponent lurched after him, to be brought to a staggering halt by his ankle chain, and two quick punches to the face almost brought him to his knees. Now he, too, was angry, and for the next four rounds the battle became a savage one that had the spectators in a frenzy, with even Delaney on his feet, shouting unintelligible encouragement.

Michael used all the skill at his command, but he was taking cruel punishment, not only from the bigger man's fists but from his knees and his bullet head, both of which were used to advantage whenever a chance presented itself. But Train had not yet managed to master the restriction imposed by his fetters, and more than once his rage overcame his caution. Twice he went down in the ninth round, but picked himself up, snarling like an animal, wild-eyed and spitting blood, to go in with his head and punching low. He continued punching after the bell sounded, and only Superintendent Delaney's intervention sent him shambling back to his corner.

In his own, with Jemmy Roberts anxiously bending over him, Michael knew that his strength was failing. A red mist of pain floated in front of his eyes, and his legs seemed no longer under his control or, indeed, capable of sustaining his weight. But he shook his head stubbornly to George Wittington's suggestion that he throw in the towel.

"He has the beating of you, Michael," Jemmy warned. "And Delaney ain't goin' to pull 'im up for hittin' low—not when he's got 'is money on 'im. You know he ain't."

He did know, Michael told himself grimly, but again he shook his head.

"I'm going on, Jem," he insisted hoarsely. "He'll have to knock me out before I'll quit."

The fight continued, less savagely now, for both antagonists were nearing exhaustion, and Train sought to avoid punishment during the next four rounds, reverting to his initial defensive tactics but mindful of the restraining fetters. In the fifteenth round, Michael got through his guard and landed several punches—one a good right to the jaw—but the blows lacked power, and Train shrugged them off. He was breathing heavily, no longer wasting energy in muttered insults, and clearly losing heart.

In the last minute of the round, he stumbled and fell to his knees, staying there for as long as he could, while Michael stood back, as thankful as his opponent for the respite. But it was short-lived. The big man lumbered to his feet at the count of

eight and came for him in a bull-like rush. As they closed, his
left fist unclenched and opened, and a handful of dust, gathered
from the ground, spread over Michael's face in a blinding
cloud. Instinctively he raised both hands to his face and eyes,
and Train hit him in a flurry of punches, which he felt painfully
but could not see.

He went down heavily just as the bell sounded, and his opponent's foot descended hard on his outstretched left arm. Then
Train turned, grinning, and in obedience to the bell went back
to his corner.

It had to be the end, Michael thought dully, as George Wittington mopped at his swollen, bloodshot eyes with a wet towel.
He could take no more, if even a remote chance of putting his
escape plan into action remained. Delaney would send him to
the quarry gang if he lost—probably as soon as the loading of
the government steamer *Hastings* was completed—and he must
either run within the next forty-eight hours or abandon any
attempt to do so in the foreseeable future. And he had to recover the Adams pistol. He—

"Well, the bell just saved you, Wexford." It was Delaney's
voice, and Michael squinted up at him, his vision still blurred.
"You fought well, but Train has the beating of you. Best throw
in the towel—there's nothing to be gained by going on, is
there?"

Had George Wittington or old Jemmy made the same suggestion, he would have agreed to it, Michael thought wearily. Indeed, a moment earlier he had been on the point of telling them
that he had had enough, but . . . Delaney's round red face
floated indistinctly in front of his half-closed eyes, wearing a
smirk of satisfaction because the outcome was obviously the one
he wanted. He was not by any means the worst of the Port
Arthur prison officials, Michael reminded himself. He could not
hold a candle to Commandant Price, but, devil take him, Delaney had permitted Train to break all the rules so that he might
rake in a sizable profit from his wager!

"No!" Michael swore softly and got to his feet. For all his
legs had turned to jelly and he was swaying dangerously, he still
towered over the stocky superintendent, and Delaney backed
away from him in alarm.

"What in hell d'you mean? You—"

"I'm not throwing in the towel, Mr. Delaney," Michael rasped. "If it had been a fair fight and I'd been beaten by a better man, I would have given him best. But it wasn't a fair fight, and you know it wasn't. I'm going on!"

Anger was rekindled and it gave him strength. The bell sounded, and he went in like a madman, careless of what his opponent might do. His left arm was almost useless, but he punched and pounded with his right, taking the tiring Train by surprise. The big man retreated, stumbled over his leg chain, and Michael's right caught him squarely on the point of the jaw.

He went down like a log and lay spread-eagled on the dusty ground, incapable of rising, his big body limp and his eyes closed. The spectators cheered themselves hoarse, clustering about Michael to offer their congratulations, even Haines and the unpleasant little Simmons among them, and Jemmy Roberts was beside himself, swearing and his eyes filled with emotional tears. At length, Tobias Train picked himself up and came shuffling over, to extend a grudging hand, and Superintendent Delaney followed after him, his smile one of genuine, if surprised, admiration.

"Well done, Big Michael," he said gruffly. "I didn't think you could do it, but, darn it, you won! I'll know better than to bet against you next time."

The overseers were herding the convicts back to their barracks, and the kerosene lamps went out, one by one, leaving the erstwhile battleground in darkness, save for the table at which the clerks were still paying out on the wagers.

"Best call it a day, Michael," George Wittington advised. He offered Michael his arm, slipping a towel over his shoulders. "I'll give you a rubdown before you turn in—you'll be stiff if I don't." He grinned at Jemmy, who was beside him. "I wonder if the commandant knows what goes on here? Let's hope he don't, for it was a great evening, and that was the best I ever saw you fight. You earned me a tidy fifteen shillings, but even if you hadn't, I'd be pleased you beat that rogue Train. You've got what it takes, Big Michael, and for all you're wearing chains and I'm not anymore, I—damn it, I envy you!"

Would the younger man still envy him, Michael wondered
dully, when the arms of the semaphore were spelling out the
news that he had absconded and when he was heading for
Eaglehawk Neck, in felon's garb, armed with a stolen pistol?
Always supposing, of course, that his aching body could throw
off the ill effects of the punishment he had taken at Train's
hands. It would take several days, he knew, but . . . the feeling had returned to his left arm, and propped up on his bunk
was a water pitcher, which he knew from past experience would
contain not water but rum. The reward from Delaney for his
victory . . . He passed the pitcher to Wittington and said,
smiling, "We'll share this, after you've given me a rubdown, Mr.
Wittington. It's just one more little thing the commandant
doesn't know about, and by heaven, it's a **lot** better than the
fare they treat you to in solitary!"

Chapter VIII

IT TOOK TWO days to load the steamer *Hastings*. Work started at 5:30 A.M. and continued until 6 P.M., with an hour's break for dinner at midday. Ordered light duties by Superintendent Delaney, Michael found himself detailed to check the timber as it was loaded onto the wheeled freight wagons that ran on the tramway from the lumberyard to the jetty.

Once a wagon had been loaded and the labor gang started to push it down the tracks, he was free and unsupervised until the next empty wagon was returned, for the process to be repeated. It seemed as good an opportunity as any to repossess himself of Ensign Bernard's Adams pistol, since the men who normally worked in the yard were transferred to the task of loading and only the two who operated the steam engine—both old, good-conduct prisoners—remained on the premises. And both, in the manner of old men, had seized on the chance to curl up beside their temporarily silent engine and sleep, paying him no heed.

Michael waited until he had seen three heavily laden wagons on their way, and then, careful to keep to the shadows lest one of the engineers should waken, he moved silently to the far end of the yard. He had chosen his hiding place with much thought, wrapping the oiled handgun in a roll of sailcloth and placing it —still loaded—in the recess between two loosened bricks in the foundation of the outer wall. The lumberyard was seldom swept, and piles of sawdust littered the ground and rose in haphazard heaps along the full length of the wall. For this reason, it was unlikely in the extreme that anyone would suspect the presence of the stolen weapon, unless they had seen him concealing it initially.

Confident in this knowledge, Michael dropped to his knees, searching for the loosened bricks behind their barrier of dust and dirt. He found them without difficulty, and after a swift glance over his shoulder to make sure that he was unobserved, he started to pry the bricks out of their setting. They came out easily enough, but the space behind them was empty—the precious Adams pistol, the key to his escape, was no longer there. Only a strip of sailcloth remained, evidently torn away by whoever had taken the weapon in order to make a less bulky package—a convict, then, Michael reasoned, sick with disappointment. Certainly a man faced with the necessity to conceal the pistol on his person . . .

He expelled his breath in a frustrated sigh, seeking to identify the man or men who had so unexpectedly thwarted his carefully laid escape plan. Haines and Simmons had been working with the lumberyard gang when he had hidden the pistol, but then so had fifty others, any one of whom might have watched him prying the loose bricks from the wall. But . . . Michael frowned, remembering. Only Haines and Simmons had, with himself, been given a week's solitary confinement. Only that pair of unprincipled rogues had returned to the Cascades at the same time as he had, the previous day . . . and Joshua Simmons was a sneak thief, who had been suspected, both here and on Norfolk Island, of stealing from his fellow prisoners. The chances were that he and Haines now had the precious pistol, and if they had, there was little doubt that they would use it. They—

The rumble of wheels on the track heralded the return of the empty freight wagon, and swearing under his breath, Michael went to meet it. Inquiry of the men preparing to reload the wagon elicited the fact that Haines and Simmons were with the jetty gang, working in the _Hastings'_ hold.

"Pretty thick, they are, the two of 'em," Jemmy Roberts volunteered. "An' in a huddle with Train, last time I clapped eyes on 'em. Seemed excited, too, like as if they'd gotten some scheme afoot. Maybe they're plannin' another match with you, Michael, an' fixin' how to lick you!"

That was hardly likely, Michael decided—Big Toby Train had looked very much the worse for wear at the morning muster, with one eye closed and a noticeable limp, but he had not petitioned for light duties, seemingly anxious to avoid any contact with his erstwhile adversary after the previous evening's battle.

"Josh Simmons was up at the yard here earlier," another man supplied. "I know, 'cause I was with the little bastard. Supposed ter be linin' up the wagons an' takin' 'em down to the jetty, we was, but 'e never done a hand's turn. Come runnin' after us, 'e did, when we was 'arfway down the jetty, puffin' an' pantin' fit to bust." He spat disgustedly into the sawdust-littered ground at his feet. "An' after that, 'e joined 'is pal on board the perishin' ship."

It was not proof positive that Simmons had taken the pistol, Michael thought, but it was near enough to confirm his suspicions . . . and it would behoove him to keep a wary eye on the two rogues, while awaiting an opportunity to recover the weapon.

To his intense annoyance, the opportunity never came. Both men, and Train with them, managed to keep well out of his way, and it was not until the last wagonload of timber had left the lumberyard for the jetty that Overseer Burke ordered him to accompany it.

"I reckon you've bin skulking here for long enough, whiles other men have bin sweating their guts out, Wexford," the overseer said unpleasantly. "Roll up them sleeves an' get ter work loading this lot when you get to the jetty, understand? An' no sliding off before your time's up. The ship'll be sailing once this load's stowed, and if it takes till dark, we'll get it finished."

Michael mumbled a suitably submissive acknowledgment and put his shoulder to the rear of the wagon, his earlier frustration lifting. Overseer Burke had done him a service, he reflected cynically, for all that had been the last thing the swine had intended. If he could manage to run his quarry to earth in the *Hastings'* hold, it should not be beyond his power of persuasion to regain possession of the stolen pistol—even if Train were to throw in his lot with Haines and Simmons. Probably their discovery of the pistol would have put the idea of escape into their minds, but they would not have had time as yet to formulate any sort of plan. Or it was to be hoped that they had not. . . . Michael pushed with the rest, and the wagon went bumping and lurching down the track.

The *Hastings* had steam up, he saw, when they reached the jetty. She was a sturdy paddle-wheeler, built at Port Arthur by convict labor about ten years earlier, before the closure of the shipyard, and she ran regularly to and from Hobart, carrying cargo and supplies. Her crew were emancipists or ticket-of-leave men, numbering a dozen, under the command of an elderly master, long retired from the East India Company's marine, who was said to be easygoing and not averse to doing a trade in tobacco with those he decided were trustworthy.

He was on deck now, a small, rotund figure with a straggling white beard, engaged in what appeared to be an argument with Overseer Burke. On the jetty, the boys from the Juvenile Establishment at Safety Cove—six husky, deeply tanned youngsters who were being transferred to the hiring depot in Hobart—were lined up at the foot of the gangplank by their overseer, where one of the ship's officers accepted their passes and prepared to call their names.

They were in high spirits, which, Michael reflected with a hint of envy, was not to be wondered at, since the decision to close down Safety Cove meant that their time at Port Arthur had been cut short. They laughed and joked as they answered to their names; the officer did not reprove them, and some of the crew joined in the repartee, their attention distracted by the merriment, and . . . Overseer Burke was nowhere to be seen.

"I'm going on board, Jem," Michael whispered to Jemmy Roberts. "Cover for me, will you, if Burke comes back?"

He swung himself onto the little steamer's congested deck, balancing on the cargo net and clinging there, as the winch lowered its burden into the after hold.

Below, after the strong sunlight outside, it was darker than he had anticipated, and for a moment or two he could see nothing. The hold was all but full, the timber stacked with methodical precision throughout its length, and at first he supposed it to be deserted, with none of the jetty gang standing by, as they should have been, to unload the net on which he had descended. But then, as his eyes became accustomed to the dim light, he glimpsed two shadowy figures a few yards to his right. He moved toward them, only to trip over a dark, recumbent form that he realized, even as he fell, was the body of a man. It lay inert, not moving despite his weight across it, and as he leapt to his feet in sudden alarm, he knew instinctively that the man over whom he had stumbled was dead. He was—*he had been*—a soldier, his white crossbelts showing up in the semidarkness against the red cloth of his tunic, his discarded shako lying, upended, beside him. The sentry, Michael thought—the one normally placed at the entrance to the hold when convicts were working there. The sentry, but without his musket . . . He drew in his breath sharply, no longer in any doubt as to the present whereabouts of the Adams pistol—or, come to that, of the soldier's musket.

"For God's sake!" he exclaimed hoarsely. "What's going on here? And who—" Two powerful arms closed about him from behind, silencing him abruptly. He attempted to struggle, to break free, sensing from their size and strength that the arms were Train's. Then the cold steel of a bayonet—the dead soldier's, his bemused mind deduced—was thrust painfully into his ribs and Simmons hissed, "Stay right where you are! Don't make a sound or you'll get this in your guts!"

"Who is it, Josh?" Haines's voice, coming from a little way away, sounded tense.

"It's soddin' Wexford," Simmons answered. "But we've got 'im, Will. What'll we do with 'im? Want me to slit 'is gizzard?"

Haines was silent for a long moment; finally he snapped, "No —let 'im go. We can use 'im, maybe." He came slithering across to join them, impeded by the planks, which, with the loosening of the rope that had held the cargo net, had spilled out to one side. "Send that bleedin' net back up, Toby, or they'll start wonderin' what's 'appened to it. Get a move on, man!"

Train obeyed him, and Simmons reluctantly lowered the bayonet, glaring at Michael as he did so.

"The bastard'll give us away, Will. We dursn't trust 'im."

"He's a lifer, same as us," Haines said with a growl. "What about it, Wexford? You with us or not?"

Michael stood his ground. "How the devil can I say, until you tell me what you're aiming to do? You're surely not going to try to run for it, are you?"

"We're takin' over the ship," Haines said. "Once she sails. We'll run 'er ashore on the mainland an' leg it into the bush. Plenty o' food, plenty o' water aboard, ain't there? We'll take what we need—they won't catch us in a hurry."

"Holy Mother of God!" Michael stared at him in shocked disbelief. For this they had murdered a wretched soldier, and the *Hastings* was still moored to the jetty, in full view of half a dozen other soldiers, the labor gangs, and their overseers, not to mention the ship's company. "The master will never sail with you on board! Have you gone out of your minds? Burke will find you missing when he calls the roll, and—"

"Burke won't find no one missin' ever again," Haines told him sourly. He jerked his head in the direction from which he had come, and Michael saw that there was another slumped, motionless body, half hidden behind a pile of timber. And the Adams was in Haines's outstretched hand. . . . Sickened, he looked away. "Did you have to kill him, too?"

"May as well be hanged for a sheep as for a lamb," Haines retorted. "An' Burke was a bloody bullyin' swine—'e had it coming, the bastard. Josh—make the signal! Quick about it— they'll be closin' the hatch any minute."

"You'll never get away with this," Michael protested. "You must be mad, Haines! There's not a chance in hell that you'll make it!"

For answer, Haines struck him across the mouth with the pistol butt. "You aimin' to give us away, Wexford? Yell for help or somethin'? D'you reckon anyone will believe you weren't in with us from the start?" He spat derisively. "You got a choice— you can join us, or I'll tell Josh 'e can slit your gizzard. Which is it to be?"

It was scarcely a choice, Michael thought dully, a hand to his swollen mouth. In any event, what had he to lose? Haines seemed confident that his crazy escape plan would succeed, and, as the fellow had pointed out, even were he to attempt to betray them and somehow gain the deck unscathed, would those in authority believe that he had had no hand in the killings? It was unlikely; he was there with the three murderers, and . . . it had been he who had stolen the Adams from Ensign Bernard's quarters.

"All right, Haines," he said thickly, "I'm with you. But how in God's name are you going to make off with this ship?"

Before Haines could answer him, Josh Simmons came scuttling down the hatchway ladder, his small, pinched face wearing a triumphant grin. "They got the signal, Will," he announced breathlessly. "An' the hatch cover's goin' on. I fixed a wedge, like you said. They'll not be able to batten it down."

"Good work, Josh lad," Haines approved. "Now lend Toby a hand an' get them bleedin' corpses out o' sight. Pile some o' the timber on top of 'em. You got the lobsterback's uniform off of 'im, Toby? Right, let me 'ave it. Look lively, lads! And Wexford—" He tossed a hammer across, to land at Michael's feet. "Get to work on them leg-irons o' yours, an' quick about it. We got to be able to move once this soddin' ship gets under way."

Haines's own irons, Michael realized, had already been removed; so had Train's and Simmons's. . . . They had wasted no time. And Haines was divesting himself of his convict's garb, evidently with the intention of donning the dead soldier's uniform. He—

From the jetty outside came the sound of raised voices and running feet and a overseer yelling commands, his voice drowned by a chorus of confused shouts and counterorders. Michael stifled an exclamation, and Haines said exultantly, as he dragged the broad-arrowed jacket over his head, "There— that's 'ow we're goin' to get this tub to sea, Wexford! Some o' the lads 'ave started a right old barney on the jetty, kiddin' the pesky overseers that a fire's broken out in the timber store. In a minute or two they'll start yellin' that it's speadin' an' the ship's in danger. Old Tarry Breeks ain't one to take no chances—I know 'im. 'E'll cast off, you see if 'e don't. An' once we're at sea an' out o' sight . . ." He chuckled, buttoning on the soldier's tunic and striking an attitude. "Like old times—me in 'er Majesty's scarlet again! Went like clockwork, didn't it, Josh? I told you it would. Worth them few quids o' baccy in the right 'ands, weren't it, eh?"

"Aye, that it was. Listen . . ." Josh Simmons, his grisly task apparently completed, held up a hand for silence. "She's puttin' off, Will! You were right."

The sudden threshing of the *Hastings'* paddle wheels bore witness to the truth of his words, and from behind him, Train gave vent to a low whoop of satisfaction. "Why, if you ain't the clever one, Will! This beats everything, by God it does! Truth to tell, though, I 'ad me doubts. I didn't think we'd make it. You—"

Haines cut him short. "We ain't made it yet, Toby," he reminded the big man harshly. "We've got to lie low till we're well clear o' the Cascades . . . an' that means keepin' quiet. You got them leg-irons off yet, Wexford?"

"Yes, they're off." Half a dozen blows with the hammer had sufficed to shatter the filed links of his fetters, and Michael discarded them with relief. Up till now, he was forced to concede, Haines's seemingly crazy plan seemed to be working successfully; but unlike Train, he still had doubts. Certainly the seizure of the ship offered a better chance than an attempt to cross Eaglehawk Neck on foot and alone, but . . . He subjected Haines's half-seen face to an anxious scrutiny.

"How do you propose to take this ship, Haines? Have you got that planned, too?"

"What'd you take me for? Course I 'ave." Haines buckled on the dead soldier's crossbelts and moved his neck in an attempt to ease the pressure from the constricting stock. "Long time since I 'ad to wear one o' these soddin' things, still less fight in 'em. An' the little bastard was a lot smaller than me. Still—will I pass muster, *Mister* Wexford?"

"You'll need the bayonet," Michael reminded him. "And you won't need that pistol."

"Think I'm goin' to let you 'ave it?" Haines mocked. He took the bayonet from Josh Simmons, a cold little smile playing about his thick, full lips as he slid the Adams into his waistband. " 'Twas seein' you hide it gave me the notion first off," he went on. "Like most o' the other lags 'ere, I thought o' tryin' to get across Eagle'awk Neck, but 'ow many ever made it that way? But with a pistol, why, that opened up a better notion. First time I 'ad a ticket-o'-leave, I worked on this tub, so I know a bit about 'er—and about 'er master. Benjamin Tarr—old Tarry Breeks—all 'e ever wants is to keep 'is nose clean an' make a copper or two on the side. He'll give no trouble, you'll see."

"Yes, but—" Michael was impatient now, his anxiety growing. "I want to know how you aim to take the ship."

Haines, however, was not to be hurried. "Weeks I been plannin' this, an' like Josh said, I was right—it's gone like clockwork. I didn't even 'ave to fire that pistol. I just jabbed it in the sojer's back an' warned 'im to keep 'is mouth shut, an' Josh finished 'im with 'is own bayonet. Never made a sound, the poor bastard—I 'ad my 'and over 'is mouth, to make sure. Then that swine Burke come below, all officious, to see what we was at, an' we served 'im the same way." There was no pity, only a brutal satisfaction in his voice. "We— 'Ang on!" He paused, listening intently, and Michael felt the slight lurch of the deck under his feet as the steamer changed course.

"He's headin' nor'west," Haines observed. "He'll hug the shore between Ironstone Point an' Whitehouse an' then run out past Green Head an' Slopin' Island. Should be in Barnes Bay soon after first light tomorrow. I reckon we'll bide our time—unless anyone pokes 'is 'ead in 'ere—an' take old Tarry Breeks in the mornin'." He smiled from one to the other of them. "I'll march you three into 'is cabin, claimin' I found you stowed away. Once we're in, we take the old buzzard, an' he'll help us round up the crew, 'cause I'll be holdin' that pistol to 'is 'ead. We're armed, and they ain't. If any of 'em give us trouble, we'll shoot 'em—or shoot one of 'em, as an example. Agreed?"

"Aye, agreed," Simmons echoed, without hesitation. Train nodded his massive head with some reluctance, and Michael, risking their concerted disapproval, made a plea for restraint.

"What about the boys from the Juvenile Establishment, the ones who are on release? You surely wouldn't shoot them, would you?" he asked. "They've done their time."

"We'll see they're locked up," Haines decided. He added, in a more placatory tone, "I don't want no more killin', Wexford. I said we'd shoot anyone as gives us trouble, that's all. An' this bunch won't, if I know anything about 'em. They'll be too scared for their own skins, an' the old man with 'em. But we're goin' to have to alter course soon after first light—run in west o' Bruny Island an' into the D'Entrecasteaux Channel, 'stead o' steerin' north for the Derwent Estuary—an' put the old tub ashore near Woodbridge Bay or Middleton Creek or thereabouts, off North Bruny. Then we'll take what we need—stores an' clothing and whatever we might find useful—an' head off for the Huon Valley. Plenty o' pickings to be had there, I guarantee."

He enlarged on his plan, and Michael listened uneasily. Haines knew the coast, that was evident, however long it had been since he had served as a member of the *Hastings'* crew. The Huon Valley was settled, and there were convict probation stations, he had heard, in the area, and a number of logging camps, as well as farms scattered throughout.

But where there were settlements and townships, there were also magistrates and constables, to uphold the law. The convict stations had guards, and with Hobart too close for comfort, it would mean that police troopers and probably military search parties would be dispatched to track them down, as soon as it was known they had escaped from Port Arthur. And when the *Hastings* failed to make port within her scheduled time, the hunt would be on with a vengeance, and rewards offered for their apprehension . . . yet Haines was talking as if it were decided that they should stay together.

Michael's uneasiness grew. Haines's mention of "pickings" made his intentions clear enough. He was planning that they should take to the bush, to prey on isolated settlers and live hand-to-mouth as bushrangers, with every man's hand against them and the inevitable death sentence facing them if—*when*— they were apprehended. Whereas he . . . dear God, he thought despairingly, had not his sole reason for attempting to escape been in order to go in pursuit of Commandant Price? Had not that been the objective in the forefront of his mind when he had stolen Ensign Bernard's Adams pistol and weighed up the risks he would incur if he tried to make the hazardous crossing of Eaglehawk Neck?

He had been ready and willing—nay, eager—to take his life

in his hands, if by so doing there might be one chance in a thousand of evening the score with the sadistic swine who had come so near to breaking him during the years on Norfolk Island. It had been *that* hope and not the hope of freedom that had kept him alive, when it would have been easier to die. But to face the life Haines and the unpleasant Simmons and Big Toby Train were now contemplating—and in their company—no, that he knew he could not do. He—

Haines said suddenly, as if guessing his thoughts or, at all events, sensing his unspoken opposition, "You got to stick with us, Wexford, understand? Once we're ashore an' clear o' the ship, you can go your own way, if you want to. But till then, you do what I say—right?"

"Very well," Michael agreed, his tone clipped. "But *you* understand, I'll have no part in any killing."

"I told you, there'll be no killing, not unless we have to." Haines exchanged a glance with Josh Simmons and then shrugged. "All right—we'll set a watch. You can take the first two hours, Wexford. Then Toby, then Josh. When we ain't on watch, we get our heads down. First thing tomorrow mornin' we take the ship an' change course, like I said. When we're off the mainland, we keep our eyes peeled for a good spot to run the ship on shore. Soon as we find one, that's what we'll do."

No one questioned the plan he had outlined, and having given Michael instructions to give the alarm if any of the *Hastings'* crew attempted to enter the hold, Haines lay down on a pile of sacking and composed himself for sleep.

There were no alarms; the ship plowed on through the night, and Michael, his watch over, slept fitfully until Haines roused him, with the information that it was dawn and time for action.

His plan worked, as he had said it would, like clockwork. The watch on deck—three elderly seamen, plus a cook's boy, engaged in emptying slop buckets into the sea—stared in astonishment when Haines, in the dead soldier's uniform, herded his three companions across the deck toward the master's cabin. But not a move was made to stop him—the seamen seemingly reassured by his claim that the three were stowaways—and old Captain Tarr, wakened blinking and bleary-eyed from what had clearly been a deep, drink-induced sleep, made no attempt at resistance. With the Adams' squat muzzle pressed into his ribs, he obeyed without argument Haines's demand that he turn out of his bunk and clothe himself.

"You was in 'er Majesty's Navy, wasn't you, Wexford?" Haines asked, as old Tarr completed his hasty dressing. Michael nodded and Haines grinned.

"Officer, was you?"

"I was a midshipman. But—"

"Then you'll know enough to make sure the captain keeps to the course I'll set 'im?"

"I think so, yes."

"Right—then on deck with you. Josh will make sure 'e don't give you no lip." He thrust the musket into Josh Simmons's eager hands, and Michael followed them on deck. Grumbling under his breath, the *Hastings'* master took the wheel and duly altered course, while Haines and Train rounded up the crew. What they did with them Michael did not know, save that, with the exception of two elderly seamen, they all vanished below. When his two fellow absconders reappeared on deck, they had evidently raided both the ship's arms chest and the old master's wardrobe, for both were clad in civilian suits, and Train was carrying two muskets. He relieved Josh, who went below once more with Haines, and on their return Josh had replaced his convict garb with seaman's ducks and a blue watchcoat, and they unceremoniously dumped half a dozen rusting cutlasses—taken, Michael guessed, from the arms chest—over the side.

"Is 'e still on course, Wexford?" Haines demanded.

"He's still on course," Michael confirmed.

"Right—then see 'e keeps on it. Josh an' me'll be in the engine room—them swine o' stokers ain't puttin' their backs into their work, so we're just goin' to show 'em what's what." Haines squinted skyward for a moment and then nodded his satisfaction. "Goin' to be a fine day, praise be! We should sight Bruny Island in—" His glance went to the master. " 'Bout a coupla hours, eh?"

"Aye, about that," Tarr confirmed sullenly.

Michael drew Haines to one side, his rancor against the man's arrogant assumption of command unconcealed. He said, lowering his voice, "I need one of the muskets, Haines. And a

change of clothing. I'm not going on the run in broad arrows.
I—"

"Use your fists," Haines sneered. "You know how to do that
well enough, don't you? I'm not trustin' you with a musket. But
you can take any clobber you want from old Tarry Breeks's
cabin once I'm sure we're in the D'Entrecasteaux Channel. We
—" He broke off, cursing, as raised voices from below and the
sound of frenzied hammering suggested that some, at least, of
the crew were bent on breaking out of their confinement. "Devil
take 'em, that's them soddin' little swine from Safety Cove. Go
an' deal with 'em, Toby. Tell 'em we'll let them go when we quit
this tub, but only if they be'ave theirselves meantime. Bust a
few 'eads if you 'ave to. Come on, Josh—let's get them bastard
stokers back into line!"

Left alone with Michael, Benjamin Tarr said slyly, "They
don't trust you, do they, Mr. Wexford? 'Cos you used to be an
officer in 'er Majesty's Navy, no doubt?" When Michael did not
answer him, he took a bony brown hand from the wheel and
grasped Michael by the sleeve of his coarse yellow shirt.
"What're you doing in the company of rogues like Haines, eh?
For that matter, what're you doing in this rig? You ain't a criminal, are you?"

What truthful answer could he give? Michael asked himself,
recalling his brief, inglorious months in the bush that had been
the reason for his having been sent to Norfolk Island. And as to
the company he kept . . . He laughed aloud.

"What's amusing you?" Tarr challenged indignantly.

"Nothing you'd understand," Michael returned. "It's just
that there'll be a price on my head, the same as on the others'
. . . and they'll hang me if I'm caught, Captain, as an accessory—that's for sure. So I'm aiming to show a clean pair of
heels, if I can—but alone, the first chance I get."

"You could be in line for a pardon," Tarr pointed out, "if you
were to help me retake my ship. I'd recommend you, and—"
He glanced at the binnacle, then questioningly to Michael.
"That's Betsey's Island, fine on our larboard bow, and the Iron
Pot light'll be in sight soon, at the mouth of the Derwent
River." He went into detail, describing a number of landmarks.
"It's getting near the time when we'll have to change course.

Which is it to be, Mr. Wexford? North to the estuary, or sou'west to weather Cape Sortie and head into the D'Entrecasteaux Channel?"

Haines would shoot him—shoot them both, probably—without compunction, if his orders were not strictly adhered to. And he would find out long before the wallowing old paddle-steamer could possibly enter the Derwent River. Haines might be no navigator, but he knew these waters and the landmarks Tarr had indicated . . . and it would not take him long to show the recalcitrant stokers what was what. Or, come to that, to scare the boys from the Juvenile Establishment into submission. Already the shouting and hammering had ceased. . . . Michael freed his sleeve from the old master's grasp.

"Steer sou'west, Captain," he said curtly.

"Then you'll not help me?"

"They're armed, Captain Tarr, and they will not hesitate to gun you down if you step out of line. I know them, and I know what they've done. The only way you can hope to save your ship and stay alive is to do what Haines wants, believe me."

"They'll wreck my ship," Tarr said with a growl. "That's what they're planning, isn't it?"

"They plan to run her ashore, yes," Michael conceded. "But if you play your cards right, you can choose where. It does not have to be on the rocks, does it?"

"No," the old man answered, his brow puckered in thought. "No, you're right, it doesn't." Again his eyes met Michael's in mute question.

"I'll do what I can, Captain," Michael responded. "But it may not be much."

The ship plowed on, and now Haines was on deck, wary and watchful, his hand always on the pistol in his belt. Even when he was satisfied that the correct change of course had been made, he did not relax his vigilance. He kept Michael at his post, standing for hour after hour at Captain Tarr's side, the ship's chart of the area spread out in front of them, each landmark checked and noted for him.

Simmons and Train brought sacks of provisions from the cook's store, carefully dividing their contents into a size and weight that each man could comfortably carry. There were three bundles, not four, Michael observed, with growing apprehension; and ammunition for the muskets was also divided into three pouches, which the other three strapped to their waists, without explanation or apology, Simmons tucking the dead soldier's bayonet into his belt, an oddly menacing smile curving his lips as he did so.

The cook, clearly terrified of them, brought food and a small ale cask on deck, and they ate, squatting cross-legged on the paddle transom, Haines studying the shore at intervals with the master's glass to his eye. Seen from the steamer's deck, it looked inhospitable enough—tall, basalt cliffs rising sheer out of the sea, with the surf dashing against their rocky outcrops and thickly wooded hills rising behind them.

Michael snatched a meal, with Benjamin Tarr to share it, and the old man observed, in a hoarse whisper, "We're coming up to a likely place." He jabbed his finger at a point on the chart. "Baker's Inlet, it's called. I could run her ashore there with a good chance of being able to get her off without doing too much damage. And Haines will like it—he'd have no trouble starting his run. No cliffs to climb, just a gentle slope and plenty of cover." He took a long swallow of the ale the cook had brought him and gestured to the sacks of provisions lying nearby on the deck. "Doesn't look to me as if they intend you to go with them."

It did not, Michael was becoming increasingly aware. Perhaps, he thought, they planned simply to leave him on board . . . although, in view of Haines's attitude toward him—which was now openly hostile—they might have other plans. He might prove an awkward witness against them if they were caught—a fact that, he was sure, had not escaped Haines's notice. But, after a prolonged study of the chart, Haines agreed that Baker's Inlet would serve well as their destination, and he ordered the *Hastings'* master to close the shore and steer for the inlet.

"How long d'you reckon it'll take us to get there?" he demanded. "Half an hour?"

"A mite longer. The tide'll be running against us when we come close inshore," Tarr told him woodenly.

"Right." Galvanized into action, Haines looked from one to

the other of his fellow escapers. "Toby, go below an' make sure the crew are all locked in—an' don't forget the cook. The stokers can go in, along o' the rest now—we don't need them no more. You'd best back 'im up, Josh, just in case any of 'em starts lookin' for trouble."

He waited, with barely concealed impatience, until his two henchmen returned to report that all was as he wanted it below.

"Not a peep out o' any of the bastards," Josh reported. He grinned derisively and gestured to the rapidly nearing shoreline. The strong afternoon sunlight shone down on a semicircle of golden sand immediately ahead, with the gentle, tree-clad slope Tarr had described forming a picturesque backcloth to the small, secluded bay. "What about it, Will? Ain't there a couple of other sods we don't need no more? An' one in partic'lar I bin itchin' to get me hands on?"

The moment he had been dreading had come, Michael realized, but . . . he had not anticipated that they would serve Captain Tarr as, it seemed, they were intending to serve himself. He had decided that, when suspicion became certainty, to dive overboard and attempt to swim ashore would be his best, if not his only, chance of survival. But the *Hastings'* master was an old man, and, like most of his generation of seamen, he probably could not swim. . . . To abandon him, whatever the cost, was unthinkable. Devil take it, he thought derisively, the instincts of a gentleman were still there. Commandant Price had not entirely obliterated them.

He heard Haines laugh, heard him bellow "Aye—have at 'im, Josh!" but had moved before Josh Simmons could free the long military bayonet from his belt. His fist landed squarely on the little man's unshaven jaw, sending him down as if he had been poleaxed, but, to Michael's chagrin, the sprawled body rested on top of the half-drawn bayonet, which he had hoped he might secure as a weapon.

"Go below!" he yelled at Tarr, "and lock yourself in! They'll kill you if you don't! I'll hold 'em off!"

Tarr tried to react to his warning, but Big Toby Train moved swiftly to block his escape, an outstretched foot bringing the old captain tumbling to his knees. The musket butt descended with hideous force, and Tarr lay spread-eagled on the deck in a slowly growing pool of his own blood.

"I thought as much—gettin' together, wasn't you?" Haines snarled. The Adams was in his hand, leveled at Michael's chest, and he waved Train aside with a harsh "No, this bastard's mine, Toby! Leave 'im to me!"

The instincts of a barefisted fighter, unwillingly acquired under Superintendent Delaney's tutelage, had not been obliterated either, Michael knew. He spun round, his leap taking him across the deck just as Haines fired, and the shot missed him by a hairsbreadth. He was over the rail an instant later, hurtling feet first into the churned-up water astern of the *Hastings'* paddle wheel. The sea opened to swallow him up, and he kicked out, holding his breath as the green water closed over his head, blindly seeking to put as much distance between himself and the ship as he could before being compelled to come up for air.

His desperate ploy succeeded. Shots rained into the sea a dozen yards from him when he rose, gasping, his lungs near to bursting. He heard Train shout "Look—there 'e is!" and the next shot came nearer as he struck out in a powerful crawl stroke for the faraway shore.

Then, to his sick dismay, when he paused for a moment to look back, he saw Train pick up Captain Tarr's limp body and fling it over the side, and the old man's despairing cry told him that he was still alive and conscious of his peril. The ship was chugging steadily toward the still-distant inlet; with no one, seemingly, at her wheel, her progress had become erratic, but she was heading away from him, drawing out of musket range with each turn of her paddle wheels.

Michael trod water, measuring the distance, and then decided to make a last attempt to save her master. Tarr was conscious when he reached him, floating on his back, the swell washing the blood from his wounded head into a scarlet patch of froth about him . . . and there were sharks in these waters, Michael knew, whether or not such dangerous predators lurked in Eaglehawk Bay. But he had been prepared to risk an encounter with them there, had he been compelled to, and so . . . He drew deep gulps of air into his lungs and, grasping Tarr by the collar, began the long, strength-sapping swim to the Huon Valley coast.

The sun was sinking when, at last, the turning tide washed him ashore with his helpless burden. No sharks had made an appearance; he would have been powerless to ward them off if they had, Michael was dully aware, and he found himself breathing a prayer of thankfulness to the God he had for so long neglected as his feet touched solid ground.

This was not the sheltered, sandy inlet upon which Tarr had chosen to beach his ship; it was seaweed-encrusted rock, with a daunting cliff face behind it, which he recognized he lacked the strength, at present, to climb. But until the tide again turned, they were safe there, and, praise be to God, he could rest his exhausted body, at least until feeling returned to his numb limbs.

It was old Captain Tarr who wakened him. The *Hastings'* master was tugging weakly at his arm, and it was again broad daylight.

"Tide's . . . turning, Wexford. We'll drown if we . . . stay here."

Michael made an effort to rouse himself. He was aching, his whole body chilled and drained of energy, his salt-soaked felon's garb seeming to cling to him in stiff, unyielding folds. Wearily he sat up and divested himself of the jacket, trying to ward off the mists of sleep and for a time unable to recall where he was and how he had come to be here.

"There's a cave . . . up the cliff a ways," Tarr whispered faintly. "If we can get to it." He pointed with a trembling hand. "But I . . . before God, I don't think I can walk!"

Memory returned, and Michael got to his feet. To have come so far, to have endured so much—even to have survived, against all odds . . . merciful heaven, the incoming tide might drive them from their refuge, but it was not going to drown them now! He braced himself and, an arm round his companion's waist, staggered toward the cave. It was perhaps twenty feet above the tidemark. Old Tarr was right—they would be safe if they could gain its shelter. A mere twenty feet, and there were handholds, footholds in the rock. . . . It wasn't beyond their reach—it couldn't be!

Somehow, a painful foot or two at a time, dragging Tarr behind him, Michael managed to reach their goal, and as the surf pounded at their heels and soaked them anew, he exerted the last remnants of his strength and lifted his well-nigh-helpless companion onto the dry cave floor.

Tarr was fighting for breath, his lined face drained of blood. Alarmed, Michael lifted him into a sitting position, propping him up against the wall of the cave and chafing the cold, limp hands between his own. The old man managed a twisted smile.

"I'll not forget what you've done for me, Mr. Wexford," he murmured, gasping hoarsely. "I'll see you're granted a pardon, if it's the last thing I ever do—I swear I will! And I'll see those treacherous villains who stole my ship are hanged for it, if it takes me the rest of my days."

Ironically, those were the last words he spoke. A sudden spasm convulsed him. His face, so pale a moment before, was suffused with hectic color, and as Michael knelt beside him, anxiously calling his name, the old man collapsed in an ungainly heap, like a puppet whose strings had been released. His breathing was stertorous, rasping in his throat, and his eyes, though open, were blank and lackluster, devoid of sight.

Michael did what he could for him, but it was little enough. The old man lapsed into a coma; his breathing became more labored, then finally ceased. Frantic efforts to revive him met with no response. Benjamin Tarr, master of the steamer *Hastings* until a few hours ago, had died as, in all probability by this time, his ship had died, smashed on the rocks that guarded the entrance to Baker's Inlet.

With the old man's death had vanished his own hope of a pardon, Michael reflected bitterly, and . . . He looked down at the still, shuttered face, his spirits at their lowest ebb. He dared not leave the body there, he knew, for if it were discovered, he might well find himself facing a murder charge, because he was a convict and because of the record Commandant Price had left as his legacy after the tortured years on Norfolk Island. His only witness could not speak up for him now. . . .

He knelt briefly in prayer, harking back to his boyhood in the half-forgotten words that he spoke aloud. Then, unable to bring himself to rob the body of its clothing, or even to go through its pockets, he steeled himself and rolled it to the mouth of the cave; a gentle push sufficed to send it, with a dull splash, into the surf below.

The cave had become untenable now. Wearily Michael stepped out into the sunlight of a new day and started to ascend the cliff, scarcely caring whether or not he reached the summit. But he reached it, after almost an hour's hard climbing, to find himself in a green expanse of pastureland, on which sheep and cattle were grazing.

There were farm buildings in the distance, perhaps two miles away, circling a white-painted dwelling house. These were the only signs of human habitation as far as the eye could see, and after some hesitation, Michael moved cautiously nearer, his need for food and a change of clothing suddenly of paramount importance in his mind.

And if that made him a bushranger and a thief, then so be it, he told himself, since fate had cast him for the role.

Chapter IX

THE SMALL STEAMER *Opossum* came smoothly alongside the wharf at Port Arthur, and as Johnny Broome waited for the gangplank to be set up to enable him to disembark, he looked about him with interest.

At first sight, it seemed a beautiful place. Low wooded hills surrounded the cove on three sides, and the buildings of the main settlement spread out in a semicircle between sea and hills, with well-kept lawns and fine, landscaped flower gardens on every hand.

The extensive, four-story penitentiary, still in the process of enlargement, was first to catch his eye; beyond it a well-constructed, stone-built church, with a graceful steeple, was approached by an avenue of symmetrically spaced oak trees. The church itself had been well designed; each of its three gables was surmounted by three small spires, the tower had four, and there was a clock set in its face.

"The work of a convict architect, the church," the *Opossum*'s master volunteered. "Feller named Laing. And it was built by the Royal Engineers—with convict labor, of course. That's Government Cottage, beside it—with the best garden on the Tasman Peninsula. And over on the other side are the commandant's and the civil officers' quarters, the soldiers' barracks, and the hospital. It's a small township these days, self-supporting and self-contained—like everyone says, a model prison. But—" He laughed shortly. "Can't say I'd want to serve a sentence here, all the same. As you can see—" He gestured to a gang of men in broad-arrowed convict garb lined up on the jetty. "There are still the chain gangs for any who step out of line."

The men, in obedience to a shouted order, hauled a railed gangway to the ship's side and set it in place.

"You can go ashore now, Mr. Broome," the master said. "And you'll find Commandant Boyd in 'is office, I expect. Follow the roadway to the church, then head for the semaphore station—see it, on top of the hill? The commandant's house is halfway up—anyone will direct you."

Johnny thanked him and, following his instructions, found the commandant in his office. James Boyd was a quiet-voiced, pleasant-mannered man—the first civilian to be appointed to the office of commandant at Port Arthur. A Scot, he had come out to Australia some fourteen years earlier with his flamboyant elder brother, Benjamin, on board the yacht *Wanderer*, but had taken no part in his brother's ill-starred commercial ventures, although for a time he had been employed by one of the banks Benjamin had founded. He read the letter of introduction from Dr. Hampton, replaced it carefully in its envelope, and eyed Johnny questioningly across his paper-strewn desk.

"I shall, of course, be happy to be of service to you, Mr. Broome. Mr. Damien Hayes is a gentleman for whom I have great respect, and I understand, from Dr. Hampton's note, that you are also on terms of friendship with him?"

"He has commissioned me to write an article on the new prison system here, sir," Johnny answered and, seeing the commandant's quick frown of displeasure, attempted to enlarge on the purpose and scope of his commission, conscious of a feeling of regret at the deception he had been compelled to practice. In his breast pocket was a second letter, written by Kitty and Patrick, which was intended for their brother Michael and which, reluctantly, he had promised to deliver should an opportunity arise. He had not read it—Kitty had insisted that he should not —but he had little trouble in guessing its contents, and when James Boyd, reassured by his explanation, agreed to accord him the virtual freedom of the prison settlement, his conscience began anew to torment him.

But it was too late to go back on his word now, he told

himself unhappily. At least he could salve his conscience by
writing a fair and unbiased report on the new model prison, and
James Boyd should have no reason for complaint on that score.
. . . He managed a smile and offered his thanks.

"You will stay with us, of course," Boyd said. "And we can
talk over dinner. Then tomorrow I will delegate one of my
officers to escort you on a tour of the establishment. There is
much to see, Mr. Broome, apart from the so-called separate
system of confinement of prisoners, adopted from Pentonville
Prison in London. There are the agricultural projects—we are
self-supporting or almost so, thanks to these—the building
work, road construction, timber felling, and a number of factories in which the prisoners turn out excellent commercial goods,
ranging from furniture to shoes. We no longer mine coal here—
the work was dangerous and the conditions deplorable, so I do
not regret the closure of the mines. But I am exceedingly sorry
that the shipbuilding yard was closed down by Governor Denison, for its record was remarkable, and the training given there
enabled men granted ticket-of-leave to obtain regular and well-
paid employment in Hobart when they left here."

He talked on, with pride and enthusiasm, and Johnny, despite his preoccupation with the real reason for his visit, found
his interest quickening. He took notes, an action that clearly
won Commandant Boyd's approval, and before they left his
office, the commandant had made out an itinerary for the two
days Johnny would spend there.

His hospitality and that of his kindly, middle-aged wife left
nothing to be desired. The room in which Johnny spent the
night was comfortably furnished and cool, and the evening
meal, served by two well-trained convicts in spotless white jack-
ets, was the best he had eaten for a long while—its ingredients,
as James Boyd smilingly reminded him, all locally produced,
from the excellent saddle of lamb to the dessert of apple tart
and fresh peaches.

Next day, escorted by the prison chaplain and accompanied
by the Boyds' two young sons, Johnny was taken to the church,
the garrison school, two of the factories, and the hospital. Boyd
himself toured the new prison with him in the afternoon, permitting him to talk quite freely to the occupants of the cells and

those in the exercise yard, and then, clearly harboring no suspicion of his visitor's motives or intentions, returned to his office, leaving Johnny in an upper messroom of the penitentiary to attend the prisoners' evening class, whose tutor was a gray-uniformed political prisoner of singular charm and erudition.

Unable to bring himself to betray the trust reposed in him, Johnny asked no questions as to the whereabouts of the man known as Big Michael. He had another day, another twenty-four hours before the *Opossum* would leave for the return passage to Hobart, he told himself. An opportunity could well arise when he would be able to obtain the information he wanted without arousing suspicion or taking undue advantage of James Boyd's kindness and warm hospitality.

That evening, Boyd returned to his quarters very late—too late to join his family for dinner—and although he looked worried, he offered no other explanation of his lateness than what he described as pressure of work. The glances he exchanged with his wife, however, suggested an emergency of some kind, and this was borne out when he told Johnny that, after all, he would be unable to accompany him on a tour of the probation stations and the visit to Eaglehawk Neck that had been arranged for the last day of his stay at the settlement.

"But this need not impede you, Mr. Broome—I'll give you a first-rate guide who has been here longer than I have, initially as a sergeant in our military guard. John Staveley is now one of my senior warders, a most excellent fellow and a mine of information about Port Arthur's early days." The commandant cast another warning glance at his wife and rejected his elder son's plea to be allowed to go with their guest. "No, no—it's school for both of you tomorrow." Turning again to Johnny, he went on, "We'll send you by boat to Long Bay and open up the tramway to take you up to Eaglehawk in comfort. Officially our splendid tram line is no longer in service—closing it was one of the former governor's many economies. But it is still quite usable, and it makes light of an otherwise tiring journey."

Once again, Johnny expressed his thanks, genuinely grateful but, as before, his conscience troubling him.

Next day, Prison Officer Staveley called for him. He soon

proved to be, as Boyd had promised, a mine of information on the early days of the prison settlement.

The onetime NCO had served under Captain O'Hara Booth for a year and was loud in his praise, claiming for him the distinction of having originated both the semaphore signal stations and the tramway, which he referred to, with a dry little smile, as the Tasman Peninsula Railroad.

"It was the first passenger-carrying line in Australia, sir," Staveley added. "And I don't reckon it ought to have been closed down. It didn't cost nothing, it moved men and supplies at a fair rate, and 'twas work the prisoners were always ready to volunteer for. A man works better if he can take a pride in what he's doing."

"Then you don't hold with the idea that work should be a form of punishment, Mr. Staveley?" Johnny suggested, thinking of the article he was pledged to write.

Staveley shrugged. "Oh, yes, indeed I do, up to a point, sir. The men we have here are pretty nearly all bad characters—second offenders, capital respites, and hardened criminals. They've got to be kept under strict discipline and undertake useful laboring work whilst they're serving their sentences here. But if we're to reform them—and that's what we aim to do—hard labor's got to be within the bounds of their endurance, sir. Teaching them a trade helps—it's reformed many men—but working them nigh to death, well, that just makes them bitter. Reward them for good behavior, punish them for bad, but don't deprive even the worst man of hope. Leastways, sir, that's my belief, and I've been here close on fourteen years. The new probation system we're operating here now—that's a good system, for it gives a man a chance."

The old man enlarged on the manner in which the probation system was organized as they boarded the oared boat, with its convict oarsmen, that was to convey them to Long Bay and the junction of the tramway. Staveley spoke to the men in friendly fashion, and it was evident from their response that they liked and respected him.

Perhaps, Johnny thought, as the whaleboat skimmed through the water, the men requiring no urging from the two overseers in charge of them—perhaps old Warder Staveley was the man to ask about Michael. If he phrased his inquiry carefully, so as not to invite mistrust or suspicion, he would at least learn Michael's whereabouts. Certainly he was not an inmate of the model prison; and he was not in the hospital—his guarded questions had elicited that much. But time was pressing; guarded questions would no longer suffice, if he were to keep his promise to Kitty Cadogan.

They made shore and soon afterward began their journey along the four-mile-long railroad, the convict oarsmen now trotting behind the single, open passenger car, pushing it up the slight incline. Seated in splendid isolation beside the old warder in the front of the car, Johnny was searching for words in which to broach the subject when, to his astonishment, Staveley himself spoke Michael's name.

"I can give you a case in point, sir," the warder said, continuing to develop his theme now that they were able to speak freely, the rumbling of the iron wheels effectively putting them out of earshot of the two men providing their motive power. "That of a man known here as Big Michael. Michael Wexford, he called himself, but I'm sure that wasn't his real name."

Johnny stiffened, controlling his shock of surprise with difficulty and scarcely able to take in what the old prison officer was saying. He was describing Michael's long ordeal on Norfolk Island, under Commandant Price's rule, offering it as an example, and Johnny gripped the wooden bar in front of him in an effort to retain his composure.

Thank God, he thought, that he was alone! Had Patrick or Kitty been with him and been taken, as he had been, completely off guard, one or other of them would surely have been in danger of betraying their secret.

"What I was telling you about trying a prisoner beyond endurance . . ." Staveley went on, seemingly unaware of Johnny's tense silence or, if he had noticed it, attaching no significance to it, "that's what was done to Michael Wexford on Norfolk Island, sir. I don't know how many times he'd been flogged or subjected to some of the forms of torture that went on under Mr. Price. When he was transferred here, just over a year ago, he came with a record, and that meant he had to serve at hard labor in chains. I tried with him, sir, I truly did try, because he was a gentleman born and they said he had been an officer in the Royal Navy at one time. And he was a political prisoner, not a criminal . . . a rebel Irishman, I believe." He sighed, seemingly with genuine concern, and Johnny's throat tightened.

"Did you—" he managed huskily. "Did you know Big Michael well, Mr. Staveley?"

"Aye, I did. Or that's to say as well as a man in my position is ever able to know a prisoner, Mr. Broome. We're not permitted to fraternize with the convicts, and they mostly don't like it if we do. But Michael was different, he . . . well, I think he liked to talk to me sometimes. And I did everything I could think of to persuade him to try for probation, but—he wouldn't hear of it, wouldn't listen to me. He rubbed some of the overseers up the wrong way, and they had it in for him. He never got out of the chain gang, never mind probation, poor young devil! And now he's absconded—absconded with three of the worst degenerates we've had here. He—"

"Absconded?" For all the tight rein he had been keeping on his emotions, Johnny almost shouted the word. "You mean," he added, in a more level tone, "that he's made his escape? From here, Mr. Staveley?"

Staveley eyed him uncertainly, on the point of regretting what he had said. "Did the commandant not tell you, sir? I thought he would have, you being his guest at the house."

Fool that he was, Johnny reproached himself. He had come within an ace of giving himself away, and—oh, God, he had to find out more, had to know how Michael had escaped and where he might have gone.

"Oh, yes, Mr. Staveley," he lied, praying that his lie would carry conviction. "Mr. Boyd mentioned that there had been an escape, naturally. He was greatly concerned about it. Upset, even, and I—well, I didn't like to ask questions and upset him further, since I'm his guest. But I'm interested, after what you have told me about Wexford—Big Michael. How did he make his escape? It's supposed to be impossible from here, isn't it?"

"It's pretty near impossible, sir," Staveley confirmed. His momentary doubts allayed, he was eager to tell the rest of his story, and he permitted himself a fugitive smile. "They got away in the *Hastings* steamer—he and three blackguards who were with him in the loading gang at the Cascades. William Haines was one—he used to be in the *Hastings'* crew at one time—and his crony, Joshua Simmons, and a fellow named Train, sent here quite recently. The Cascades is an inlet of Norfolk Bay, on the north of the peninsula. It's where the lumberyard and sawmill are, and the ship was taking on a load of timber. They jumped the sentry and an overseer—killed them, very probably, though it's not known for sure. They've both vanished, and so has the ship. She's more than a day overdue in Hobart—that was the news the commandant received last night, sir—and there's a search being made for her now. I don't doubt, sir, that the vessel that brought you here, the *Opossum*, will be required to join in. She's due to sail first thing tomorrow, is she not, sir?"

Johnny drew in his breath sharply. If old Staveley was right and the *Opossum* were ordered to take part in the search, it might prove a totally unexpected stroke of luck, so far as he was concerned. It would give him a chance, however slender, of finding and making contact with Michael. Of telling him that his brother and sister were in Hobart and that they had made—or were making—arrangements to send him to New Zealand, if he could make his way to join them. But . . . A sudden nagging doubt assailed him.

If Michael *had* had a hand in the taking of the ship, and if, as Staveley feared, the overseer and the sentry had been killed, then a charge of murder would be laid against him and, very probably, a reward offered for his capture. Even if no one had been killed, the seizure of a ship at sea was piracy—a crime that carried the death penalty. The fugitive would be taking his life in his hands if he attempted to enter Hobart, so that . . . Johnny inclined his head in answer to the old prison officer's question.

"Do you believe," he asked impulsively, "that this man, the man you call Big Michael, would commit murder? Do you believe him capable of it, Mr. Staveley?"

Staveley frowned. "It's hard to say, sir. Like I told you, Michael Wexford was tried beyond endurance before he was ever transferred here. He was a gentleman, in my view, but he had been—well, I suppose you'd call it brutalized. I'd like to be able to tell you he's not capable of taking another man's life, but I'm not sure. But the men he's absconded with—that's a different story. None of them would think twice about it. Indeed, I'm astonished that Michael went with them. It's possible that he didn't do so willingly, of course, but if they murdered the sentry and Overseer Burke—and if Michael was with them—then he would be an accessory to murder. No two ways about that, sir."

As he had feared, Johnny reflected glumly. Indeed, although he had not given his support to the younger Cadogans' fool-hardy attempt to organize their brother's escape, he was compelled to recognize that, had they succeeded in smuggling him aboard the sealer *Mary Ann,* the poor, unfortunate fellow would have been very much better off than he was now . . . even if, because of his previous naval service, his villainous companions had given him command of the *Hastings.*

"They'll not get far, sir," Staveley observed, as if guessing his thoughts. "The *Hastings* is coal-burning—a paddle-steamer, and she—" He broke off. "Somebody's hailing us, Mr. Broome. Aye, look—" He pointed along the track behind them. "There's a car coming after us, with one of our officers in it, and he's waving. Hold hard, lads," he bade the two convicts, who had just thankfully hauled themselves onto the rear of their own car, ready to glide down the slight slope to Eaglehawk Neck.

The men obediently applied the brakes, and they waited for the second vehicle to catch up with them. When it did so, its occupant came hurrying to join them.

"Message from the commandant, sir," he told Johnny. "Sent by semaphore to us at Long Bay. You're to return at once—the *Opossum*'s ready to sail." He added, lowering his voice and addressing Staveley, "I reckon she's bein' sent to search for them absconders that stole the *Hastings,* don't you, Mr. Staveley?"

"I reckon she is, Martin," old Staveley agreed. "Well, we'd best get you back to her, Mr. Broome, unless you want to stay here for the next three weeks." He gestured to the foot of the slope, still half a mile distant. "I fear that's all you'll see of Eaglehawk Neck, but it's enough, maybe, to prove that stealing a ship is easier than getting across the Neck, the way it's guarded. That's the guardhouse, sir—the white stone building —with the soldiers' quarters behind. Thirty men are always stationed there, with one officer. And then there're the dogs— you can just see them, chained right across the rocks in a line, with their kennels behind them, and on that wooden platform that floats in the bay. It takes a brave man—or a foolish one— to try and get past that lot, sir. But still some of them try. One fellow wrapped himself in a 'roo skin and tried to hop across, but the sentry yelled he was going to bag a 'roo for supper and opened fire!"

On the way back to Long Bay, the old man regaled him with droll and sometimes tragic stories of escape attempts that had failed, ending with an account of the only successful one, made by Martin Cash, and Johnny listened with what patience he could muster.

Returning at last aboard the *Opossum,* he found a note of apology from the commandant, which very briefly described the circumstances of the escape:

> I am sorry to cut short your stay, but as no doubt you will have learned from Mr. Staveley, four of our prisoners have made a very daring escape, as a result of which we fear that at least two men have lost their lives and the government steamer *Hastings* has been seized by the miscreants and has not returned to port.
>
> As Captain Jones of the *Opossum* has expressed his willingness to join in the search for the missing vessel and believes he can hazard an accurate guess as to her present whereabouts, I decided to delay him here no longer. He will sail as soon as you board. I have taken the liberty of sending your bag to the ship.

The letter ended with cordial good wishes and the hope that Johnny had seen enough of the Port Arthur penal settlement to enable him to complete the writing of his article for the newspaper that had commissioned it.

The escapers had not been named in the commandant's note, but Captain Jones had been informed of them and supplied with descriptions, and over dinner that evening, with the *Opossum* steaming south through Carnarvon Bay and heading for Cape Raoul, he talked at length of his intentions.

"I've known Benjamin Tarr a good few years, Mr. Broome," he said. "He's a good man, and I pray that no ill has befallen him. The swine who escaped on board his ship are lifers, all four of 'em, and seemingly men of bad character, especially the bastard named Haines. And they'll be armed—*Hastings* carried an arms chest, like we do—so poor Captain Tarr won't have stood a chance against them. I just hope we can find the ship before those devils wreck her."

"Mr. Boyd told me that you had an idea where they might have taken her," Johnny said.

"Well, I can make a shrewd guess," the master answered. He pushed his empty plate away and spread a chart across the table in front of them. "They don't have much choice, really. They sailed from Cascades Bay into Norfolk Bay—on the north of the peninsula, see?" He jabbed a finger on the chart. "And we sailed from here, by the longer route, where it's liable to cut up rough between Cape Raoul and Adventure Bay. The *Hastings* doesn't carry more coal than she needs for the shorter passage, between Hobart and Norfolk Bay. She carries sail, of course, but she's a poor sailer at the best of times, and I doubt if any of the escapers could handle her under sail. They can't go to Hobart, that's for sure, and they can't replenish the coal she'll have used. So they can't go very far, can they?"

"No," Johnny conceded, studying the chart with frowning brows as the master pointed out the places to which the missing steamer was unlikely to have gone. But would Michael Wexford, with his naval training—for all it was a long time ago—could he or would he have been able to handle the *Hastings* under sail? It was possible, he supposed, but unlikely—Michael had been only a midshipman, not a watchkeeping officer.

"Right, then," the *Opossum*'s master went on. "My guess is that they'll run in between Bruny Island and the mainland—here, d'you see, Mr. Broome? The Huon Valley's fairly sparsely settled. I fancy they'll beach the ship or run her ashore round about this area and leg it inland. What happens to the swine after that is not my affair. They'll post rewards on them and send troops and police to hunt for them. What concerns me is the ship and her people, more particularly Captain Tarr, because it's anybody's guess what state they'll have left her in or what they'll have done to the ship's company. So—" He sighed and folded the chart. "The glass is falling. But I'm going on, whatever the bloody weather's like. I'd go below, if I were you, Mr. Broome, and get your head down. We'll sight Cape Raoul before dark, and we'll probably be in for a rough night."

His forecast proved to be correct. Johnny took his advice and, having no duties on board, slept fitfully until well after dawn, as the stout little *Opossum* buffeted her way through heavy seas and a rising wind. His thoughts troubled him more than the storm itself, and when sleep eluded him, he was tormented by doubts concerning what he must tell Kitty Cadogan of her elder brother's escape attempt and of the fate that would await him, were he to be caught by the forces of the Crown.

He mulled over a hundred and one brief speeches and explanations, conscious that, whatever he said or however he might try to soften the blow, the news he had to give her would come close to breaking her heart.

Toward noon of the following day, the wind lessened and the weather began to moderate; by late afternoon, when the ship was under the lee of North Bruny Island, rain set in and visibility was so greatly impaired that, although Captain Jones was in a fever of impatience, he announced that he would have to lie-to until light next day.

But the next day, soon after the *Opossum* had again got under way, the lookout on her masthead hailed the deck, a note of excitement in his voice as he claimed to have sighted the missing vessel in an inlet ahead and to starboard.

"Baker's Inlet," Jones announced, after a hurried search of his chart. "Sandy beach, rocks at the entrance, but no cliffs. That's the sort of place Ben Tarr would've chosen, if he knew he had to run his ship ashore. Maybe he's still alive." He shouted a string of questions to the lookout, and the man did his best to answer them.

"It's her all right, Cap'n—it's the *Hastings.* She's aground in shallow water, with her larb'd side awash. I can't see no one on deck. No one on the shore, neither."

Captain Jones rang for full speed ahead, and as the *Opossum* neared the entrance to the inlet, he joined the lookout aloft, his glass sweeping the shore.

"No sign of life, Mr. Broome," he told Johnny grimly, when he regained the deck. "We'll just have to hope the crew are below—locked up, probably, when those villains abandoned ship. Well, we'll soon find out."

He brought-to at the entrance to the inlet, and as the *Opossum*'s paddle wheels were stilled, he ordered the quarterboat lowered, nodding his acquiescence to Johnny's request that he be permitted to accompany the search party.

The sound of voices, coming from the stranded ship, raised their spirits as the boat came alongside the *Hastings'* listing stern and the bowman steadied her with his boat hook.

"Well, some of 'em are alive," Captain Jones observed, with relief. "Alive and kicking, judging by the hullabaloo they're making! Must have heard us." He gave an encouraging hail, which was answered with wild cheering and a chorus of excited shouts. He smiled. "Thank God for that! Right, lads," he bade his boat's crew. "Make fast, and let's have those axes aboard. I don't doubt we'll have to hack our way through to them— they'd have been out otherwise."

Once again, his forecast proved to be correct. Nine of the *Hastings'* crew were battened down in the forward hold, with planks nailed across the hatch, and the mate was locked in his cabin, the porthole boarded over. The cook, the ship's engineer, and the two stokers were confined in the after hold, with the boys from the Juvenile Establishment. All of the latter were cold, hungry, and soaked to the skin, for the hold was partly flooded, and the stench emanating from it caused the rescuers to retch uncontrollably.

"There's two bodies down 'ere," the elderly cook stated plaintively. "Wouldn't let us move 'em, the miserable black-guards! And they wouldn't give us no food nor water, neither— we'd 'ave bin dead if you hadn't found us when you did, Cap'n, an' that's the God's truth! As it was, they done poor Cap'n Tarr in. Smashed 'is skull, one of 'em did, 'an threw 'im over the side."

"Which one?" Johnny demanded hoarsely. "Which one of them killed your captain?"

"A big fellow, sir," the cook answered. "Haines called 'im Toby." He shivered. "I'd 'idden in one o' the boats, hopin' they'd forget about me, see? But they didn't—that bastard Haines remembered, 'fore they battened us down an' left the ship. An' they was firin' their muskets at the other big fellow—a convict, sir, who absconded with 'em. 'E jumped overboard, but I didn't see if they 'it 'im."

Michael, Johnny thought, his heart sinking. Big Michael, he could only suppose, must have fallen out with his fellow escapers, or they with him.

"I don't reckon they did, though," the cook added. "Last I seen of 'im, 'e was swimmin' pretty strong, for all they must've fired a dozen times at 'im when 'e was in the water." He spat disgustedly on the deck. "But they killed the cap'n, no doubt o' that."

Captain Jones said bitterly, "What a way to die!" He waved the shivering cook into the boat. "All right, lad, I'll take a report from you after you've had a meal and got yourself into dry clothes. Cut along."

It required three trips to convey the imprisoned men by boat from the wrecked vessel to the anchored *Opossum.* Several of them were in a bad way—the stokers had been beaten severely, the mate had what looked like a gunshot wound in the leg, and the ship's engineer's face was a mass of bruises, his left eye closed.

"I'm making for Hobart, Mr. Broome," the *Opossum's* master said when he returned on board with the last boatload. "Some of the men are in urgent need of a surgeon, and there's nothing more I can do here. I don't think the *Hastings* is too badly damaged—she can probably be salvaged, but I don't have the equipment to haul her off. I'll notify her position, of course, and they'll send a salvage tug. And—" He made a grimace. "We gave the bodies Christian burial before we left. It was a ghastly job."

"What about the escapers, Captain?" Johnny nerved himself to ask.

Captain Jones shrugged. "They're not my concern. It'll be up to the police and the military to hunt for them. In any case, they've had too much of a start—they'll be miles from here by now."

"May I question the *Hastings'* men, sir? I'd like to hear their full story."

"For your newspaper?" Jones suggested.

"I . . . yes, for my paper, Captain." Johnny kept his voice level.

"I've no objection, Mr. Broome," the captain assured him. "Ask all the questions you want to, and . . ." His face darkened. "Write a decent obituary for old Bengy Tarr, will you? I'll give you all the information you need for it."

"I will indeed," Johnny promised. "Thank you, Captain."

But all his questioning elicited little more than he had learned already. The cook told him that the big convict who had jumped overboard had, from the outset, appeared to be regarded with hostility by the other three. They had exchanged their yellow convict uniforms for clothes stolen from the *Hastings'* people, but the big man had not been allowed to discard his.

"They made 'im stay on deck with Cap'n Tarr, sir, all the time, and—aye, 'e wasn't armed, like they was. 'Im an' the cap'n, I reckon they was plannin' somethin', the two of 'em, an' Haines must've got wind of it. 'E's a real bastard, Will Haines, sir . . . I knew 'im from way back, when 'e was a deck'and aboard this ship. Used to be in the army once, I believe, but 'e got thrown out. Served a year or two on Norfolk Island, got 'is ticket-o'-leave, an' then made more trouble an' they give 'im life at Port Arthur." The cook's voice shook. "There's nothin' I wouldn't give to get me 'ands on the blasted swine, after what 'e done to us. An' the poor old cap'n. 'E was a real good bloke, Cap'n Tarr, sir. I 'ope you'll write that in your newspaper."

He would, Johnny resolved. If he did nothing else, he would write Captain Benjamin Tarr's obituary. But . . . the problem of Michael Wexford was unsolved. The chances were that he had survived, if the cook's story was true—and there was no reason to disbelieve it. But survival meant that he was on the run, somewhere in the Huon Valley, probably, if he had managed to make his way there. On the run, hunted for by military search parties and . . . dear God, by Haines and his villainous companions as well, perhaps! Michael could not have landed far away. . . .

Johnny passed another almost sleepless night, his conscience plaguing him. Should he perhaps have stayed on shore, where the *Hastings* was beached, he asked himself, and gone in search of Michael, instead of returning to Hobart? Was that what Kitty would have expected of him, however slim the chance of catching up with the fugitive? But . . . no, alone and unarmed, without any knowledge of the country, it would have been madness to attempt it. He would simply have been risking his life in vain, quite apart from arousing grave suspicions as to his motives, had he demanded to be set ashore. And even had he managed, by some miracle, to find him, Michael would in all probability not have trusted him. To Michael he was a stranger and would have seemed a potential enemy, to be avoided at all costs.

But how to explain all this to Kitty? How, God help him, could he tell her the awful, well-nigh unbelievable story? Rack his brains though he might, Johnny was no nearer to a solution when the *Opossum* nosed her way alongside the Elizabeth Street pier and set him ashore in Hobart. From the dockside, it was a mere stone's throw to the Customs House Hotel, and he covered the short distance on leaden feet. To his glum inquiry, the porter replied that Mr. Cadogan was out but her ladyship was in their suite.

"And in a rare good humor she is, sir," the man added. "They both lunched with His Excellency at Government House, and they must have received good news, for her ladyship's been singing ever since she came back." He grinned, clearly the recipient of Cadogan generosity. "I'm to show you right up, Mr. Broome, on her ladyship's orders. She saw your steamer come in, sir, and she told me she wanted to see you at once."

Johnny hesitated for a long moment outside the door of the sitting room, bracing himself, but the porter flung open the door and announced him, and, unable to delay any longer, he went in.

Kitty, looking radiant with happiness, jumped up and flung herself impulsively into his arms.

"Oh, Johnny—dear, dear Johnny, I am so glad you're back at last!" She was half laughing, half crying, her soft, fragrant cheek laid on his. "The most wonderful news—the governor told us that Michael has been pardoned! He's received a royal pardon, Johnny, which means he'll be freed at once! Our appeal to the English High Court was successful . . . isn't it truly the answer to prayer? Pat has gone to see Dr. Hampton to try to arrange for Michael's release to take place expeditiously. He could be here—here with us, Johnny—within the next few days! Can you believe it? And he'll be able to go home. He—" Johnny's silence, his failure to respond to her joy, seemed suddenly to alarm her. Kitty drew back from his embrace, a hand to her throat. "Johnny, what is wrong? Why aren't you pleased for us? Surely you—oh, Johnny, for God's sake, what *is* it?"

There were no words, Johnny knew, save a blunt, unvarnished statement of the truth. For all it must shatter her bright and short-lived dream, he could not soften the blow, could not allow her to go on hoping.

He reached for her gently and held her close.

"Dearest Kitty," he managed huskily, "I have to tell you—Michael made his escape from Port Arthur several days ago. He—he's on the mainland, to the best of my knowledge. On the run, Kitty. I wish—oh, God, *how* I wish that I could give you any news but this! But you have to know. . . . Kitty, the pardon has come too late."

There was no sound in the sunlit room save Kitty's bitter, heartbroken sobbing. But then she raised her face to his, and Johnny saw the brave determination in her lovely, tear-filled eyes.

"We must find him, Johnny—wherever he is, we must find him! You'll help us, won't you?"

What could he say, when she looked at him like this? How could he, how could any man refuse such an appeal?

"Of course I will, Kitty," he promised. "Sweetest, dearest Kitty, I love you! I—"

She seemed not to have heard him or taken in his declaration, and as Johnny's lips sought for hers, she eluded them, instead brushing his cheek lightly and again drawing away from him.

"I must go to Patrick," she said urgently. "There's no time to be lost. Take me to Dr. Hampton's, will you please?"

Already she was donning her bonnet, one of the pretty, frivolous, flower-decked bonnets he had come to associate with her. Johnny controlled himself and, his face expressionless, wrapped a shawl about her and offered her his arm.

They went out into the street together.

Chapter X

CROUCHING IN THE shelter of a clump of bramble bushes, fifty yards from the farm buildings, Michael watched and waited, like an animal of the wild, fearing to approach the house until he could be certain it was empty of its human inhabitants.

There did not appear to be anyone left in the pleasant, white-painted building, as far as he could judge. Ten minutes earlier two women had come out, bearing a laden basket and two heavy earthenware jugs between them, to make their way to a field, some distance beyond the fenced sheep paddock, where the wheat harvest was being gathered in.

Michael had counted three men working there with sickles. The two women followed behind the reapers, gathering up and binding the sheaves, which they formed into small pyramid-shaped stacks with the ease and skill of long practice.

All toiled without pause, seldom glancing up from what they were doing, but the women were singing—their voices carried to him faintly on the breeze. It was a happy, carefree sound, and as he listened, Michael found himself envying the settler and his family, whose lives were so much less complicated than his own. He hated the thought of robbing them, but he knew that if he were not to be caught, he must rid himself of his convict garb and, having done so, put as great a distance as he could between himself and the rocky shore on which he had landed the previous day.

It would, of course, not be long before a military search party was sent out—the *Hastings* had probably been reported overdue by now—but . . . He frowned, shading his eyes with his hand as he again looked about him. Haines and his two companions constituted the most immediate danger, particularly if they had beached the steamer in the inlet of which old Captain Tarr had told them, for that could not be very far away from where he now was.

He wondered, fleetingly, about the crew. No doubt the poor devils had been left locked up on board, to discourage pursuit; but without a weapon, he dared not make an attempt to release them, lest they turn on him. But perhaps the farmhouse might yield a hunting rifle or a bird gun, as well as the clothing he hoped to find there, and . . . He turned his gaze once more on the distant wheat field. The house *must* be empty—the settler and his family were safely out of earshot and busy with their harvesting, which was a stroke of unexpected luck that he would turn to his advantage.

Michael got to his feet and, crouching low, made for the rear of the house at a run. The back door was unlocked and opened at a touch. He went inside, reminded of his hunger as the aroma of fresh-baked bread greeted him from what was evidently the kitchen. A wood-burning oven and hob took up most of the space on the outer wall, and a well-scrubbed table, with benches drawn up to it, stood in the center of the room. On the table was the remnant of a loaf of bread, plus a flagon of milk, and, to his joy, the better part of a leg of mutton, from which only a few slices had been cut.

Unable to resist the temptation, Michael pulled out one of the benches and, seating himself, fell on the food hungrily, the milk tasting like nectar as he poured it down his parched throat.

"You are hungry?"

The voice, soft and feminine, came from behind him and he leapt up, wary and startled, to see a girl of about fifteen or sixteen framed in the open doorway. She was very pretty, her small, childish face wreathed in a smile, and as she came toward him, Michael saw that she was severely crippled, one of her legs seemingly twisted beneath the striped gingham dress. She moved awkwardly and with a pronounced limp—the reason, he decided, why she was not out in the harvest field with the rest of her family—and he relaxed, realizing that he had nothing to fear from so small and helpless a being.

"I—I do beg your pardon," he began, and then, conscious of the absurdity of such an apology, he broke off and, anxious above all to reassure her, added quickly, "You have nothing to fear from me, I give you my word."

"I asked if you were hungry," the girl repeated. She continued to smile at him, and despite his unkempt appearance and the prison garb that marked him an absconder, she showed no sign of being afraid of him, Michael realized, with astonishment. He answered her question truthfully.

"Yes, I'm hungry. It is a long time since I have eaten."

"Then please sit down, sir," the crippled girl invited, "and I will prepare a meal for you. My father, Mr. Amos Meldrum, always gives hospitality to passing travelers. We are isolated here, you see," she added engagingly, "so we do not see many travelers. Would you care for a glass of cider? It is home brewed."

Still trying to recover from his initial astonishment, Michael thanked her. Deftly she cut slices from the loaf and placed them, with an appetizing-looking hunk of cheese and some slices of meat, on a plate in front of him. The cider was poured from an earthenware jug, which she fetched from the pantry, and as she gave him the brimming glass, she said, eyeing him with the first hint of curiosity she had displayed, "My name is Prudence Meldrum. What is yours, if I may ask?"

"Michael—Michael Wexford."

"I suppose that you have escaped from one of the convict stations?" Prudence Meldrum suggested. Neither fear nor condemnation sounded in her voice; her suggestion was logical, rather than critical.

"From the Port Arthur Penitentiary, Miss Meldrum," Michael answered truthfully, and this time his answer clearly surprised her, for her dark eyes widened and she stifled an exclamation of what might have been puzzlement or even doubt of his veracity.

"But I thought it was impossible to escape from Port Arthur! My father always said it was." She hesitated, reddening, and then swiftly apologized. "It's not that I don't believe you, Mr. Wexford. But my father—that is . . ."

"Does Mr. Meldrum know the penitentiary?" Michael asked. He drained the glass of cider, which was remarkably good, and without waiting for him to request it, Prudence Meldrum re-filled it for him.

"Oh, yes," she asserted. "Poor Dad was a prisoner there him-self, three years ago. He wasn't there long—only a few months, and then they gave him his ticket-of-leave and finally a full pardon. Because he was convicted on what they said was per-jured evidence, you see. And he was given this land as compen-sation."

Like his own conviction, Michael thought wryly—only the perjurer, in his case, had never retracted his evidence . . . and probably, damn his soul, he never would!

"How did you escape?" the girl asked. Seeing that he had finished the meat and cheese, she took his plate, replacing it with a bowl of apple pie, sprinkled with curds. "I hope this will be to your taste, Mr. Wexford. I made it myself, from our own apples."

"It is delicious," Michael told her. He finished the pie and released a sigh of satisfaction. "I haven't tasted pastry like yours since—oh, heavens, since I was a boy in Ireland! You must be a very expert cook."

"It is all I can do," Prudence answered regretfully. "Because of this—" She touched her crippled leg, but without any vestige of self-pity. "I cannot work on the land, you see. So I help my mama with the cooking, so that she may tend the lambs and milk the cows and help with the harvest, as she is doing now. She and my family—they all work the land." She shrugged her slim, bowed shoulders, dismissing the subject of her infirmity, and repeated her earlier question. "Mr. Wexford, how *did* you make your escape? Did you brave those terrible dogs that guard the Eaglehawk Neck?"

It was an oddly unreal conversation, Michael thought, but this girl, with her smiling frankness and her ready trust, was unlike anyone he had ever met before, and he found himself wondering whether, perhaps, she was a trifle simple. Certainly she was naive, and— He was conscious of a sudden fear. Suppose Haines and Big Toby Train and the ratlike Josh Simmons had chanced on this isolated place, instead of himself . . . how would they have reacted to Prudence Meldrum's warm and kindly hospitality? The mere thought caused him to shudder as, with cold bitterness, he visualized their response. And they might well be in the area, all three of them.

"It's a long story, Miss Meldrum," he said, evading her question concerning his escape from the Tasman Peninsula. "I'll tell your father about it when he comes in. I wasn't alone, you understand, and—the men I escaped with are evil, dangerous rogues. If they were to come here, it would be unwise to let them in. Perhaps you should bar the door." There was an ancient flintlock musket hanging on the wall, and Michael glanced at it, frowning. He would probably frighten her if he attempted to take possession of it, but at least it was there, should the necessity arise—although he could see no evidence of powder and shot in its vicinity.

Prudence smilingly shook her head to his suggestion that she bar the door.

"It's never barred, Mr. Wexford. My father likes to think that his door is open to passing travelers, as I told you. He would be displeased if I were to go against his wishes."

"Then maybe," Michael urged, "you should go to the wheat field and tell him to be on his guard."

"I cannot walk so far," Prudence said apologetically. "Or at least it would take me a very long time. But you could go and find him, if you are worried." She studied him, her smooth brow puckered, as if for the first time noticing his convict dress and his unshaven cheeks. "You might alarm him, if you go to him as you are. I will bring you a razor and hot water and find you other clothes, shall I?" She hesitated, drawing in her breath sharply. "Are these men, the men you escaped with—are they really bad men who would do us harm?"

"I fear so, yes."

"But you are not, although you escaped with them?"

Faintly exasperated, Michael shook his head and saw her smile return, in all its trusting innocence.

"I knew you were not," she asserted.

"How did you know?"

"I watched you," Prudence confessed. "I watched you for a long time, whilst you were hiding beyond the apple orchard. You were afraid of discovery, and it took you a long time before you thought this house was empty and that it would be safe for you to enter. But you brought no weapon with you—not even one of the fence posts, which were lying near you—so I knew that you intended no harm. And you looked ill and hungry, and your clothes were wet. I decided that I would help you or at least give you a meal. And then when we talked—your voice is the voice of a gentleman, Mr. Wexford. I knew you would do nothing to harm me."

Her logical reasoning defeated him. Yet it *was* logical, Michael decided ruefully. Whatever she had done when she found him in her kitchen, he would not have laid a hand on her, poor little soul, because of her crippled state. But Will Haines would have no such qualms—it was essential that the girl's father be warned that Haines and the others might also pay a visit to his farmstead. He had no means of knowing whether or not they were still in the vicinity—it was possible that they had gone long since, for they had clothing and provisions, which they had taken from the *Hastings,* and Haines had talked of making for the Huon Valley.

"*I* had a weapon under my apron," Prudence told him. She laughed at his discomfiture as she brought a heavy wooden rolling pin from its concealment and laid it on the table. "In case my judgment should be wrong!" She gestured to him to rise. "The washhouse is outside in the yard, Mr. Wexford. You will find soap and a razor there, and here is your water, in the kettle. Whilst you are shaving, I will see if I can find any garments that will fit you. You are much bigger than my father and brothers, I'm afraid, but we once had a seafaring man working for us who was almost as tall as you are. He is dead, poor man, so he will not mind if I give you the clothing he left here."

By the time Michael had washed and shaved, she had kept her promise, and he found a little heap of clothing by the door of the washhouse. The trousers were canvas, clearly the property of a onetime seaman, as was the brass-buttoned blue jacket, and both fitted him tolerably well. The shirt, which was of good linen, was too small, but Prudence had thoughtfully provided a wide neckerchief and what looked like a woolen scarf, which had stretched, in numerous washings, to several times its intended length, and which he was able to use as a cummerbund.

Respectably clad, after more years than he cared to count, Michael made his way back to the kitchen, feeling absurdly lighthearted at the prospect of appearing as a free and civilized man—if, perhaps, not yet a gentleman. The sound of voices, coming from inside the house, brought him warily to a halt, but then, hearing Prudence's soft laughter, he continued on his way. There was a stocky, dark-bearded man in the kitchen, talking to her in clipped, disapproving tones, and as Michael entered, the newcomer turned on him wrathfully.

"My daughter tells me you're an absconder from Port Arthur Penitentiary," he accused, without preamble. "Is that true?"

Michael faced him unsmilingly. "Yes, sir, it's true. My name is Wexford, Michael Wexford, Mr. Meldrum. Your daughter, sir, has been kind enough to take pity on me and provide me with the clothes I am wearing. She—"

"I fell into a grave error when I christened her Prudence," the farmer said gruffly. "Prudent is the last thing she is . . . she gives her trust to any stray down-and-out who passes this way! Not that many do, and none of them have been absconding convicts, up to now."

"I did not betray Miss Meldrum's trust, sir," Michael defended.

"Just as well you did not, or I'd have had you horse-whipped and thrown off my land!" Meldrum retorted. He looked Michael up and down with narrowed, searching eyes, and added grudgingly, "Well, poor old Tom Blaney's clobber seems to fit you well enough, so I'll not take it off you. But I'll thank you to be on your way, mister. We don't want absconders here."

"I'm grateful for the clothing," Michael assured him. "And of course, sir, I will not abuse your hospitality. But—"

Amos Meldrum cut him short. Turning to his daughter, he swore softly. "Damme, Prue, you're right on one count! He does talk like an educated gentleman, and no mistake!"

"I told you he was, Papa," Prudence responded, smiling. "And he wanted to warn you, he—"

"Warn me? What about, for the Lord's sake?"

"About the men who absconded with me, Mr. Meldrum," Michael put in. Gravely he explained the circumstances of his escape, ending with Haines's attempt on his life when he had jumped overboard from the *Hastings'* deck. "Her master—Captain Tarr—is dead, sir. We managed to reach the shore, not far from here, but Captain Tarr had been badly injured, and he— he died. There was nothing I could do for him, alas. But the convicts—Haines and the other two—they've murdered an overseer and a soldier already. They are desperate men, Mr. Meldrum, and it's possible that they may come here."

Amos Meldrum scowled. "You say they were intending to run the ship—the *Hastings* steamer—ashore in Baker's Inlet?"

"Yes. That was where Captain Tarr advised them to make for, but I don't know whether or not they did. He chose it because it has a sandy foreshore—he was hoping they would not damage the ship too severely."

"Hmm." Meldrum was thoughtful. "Baker's Inlet is a ways from here—about fifteen miles, as the crow flies, and these fellows aren't crows. The Huon Valley's west of here—we're north of Baker's Inlet, and Hobart's to the north. I can't see them coming this way, especially if they've got provisions looted from the steamer." He paused, again eyeing Michael from beneath frowning black brows. "Which way do you plan to go, Mr. Wexford?"

Michael hesitated, taken by surprise at the question. Which way *did* he intend to go? he asked himself, realizing that he had made no plans since leaping headlong from the *Hastings'* deck. But his aim and object in escaping from Port Arthur had always been clear enough, when he had made his initial plans during the long hours he had spent in solitary confinement. Had it not been the thought of tracking down Commandant Price that had kept him going, sustained his courage and his stoic endurance? And Price was in Victoria, as commandant of Pentridge Gaol and inspector general of the State Prison Service. . . .

Michael met his interrogator's frowning gaze and answered quietly, "I'm aiming to get to Victoria, so . . . I'll head for Hobart and try to pick up a ship there, if I can." He smiled wryly, gesturing to the seaman's clothes he was wearing.

"These should help, should they not? I could sign on as a seaman."

"You'd need papers," Meldrum warned. He relaxed a little, and his frown vanished. "Maybe I could help you there. The fellow those clothes belonged to—old Tom Blaney—was a sailor before he came to work for me. I've got his papers somewhere—put 'em away, after the old fellow died. I'll find them for you, before you leave." He glanced at Prudence, his smile affectionate, and then went on. "I'm not being uncharitable, Mr. Wexford—I had a spell in the Port Arthur Penitentiary myself a few years back, for something I didn't do. I'd have run if I'd been able to, but luckily my pardon came through before I even thought of trying it. But you'll understand why I can't afford to risk harboring an absconder. Anyone who's ever been a convict rates suspicion, and when the search parties start hunting for you and the others, it's a hundred to one they'll come here and turn the whole place upside down."

"I understand, sir," Michael answered, without rancor. "If you'll oblige me with Blaney's papers, I'll leave you in peace. And with gratitude, particularly in Miss Prudence's case."

"Good," Meldrum acknowledged. He took a heavy, old-fashioned timepiece from his pocket and sighed, as he replaced it. "I must get back to the harvesting. Bide here for the evening meal —I'll hunt up those papers when we've eaten. My wife'll be along soon—I'll tell her to find you somewhere to sleep for a couple of hours. You look as if you need a sleep." He clapped a hand on Michael's shoulder. "You're Irish, aren't you?"

"Yes, I am, sir. I—"

"A political prisoner, were you?" Meldrum suggested shrewdly. "A rebel?"

"You could call me that, yes. The judge did. But if I was not a rebel when they tried me, then—" Michael shrugged, the old, remembered bitterness creeping into his voice. "I am now. I hold no brief for Her Majesty's government, Mr. Meldrum, and I doubt I ever shall!"

"That's hardly to be wondered at, Mr. Wexford," the older man conceded. "But what's done can't be undone, can it?" He drew Prudence to him and kissed her gently on the cheek. "All right, my dear lass, I'm not blaming you for what you did. This time you were right, so why don't you pack up a few things Mr. Wexford may need, on his way to Hobart, while he has a little shut-eye, eh? We'll not send him away empty-handed, at least, will we?"

At the door, he turned and added, as if it were an afterthought, "We'll keep our eyes peeled in case your late companions show up. But I don't reckon they will."

"How about taking that musket, sir?" Michael gestured to the old flintlock hanging on the wall. "In case they do?"

Amos Meldrum gave him a wry smile. "That old thing? You couldn't hit a haystack at forty paces with it. But it'll still fire, and there's powder and buckshot in the dresser drawer. I'll leave it in your charge. You can fire a warning shot if you see 'em coming."

With that he was gone, and Michael, after a momentary hesitation, left the ancient weapon where it was. As if she had read his thoughts, Prudence said quickly, "Go and rest, Mr. Wexford, as my father advised. I'll keep a careful lookout, and I'll call you if I see anyone coming to the house."

Her mother, a tiny, apple-cheeked woman with graying hair and a friendly, bustling manner, returned to the house shortly afterward. Before beginning her preparations for the evening meal, she made up a bed for him on a horsehair sofa in the room she called the parlor, and Michael stretched out on it gratefully, only then realizing how tense and exhausted he was. The pleasant, half-forgotten sound of feminine voices—hushed on his account but still just audible—reached him from the kitchen and swiftly lulled him into sleep. His tension drained out of him, and he let himself relax, conscious of a sense of well-being that he had not experienced for years.

The dream he had was hauntingly nostalgic. In it, he was transported back to the home of his childhood and first youth . . . Castle Kilclare, the rambling old house at the lake's edge, with its enchanting glimpses of windswept gray water and distant hills—green, as only Irish hills ever were—the trees ablaze with the golden-orange of autumn foliage.

The blood-stirring echo of a hunting horn, sounding the "Gone away!" was suddenly music in his ears, and Michael smiled in his sleep. He saw again the field of the Kilclare hunt streaming across the parkland at the rear of the castle, hounds in full cry and his gallant old father, top hat crammed down over his white head, galloping after them at full stretch. He was mounted on the big chestnut weight-carrier he always rode—a vicious animal, which the grooms called Satan. And there was Kitty—a girl of barely fifteen, as he remembered her—tearing after the old man on the aging chaser to which she had just been promoted and being rebuked for her thrusting recklessness. Madcap Kitty . . . it had not only been the grooms who had called her that—the whole hunt knew her for the fearless little creature she was, and once again Michael was smiling at the memories his dream evoked.

He saw her twin, Patrick, as ever chasing her shadow, devoted as twins seemed to be, and ready to follow her lead, wherever it might take him and however dangerous it proved. Their mother had died when they were born. All that was left to remind him of her was the oil painting of a slender, exquisitely beautiful woman in a red velvet gown, which hung over the great stone fireplace in the entrance hall. Lady Caitlin Cecilia Fitzgerald she had been, before her marriage to his father . . . Kitty had been named after her and, indeed, had taken after her, for she, too, by all accounts had been a brilliant horsewoman before her untimely and tragic death.

The sound of the huntsman's horn faded into silence and the dream faded. But it had been so vivid, the illusion of being back at Kilclare so intense, that Michael pushed away the hand that was gripping and shaking his shoulder, reluctant to return to wakefulness, his mind and his thoughts still in the past. Undeterred, the hand went on shaking him, and a woman's voice called him by name.

"Mr. Wexford—wake up! Supper's ready, and we're all at the table."

Michael opened his eyes at last, to recognize Mrs. Meldrum bending over him, a spotless white apron—several sizes too big for her tiny frame—girt about her, and her cheeks pinker than ever from her exertions in the kitchen.

" 'Tis a fine meal, though I do say it myself," she told him, smiling. "And I'd not want you to miss it."

Michael jumped up at once, swiftly apologetic, and her smile widened, lighting her faded blue eyes. "You needed your sleep, Mr. Wexford," she said indulgently, and gestured to his discarded jacket. "Come in when you're ready. It's not that often we entertain a guest."

The family were seated round the kitchen table when Michael joined them. Two young men, stocky and dark-haired like Amos Meldrum, were introduced as his sons, Oscar and Peter, and a young woman, Martha, who was Oscar's wife, greeted him shyly. But their shyness evaporated as the excellent meal progressed, and the young men questioned him excitedly concerning his escape.

"They reckon it's impossible to escape from the Tasman Peninsula," Peter exclaimed. "Only three fellows ever made it, by all accounts, and that was years ago. And I don't think anyone stole a ship before."

There was admiration in his voice, and Michael, observing a frown of disapproval on Amos Meldrum's face, endeavored to reduce his exploit to the chance happening it had been.

"I'd no intention of seizing the ship when I went on board," he said gravely. "I'm no hero, lad, and the idea did not enter my head. Certainly I would not have chosen the men who escaped with me as my companions, had I been given a choice."

"Are they such villains, sir?" Oscar asked, evidently not quite convinced.

"They are killers," Michael told him, with quiet emphasis.

"But you've never killed anyone?"

"No, I have not."

"Mr. Wexford is what they call a political prisoner," Amos Meldrum put in, continuing to frown, as if regretting the turn the conversation had taken. "But those villains will be caught in the end—the authorities will not rest until they are. There will be rewards for their capture posted and, never fear, a high price set on their heads. They committed piracy as well as murder— they'll be hanged for sure if they are brought to trial."

As would he, Michael reflected, with a sinking heart. He had been with them—that would be enough where the authorities were concerned, since he had no means of proving that Haines, with the same ruthlessness that he had displayed when taking the lives of the others, had also attempted to kill him. Haines

. . . and Josh Simmons, the bloodthirsty little swine who was his willing tool.

He glanced across at Prudence, surprised to see that her eyes had filled with tears. She said, as if guessing his unspoken thoughts, "But they will hunt for you, too, will they not, Mr. Wexford? They will put a price on *your* head, as well as on those rogues?"

Touched by her concern, Michael smiled at her reassuringly. "Oh, probably they will," he conceded, with deliberate lightness. "But I don't intend to be caught, Miss Prudence. And if I can avoid it, I don't intend to set eyes on those three rogues again. I shall quit Tasmania by the first ship that's willing to take me."

"That reminds me," Amos Meldrum said, his expression relaxing. "I must make a search for Tom Blaney's papers, as soon as we finish our meal. They're of no use to me, Mr. Wexford, but they might serve your purpose very well." He passed his empty plate across the table. "I could do with another helping, wife. Harvesting's hungry work."

"To be sure it is, Amos," Mrs. Meldrum agreed. "You—" Her serving spoon poised over the steaming pot of stew on the hob, she broke off a strangled cry, the spoon falling with a metallic clatter from her hand. The door from the yard burst open, and to his shocked dismay Michael saw Train framed in the aperture, a musket held purposefully in front of him.

He came into the lamp-lit kitchen, calling out over his shoulder, and Josh Simmons followed, similarly armed but limping, with Haines a few paces to his rear.

Train was the first to see and recognize Michael. He let out a yell of mingled surprise and indignation.

"Sweet Jesus, look who's here, Will! It's Wexford! The bastard didn't drown after all!"

Haines thrust past him, swearing. "What the devil are you doin' here, Wexford?" The muzzle of the Adams pistol made painful contact with Michael's ribs. "An' where's Tarr?"

"He's dead—and you can add him to your score!" Michael flung at him angrily. "That adds up to three that I know of, Haines. How many more have you murdered? And what's happened to the *Hastings* and her people?" When Haines ignored both questions, he asked, in a quieter tone, "Why are you here, and what do you want of these good people?"

"Ah, now you're talkin'! We're here because we ran into a bunch of bloody police troopers an' Josh did in his ankle when we was tryin' to keep out o' their way. An' we seen lights burnin' here, so—" Haines looked about him, an odd little smile playing about his lips. "We reckoned we ought to sample the local 'ospitality. We could do with a good 'ot meal, an' Josh could do with a woman's care for 'is ankle. What about it, you ladies? You gonna give us what you seem to have given our mate Wexford, eh?"

He leered at Martha, and her husband leapt furiously to his feet. But before he could speak, Train's musket butt caught him on the side of the head, felling him instantly. With a sob, Martha dropped to her knees beside him, pillowing his head on her lap. Haines snapped shortly, "So it's to be that way, is it? Josh—Toby, tie the men up! There'll be some ropes somewhere about, but use their belts if you can't find any."

Amos Meldrum, who had said nothing until now, rose with dignity to confront Haines. "There is no need to tie us up, Mr. Haines. We are simple, God-fearing folk, and we will give you food. And I am sure my wife will attend to your companion's injured ankle, provided the three of you leave as soon as it is light, which Mr. Wexford agreed to do. We want no trouble, with you or with the law."

Haines laughed. "That's a fair offer, mister, an' we'll take it. All the same, I'll feel safer if you an' your lads are tied up, so's we can relax, understand? Get on with it, Josh—sit 'em in their chairs an' make sure they stay in 'em. Now, how about some liquor, eh? You got any rum? It's a long while since I tasted any rum, an' I'm parched."

"There is a small keg in the pantry," Amos said. "And a cask of cider. That's all we have." In response to a jerk of the head from Train, he resumed his seat and submitted to having his hands tied behind the chair back with his belt. "Mr. Wexford knows where it is—he can fetch it."

"No 'e can't," Josh objected venomously. "Mr. bloody Wexford's 'aving 'is 'ands tied and 'is feet, like the rest of you!" He advanced on Michael, grinning, but Haines shook his head.

"Leave the bastard be, Josh. He's on the run, same as us, ain't 'e? An' we're takin' 'im with us when we go. Fetch the liquor, Wexford."

Bewildered by his attitude, Michael obeyed him. The pantry, from which Prudence had earlier brought the cider she had poured for him, was a small, windowless addition opening from the kitchen. As he crossed the kitchen, he noticed that the old flintlock musket had been removed from the wall on which it had formerly hung, and his flagging spirits lifted. Amos Meldrum, as clearly as he could, had directed him to the pantry, counting on his being left at liberty, and . . . He opened the door, his heart suddenly pounding as he saw the old weapon propped up against the wall to his right.

It would be noticed immediately, were Haines or either of the others to enter the pantry; despite the absence of a light, the glow from the kitchen lamps would reveal it, and . . . Michael quickly scooped up the gun, seeking for a safer place in which to conceal it. There was no time now, he knew, to look for the powder and shot with which to load the rusting musket, but . . . he pushed it hurriedly into a small space between a laden dresser and the wall, reminded of the manner in which—it seemed almost a lifetime ago—he had hidden the stolen Adams in the Cascades lumberyard.

He found the small rum keg without difficulty and carried it into the kitchen, meeting Amos Meldrum's questioning gaze with a barely perceptible nod. Prudence, in response to her father's gesture, took three pewter tankards from their hooks on the kitchen dresser and set them on the table, and Haines thanked her, with mock politeness. He took the keg, grinning, and splashed generous measures of rum into each of the three tankards.

Oscar, Michael saw, had been tied to his chair like his father and brother. He slumped there, barely aware of what was going on, his pretty young wife trying vainly to stem the bleeding from the ugly wound on his face with her apron. Josh, who had found a length of rope, completed the bonds that secured the injured young man's feet and, with a grunt of satisfaction, accepted the brimming tankard Haines was holding out to him.

"God, Will, this tastes good!" he exulted, swallowing his portion almost at a gulp. "Any more where that came from?"

"Course there is, boy—but go easy, will you? We ain't accustomed to this stuff where we've bin. I reckon we better eat 'fore we do any heavy drinkin'." Haines turned to Mrs. Meldrum and asked impatiently, "How about it, missus? Ain't you got our grub ready yet?"

The little woman, as quietly dignified as her husband, inclined her gray head. "If you will draw that bench up to the table," she said, "I will serve your meal. I was not expecting to have to feed so many—there is not much of my stew left. But there is a ham and cheese, if it does not suffice. And bread-and-curd tart."

Haines thanked her, faintly abashed by her manner. But he swiftly recovered his confidence, and forgetful of his earlier insistence that they should drink only in moderation, he was soon filling and refilling the tankards, while all three men wolfed every scrap of food that was put in front of them, their appetites seemingly insatiable.

Michael watched them covertly, waiting for drunkenness to set in and, perhaps, manifest itself in a slackening of their vigilance. Train was already lolling, head in his two big hands and elbows on the table, his speech slurred and his language becoming increasingly obscene, and Josh Simmons's narrow, bony face was flushed, as he continued to take great gulps of the rum and hiccup loudly when he emptied his tankard. But Haines kept his head, for all the liquor he consumed . . . and, for his own cynical amusement, he kept Prudence at his elbow, plying her with tidbits from his plate and stroking her dark curls with every appearance of affection, as if she were some small, petted dog.

Michael trembled for her when Haines, his meal finished, took her onto his knee and started to question her as to the cause of her infirmity.

"Was you born like this?" he asked her, his arm drawing her closer when the girl attempted to shrink from him. "There, I don't mean you no harm. It just seems sad, a pretty young thing like you to be the way you are."

Both Amos Meldrum and his wife were showing ominous

signs of strain, but when Mrs. Meldrum sought to intervene, Haines pushed her roughly away, repeating his assertion that he intended the girl no harm. Young Peter, driven to fury by this treatment of his mother, yelled out in protest—whereupon Josh, swearing unpleasantly, got up and staggered unsteadily across the room, to silence him with a brutal blow across the mouth.

He, at least, was drunk, Michael decided, and Train was not far from lapsing into befuddled sleep. Before much longer, they would empty the rum keg, and he could offer to bring them the cider. He met a terrified, pleading glance from Prudence and, sensing the danger she was in, was hard put to it to retain the iron control he had imposed on himself. But to act prematurely was, he knew, to court disaster. Up till now, to his own surprise, all three of his fellow absconders had acted as if he were still one of them, in equal peril from outsiders—or settlers, like the Meldrums—and therefore bent, as they were, on escape. While they had not shared their liquor with him, they had left him free to move about the kitchen, instead of being bound, hand and foot, as were Amos Meldrum and his sons.

No doubt Haines had a reason for doing so; certainly none of them trusted him, and a false move would bring a bullet from the Adams or a rifle butt smashing down on his head, but . . . He saw Josh go back to the table and tip the last drops of rum into his tankard.

"It's finished, Will," he said plaintively. "The bloody rum's finished. Ain't there any more?"

"There's a cask of cider in the pantry," Amos Meldrum offered. His eyes sought Michael's, as Prudence's had done, a mute plea in their depths. "It's good stuff, home brewed. I made it to sell, but if you want it, you're welcome." Then, fearing, perhaps, that he might have appeared too eager, he added sourly, "If it will start you on your way out of my house and off my land, take it and go! You know where I keep the cask, don't you, Mr. Wexford?"

"The night's still young," Haines reminded him. He continued to stroke Prudence's dark head, the expression on his lined brown face half tender, half lascivious as he looked down at her.

"All right, go get it, Wexford," he ordered, without looking up. "It'll be better than nothin', I suppose."

Michael nodded, not trusting himself to speak, and he was trembling violently as he made for the pantry door. Pray heaven he was able to find the powder and shot and that he would have time to load and prime the ancient flintlock before one of the three convicts became suspicious! In the drawer of the dresser, Amos Meldrum had said, but . . . had he meant the kitchen dresser, or the one in the pantry?

He had been standing in the kitchen when he said it, and the kitchen dresser—a heavy, carved family heirloom, with crockery lining its shelves—was just a few feet away, close by the outer door. The logical place, surely, for the ammunition to be kept, rather than in the dark pantry . . . Michael took the three paces that separated him from the dresser and, pretending to stumble, opened the top drawer.

He was sick with relief when his fingers closed on powder horn and cartridge bag. No one had noticed his action; no shout of alarm came from the men at the cluttered table, and when he glanced anxiously over his shoulder, he saw that Josh was moving across to confront Oscar Meldrum's young wife, his intentions all too plain. Amos Meldrum himself was not looking toward him, all his attention centered on his daughter—and she, poor child, seemed numb with fear as Haines leaned forward to whisper to her, his mouth close to her ear.

He must memorize their positions, Michael told himself, for he would have only a few seconds when he came back with the gun loaded . . . and only one shot, if he was compelled to fire. Train was asleep—that narrowed the odds a little—and, yes, Josh had left his musket propped against the bench from which he had just risen. Haines must be his target, then; he was apparently sober, and he carried the Adams—the six-shot Adams revolver—at his waist. Somehow, Michael thought, he would have to prevent him from drawing the Adams—or shock him into standing up, so that poor little Prudence did not impede his own aim . . . if he *could* aim, in that congested, dimly lit kitchen, with a rusting flintlock, whose owner had decried its accuracy in scornful tones.

He heard Josh demand, "How about some womanly care for

my busted ankle, Martha Meldrum?" and then he was in the pantry, groping for the hidden flintlock. It took him longer to load it than he had anticipated, for his hands were clumsy and unsteady, and he dropped the paper wad when trying to insert it in the muzzle. But at last it was done, the charge rammed home, and Michael forced himself to pause for a moment to gain his breath before cocking the weapon and moving to the door.

The cider cask, a heavy, iron-bound wooden barrel, stood by the door, and as a precaution he turned it on its side and rolled it in front of him into the kitchen, making as much noise as he could. Haines turned at the sound, growled something Michael could not hear, and then turned back to Prudence, who was struggling to escape from his arms. He raised a hand to slap her viciously across the face, and her cry of pain galvanized Michael into action.

He was across the room, the muzzle of the flintlock jammed into Haines's unprotected back, and as the convict's hold on her loosened, Prudence broke free of him, flinging her frail body down at her father's feet and sobbing her fear aloud. Meldrum strained at his bonds but could not move to help her, and his wife, showing courage and a swift appreciation of what was happening, pulled the terrified girl to safety, then seized the musket Josh had carelessly abandoned. Holding it, her finger on the trigger, the little woman placed herself in front of her husband and child, and Josh, who had made a belated attempt to recover his weapon, came cursing to a halt when he found himself confronted with it.

Haines, not unexpectedly, was quicker and more resourceful. Despite the gun muzzle at his back, he contrived to seize the Adams pistol and aim it at the semiconscious Oscar, who was directly opposite him—but before he could fire or even threaten to do so, Michael knocked it from his hand. The pistol skidded across the floor, to vanish beneath young Peter's chair, and the boy moved his pinioned legs so as to keep it there.

Train wakened and looked about him owlishly, unable to comprehend the situation in which he found himself.

"Don't move!" Michael warned him. "Or Haines gets it. My gun's loaded with buckshot—I could blow him to pieces!"

The warning had its effect. "I'm getting to hell out o' here!" the big man grunted. He started for the outer door at a shambling run, ignoring Josh Simmons's frantic efforts to stop him and leaving his musket on the bench. Bravely, at her father's bidding, little Prudence scrambled to her feet and retrieved it, while Martha, taking a knife from the table, no less bravely set about freeing the captives.

The battle, such as it was, seemed to be over, and even Haines was ready to accept defeat.

"All right, Wexford," he managed, in a choked voice. "We'll go an' we won't trouble none o' you no more. You ain't a killer, are you? Don't want my death on your conscience, do you?"

Michael kept the muzzle of the flintlock pressed firmly into his back. "It wouldn't in the least concern me, Haines," he returned indifferently. "I'd as soon kill you as turn you in."

"You're one of us," Haines reminded him. "Turn us in an' you'll be signin' your own death warrant. I trusted you, Wexford, don't forget that. I should have listened to Josh an' hogtied you with the rest."

His admission was too much for Josh. "That you should, Will!" the little man accused him furiously. He was beside himself with rage and frustration and, in that moment, Michael sensed, more dangerous than Haines had ever been. Mrs. Meldrum still faced him with the musket she had seized, but it was wavering, and her face had drained of color. Probably, Michael thought despairingly, she had never fired a musket in her life, and Josh, evidently coming to the same conclusion, brushed her contemptuously aside.

He had the long bayonet in his hand now—the one he had kept in his belt—and he was screeching incoherent threats.

"If I'm for the chop, Wexford, I'm takin' you with me and be damned! You ain't got the guts to pull that trigger—an' you know I'll get you if you do! Make a run for it, Will, d'you hear me? The bastard can't get us both!"

Haines flung himself forward on his face and the next instant was scrambling on all fours for the door. Michael closed his finger about the trigger, only to realize that the old flintlock had misfired, and then Josh Simmons was upon him, the bayonet jabbing at him savagely and aiming for his throat. He was con-

scious of excruciating pain in his right shoulder. The musket
fell from his grasp, but he managed somehow to ward off a
second blow, and with his left hand he wrested the bayonet
from his assailant and flung it away.

His senses reeling, he heard Haines yell from the door for
Josh to join him. As he slipped to his knees, there was a loud
explosion and he guessed that someone—Amos Meldrum, perhaps, or one of his sons—had fired the musket Josh had left
behind. When he staggered to his feet, he saw Amos coming
back into the house, a smoking musket in his hand, shaking his
head disconsolately.

"They got away, all three of them, devil take them! And I
missed the big fellow by a hairsbreadth!"

"We could ride after them, Pa," Peter urged. "It'll only take
me a few minutes to saddle a couple of horses. We—"

"No," his father said reluctantly. "Best leave the troopers to
hunt for them. They won't get far, and at least they're not
armed now, so they won't do much bushranging. Thanks to our
good friend Wexford here, we're rid of them, praise be to God!"
He held out his hand, beaming and clearly greatly relieved.
"We're in your debt, Mr. Wexford. We—" Michael attempted to
take the proffered hand, but there was a red mist floating in
front of his eyes, and Amos Meldrum's face abruptly vanished.

Peter's voice, seeming to come from a long way away, exclaimed, "He's been hurt, Pa! He's bleeding like a stuck pig!"
Hands clutched at him as he slithered to the floor, the mist
closing over him to blot out sight and sound, only the awareness of pain remaining and a nightmare vision of Josh Simmons's face, contorted with rage, as he plunged in with his
bayonet.

Chapter XI

FIFTEEN DAYS AFTER he had first arrived at the Meldrums' farm, Michael climbed down from the wagon in which Oscar had driven him to the outskirts of Hobart and prepared to make his way on foot to the harbor. The promised seaman's papers, made out in the name of Thomas Albert Blaney, reposed in the breast pocket of Blaney's old brass-buttoned jacket, together with a note from his employer, releasing him from his assigned service. They would not bear too close an inspection, since Blaney had been in his late fifties when granted his ticket-of-leave, but . . . Michael tried to dismiss the worry from his mind.

A ship's master, short of his complement, would probably refrain from asking too many questions, and he did not intend to linger in Hobart for any longer than he could avoid. His injured arm was still bandaged, but the wound had healed quickly and now incommoded him very little. Mrs. Meldrum and her daughter Prudence had been excellent nurses, he reflected, conscious once again of the regret he had felt when, no longer needing their services, the time for his departure had finally come.

Amos Meldrum had not pressed him to stay, and he understood the farmer's reasons. Two different search parties had come to the house in the space of a week—one military, the other composed of mounted police troopers and local constables. They had both announced that they were seeking four escaped convicts from the Port Arthur Penitentiary, desperate men who had committed murder and piracy and were wanted —dead or alive—in return for a substantial reward.

Meldrum had, perforce, told them of the raid by Haines and his companions, insisting, however, that there had been three men, not four, and both parties had made extensive searches of his land and buildings before moving on. Michael had remained hidden in an attic, and the family had made no mention of his presence there, but the sergeant in charge of the military party, a conscientious man, had come perilously close to discovering his hiding place. He had, furthermore, a note to the effect that Thomas Albert Blaney, a ticket-of-leave convict, had died while in assigned employment on the Meldrum property, and had demanded confirmation, even going so far as to inspect the old seaman's grave. And he had taken the stolen muskets. . . . Michael touched the Adams revolver, which was tucked into the belt of his trousers, just as Haines had carried it. At least the conscientious sergeant had not known of its existence, and Amos Meldrum had insisted that the weapon was of no use to him.

"You might run across those blackguards, Michael, before the search parties catch up with them," the older man had said gravely. "And if you should, you'll have to defend yourself. So take the pistol—I don't imagine they're likely to come back here. But that sergeant may—it's evident that he wasn't entirely satisfied, or perhaps my story didn't ring quite true. We're not ungrateful for what you did, but you're not safe here, and . . . there's Prudence. For her sake, lad, it will be best if you leave as soon as you're fit to travel."

He had added, with genuine sadness, "She has lost her heart to you, poor child. But there's no future in it for either of you, is there? Not in the circumstances. She'll get over it, once you're gone."

He was probably right, Michael thought. Certainly there could be no foreseeable future for a little cripple girl of barely sixteen and an escaped convict with a price on his head . . . who was almost twice her age. All the same, the memory of her stricken face, when he had bidden her farewell, tore at his heartstrings. She was so gentle and sweet, so trusting and so blind to what the years of his imprisonment had made of him.

To Prudence Meldrum he had been, however briefly, a hero
. . . and a wounded hero, at that, as much in need of her care
and pity and, yes, her love as an orphaned lamb or a stray dog.
Or even the injured nestling—a bronze-wing pigeon—that she
had reared, with infinite patience, from featherless infancy to
healthy adulthood, and which she had proudly displayed to
him, perching on her outstretched arm, after it had flown down
from a tree in response to her call.

"He knows me, Michael," she had told him, eyes bright with
pleasure at the bird's tameness. "And even though he has long
ago returned to the wild and found a mate, he still comes back
to me when I whistle to him. He doesn't forget me, and I—oh,
Michael, I shall never forget you! As long as I live, I shall think
of you and pray for you. And I—I shall hope, one day, to see
you again."

But he had not been able, in honesty, to promise her that,
Michael recalled, with sudden bitterness. For was he not, even
now, about to seek for a ship that would take him to Melbourne
for the purpose of killing a man? And had not the thought of
taking John Price's life been all that had sustained him throughout the long, tortured years of his convict exile? His fingers
closed on the butt of the pistol at his waist. For God's sake, had
not the initial theft of the Adams been for that purpose? When
he had taken it, he had seen the weapon solely as a means to
accomplish his escape and the escape itself as a means to seek
out the erstwhile commandant of Norfolk Island and exact his
revenge.

What then, he asked himself, had such a man as he to give to
a little, innocent girl, whose name was incongruously Prudence
and who, all unwittingly, had wanted to give him the most
precious gift she had to bestow? Her father had been right—
there could be no future for either of them, in the circumstances, and, in all probability, as Amos Meldrum had also said,
Prudence would get over it, once he had gone.

Michael quickened his pace. Oscar had set him down only a
short distance from the center of town, at the start of a long
street named after one of the earlier governors, Macquarie, with
instructions to follow it until he came to the intersection with
Murray Street.

"That will take you to the docks. There are a good many taverns in the dock area, as you might expect, and most of them are patronized by seagoing folk. You should be able to make inquiries over a drink or two without inviting attention. Pa gave you enough money, didn't he?"

Indeed, Amos had been generous; he had enough for a night's lodging, as well as for the drinks he might have to buy, but, Michael decided, stepping into the shadows as a mob of men emerged from the gate of a nearby shipbuilder's yard, it would still be wise to use care in choosing the hostelry he patronized. A small, quiet place, whose clientele did not include the military, he thought—and gave a wide berth to one in whose lamp-lit taproom he glimpsed half a dozen scarlet coats. But, even as he moved away from it, the rhythmic thud of steel-shod boots on the cobblestones of the road behind him set his pulses racing, and he again sought the shelter of a shadowed doorway. A squad of soldiers marched past him with shouldered arms, heading for the docks and scattering a knot of loud-voiced revelers—seamen, by their garb—who had gathered in the roadway outside the tavern they had just left.

"Bloody lobsterbacks!" one of the seamen exclaimed, shaking his fist at the soldiers' retreating backs. "It ain't enough that they've bin in every tavern between 'ere an' Battery Point, makin' a flamin' nuisance o' theirselves! Now it seems they're goin' to search the ships at the bloody anchorage. If some o' the poor devils of convicts got away from the Tasman Peninsula by makin' off with a bleedin' gover'ment steamer, good luck to 'em, I say! Got the steamer back, didn't they?"

The speaker, who had addressed no one in particular, concluded with a loud hiccup, and one of his shipmates gave him an ironical cheer.

"Better not let 'is Excellency 'ear you sayin' things like that, Davie boy! I reckon 'e'd have you clapped in irons an' shipped off to whatever they call the place—Port Arthur, ain't it? An' *you* wouldn't know 'ow to set about piratin' no gover'ment steamer to get away from there, would you, now?"

"I'd 'ave a bleedin' good try," the man called Davie retorted defiantly. He hiccuped again and then, noticing Michael stand-

ing a few yards away, turned to grin at him with drunken good
humor. "Evenin', matey. On yer tod, are you?"

He was English, Michael decided—an English Cockney by
his accent—and probably a member of the crew of one of the
mail steamers that berthed at the customs wharf, according to
what Oscar had been able to tell him of the layout of the Hobart
dockside.

"Why, indeed I am, friend," he confirmed, slipping easily
into the suggestion of an Irish brogue. He started to explain
that he was aiming to sign on with any ship's master who was
looking for hands, but one of the other men, even drunker than
the friendly little Cockney, came staggering unsteadily toward
him and clapped a muscular arm about his shoulders.

"Jaysus!" the newcomer greeted him. "Amn't I knowin' a
Wexford voice when I'm hearin' it? Ye're from t'ould country,
surely? From de beautiful county o' Wexford, I'd swear t' God!"

Conscious that he might be treading on dangerous ground,
Michael admitted the truth, and the big Irish seaman continued
to extol the beauties of his native land, his eyes filled with senti-
mental tears.

"Sure and we must drink on it," he insisted.

It would be a way of avoiding notice, Michael thought. As
one of a crowd of seamen on a run ashore, he would not be
given a second glance by the military search parties. A police
patrol might pick up the whole mob, if they became too riotous,
and lodge them in jail for the night, but if there were any risk of
that happening, he could quickly part company with them at
the first sign of trouble.

He spent the next hour with his newfound companions, in a
dockside tavern near the waterfront, contriving—not without
difficulty—to limit his drinking to a few glasses of rum punch.
It was time well spent, for they located a number of vessels in
the port, with their names and destinations, and gave him chapter and verse of the hunt for the absconders from Port Arthur,
which had apparently been going on for most of the day.

"First 'twas reckoned as they'd shown a clean pair o' heels
and was off bushrangin' or whatever it's called in some place
called the Huon Valley," the little Cockney seaman called Davie
volunteered. "But then the people from the gover'ment steamer,

the *Hastings,* was brought in, an' they spotted one of 'em 'ere in town, so the 'unt was up wiv' a vengeance. There's big rewards out for 'em, see, so everyone's trying ter nab the poor sods. An' now they're searchin' all the ships in the anchorage that's due to sail in the next coupla days." He eyed Michael thoughtfully. " 'Ave to be a mite careful if you're lookin' for a berth, mate. They're checkin' papers real carefully, from what I've 'eard."

What, Michael wondered, as he listened—what in the world could have induced Haines, of all people, to return to Hobart, where he was known by sight? The fact that he and his companions had no weapons, save for Josh Simmons's bayonet? Or had the search parties in the Huon Valley been closing in on them, rendering the risk of capture even greater there than in the town? With the rewards as inducement, probably the settlers had joined the hunt, rendering their position untenable, and . . . He smothered a sigh. His own also, of course. Even with the late Thomas Blaney's papers, he would have to move with extreme caution.

Davie ordered another round of drinks, and then, to Michael's relief, his friend Geordie, a tall, rawboned North-countryman, announced that it was time they went back to their ship. They had to half carry the homesick young Irishman, who had drunk himself into a paralytic stupor, and their return to the docks was noisy. Michael stayed with them until they were in sight of their brightly lit mail steamer, the guard on duty at the dock gates letting them through with indulgent admonitions to sober up and hold their tongues. He slipped away from them unnoticed and, after a wary search, found a deserted and virtually empty warehouse from where he could watch what was going on without himself being seen.

There were half a dozen ships, of varying sizes, within his range of vision, and he studied them carefully, while keeping track of the three boatloads of armed soldiers that were now plying between them. The search was well coordinated, the boats maintaining contact by means of signal lamps, and on the customs wharf two officers were pacing up and down, directing the boats and receiving their signals.

After a while, one of the officers crossed to what Michael realized was a hotel, to return to his post a little later, accompanied by two civilians in evening dress. He was too far away to be able to see their faces, but one was a tall, broad-shouldered man, with a fair beard, his companion slight and dark. Both were watching the boats' progress with even more intensity than himself, and when one boat—tied up to the lee chains of a small sealer—started to flash a lengthy signal to the shore, their excitement became evident. Minutes afterward, a woman, muffled in a dark cloak against the misty chill emanating from the river, came running from the hotel to join them, the bearded man solicitously putting his arm about her as they waited together.

Then the boat put off from the sealer's side, and when it emerged from the shadow the ship had cast and into the moonlight, Michael saw, with a quickening of his pulses, that the soldiers' search had been successful. Huddled in the sternsheets, their arms pinioned, were three dark figures, and even at that distance it was not hard to recognize them. Haines—whatever had been his reason for coming to Hobart—had made a fatal error, and now all three men would pay for it with their lives, for they would certainly not be allowed to escape again.

Illogically, for a brief moment, Michael found it in his heart to feel compassion for them, but then, remembering what they had so nearly done to little Prudence Meldrum and her family, the impulse faded. They were foul, insensitive brutes, and hanging was no more than they deserved, he told himself, and shifted his position in order to gain a better view of the customs wharf and the reception the captives were accorded.

The three civilians moved across to the head of the landing steps; one of the officers barked a brusque order, and as Haines and his two companions came ashore, they were hustled into line, their guards grouped about them to cut off any attempt they might make to break away. The civilians' inspection was cursory; Michael saw all three heads shake, almost in unison, and they turned away, the woman seemingly distressed, for he saw her hide her face with her hands and then, picking up her skirts, run back to the hotel as if all the fiends of hell were at her heels.

Absurdly, just for an instant, she reminded him of his sister Kitty, who had been wont to run in that same swift, abandoned fashion when anything hurt or frightened her. But it *was* absurd, he chided himself—Kitty was twelve thousand miles away, in the lovely homeland, the mere thought of which had reduced the big Irish seaman to maudlin tears a little while ago.

Haines and the others had been apprehended; he was no longer in danger from them, and now it behooved him to find a ship—any ship—that would take him away from Hobart, God willing, forever.

Michael again moved cautiously, inching to the front of the warehouse to enable him to study the vessels crowding the anchorage. The soldiers' boats had been recalled, he realized; the other two were on their way back to the customs wharf, their search having evidently been called off. It would be best to wait until all three parties and the officers withdrew, and then . . . His gaze went to a small, white-painted brig riding at anchor some sixty or seventy yards from where he stood. She had earlier been boarded and searched, and since the search had been abortive, she was probably unlikely to merit the attention of the military again. And he could swim out to her; that was no problem, so long as the watch on her deck did not see him and he could contrive to scramble aboard her unobserved. He measured the distance with his eye; in darkness, distances were deceptive, and she might be farther out than he had judged. It might be wise to wait, however, until the excitement occasioned by the search and the fugitives' capture died down, and then try to board her. If— Michael tensed, cursing under his breath, as the sound of ribald laughter and a chorus of catcalls reached his ears, interspersed with approaching footsteps.

The sound came nearer. Another party of drunken seamen, he thought irritably, on their way to rejoin their ship—and they were coming toward the warehouse. He looked about him for a hiding place and found it behind some bales, piled against the wall of the warehouse.

There were about a dozen men in the party, and they were almost all cheerfully inebriated, the exceptions being a big, tough-looking fellow with a dark beard—the ship's bo'sun, Michael decided—and a younger man, in the pea jacket of a mate. Evidently their vessel was due to sail early the next day, for the bo'sun cursed them roundly for the trouble he had had in finding them, adding the warning that if their behavior were repeated, he would see to it that the *Mercedes* sailed without them.

Michael's interest increased when the big man strode to the end of the wharf and his waving lantern was answered by one on the deck of the white-painted brig—the one to which he had contemplated swimming—and he saw that her people were lowering a boat, presumably with the object of picking up the absentees. A husky seaman, in a woolen cap and salt-stained ducks, started to complain ill-temperedly to all who were in earshot. His voice was slurred and his indignation such as to make his remarks all but unintelligible, but Michael listened, buoyed by a sudden hope. The fellow, it seemed, did not wish to return to the ship, and he hung back from the others, only a few feet away from Michael's hiding place. Apparently the man had formed an attachment to a woman on shore, who had promised him marriage and a job in one of the shipyards if he remained in Hobart.

"Have a heart, Bo'sun!" he pleaded. "Talk to him, for the Lord's sake, Mr. Murphy—sure and isn't it the chance of a lifetime, now? Dere's dis young woman—a beauty, if ever I seen one, so she is—an' she willin' to wed me and—"

"She's a whore, O'Hara," the bo'sun told him harshly. "And you are not only drunk—you're out of your mind! We're saving you from yourself, lad, and you'll be grateful when you sober up."

"I will not!" the man called O'Hara retorted with sullen obstinacy and, as soon as the bo'sun turned his back, mumbled, "Sure an' I'll curse de pair o' ye till me dyin' day, so I will!"

On impulse, Michael leaned forward and grabbed his arm, drawing him into the space behind the bales and silencing his startled protests with a hand over his mouth.

"Keep quiet," he warned. "Now—tell me. Do you really want to stay in Hobart? Nod your head if you do." O'Hara nodded vigorously, and Michael removed his hand. "All right then—bide here till the boat puts off and then run. I'll take your place."

O'Hara stared at him owlishly. "You mean it?"

"Aye, I mean it. I'm as anxious to get away from here as you are to stay."

"You're a bleedin' escaped convict, aren't you?" The accusation was without malice; O'Hara was grinning.

"I'm ticket-of-leave," Michael told him. "And I want to quit Tasmania. Where's your brig bound?"

"Geelong. Wid a cargo o' New Zealand timber." The grin widened, and O'Hara, swaying a little, extended a big, callused hand. " 'Tis a bargain, an' God bless yez!"

Geelong, Victoria, Michael thought, elated, and scarcely able to believe his good fortune . . . the *Mercedes* was bound for Geelong, Victoria! He shook the young Irishman's hand and then plucked his woolen cap from his head.

"I'll need this, so that they won't spot me. You'll bide here quietly, will you not?"

"Like a wee small mouse," O'Hara assured him, with drunken earnestness. "Not a sound shall they hear, I swear it!" He slumped down among the bales, still grinning. " 'Tis a happy man you've made me."

Michael crammed the woolen cap onto his own head and, in a fair imitation of a tipsy gait, joined the others as the boat from the *Mercedes* came alongside the jetty. He received a good-natured cuff from the big bo'sun as the men piled into the boat.

"You should lay off the liquor, O'Hara, you damned young fool!" the bo'sun reproached him, but neither he nor the mate took any further notice of him, and in the darkness the woolen cap proved an effective disguise.

On board the *Mercedes,* the truants from the shore were herded below, with a stern injunction from the young mate to "Sleep it off, you miserable rogues!" Michael stumbled into a vacant bunk in the crew's quarters and, without undressing, turned his face to the bulkhead and feigned sleep.

A bellow from above of "All hands!" roused him just before dawn the following morning, to find the master on deck and the brig preparing to weigh anchor. All was orderly confusion in the darkness, with the *Mercedes*' two mates and the big bo'sun hustling the seamen about their various tasks. To Michael's relief, the man whose place he had taken, Sean O'Hara, had not been a prime seaman, and he found himself performing strenuous but comparatively unskilled work, lending his weight to the capstan as the anchor was hove in, tailing on to sheets and halyards when sail was set and trimmed, and earning a few curses as he tried to remember lessons he had learned years before as a midshipman and had long since forgotten.

But no one questioned his identity. The curses came mainly from the other seamen, who addressed him as Sean and, attributing his lapses to the previous night's heavy drinking, impatiently pushed and elbowed him into the positions he was supposed to occupy in the tasks required of him. As yet the sun had not risen, and a swirling mist hung over the anchorage, blotting out men's faces and obscuring both the land and the towering sails above, now slowly filling as the breeze caught them and the brig got under way.

"Jump to it, Sean!" one of his fellows exhorted him. "Holy God, man, you must've had a bloody barrelful on shore last night! What d'ye think you're doing?"

"Numbskull, you heard the order—man the lee braces! What's got into you? The bo'sun'll have your hide if you don't watch out!" Another man fumed, thrusting past him, bare feet slithering on the wet deck.

It was coming back to him—the familiar routine, the instant obedience to the shouted commands—but he was still too slow, Michael realized, still having to think. As a mid, he had been a foretopman, despising the landsmen and the marines who had formed the afterguard, but—

"Ready about! Ease the helm down!" The master's orders boomed from his speaking trumpet, and there was a concerted rush across the deck, carrying Michael along with it, to bring him up beside the young mate—Murphy, he recalled; yes, that was his name—who had been on the landing stage the previous night.

"Tacks and sheets! Let go to'gallant bowlines! Mainbrace . . . ." The orders followed thick and fast, as the brig came about to settle on the starboard tack. Michael hauled on the lee brace with the other men, putting his back into it and conscious that Murphy was watching him, a faintly puzzled frown creasing his brow.

"Head braces!" the mate snapped, and once again there was a

rush across the canting deck to the weather side. "Of all haul! Look lively, lads! Brace sharp up there!"

It was not until the brig was running before a brisk beam wind that the order came for the men of the watch below to break their fast. Michael paused to wipe the sweat from his streaming face, and Murphy caught up with him, to grasp him by the shoulder with a quiet "Hold hard."

He turned, realizing that the woolen cap no longer hid his face and that the early-morning mist had dispersed, putting an end to his deception.

"You're not Sean O'Hara," the mate accused.

"No, I'm not, Mr. Murphy."

"Then who the devil are you?"

Michael hesitated and then answered evasively, "My seaman's papers are in the name of Thomas Albert Blaney, sir."

Murphy studied his face with watchful, narrowed eyes. "But that isn't your real name?" he suggested. His tone was not unfriendly, but it was wary. "I think I have it. You are one of the fugitives they were hunting last night—the one the military patrol failed to catch. You escaped from Port Arthur?"

It was useless to deny it, Michael knew. Clearly, though, the *Mercedes* would not at this point return to Hobart in order to hand him over to the authorities there. Yet equally clearly, that would be his fate when she made port in Geelong. Her master would have no choice, Michael was certain—even if he were to persist in claiming the identity of Thomas Blaney, whose ticket-of-leave did not entitle him to quit his employment in Tasmania. He shrugged and inclined his head.

"Yes, that is so," he admitted.

"Then your name is Wexford—Michael Wexford? They caught the other three."

"Yes," Michael confirmed flatly. "I saw them bring in the other three."

Murphy continued to study him thoughtfully. "The hunt was particularly for you," he volunteered. "We were all given your name, and there were special instructions, to be followed if you were found."

"Special instructions, sir? In my case?"

"Yes." Murphy jerked his head in the direction of the after

companionway. "We can't talk here. Come to my cabin. I shall have to report you to Captain Deacon, but—well, I'd like to hear what account you can give of yourself first, Mr. Wexford."

In the privacy of his cabin, the young mate waved Michael to a seat on the berth and took up their conversation at the point where it had left off on deck.

"The instructions were that, if you were apprehended, you were to be taken to the customs wharf to be identified. There were military officers there and two civilians—a young couple, people of quality, I was informed, who had authority from the governor, no less. Which seems to put you in a different light from an ordinary escaper, doesn't it?"

Michael stared at him in frank bewilderment.

"A couple? You mean a married couple—a man and a woman? I thought I saw them last night."

"But you did not recognize them?"

"No, they were too far away. I've no idea who they were."

Murphy smiled. "Perhaps you *should* have known them, Mr. Wexford—because you are a gentleman, aren't you? You speak like one. Were you a political prisoner?"

"Initially, yes. And I used to be a gentleman and a midshipman in Her Majesty's Navy. However—" Michael shrugged. "After serving time on Norfolk Island under Commandant Price and then at the Port Arthur Penitentiary, the most I can lay claim to is that I'm a useful prizefighter." He hesitated, the memory of the previous night's happenings vivid in his mind. There was the young woman who had wept and then run so swiftly and recklessly back to the hotel—the young woman who had stirred his imagination because of the likeness she had borne to his sister Kitty. But it was so long since he had seen Kitty; she would have changed, grown up and become a young lady, instead of the girl, the child he remembered.

"Mr. Murphy," he asked tensely, "do you know the names of the two civilians who were on the customs wharf yesterday evening?"

Murphy shook his head. "No, we weren't given any names, except yours and those of the other escapers. They told us to proceed carefully because you were desperate men, wanted for murder and piracy, and would be likely to resist capture."

"I see." Michael hid his disappointment. It was, he thought ruefully, too much to expect that Kitty and Patrick would have come to Australia in search of him, although . . . He smothered a sigh. They would be capable of it, they—

"Mr. Wexford, were *you* involved in murder and piracy?" Murphy demanded.

"I was involved in the taking of the *Hastings* steamer—with a gun at my head. The murders were committed before I boarded her. Perhaps I should explain what happened, if you've time to listen. It's quite a lengthy tale."

"We're both off watch," Murphy said. "I've time to listen, Mr. Wexford."

Encouraged by the young mate's attitude, Michael gave him as brief and unvarnished an account of the circumstances surrounding his escape as he could, and Murphy listened without interruption until the story was concluded. Then he asked a few questions about the death of the *Hastings*' master, shaking his head regretfully when Michael told him that he had been compelled to consign the old man's body to the sea.

"Then you've no proof of how he died? No proof that you tried to save him?"

"No, alas—none. And the crew were all below when Captain Tarr and I went over the side and Haines fired on us. They would have seen nothing."

"How about—what is their name? The folk you stayed with after you went ashore?"

"Amos Meldrum and his family, you mean?" Michael shook his head. "I'd not want to involve them, Mr. Murphy. Technically they broke the law in giving me shelter and not handing me over to the military search party when they came to the farm. And, I fear, giving me a dead man's papers and his ticket-of-leave would be an offense equally heinous."

Murphy frowned, mulling over his reply. "You understand, don't you," he said at last, "that if I report your presence on board this ship to the master, he'll be legally bound to hand you over to the police in Geelong as an escaper? Old Silas Deacon is a good man, as straight as they come, but they'd take his master's ticket off him if he failed to hand you over."

"Yes," Michael conceded, tight-lipped. "I understand that."

"On the other hand, Mr. Wexford," the mate said, his frown lifting, "I believe what you've told me, and I'd like to help, if I can."

"You've no call to help me, Mr. Murphy," Michael felt obliged to say. "I'm grateful, but you could get yourself into a great deal of trouble if you do. And there's no way I could repay you. I—"

"I've been in trouble myself," Murphy told him. "Plenty of trouble, and I—I lost my wife, a few months ago. She died in childbirth, and I—well, I suppose I've been running too, trying to escape from the—oh, damn it, the knowledge that I was responsible for her death. If she had not married me, she would still be alive, Wexford. And I loved her. She was the sweetest, most beautiful woman in the world!"

"Yes, but—oh, for God's sake, you cannot be responsible for her death in childbirth," Michael began, surprised by the depths of the young mate's grief. "You—"

It was as if Murphy had not heard him, for he went on, in a low, bitter voice, "I ran to the first place that offered escape—this ship. I thought if I could get away from the places I'd shared with Elizabeth, her family, our home, that it would be easier to forget. It hasn't been much easier, and I haven't forgotten. Deacon made me second mate because I'd sailed with him before, as a deckhand, and I'm related to the ship's owner—and I know a little about navigation. But I'm not much use to him, if the truth were known. My heart's not in it, you see. I'd more or less made up my mind to quit when we make port at Geelong and go to the goldfields. I've done a spell as a digger, and I've enough for a grubstake."

His tone changed and he managed a wry smile.

"We could tell Captain Deacon a different tale from the one you've just told me, Mr. Wexford."

Michael eyed him uncertainly. "What sort of tale?"

"Well, that you are a new immigrant, anxious to get to the goldfields and—yes, without the money for your passage. So you smuggled yourself on board this brig, hoping to pass yourself off as a seaman in place of the lad who deserted—O'Hara. Those seaman's papers of yours—would they pass muster?"

Michael shook his head. "The man they belonged to is dead

—and he was a ticket-of-leave convict assigned to Amos Meldrum. So I fear they would not bear close inspection."

"Let me see them, will you?"

"Yes, of course." Michael produced the grubby, much-faded seaman's book from his pocket. "Thomas Blaney's ticket-of-leave and a note from Amos Meldrum are inside."

Murphy studied all three documents with frowning care. "Well," he said, returning them, "I reckon the seaman's book would get you ashore, and it might satisfy Captain Deacon, if you don't show him the ticket-of-leave. They don't worry too much in Geelong. There's a steady flow of gold seekers entering the port, some with money and papers and some without much more than the clothes they stand up in. All they want is to get to Ballarat or Bendigo or to the new fields in the Murray Valley. There are hundreds, thousands, of men, from every country in the world, working in the fields still, although the first mad rush is over. There aren't many fortunes made these days, but . . ." Murphy's expression relaxed. "I still have a mind to go back. It's been in my blood, I suppose, ever since I made a lucky strike in California, years ago, when I was just a kid."

"You were in California?" Michael questioned, surprised.

"I hail from there, Mr. Wexford."

"And Murphy?"

"Oh, that's my real name—Luke Murphy." The young mate was smiling now, suddenly eager and excited. "We could team up together for a while, if it would help you to make good your escape. I'd get you to Ballarat, anyway, and we could part company there, if you want."

"You would be taking a chance, Murphy. I cannot ask that of you," Michael began. "You—"

Luke Murphy cut him short, still smiling. "You have not asked it of me—I've offered. There's a difference. I've learned to judge men since I came out here, and you're no villain—I'd stake my life on that. And I'd be right, wouldn't I?"

A second human being had taken him on trust, Michael thought—the little crippled girl Prudence Meldrum had been the first, and now this young Californian was prepared to do so. He felt humbled, momentarily bereft of words, tempted to confess to Luke Murphy the real reason for his determination to make his escape from Port Arthur—but no sooner had the thought occurred than he dismissed it from his mind. This boy, who had lost his wife and gone to sea in a vain attempt to find forgetfulness, could not be expected to understand, any more than the gentle little Prudence would have understood, had he made his confession to her. She, who had nursed an orphaned wild bird and restored it to life, with infinite patience and devotion, would have been hard put to it to sympathize with his obsession for revenge on the man who had robbed him of his pride, his manhood, and—perhaps even of his soul. And Luke Murphy was like her, in a way.

Michael forced an answering smile, accepting the hand Murphy was holding out to him.

"I was not born a villain," he said quietly. "And I'll not betray your trust. We'll go to Ballarat together, and I thank you, with all my heart, for your offer."

"We shall have to square Captain Deacon first," Murphy reminded him. "I think I'd better take you to him now. You—" He paused, eyeing Michael uncertainly. "Is Wexford *your* real name?"

"No," Michael admitted. It was a long time since he had used his real name, but to his own surprise, he was able to admit to it with pride. Price had not, after all, stolen that from him. "It is Cadogan," he said. "Michael Cadogan. Wexford is where I come from."

Chapter XII

DOMINIC HAYES WAS in the *Chronicle* office when Kitty was announced, the newspaper's front page spread out across the desk. He rose at once and, having ushered Kitty to a seat, gestured to the page of newsprint he had been studying.

"Look at this," he invited, in an oddly tense tone of voice. "The mills of God, it would seem, *do* grind exceeding small!"

Kitty picked up the page and drew in her breath sharply as she took in the banner headline.

NORFOLK ISLAND'S EX-COMMANDANT MURDERED

Shocked, she read on:

We have just received the tragic news from Melbourne that, on March 27, at Pentridge Gaol, Mr. John Price, Inspector General of Penal Establishments in the State of Victoria, was set upon by seven of the gaol's inmates. Taking him unawares, they stoned and savagely attacked him with their quarrying tools, battering him with such severity that he died shortly afterward.

The miscreants responsible have been placed under arrest and are to be brought to trial, whilst two convicts, who went to Mr. Price's assistance but were unable to revive him or stanch the fatal bleeding, have been commended for their prompt and compassionate action.

The late Mr. Price was, of course, well known in Hobart, having settled initially in the Huon Valley District in 1836, on his arrival in the colony, later being appointed a police magistrate and muster master in the Convict Department.

He and his wife, the former Mary Franklin, niece of our Lieutenant Governor, resided here until, following an attempted mutiny by the Norfolk Island convicts in July 1846, the Executive Council recalled the military commandant, Major Joseph Childs, and appointed Mr. Price civil commandant in his place. Accompanied by his wife and their five young children, Mr. Price sailed from Hobart to take up his appointment, which he held until January 1853, when the decision to wind down the penal colony was reached.

A year later, with the increase of lawlessness in the State of Victoria due to the gold rush, Mr. Price was appointed Inspector General of Penal Establishments and took charge of Pentridge Gaol—where he met his death—and the prison hulks off Williamstown.

He was born on October 20, 1808, the fourth son of Sir Rose Price, of Trengwainton, Cornwall, England, and was educated at Charterhouse School and Brasenose College, Oxford. . . .

She skipped down toward the bottom of the page:

Mr. Price will be sadly missed by his many friends in this town, and our sincere condolences are offered to his widow in her tragic bereavement. . . .

There was still more, but Kitty could read no more, the words that the convict O'Brien had written in his diary dancing before her eyes and blotting out those printed in the newspaper:

Price ordered Big Michael fifty lashes for making his complaint insolently and doubled the sentence when Michael laughed at him. They flogged him, with a dozen others . . . he took the flogging without making a sound, and then spat at Price's feet when they cut him down. Price put his damned eyeglass in his eye

*and shouted "Give him the gag!" And then put him back in
solitary for ten days. . . .*

How, she wondered bitterly, could anyone grieve for a man
like John Price? Had he not been given his just deserts by the
poor wretches who had attacked him in the quarry at Pentridge? Poor tortured souls, as Michael had been, they had rebelled and murdered their tormentor, and no doubt the law
would exact retribution and hang them for what desperation
had driven them to do. At least, God be thanked, Michael had
not been of their number.

"Do you really think," she asked Dominic coldly, "that
Commandant Price will be sadly missed by his Hobart friends?"

"He *had* friends here, Kitty," Dominic defended. "And
Mary Price was very well liked." He shrugged his broad, well-
tailored shoulders. "Such—er—sentiments are expected of a local newspaper, you know."

He was right, of course, Kitty had to concede. Dominic took
the page from her and, carrying it to the door, handed it over to
one of his employees with a crisp "Yes—print it as it stands."
Returning to his desk, he asked, a faint edge to his pleasant
voice, "I gather you met with no success last night? Your
brother Michael was not with the absconders they apprehended?"

Kitty shivered at the memory his question invoked.

"No, Michael was not there. I—oh, Dominic, I don't know
whether to be glad or sorry! They were dreadful men, the ones
they say escaped with him. One of them—they said his name
was Haines—was *evil.* I don't think I have ever come across
anyone who personified evil as he did. And the two others—one
was very tall, and just for a moment I thought it might be
Michael—they were brutes."

"The type who attacked and killed John Price?" Dominic
suggested. "That's what most of them are like, Kitty. Hardened
criminals, incapable of reform, who must be locked away for
the good of humanity."

And Michael, Kitty told herself wretchedly, had been compelled to live his life with such men. . . . She bit her lip
fiercely, stifling an angry rejoinder. Dominic did not understand; he saw all convicts in the same light, and despite his

efforts to help her—which had been considerable—he had no
real sympathy for Michael's cause. Rather he had made those
efforts for *her,* and it was becoming increasingly evident that he
expected favors in return. And that spelled danger, for he was a
married man and Hobart had more than its share of clacking
tongues.

"Then it would appear that your brother has made good his
escape," Dominic went on, breaking the little silence that had
fallen between them. "Or perhaps he hasn't yet come to the
town. Did the villains who were captured give any information
as to his whereabouts?"

"They told Captain Brown, the officer who questioned them,
that they left Michael at a farmhouse close to where the steamer
—the *Hastings*—went aground," Kitty answered. "But that was
three weeks ago. They claimed that Michael was holding a family called Meldrum to ransom—but they were lying, they were
trying to implicate him in their crimes."

"How do you know that?" Dominic's tone was skeptical.

"Because a search party of Captain Brown's men had been to
the farm," Kitty explained. "They went on board the *Tamar,*
the ship that was sent to tow the *Hastings* back to port. They
reported that all the Meldrums were at liberty and going about
their business quite normally. Michael may have been there, but
he's not there now."

"Then you think he's here, in Hobart?"

"I don't know," Kitty admitted reluctantly. "Patrick and
Johnny are both convinced he is—they are scouring the town
now, on the chance of finding him or finding someone who's
seen him. We *must* find him, Dominic. He doesn't know that
he's been pardoned, and—well, it's essential that he's told about
the pardon. Before—that is—" She broke off, flushing.

"Before he commits any—er—any act that might be con-
strued as a crime?" Dominic finished for her. "Such as robbery
under arms—bushranging?"

"Yes." Kitty felt her color deepening. "That is the only
course open to escaped convicts, is it not? In the end. And all
poor Michael will be thinking of is—it must be—how to avoid
capture."

"I thought the search for him had been called off," Dominic said.

"The offer of a reward for his apprehension has been withdrawn," Kitty told him. "John Broome saw to that. He called on the governor and on Dr. Hampton this morning. But the search is to continue. As I told you, Patrick and Johnny are scouring the town, and—"

"It's a big town now," Dominic reminded her. "Close on a quarter of the population of Tasmania resides here. It will be like looking for a needle in a haystack, so if I were you, my dear, I would not build my hopes too high." Dominic paused, looking up at the wall clock above his head. "Time marches on. Will you take lunch with me, Kitty?"

"At your house?" Kitty asked uncertainly.

He shook his head. "I seldom take luncheon at home. Marion entertains her lady friends to luncheon, and I'm not welcome, if I turn up when I'm not expected. Besides, I—oh, Lord, Kitty, you must know how much I enjoy your company! There's a pleasant little eating house in the next street, kept by a Frenchman, so I promise you the food is excellent. And afterward, if you would care to, we could go for a ride—out in the country. It's a while since my horses had a pipe-opener—they're just eating their heads off in the stables. And you handle the gray filly, Snowgoose, so beautifully."

Kitty was tempted. The occasional rides on Dominic's fine horses were always a pleasure to her, but usually Patrick came with them, and in his presence Dominic behaved circumspectly. Alone and unchaperoned, he might be less so. She had been aware for some time of the feelings he had for her, although up till now he had been careful to restrain himself. He was an attractive man—handsome and erudite, always good company, and a practiced horseman—yet . . . her conscience pricked her. He *had* helped immensely in the search for Michael, sometimes at considerable personal risk, for had it not been he who had arranged the meeting with Martin Cash—the man who had succeeded in escaping from Port Arthur—well knowing the purpose for which she and Patrick had wanted to make contact with him?

"Then thank you," she acknowledged, smiling. "I'd particularly like to ride out into the country, Dominic. I—"

"In the hope, no doubt, of finding some clue as to your brother's present whereabouts?" Dominic challenged, a hint of sullenness in his deep voice.

"That, of course," Kitty agreed. "It's why we're here, is it not—to try to find Michael? It's more urgent than ever now."

"He may have left Hobart—left Tasmania, Kitty. Have you considered that as a serious possibility? He's had time to find a ship—some of the masters aren't too particular. I mean—"

"I know what you mean," Kitty retorted with asperity. "But Michael was an officer in the Royal Navy, you know. And if he *has* taken passage to—to New South Wales or Victoria or even to New Zealand, Patrick and I will follow him."

"Then *I* hope he's still in Tasmania," Dominic said. "It will break my heart if you leave here, Kitty. You're—oh, God, you're the most beautiful woman I've ever known! Meeting you has—has changed my life."

He looked so downcast that Kitty stifled the impulse to reprove him. Instead she said gently, "You should not talk like that, Dominic, truly you should not. You know it cannot lead anywhere, even if I wanted it to—and I don't. I'm committed, you must understand that."

"Committed to your other admirer, John Broome?" Dominic challenged with a bitterness he made no attempt to hide. "Is that it, Kitty?"

She denied his accusation with a flash of anger.

"No—to finding my brother Michael! John is a good friend, a very good and generous friend. Like you, he has gone out of his way to help us. And he—"

"And he is free, of course—free to marry you. Whereas I am not." Dominic's anger matched hers, and Kitty rose quickly to her feet.

"I have no intention of marrying anyone," she told him, with icy restraint. And it was the truth. Johnny Broome was also an attractive man, and one of great integrity and charm—but so far as marriage was concerned, she had scarcely given it serious consideration since arriving in Australia. It was on Michael's account that she and Patrick had come to Australia, for his sake that they had gone to Norfolk Island and then come here. She could not, *would* not permit herself to be diverted from the search, by Dominic or Johnny Broome or any man, until they found Michael and were able to give him the glad news that he had been granted a royal pardon.

"I think," she began, picking up her parasol and moving toward the door, "I think perhaps it might be best to postpone our luncheon, Dominic. You—"

Raised voices from the outer office caused her to break off; a moment later the door opened and Patrick and Johnny appeared, ushering between them a young man in the garb of a farmer, stocky and dark-haired and plainly exceedingly nervous and ill at ease.

"We struck it lucky at last!" Patrick exclaimed excitedly. "And by the purest chance." He turned apologetically to Dominic. "Forgive us for bursting in here like this, all unheralded, Dominic, but I knew Kitty was coming here, and I simply had to give her the good news. This lad"—he gestured to the stocky young farmer—"is Oscar Meldrum. It was at his father's holding that Michael found refuge. Oscar, this is Mr. Dominic Hayes, editor and proprietor of the Hobart *Chronicle.*"

Oscar Meldrum touched his straw hat and then hurriedly removed it from his head, murmuring an acknowledgment of the introduction in awed tones. He seated himself on the edge of the chair Dominic drew up for him, clutching the hat nervously in big, work-scarred hands. There was a faded bruise on his forehead, Kitty noticed, and anxious to put him at ease, she went to him, holding out her hand.

"I'm Michael's sister," she told him, smiling. "And I think we must be in your family's debt, Mr. Meldrum, on Michael's account."

The young man found his voice then. "Oh, no, ma'am," he denied. "It's the other way about—we're all in Mr. Wexford's debt. We reckon he saved our lives."

"Saved your lives?" Dominic echoed, unable to hide his astonishment. "How in the world did he do that?"

Oscar Meldrum started to explain, but Johnny cut him short. "Maybe we should begin at the beginning, Oscar. Mr. Hayes has not yet heard how we found you. It really was the most stupendous slice of luck, you see." He was addressing her, Kitty realized, and there was elation in his voice. "We'd been asking questions all over town, Patrick and I, without any glimmer of success, and then, passing an agricultural supplier's, we noticed Oscar's wagon in the yard. It had the name on it—Amos Meldrum, Baker's Creek Farm—and Patrick remembered that was where those rogues who wrecked the *Hastings* steamer told Captain Brown they'd last seen Michael. So we made ourselves known—just in time, wasn't it, Oscar? For he was making his last call for stores and was about to set off for home."

Oscar nodded. "Yes, that's right, sir."

"Tell your story," Johnny invited. "Just as you told it to us. And don't worry about getting your family into trouble, lad. We'll see to it that you don't."

Nervously at first, Oscar obediently launched into his account of what had occurred at his father's farm following Michael's sudden appearance there.

"We was out harvestin', so we never seen him when he first turned up. My little sister—she's badly crippled, so she wasn't working with the rest of us—Prudence let him in. He was wet and cold. He'd swum ashore, seemingly when them absconders turned on him and the ship's master and tried to kill them. But the master, Captain Tarr, was hit bad and he died. . . ." Gathering confidence from the concerted interest of his listeners, Oscar continued his story, describing in stark detail the raid by Michael's three fellow convicts.

"There was nothin' we could do. They was all armed, and my pa had put the only weapon we had—an old flintlock musket— in the larder. They tied me and my brother and Pa to chairs, but they didn't tie Mr. Wexford up, or my wife or my ma or Prudence. The rogue they called Haines kept a gun on Mr. Wexford and made him fetch liquor for them, while my ma was fixin' them a meal. One of them hit me with his musket butt—" Oscar gingerly touched the bruise on his forehead. "So I was pretty well out of my senses when they was eatin' and drinkin'. I only came to when Mr. Wexford fetched the old flintlock out of the larder and went for Haines with it."

Warming to his subject, he gave a graphic description of the struggle that had ensued in the lamp-lit kitchen of the farm-house, and Kitty listened, her throat tight.

"Haines would have shot me, if Mr. Wexford hadn't knocked the pistol out of his hand," the young farmer went on. "One of them lost his nerve and legged it out of the house, which narrowed the odds a bit, and my ma got hold of one of their muskets, while Martha, my wife, and little Pru was tryin' to cut us free. Haines saw he was licked and said they'd go and no' trouble us no more, but the little man—the one they called Josh —he seemed to go crazy. Haines was makin' for the yard when Josh went for Mr. Wexford with a bayonet he had, and the flintlock misfired. He stabbed Mr. Wexford in the arm, screechin' an' yellin' like a banshee, and then, when he seen him fall, he legged it outside after the others. We didn't see no more of them, thank God!"

"What happened to Mr. Wexford?" Kitty asked anxiously. "Was he badly hurt?"

"He was bleedin' badly," Oscar answered. "But my ma took care o' that and put him to bed. He was with us for a couple of weeks, and then he said he wanted to come here, to Hobart. He was aimin' to sign on a ship if he could find a master to take him—wanted to quit Tasmania, he said, and get to Victoria if he could. He had some reason why he had to go to Melbourne, but he never told us what it was. All I know is that he mentioned havin' to find someone there, a man who owed him somethin'. He—" Oscar hesitated, looking from one to the other of them uncertainly. Finally he appealed to Johnny. "You did say you'd see my family didn't get into trouble over helpin' Mr. Wexford, didn't you, sir? 'Cause they *did* help him. *I* helped him—I drove him to the outskirts of town. We owed him our help, sir."

"You shall not be blamed for that, Oscar," Johnny assured him. "I'll intercede on your behalf with His Excellency the governor, if necessary." He laid a hand on the young man's shoulder. "How else did you help Mr. Wexford? Speak freely, lad . . . Mr. Wexford has been granted a pardon—that's why it is so important that we find him. He doesn't know, you see."

Oscar looked relieved. "That's good news, sir, about the pardon. As to how else we helped him—well, my pa gave him clothes and seaman's papers that had belonged to an old ticket-of-leave convict who died after working for us for a couple of years. His name was Blaney—Thomas Albert Blaney. Mr. Wexford had his ticket-of-leave, too, sir, and a letter from my pa givin' him permission to come to Hobart for stores. None of 'em would have held water if the police had checked the records, of course, but Pa reckoned the seaman's papers would get Mr. Wexford a berth."

Kitty, who had followed his account with rapt attention, gave vent to a little cry. "Do you think, then, that he has left Hobart? Do you think he found a vessel to give him passage?"

Oscar met her gaze uneasily. "Truth to tell, I don't know, ma'am. But he was right determined—I reckon he'll have made a good try."

Dominic got to his feet. "My people will have a list of ships departing this port and their destinations. I'll get it. We might be able to narrow the search, at least. Michael may still be on board one that hasn't yet sailed."

It was a slim hope, Kitty reflected, but . . . perhaps it *would* narrow their search.

"Can I go now, Mr. Broome?" Oscar asked diffidently. "They'll be expectin' me back home, and—"

"Wait a minute, Oscar," Patrick said quickly. "There's one other thing—one other service you could perform that will help Mr. Wexford. Johnny—" He looked across at Johnny for confirmation. "If Oscar were to tell the story he's just told us to the police or, better still, perhaps, to a police magistrate, it might save Michael from being charged with any offense against the Meldrums."

"Swear an affidavit, you mean? Yes." Johnny nodded emphatically. "Indeed it would. We could go and find a magistrate right away, if you are willing, Oscar. Then you can set off home —it shouldn't take too long."

Dominic returned with a list in his hand.

"My father's a magistrate," he offered. "And he'll be at home for luncheon. And I agree, Pat—it would be a wise precaution, in view of the false claims made by the rogues they arrested." He spread the handwritten list on the desk in front of him. "Here we are . . . the choices aren't great. Only two vessels left port this morning—the brig *Mercedes,* master Silas Deacon, destination Geelong, with a cargo of New Zealand timber. And the wool clipper *Avalon,* master Joseph Mercer, destination Port Jackson, cargo trade goods and machinery." He frowned. "One of my people said that the *Avalon* was taking on hands. A number of her crew deserted, and two were injured in a storm. Sounds the more likely, don't you think?"

"Perhaps," Patrick conceded. He turned to Oscar. "Are you sure Mr. Wexford was aiming to take passage to Victoria?"

Oscar shrugged. " 'Deed I'm not certain sure, sir. He just mentioned it, that was all. I reckon though—well, I reckon he'd have signed on any ship, whatever its destination, just to get clean away from Tasmania."

"There are five other vessels in port, due to sail within the next ten days," Dominic put in. He read the names from his list and then looked up, brows raised in mute question. "I can send one of my reporters out to the ships that are still in the port. He can make discreet inquiries as to whom they've signed on."

"Oh, thanks, Dominic," Patrick acknowledged. He hesitated. "I think I'd better go with your man, just in case Michael *is* on board one of these ships. There are two or three sealers, too, that might bear investigation. Can you arrange for Oscar to swear an affidavit, Johnny, if I go? We don't want to hold him up."

"Yes, gladly," Johnny agreed. "You ready, Oscar? If we can settle the matter now, you'll be able to leave well before dusk." Receiving Oscar's assent, he glanced inquiringly at Kitty, but Dominic swiftly intervened.

"Kitty is lunching with me, John, and then we're going for a ride. You promised," he added, lowering his voice, as Kitty started to demur. "Please, Kitty, don't deprive me of the pleasure. It may not be mine for much longer. If Michael has managed to reach Sydney or Melbourne, you said yourself that you'll follow him." His tone was almost pleading, bereft of the arrogance he habitually displayed, and Kitty found herself once again reluctant to hurt him.

She gave her assent, avoiding Johnny's gaze but conscious of his unspoken reproach, and Dominic, seizing on his momentary advantage, said with a swift change of tone, "I'm giving you another chance to ingratiate yourself with my father, John. He's thinking of setting up in competition with the *Chronicle,* I've heard, with *you* as his right hand! This story will delight him."

Johnny stared at him in surprise. "I didn't think—"

"You didn't think I knew? Good God, there are no secrets in Hobart, and the old man's been talking to my printers. It's true, isn't it?"

"It's a possibility, yes," Johnny admitted. "But that's all it is, and I haven't come to any decision yet. It depends on—oh, a number of things. But mainly, of course, it depends on Kitty, as I'm sure you are aware." He grasped Oscar's arm and left the office before either Kitty or Dominic could reply.

"The devil take him!" Dominic swore softly under his breath. Then, realizing that Patrick was scowling at him, he recovered himself. "You'll join us, won't you, Pat? It will be time enough to go out to the anchorage after we've eaten."

"Yes, do, Pat," Kitty urged, and the awkward moment passed. Over an excellent luncheon, they talked amicably enough, but Kitty was tense and unhappy, wishing that she had not agreed to the ride and seeking for some excuse to break her promise, without giving Dominic cause to reproach her. He, however, behaved with punctilious courtesy throughout the afternoon, making no mention of his feelings, and finally Kitty gave herself up to the sheer exhilaration of their ride together in the beautiful, deserted country beyond the boundaries of the town. She had always loved horses and was happily at her ease on the mettlesome filly Snowgoose as she galloped at Dominic's side, now passing him, then reining in to enable him to draw level with her, hair flying loose in the wind and cheeks aglow.

"It will be a thousand pities if you have to leave here just as our racing season is beginning," Dominic told her, when they pulled up and prepared to turn for home. "You'd make a superb jockey for that filly, you know. She's entered for a sweepstake race over at Bell Farm on Saturday. It's a private affair, organized by the Hunt, but there are some pretty substantial wagers on it."

"But women do not ride in races here, do they?" Kitty suggested.

"No. Do they in Ireland—in County Wexford?"

She laughed. "No, not officially. But I've ridden in a few races—in Pat's name, with my hair tucked under my cap. It was wonderful! I never won, but I enjoyed every moment of it—until my father found out and put a stop to it. We rode over fences, not on the flat, of course—and there was always the hunting, even if I wasn't allowed to race anymore. I loved the hunting."

"I don't imagine there were many who could match you," Dominic said.

"Michael was better than any of us," Kitty asserted.

"That's hard to believe!"

"Ah, but you've never met Michael."

"True," Dominic answered thoughtfully. "But there must be something very special about him to inspire such devotion in his brother and sister. To bring you and Pat to the other side of the world in search of him, I mean."

It was true, Kitty thought. She said, with quiet conviction, "I don't regret coming. How could I, after reading that diary we found on Norfolk Island? You read it—you know what Michael endured at the hands of Commandant Price. In his case, as you said this morning, the mills of God did grind exceeding small, and I cannot feel the smallest pang of sorrow for his death or the manner of it. I wonder if Michael knows that Mr. Price is dead?"

"It will be in all the papers, Kitty—the *Chronicle* will publish the obituary I showed you. And there'll be talk, of course. Wherever he is," Dominic offered consolingly, "I'm sure that your brother will get to know. And he'll feel no sorrow."

"No. I just pray to God that we may find him, Dominic, before—" A lump rose in Kitty's throat, and she could not go on.

"Before it's too late," Dominic finished for her, as he had done earlier, when they had talked in the *Chronicle* office. This time she sensed genuine pity in his voice as he added gravely, "Perhaps he hasn't left Hobart yet, Kitty—perhaps he's on board one of the ships in the anchorage and Pat will find him." His hand closed about hers. "Come with me to Bell Farm on Saturday, my dear. It will take your mind off your worries, at least for an afternoon. Please, Kitty!"

She consented abstractedly, her thoughts elsewhere, but when she returned to the hotel, neither Patrick nor Johnny had any news to give her.

"All I know," Patrick said despondently, "is that Michael's not in this harbor. We visited every ship. The only information I was able to glean was that the wool clipper, the *Avalon,* signed eleven men before she sailed. Her master interviewed men yesterday, in a waterfront tavern. There's no record of the *Mercedes'* signing anyone—only that one of her mates came ashore last night, to round up drunks. Johnny says she's owned by a very old friend of his, a man named Claus Van Buren, who owns several trading vessels. And—" He turned to Johnny. "You tell her the rest, Johnny."

"Claus just came into port," Johnny said eagerly. "In his American-built clipper, the *Dolphin.* I went out to her, and Claus told me he would be sailing for Sydney within the next two or three days. He offered to give us passage, and—she's a very fast sailer, Kitty. We could not hope to catch the *Avalon,* but we shouldn't be far behind her. And—I think the chances are that Michael was one of the men who signed on as deckhands, so—" He looked at her expectantly. "What do you say? Shall we go back to Sydney and hope our guess is the right one?"

"We?" Kitty echoed uncertainly. "Do you mean—"

Patrick answered her. "You and Johnny. He has to go back to Sydney to square things with his editor. But we cannot be sure Michael sailed in the *Avalon,* Kit. It's within the bounds of possibility that he managed to get a berth on board Claus Van Buren's *Mercedes,* so . . ." He came to take both her hands in his. "We'll have to divide our forces. I'll stay on here and continue the search until I can take passage to Geelong or Port Phillip. And—"

"Why can't I stay with you?" Kitty objected.

"The Victoria goldfields are no place for a lady, Kit," Patrick pointed out gently. "And that's probably where I'll be headed, if Michael *did* sail with the *Mercedes* after all. I'd let you know, of course, if I manage to find any trace of him. There's a regular mail service between Melbourne and Sydney, and we could arrange a rendezvous."

"Yes, but—" Kitty faced him, tears in her eyes. "We've always been together, Pat, and we—we started this search together. I want to stay with you."

"Kit, Michael's going to need a home, someone to care for him if he's in Sydney—and I'm pretty sure that's where he'll be. Mine could well turn out to be a wild goose chase, you know, but we can't take the risk of *not* looking for him in Geelong. And again, love, he might decide to stay with the *Mercedes*— she's bound for Sydney, after she's discharged her cargo in Geelong, Van Buren told us. . . ." He talked on, his arguments and his reasoning impossible to refute, and finally Kitty gave her unhappy consent to the change in their plans. Johnny, she knew, could not be the one to stay in Hobart, without risking the loss of his job on the Sydney *Morning Herald*. And old Mr. Hayes had not yet launched his new paper. There were unexpected holdups, Johnny told her, and in addition there was strong opposition from Dominic, which, understandably, worried his father.

"I've my living to earn, Kitty," he added apologetically. "And Pat's a free agent. It has to be this way, I'm afraid."

His tone, Kitty realized, was more than a little hurt, and her conscience pricked her on his account, not for the first time. Even more than Dominic had done, Johnny had gone out of his way to help their search, she reminded herself, and she was swiftly contrite.

"I understand, Johnny," she assured him. "And I'm truly grateful to you. Both Pat and I know how much we owe you. It's just that, as I said, Pat and I have always been together. We're twins, you see, and—"

"It won't be for long, Kit," her brother assured her. "And of course, if you *do* find Michael in Sydney, I'll be on my way back there the instant you tell me so."

Johnny left them to go out again to the *Dolphin* to confirm with Claus Van Buren the passages he had provisionally been offered, and on his return to join Kitty and Patrick for dinner, he was waving a letter in his hand.

"The Sydney mail's just in," he told them, "and there's a letter from Red. He writes that he was back in time for the arrival of his firstborn. I'm now the proud uncle of a lovely little girl, weighing seven pounds, two ounces, at birth, who is to be christened Jessica. But, alas, Red will not be there when we arrive—the *Galah* is ordered to Singapore, to pick up troops for China, where, it seems, the war goes on. And there is trouble in India, Red says, but so far it's only a rumor, and it may not amount to anything serious."

Kitty was suddenly reminded of Colonel William De Lancey and his wife—Johnny Broome's sister—whose farewell reception she had attended in Sydney. She looked at Johnny and guessed, from his expression, that he too was thinking of the De Lanceys. "Perhaps," she offered sympathetically, "the trouble in India will blow over. There are always rumors, Johnny."

"Yes," Johnny agreed, tight-lipped. "There are always rumors, Kitty. I hope and pray that is all there are." He shrugged and added, "Claus Van Buren won't be sailing until Monday—he has to fit a new foretopmast, he told me. But our passage is confirmed, and we can go on board any time we like on Sunday."

Which would leave her free to attend the race meeting to which Dominic had invited her, Kitty thought, recalling the invitation with some slight misgiving. But perhaps it *would* distract her from her worries; and if Pat came with her, there would be no risk of giving offense to Marion Hayes, if, as seemed probable, she accompanied her husband to . . . what had Dominic called the place? Bell Farm—that was it. A private meeting, organized by the Hunt, could well be very entertaining, although it was unlikely to engender the excitement and friendly informality of a similar meeting in her native Ireland, where everyone knew everyone else and the wagers were in sixpences and shillings, rather than pounds.

On Saturday, however, Kitty found herself alone when Dominic Hayes arrived in his carriage to pick her up, Patrick and Johnny having ridden out to interview the master of a sealer who was said to have signed on three men suspected by the police of being ticket-of-leave absconders.

And Dominic, too, was by himself.

"Marion is bored to tears by anything to do with horseflesh," Dominic said lightly, sensing Kitty's unspoken thoughts, as he handed her into the carriage. "And she disapproves of my betting." He grinned, with boyish bravado. "I've fifty sovereigns on Snowgoose in the Master's Cup and a hundred on my other entry, running in the first race, Lucifer. But he should win pretty comfortably—I've the lad who rides for Edward Rowe on him, and the opposition isn't up to much, apart from a horse called Flying Buck. But he's a four-year-old, and Lucifer's seven, so we have an advantage in the weight for age handicapping." His smile widened when he saw Kitty's look of mystification. "That's how we do it here, so that an older horse isn't penalized, even if it's won a few races."

He explained the system, as he took his place beside her and the carriage moved off. "The Hunt races are restricted to home-bred horses—bred in Australia, I mean, not necessarily in the state. Snowgoose's sire was a purebred Arab named Afghan Hawk, owned by the Rowe brothers of Melbourne, which won the Victoria Turf Club Derby." Dominic sighed. "But my little filly will be up against it this afternoon, Kitty—that's why I'm only risking fifty on her. The Master's Cup has attracted some formidable entries. There's Rose of April and Tomboy, for a start, and Cooramina and a very fine mare called Starflight, which Rowe's lad is riding. They're all quality horses over two miles. Lord, how I wish you'd agree to my putting you up on Snowgoose! The filly goes for you—you have such magical hands. My boy is all whip and heels—he does not bring out the best in her. But you would romp home, I know you would."

Kitty looked down at her flowing skirts and shook her bonneted head, her smile rueful. "In Pat's name, I suppose? But hardly attired like this, Dominic."

"You've taken Pat's name before," Dominic reminded her. "You said so yourself. And as to your attire—I have the silks with me, as it happens, and we'll be passing the *Chronicle* office in a few minutes. It's Saturday, so there will be no one there except the caretaker. You could change in my private office, and not a soul would be the wiser. Please, Kitty!" He leaned toward her, and Kitty saw, from the expression on his good-looking face, that—far from jesting—he was in grim earnest. "This race means a great deal to me, apart from the money—although that counts too, I admit, because the *Chronicle*'s going through a sticky patch at the moment and I could use some ready cash."

She hesitated, taken by surprise at his seeming urgency and tempted, in spite of herself, by the prospect of riding in a race again. It was not for nothing that the good folk of Kilclare had called her Madcap Kitty, but—

"Look," Dominic said, breaking into her thoughts. "I'll make you an offer. Win the race for me and I'll withdraw my opposition to the new paper my father wants to launch. That would ensure that John Broome lands a job here. Or if you prefer it, the *Chronicle* will commission him to find your brother Michael and write his story, all expenses paid. Kitty, I'm begging you!"

Both were incredible offers, and Kitty stared at him, momentarily bereft of words. "But would it not be breaking the Hunt rules?" she finally managed uncertainly. "My riding, I mean?"

Dominic shook his head. "There's nothing in the rules to preclude you from riding. The race is open to amateur riders, sex unspecified. As long as you make the handicapper's weight and I enter you in Pat's name, for your own protection—not to conform to any rules—there could not be any objection." They were nearing the *Chronicle* office and he called to the coachman to slow down. "Come on, Kit, say you'll do it! Damn it, with you in the saddle Snowgoose will win!"

Perhaps if she had not been booked to leave Hobart the next day, Kitty would have thought twice about it, but as it was . . . She drew in her breath sharply and then gave her assent, conscious of a quickening of her pulses. There was a risk, she knew, that someone might recognize her. But her resemblance to Pat was very close; and in racing silks, with a cap pulled down over her hair, the risk was small. And perhaps . . .

Dominic gave her no time to reconsider. He rushed her into the office, dismissed the caretaker, and laid out breeches, boots, and gaily colored silk jacket on the desk in his private room. When she had changed, he brought her an overcoat, wrapped it about her, and hurried her out to the carriage.

When they reached their destination, he bade her remain in the concealment of the carriage.

"I'll come for you when it's time to weigh in. Until then, don't show yourself, just in case. Pat has made a good many friends, and some of them are probably here."

He was gone for what seemed to Kitty a very long time, and as she crouched in the dark interior of the carriage, hearing the distant sound of raised voices and galloping hooves, her earlier excitement faded and she began bitterly to regret her impulsive promise. This was different from the happy-go-lucky racing of Kilclare; a picnic race meeting it might be called, but large sums of money would be changing hands. Had not Dominic told her that he had wagered 150 pounds on his two horses? Probably, such was apparently his faith in her horsemanship, he had increased that sum—doubled it, even, and backed Snowgoose to win. And she could fail . . . she had no experience of race riding in Australia. She had not walked the course—had scarcely done more than glimpse it, from the curtained window of the carriage. She—Kitty tensed, guessing from the shouts and cheering reaching her from outside that the first race had been run, the winner decided.

Dominic returned at last, glum and despondent.

"Flying Buck won by twenty lengths," he told her. "Lucifer was not even placed. That's my hundred sovereigns down the drain. But never mind, I'll recoup my losses on Snowgoose, Kit. You've got to win!"

"I may not even be placed," Kitty warned him miserably. "Oh, Dominic, this is madness! I don't know the course, and I've only hacked the filly. Find someone else to ride her, please. You—"

"It's too late now, Kitty." Dominic got in beside her and, taking a used envelope from his pocket, made a quick sketch of the course. "Only the start and finish are fenced—the rest is flagged. You've a sharp left-hand turn here at three furlongs, see? Keep on the outside and then work your way into the center after the turn, and try to get out in front, if you can, when the ground rises. The filly should get her second wind after that, but don't push too hard until you're on the flat again."

He went carefully into every aspect of the tactics he wanted her to employ, and Kitty tried, with a sinking heart and a sick sensation in the pit of her stomach, to take it all in. There were two circuits of the track—that much she understood—and then there was a straight run in, on level ground, to the finish. And there were twenty-three horses entered for the Master's Cup. The gray Starflight, ridden by the owner's son, presented the greatest danger, in Dominic's opinion. Rose of April, a chestnut with a white blaze, had won some good races; and the two bays, Tomboy and Cooramina, would need to be reckoned with. The last named would almost certainly go into the lead early on.

"She's not a stayer. You can afford to let her make the pace on the first circuit," Dominic ended. He smiled at her and then impulsively drew her to him, his lips seeking hers hungrily. He had been drinking, Kitty realized, suddenly sickened and angry with herself for having let him talk her into such an act of madness as riding in this race undoubtedly was. She freed herself and snapped back at him with a flash of temper.

"Leave me be, Dominic. You have no right, you—"

"Very well," he retorted sullenly. "It's a bit like embracing one of my own sex with you in those silks, anyway. No one will recognize the Lady Kitty Cadogan, that is certain." He took out his pocket watch and forced a smile. "It's time you weighed in. And, if it's any satisfaction to you, I've got cold feet, too!"

But the weighing-in was accomplished without incident; they went into the paddock, Dominic careful to keep her apart from the other riders as they trooped out of the tent to where the twenty-three horses were being led round by their grooms. Once in the saddle and on the way to the start, Kitty felt her nervousness vanish. The die was cast; there could be no going back now, she told herself. The ordeal would soon be over, and win or lose, she could only do her best.

"Good luck to you, Pat!" A voice shouted from the crowd of spectators, and she had the presence of mind to wave briefly in response. The starter, mounted on a stout cob, bawled at them to get into line, and she recalled Dominic's advice and took Snowgoose to the outside, finding the chestnut Rose of April beside her. The other gray, Starflight, was in the center. Rose of April's rider, a pleasant-faced youngster in red-and-green hooped colors, gave her a friendly grin.

"It's quite a turn, by the three-furlong post. Let's hope they don't rush at it hell for leather, eh?"

The starter raised his flag before Kitty could reply, and as the line of horses wavered, he let it fall and they were off, thundering across the green turf like a flood suddenly released.

Kitty afterward could remember little of the first part of the race. She did not press Snowgoose, letting her tuck in just behind Rose of April, both horses keeping to the outside. The curve negotiated, she eased the filly into a gap that conveniently appeared a dozen lengths behind a big, long-striding bay, which —in the light of Dominic's forecast—she took to be Cooramina. Rose of April came with her, and together they breasted a gentle slope, the chestnut's friendly young rider calling out something she could not catch, save for the name by which he addressed her—Mr. Cadogan.

He, at least, did not harbor any suspicions as to her identity, Kitty thought, and, taking comfort from this realization, began to enjoy the heady exhilaration of the breathless, headlong race down the slope. They entered the second circuit, and now, out of the corner of her eye, she glimpsed a gray shape starting to forge ahead—Starflight had emerged from a knot of tiring horses and was gaining ground with seemingly effortless speed, passing Cooramina as if the big bay mare were standing still. Recalled to Dominic's need to recoup his betting losses, Kitty urged Snowgoose forward in pursuit, and the filly responded instantly, Rose of April a yard or so behind but keeping pace with her.

They were approaching the turn at the three-furlong post when, without warning, disaster struck. Starflight's rider took the turn too fast and, in an effort to increase his lead, a shade too sharply, and the gray went down in a tangle of flailing legs, flinging its rider heavily to the ground. He fell squarely in Snowgoose's path, and instinctively the filly tried to swerve to avoid trampling him. But they were too close, and with Rose of April almost level, a multiple crash would have been inevitable. Kitty did the only thing possible, her reaction as instinctive as that of her mount. With hands and heels she lifted her, and Snowgoose responded with a wild leap that carried her over the prostrate man, leaving him untouched and able—though Kitty did not see him—to roll clear of the following horses.

Rose of April had swerved and lost ground in consequence, and suddenly Kitty found herself alone, her lead unchallenged, the slope rising in front of her, and she sensed that she had only to keep going and she would win. For a moment she was undecided; it seemed an injustice to snatch victory that might well not have been hers, had it not been for the accident to Starflight —but then she heard the other horses pounding after her and heard Rose of April's young jockey shout a challenge.

"I'm after you, Cadogan!"

Pat would not have pulled up, she told herself. He would have made a race of it, and since she had stolen his name . . . Kitty leaned out on Snowgoose's sweat-damp neck and urged her down the slope, again using hands and heels to best advantage. The brave little filly quickened her stride and, regaining the rhythm she had lost during her rider's moment of doubt, galloped smoothly past the winning post with Rose of April laboring a clear three lengths behind her.

The cheers were deafening, and as Dominic led her in, hands reached out to pat Snowgoose's neck and nose and even her quarters, while others sought to shake Kitty by the hand, calling out congratulations.

"Well done, sir, well done indeed!"

"That was a fine bit of riding, Mr. Cadogan!"

"Well ridden, Pat! You excelled yourself!"

Kitty saw Starflight come in, her rider on foot, leading her, and both apparently unscathed.

"I knew you'd do it," Dominic exulted, turning to look up at her, flushed and almost beside himself with excitement and relief. "But by heaven I didn't know how well! That truly was a fine piece of riding, Kit!"

In his excitement he had addressed her by name, and as she slipped from the saddle, Kitty whispered tensely, "You must get me away—at once, as soon as I've weighed in."

Somehow, Dominic contrived to usher her through the crowd, draping his coat over her shoulders and walking with his arm about her, fending off those who continued to offer their plaudits and answering for her, as people milled about them, eager to talk to her. The start of the parade for the next race focused the crowd's interest elsewhere and eased the congestion at last, but Kitty was spent and breathless when they reached the carriage, and she stumbled thankfully inside, her taut nerves strung to the breaking point.

"I shall have to stay for the presentation of the cup," Dominic told her. "It would look odd if I didn't. My coachman can drive you back to the hotel, and you can rely on his discretion. He's well paid to keep his mouth shut. Or—" He gestured to a bundle on the seat beside her, and a slow smile spread across his face. "Kit, your own clothes are here. You could change and reappear as Lady Kitty Cadogan, if you had a mind to, and stand proudly at my side as I accept the cup. That would scotch any suspicion, would it not? We could say you were representing your brother, who had urgent business elsewhere."

But Kitty had borne enough. Close to tears, she shook her head. "Tell your coachman to drive me back to town," she pleaded, and cut short Dominic's effusive attempts to thank her. "I won your race for you, so don't forget that bargain you offered."

He looked crestfallen. "You mean I should withdraw my opposition to my father's rival newspaper? Is that what you want?"

"No." Kitty blinked back the tears, recovering her composure. "You said that the *Chronicle* would commission Johnny Broome to find my brother Michael and write his story. *That's* what I mean, Dominic!"

"It's all you've ever wanted, isn't it?" Dominic accused with bitterness. "All you've ever wanted of me or anyone else—even John Broome."

It was, Kitty thought. She inclined her head wordlessly, and Dominic stepped back, defeated, slamming the door of the carriage shut behind him. She heard him shout an order to the coachman.

The carriage moved off, and as the sound of the racegoers' voices faded into silence, she stripped off the silks in which she had aped her brother and, bracing herself against the rolling of the fast-moving vehicle, redonned her own garments and pinned her small, flowered bonnet back on her head.

When the coachman drew up outside the door of the Customs House Hotel, it was with perfect composure that Lady Kitty Cadogan emerged from the carriage, and, with a brief word of thanks—which the man accepted, wooden-faced—she entered the foyer, to find Patrick waiting for her with ill-concealed impatience.

"Thanks be to heaven that you're here, Kit!" he greeted her. "Van Buren's sent word that he wants to sail at first light and that you're to go on board the *Dolphin* right away. I've seen to your baggage, and John's taken it down to the wharf." He eyed her, frowning. "What in the world have you been doing, little sister?"

"It's a long story, Pat," Kitty evaded. "But—" Recalling Dominic's accusation, she smiled. "Helping in the search for Michael, perhaps."

PART TWO

The True Patriots

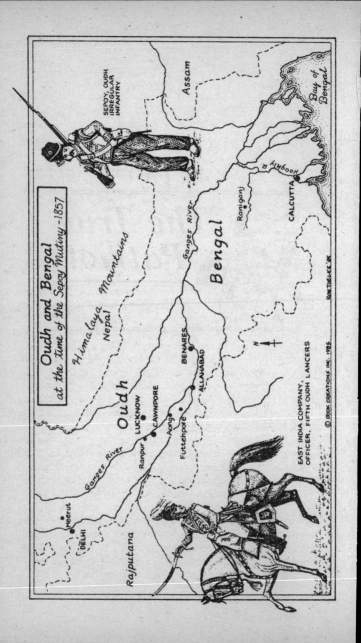

Oudh and Bengal
at the time of the Sepoy Mutiny - 1857

SEPOY, OUDH
IRREGULAR
INFANTRY

Assam

Bay of
Bengal

Himalaya
Nepal Mountains

Ganges River

HOOGHLY R.

Ranigonj

Bengal

CALCUTTA

Oudh

LUCKNOW

Ranpur

CAWNPORE

Anga

Futtehpore

BENARES

ALLAHABAD

N

S

EAST INDIA COMPANY,
OFFICER, FIFTH OUDH LANCERS

© BOOK CREATIONS, INC. 1985.

RON TOELKE '85.

Rajputana

Ganges River

Meerut

DELHI

itapur, Ranpur . . . it was something like that,
some fifty or sixty miles from Lucknow, the capi-
, William had said.
as enlarging on the military situation, talking with
ity of the British troops presently quartered through-
rovince of Bengal and in its capital city, Calcutta.
has been drained of white troops—they have had to be
China, to Burma and Persia, and to the Afghan border.
are barely forty thousand in the whole of India, Com-
er Broome, and about five thousand British officers serv-
ith the East India Company's native regiments." He shook
ead in a despairing gesture. "The sepoys in the three presi-
cy armies—in Madras, Bengal, and Bombay—number in
cess of three hundred thousand, with the bulk of the artillery
their hands. As yet it appears that only the Bengal Army has
narrows the odds to a certain extent, provided
main loyal. But you will un-
y of the governor gener-

ars on

Chapter XIII

HAVING FIRED THE customary salute, the *Galah* steered a careful course through the crowded roadstead and came to anchor in Singapore's harbor.

The passage from Sydney had been uneventful, save for three days and nights of gale-force winds in the Java Sea, when the frigate had been reduced to a close-reefed main topsail and had lost a young seaman in a fall down the after hatchway at the height of the storm. Earlier, in the Sunda Strait, a sudden tropical thunderstorm of unusual violence had turned day into the blackest of nights, taxing Red Broome's navigating skill to the limit. But, staunch vessel that she was, the *Galah* had come through these not-expected perils undamaged and without the loss of a spar, and Red was well pleased with her performance and that of his ship's company.

He had left Sydney with regret, when the survey ship *Herald* had arrived as his relief, bringing orders for him to proceed to Singapore to pick up troops destined to augment the military force engaged in the war with China. He was to convey them to Hong Kong, where the *Galah* would join the flag of Rear Admiral Sir Michael Seymour.

It had been a wrench leaving Magdalen, so soon after the birth of their daughter, whose christening, in the names of Jessica Rachel, had had to be brought forward to the day before his departure, to enable him to attend. . . . Red smothered a sigh. Mother and child had been pictures of health, but Magdalen, understandably, had been distressed and had hinted, for the first time since their marriage, that perhaps the time had come to bring to an end his naval career.

Red repeated his sigh and banished the unwelcome thought. The sea was his life, and for all Magdalen's wistful hints, he could not imagine himself existing permanently ashore . . . and certainly not as a farmer, which had been one of his wife's tentative suggestions. Besides, there were compensations to be considered; the war with China promised opportunities that were lacking in peacetime, and he had battled with the Chinese before, as a young officer serving under Henry Keppel in the frigate *Dido.* There was a rumor, Denham of the *Herald* had told him, that Keppel was on his way out to China in command of the fifty-gun *Raleigh* and with the rank of commodore. It would be more than good to see—aye, and fight with—his old chief again.

"Sir—" His first lieutenant and brother-in-law, Francis De Lancey, broke into his thoughts. "There's a boat putting off to us. Looks like the governor's barge, unless I'm much mistaken, sir."

Surprised, Red turned his glass on the approaching boat. There was a civilian, in a white tropical suit and panama hat, seated in the sternsheets. A young man . . . too young to be the governor, but probably an aide or a secretary, he decided, after a brief scrutiny.

"Be good enough to receive our visitor, Mr. De Lancey," he instructed. "I'd better change, in case I'm required to call on His Excellency right away. I'll be in my cabin if I'm wanted."

The visitor proved, as he had supposed, to be a civilian secretary, a friendly, good-looking young man, who gave his name as Mark Adamson. He accepted the offer of a glass of Madeira, and then—again as Red had anticipated—he voiced the governor's desire to see the *Galah*'s commander at once.

"Fresh orders for you, I believe, sir, and rather urgent ones. So if you could come with me to Government House now, H.E. will be greatly obliged."

There was a carriage waiting on the wharf when they landed, with a Chinese coachman on the box, and they drove up to what was known as the Hill at a spanking pace, passing the

pleasant residences of Si
with its well-kept, luxur
Government House stood
a rambling, commodious e
town and harbor, and uniforme

The governor was waiting in
introduced Red to him. With him
of the 14th Regiment, Colonel Poo
looked grave-faced and worried, as if th
to impart to him was anything but good.

"India, Commander Broome," Gove
nounced grimly, "is in the grip of anarchy.
sepoy regiments of the Bengal Army have bro
tiny. In Meerut, after some disaffection concerne
issue of greased cartridges, all three sepoy regiments
the Europeans, cut down their officers, and
women and children in what a
slaughter and arson. The B
heavily outnumbered
of the gen

murdered white
appears to have been an orgy of
British regiments stationed there were
and—due, it is rumored, to the ineptitude
eral officer in command—the mutineers were permitted to march on Delhi. There they were joined by the native garrison, and similar ghastly scenes of carnage took place. The surviving British civil and military officers and their families were compelled to flee for their lives, leaving the mutineers in possession of both the city and the fort. It is understood that they have proclaimed the last of the Moghuls, the Shah Bahadur, as emperor, and—" He glanced at Colonel Pooley and added somberly, "As may be imagined, Commander, British prestige in India has suffered disastrously, and the governor general, Lord Canning, has made an urgent appeal for troops to be sent to his aid."

Red heard him with a sick sensation in the pit of his stomach, his first, panic thought of his sister Jenny, who, with her husband, William De Lancey, must by this time have reached the station in the recently annexed kingdom of Oudh, where William's new command was garrisoned. What had been the name of the place? He frowned, trying to recollect the address Jenny had given him, written on a scrap of paper, which he had stowed with his personal journal in his cabin on board the *Ga-*

mutinied, which ha[...]
the Madras and Bombay ar[...]
derstand, I am sure, the extreme urgenc[...]
al's request for more British troops."

Red inclined his head, still conscious of his own re[...]
Jenny's account. She had not wanted to go to India, he recalled,
but she had gone, because Will De Lancey had expected it of
her and because she loved him. Lucknow was in Bengal, Will's
regiment a company regiment of Oudh Irregular Cavalry,
and—

"Lord Elgin, the new plenipotentiary to China, left here two
days ago for Hong Kong on board Her Majesty's ship *Shannon*," the governor said. "Before leaving, he instructed me to
hold troops bound for China, pending their redirection to Calcutta. The troopships *Himalaya* and *Simoon,* with the Fifth and
Ninetieth regiments on board, have already been so redirected.
Only the troops *you* were ordered to pick up here and convey to
Hong Kong have proceeded to their original destination. Lord
Elgin took them with him on board the *Shannon,* which, as I
mentioned, left here two days ago. However, before he departed, his lordship confided to me that he ultimately expected
to go to Calcutta himself, in order to assess the situation in
India and consult with the governor general. The news from
China is good . . . you probably have not heard that Commo-

len, understandably, had been distressed and had hinted, for the first time since their marriage, that perhaps the time had come to bring to an end his naval career.

Red repeated his sigh and banished the unwelcome thought. The sea was his life, and for all Magdalen's wistful hints, he could not imagine himself existing permanently ashore . . . and certainly not as a farmer, which had been one of his wife's tentative suggestions. Besides, there were compensations to be considered; the war with China promised opportunities that were lacking in peacetime, and he had battled with the Chinese before, as a young officer serving under Henry Keppel in the frigate *Dido*. There was a rumor, Denham of the *Herald* had told him, that Keppel was on his way out to China in command of the fifty-gun *Raleigh* and with the rank of commodore. It would be more than good to see—aye, and fight with—his old chief again.

"Sir—" His first lieutenant and brother-in-law, Francis De Lancey, broke into his thoughts. "There's a boat putting off to us. Looks like the governor's barge, unless I'm much mistaken, sir."

Surprised, Red turned his glass on the approaching boat. There was a civilian, in a white tropical suit and panama hat, seated in the sternsheets. A young man . . . too young to be the governor, but probably an aide or a secretary, he decided, after a brief scrutiny.

"Be good enough to receive our visitor, Mr. De Lancey," he instructed. "I'd better change, in case I'm required to call on His Excellency right away. I'll be in my cabin if I'm wanted."

The visitor proved, as he had supposed, to be a civilian secretary, a friendly, good-looking young man, who gave his name as Mark Adamson. He accepted the offer of a glass of Madeira, and then—again as Red had anticipated—he voiced the governor's desire to see the *Galah*'s commander at once.

"Fresh orders for you, I believe, sir, and rather urgent ones. So if you could come with me to Government House now, H.E. will be greatly obliged."

There was a carriage waiting on the wharf when they landed, with a Chinese coachman on the box, and they drove up to what was known as the Hill at a spanking pace, passing the

Chapter XIII

HAVING FIRED THE customary salute, the *Galah* steered a careful course through the crowded roadstead and came to anchor in Singapore's harbor.

The passage from Sydney had been uneventful, save for three days and nights of gale-force winds in the Java Sea, when the frigate had been reduced to a close-reefed main topsail and had lost a young seaman in a fall down the after hatchway at the height of the storm. Earlier, in the Sunda Strait, a sudden tropical thunderstorm of unusual violence had turned day into the blackest of nights, taxing Red Broome's navigating skill to the limit. But, staunch vessel that she was, the *Galah* had come through these not-unexpected perils undamaged and without the loss of a spar, and Red was well pleased with her performance and that of his ship's company.

He had left Sydney with regret, when the survey ship *Herald* had arrived as his relief, bringing orders for him to proceed to Singapore to pick up troops destined to augment the military force engaged in the war with China. He was to convey them to Hong Kong, where the *Galah* would join the flag of Rear Admiral Sir Michael Seymour.

It had been a wrench leaving Magdalen, so soon after the birth of their daughter, whose christening, in the names of Jessica Rachel, had had to be brought forward to the day before his departure, to enable him to attend. . . . Red smothered a sigh. Mother and child had been pictures of health, but Magda-

pleasant residences of Singapore's wealthy merchants, each with its well-kept, luxuriant garden and wide expanse of lawn. Government House stood at the summit of Flagstaff Hill; it was a rambling, commodious edifice, with a magnificent view of town and harbor, and uniformed Sikh sentries on guard outside.

The governor was waiting in his office, and Mark Adamson introduced Red to him. With him was the commanding officer of the 14th Regiment, Colonel Pooley, and both, Red saw, looked grave-faced and worried, as if the news they were about to impart to him was anything but good.

"India, Commander Broome," Governor Blundell announced grimly, "is in the grip of anarchy. Most of the native sepoy regiments of the Bengal Army have broken out in mutiny. In Meerut, after some disaffection concerned with a new issue of greased cartridges, all three sepoy regiments turned on the Europeans, cut down their officers and murdered white women and children in what appears to have been an orgy of slaughter and arson. The British regiments stationed there were heavily outnumbered, and—due, it is rumored, to the ineptitude of the general officer in command—the mutineers were permitted to march on Delhi. There they were joined by the native garrison, and similar ghastly scenes of carnage took place. The surviving British civil and military officers and their families were compelled to flee for their lives, leaving the mutineers in possession of both the city and the fort. It is understood that they have proclaimed the last of the Moghuls, the Shah Bahadur, as emperor, and—" He glanced at Colonel Pooley and added somberly, "As may be imagined, Commander, British prestige in India has suffered disastrously, and the governor general, Lord Canning, has made an urgent appeal for troops to be sent to his aid."

Red heard him with a sick sensation in the pit of his stomach, his first, panic thought of his sister Jenny, who, with her husband, William De Lancey, must by this time have reached the station in the recently annexed kingdom of Oudh, where William's new command was garrisoned. What had been the name of the place? He frowned, trying to recollect the address Jenny had given him, written on a scrap of paper, which he had stowed with his personal journal in his cabin on board the *Ga-*

lah. Pirpur, Sitapur, Ranpur . . . it was something like that, an outstation some fifty or sixty miles from Lucknow, the capital of Oudh, William had said.

Pooley was enlarging on the military situation, talking with equal gravity of the British troops presently quartered throughout the Province of Bengal and in its capital city, Calcutta.

"India has been drained of white troops—they have had to be sent to China, to Burma and Persia, and to the Afghan border. There are barely forty thousand in the whole of India, Commander Broome, and about five thousand British officers serving with the East India Company's native regiments." He shook his head in a despairing gesture. "The sepoys in the three presidency armies—in Madras, Bengal, and Bombay—number in excess of three hundred thousand, with the bulk of the artillery in their hands. As yet it appears that only the Bengal Army has mutinied, which narrows the odds to a certain extent, provided the Madras and Bombay armies remain loyal. But you will understand, I am sure, the extreme urgency of the governor general's request for more British troops."

Red inclined his head, still conscious of his own fears on Jenny's account. She had not wanted to go to India, he recalled, but she had gone, because Will De Lancey had expected it of her and because she loved him. Lucknow was in Bengal, Will's regiment a company regiment of Oudh Irregular Cavalry, and—

"Lord Elgin, the new plenipotentiary to China, left here two days ago for Hong Kong on board Her Majesty's ship *Shannon,*" the governor said. "Before leaving, he instructed me to hold troops bound for China, pending their redirection to Calcutta. The troopships *Himalaya* and *Simoon,* with the Fifth and Ninetieth regiments on board, have already been so redirected. Only the troops *you* were ordered to pick up here and convey to Hong Kong have proceeded to their original destination. Lord Elgin took them with him on board the *Shannon,* which, as I mentioned, left here two days ago. However, before he departed, his lordship confided to me that he ultimately expected to go to Calcutta himself, in order to assess the situation in India and consult with the governor general. The news from China is good . . . you probably have not heard that Commo-

dore Elliot destroyed the Chinese fleet in Escape Creek, and
Commodore Keppel, a very short while afterward, fought a
brilliant action at Fatshan. Indeed—"

Colonel Pooley spoke up, a hint of impatience in his voice.
"Your Excellency will recall the reason why Commander
Broome was summoned in such haste—the engineer detach-
ment at present under my command, sir."

"Ah, yes, the engineers," the governor echoed. "Eighty men
of the Royal Engineers, to be exact, whose commanding officer
is a railway expert, Colonel Pooley tells me. They too were en
route to Hong Kong, but it seems to both of us, in view of the
governor general's appeal and Lord Elgin's parting instructions,
that there is a greater need for them in India than anywhere
else. I understand that a rail link between Calcutta and Allahabad is in the process of construction—isn't that so, Colonel?"

"I believe so, sir, yes," Pooley confirmed. "I am not sure
whether the line has yet reached Allahabad, but to the best of
my knowledge, it is the intention of the Indian government that
it should. And these men, these Royal Engineers, would provide skilled help to that end, if they can be conveyed at once to
Calcutta."

"You want me to give them passage, sir?" Red questioned.
"Aboard the *Galah?*"

"Precisely," the governor returned. "I shall take it on myself
to change your orders, Commander. Your ship, if she is required on the China station, can proceed to Hong Kong as soon
as you have set the engineer detachment ashore in Calcutta.
Unfortunately there is no senior naval officer here at present,
whose agreement I might have sought, so that I must act on my
own authority in the matter. Er—I trust you will accept my
authority?"

Red's hesitation was brief. The change in his orders was admittedly unorthodox, but the governor's argument was entirely
convincing, and he signified his willingness to accept the
change.

"Of course, Your Excellency. I can take on water and supplies and be ready to sail as soon as the engineer detachment is
embarked. By noon tomorrow, sir, if the detachment is ready
and my supplies can be made available at once."

"I will ensure that they are, Commander. And the men, Colonel?"

"They will be at the quayside tomorrow morning, sir," Pooley promised. "Their commanding officer is a young Scotsman —Captain Fergus Maclaren. I'll send him out to your ship this evening, Commander, if that is agreeable to you."

"I will have him to dinner on board the *Galah,*" Red offered. He prepared to take his leave, by no means ill pleased, in the circumstances, by his enforced change of destination. It was likely that, in Calcutta, he might obtain news of the situation in Oudh and of Jenny and her husband; of necessity, the governor's information could not be up to date, and perhaps, God willing, by this time the mutiny in Bengal might already have been quelled.

The Meerut outbreak had clearly been serious enough, and the fact that Delhi had fallen to the rebellious sepoy regiments did not augur well, but . . . Red accepted the written order Governor Blundell offered him and came formally to attention.

Returning to the quayside in the carriage that had brought him to Government House, he had no eyes for the ordered beauty of his surroundings, as he attempted to bring to mind the map of India. Delhi was hundreds of miles to the northwest of Lucknow, he thought, and Sitapur . . . Ranpur—devil take it, why couldn't he remember the address Jenny had given him? At all events, William's native regiment formed part of the garrison of an outstation, fifty or sixty miles from Lucknow, and there were surely British troops, a British regiment, in Lucknow. It was the capital of Oudh, with—yes, had not William said that Sir Henry Lawrence had been appointed chief commissioner of Oudh, with his headquarters in Lucknow? Sir Henry was a man Will had appeared greatly to admire.

"He is held in high esteem by both Indians and British," Will De Lancey had said. *"If any man can reconcile the adherents of the old King to the annexation of his kingdom, that man is Lawrence. . . ."*

Red learned more during the meal to which he entertained Captain Fergus Maclaren on board the *Galah.* The Royal Engineer officer was a tall, dark-haired man of about thirty-four or -five, with a grave manner and the soft, lilting accent of a Highland Scot. It turned out that he had served for seven years in India, two of those years in a military station fifty miles from Lucknow—Cawnpore, on the Ganges River. He was able to locate Ranpur and, as befitted his profession, drew an excellent sketch map of the area, offering illuminating comments as his pen moved deftly across the paper. He noted place names, roads and rivers, and the site of the proposed railway, which, it seemed, had been planned during the time he had been stationed in Cawnpore.

"The Ganges River and the Great Trunk Road are the principal means of communication between the port of Calcutta and the northwest," he explained. "As yet the rail system covers barely a hundred miles—the railhead is here, at Raniganj, d'you see, sir? After that, all troop reinforcements going inland to Benares and Allahabad will have to proceed by river steamer, or by elephant or bullock stage, or they'll have to march . . . and that takes time. There is a proposed rail link between Allahabad and Cawnpore, further inland, but to the best of my knowledge it ends here, at Lahonda—forty miles from Allahabad. It had just been started when I left to go to Scotland on furlough. And you'll realize the distance between Calcutta and Lucknow is seven hundred miles by road and about a thousand by water. And in the monsoon, when the rivers flood and the roads become well-nigh impassable for wheeled traffic, delays are inevitable."

"What have you heard of the present situation in Delhi and Meerut?" Red asked. "From what the governor and Colonel Pooley told me, that's where the mutiny began. And the mutineers took Delhi almost a month ago."

The engineer officer shrugged. "H.E. is probably in possession of more up-to-date information than I am, Captain Broome. But Delhi is, of course, likely to become the focal point of any uprising—if it's not that already. I imagine that every conceivable effort will be made to recapture it. But not from Calcutta—the distance is too immense. I understand that there's a force being assembled at Ambala, which is here—" He pointed to the map. "It's in the hills, near Simla, where the commander in chief, General Anson, has his hot-weather headquarters. But again, sir, transport will be the problem. An army, even a relatively small army, on the move in India requires a vast number of coolies, beasts of burden, carts, ammunition tumbrils, tents, water tankers. Stores have to be carried, forage for the animals, and—" He repeated his despairing shrug. "It will, I fear, be a good long while before Delhi can be retaken. And until it is once again in British hands, there's just no knowing what will be the effect on the sepoy troops throughout India and particularly in Bengal. Oudh could go up like a powder keg when a naked flame is applied to it!"

He talked on, giving the facts as he knew them and continuing to illustrate his words by recourse to a swiftly sketched map.

Returning to the situation in Oudh, he laid stress on the dangers where most outstations were garrisoned exclusively by sepoy troops.

"Cawnpore had the Queen's Thirty-second when I was there, Captain Broome, but I understand the regiment has been posted to Lucknow—which augurs well for Lucknow but badly for Cawnpore, which will be left with three native regiments and"—Maclaren made a wry grimace—"the so-called Nana of Bithur, claimant to the throne of the Mahrattas."

"What of him?" Red questioned. "He's an Indian prince, isn't he—a rajah?"

"A very embittered one, I fear—although he affected great friendship for our countrymen in the garrison when I was there. In fairness to him, I have to concede that he has reason for bitterness. He was the adopted son of the last Maharajah, Baji Rao—the Peishwa—but because he was not related by blood, the title and the old Peishwa's very lavish pension were denied him, in line with the former governor general's policy, of which you've no doubt heard. Annexation and lapse, it was called." He went into brief detail, an odd little smile curving his lips.

"It sounds like barefaced robbery," Red exclaimed.

"It was indeed, sir," Maclaren agreed cynically. "Under Lord Dalhousie's governorship, the East India Company added something like two hundred and fifty thousand square miles to British-Indian territory in eight years. We—the British—have something to answer for, I'm afraid. The Nana made numerous appeals to the East India Company's Court of Governors, but all were dismissed. All he inherited from Baji Rao were his debts—which were considerable—his palace at Bithur, a private army, and a host of retainers and aging dependents, said to number about fifteen thousand. Frankly, sir, if there *is* an uprising and the Army of Bengal does mutiny, I'd repose no trust whatsoever in the Nana. He has nothing to lose and everything to gain if he throws in his lot with the sepoys."

It was logical, Red reflected, his anxiety for his sister and her husband in no way assuaged by the picture Fergus Maclaren had painted. Poor little Jenny! God grant that she would not live to regret her decision to accompany Will De Lancey to India. Uneasily, he questioned Maclaren as to the likelihood of mutiny breaking out in the Oudh outstations, which, like Ranpur, had entirely native garrisons.

"It's impossible to predict, sir," the engineer officer answered flatly. "Every Company officer I've met believes heart and soul in his own regiment's loyalty, and it remains to be seen if their faith in their men will be justified. A lot depends on individual officers and the relationship they've built up with the men they command. But even before I went on furlough, attempts were being made to stir up sedition among the native troops. Hindu priests were secretly visiting the sepoys, warning them that the Company policy was to convert them to Christianity by destroying their caste system. And it was rumored that they had revived an old prophecy, which forecast the end of the Company's rule on the hundredth anniversary of the Battle of Plassey. Which—" Maclaren swore, and brought his clenched fist down on the mess table in sudden alarm. "For God's sake, that's today, isn't it? Today's the twenty-third of June, and Clive's victory was exactly a hundred years ago, unless my memory's at fault. June the twenty-third, 1757!"

Red stared at him, startled by his vehemence. "No," he corrected. "Today is the twenty-fifth."

"Then the day will have come and gone. There was some talk of a comet that was to be seen in the night sky—I wonder if it was? And *if* the uprising was timed for the twenty-third?"

"They did not wait for any damned comet in Meerut," Red reminded his guest. "Well, I suppose we shall soon find out, my friend. We'll sail as soon as your detachment is embarked, and granted fair winds, we should be setting you ashore in Calcutta within a couple of weeks. Less, if we pick up a decent wind in the Straits of Malacca—which is not beyond the bounds of possibility."

Red's forecast proved to be accurate. A strong and favorable wind was picked up in the Straits of Malacca and carried all the way to the mouth of the Hooghly River. On July 8, the *Galah* anchored for the night in Diamond Harbor, and the next day, under the direction of a Bengal marine pilot, she proceeded slowly up the dull and muddy waters of the great river. There was thick, luxuriant jungle on either bank, broken by mudflats and innumerable small islands, which, with their tangled vegetation and basking crocodiles, looked anything but inviting.

As they neared the city of Calcutta, the east bank of the river —known as Garden Reach—became more attractive, with its well-kept gardens and pleasure grounds and white-painted bungalows, occupied, the pilot said, by officials and well-to-do merchants, who appeared to live in considerable style. On the opposite bank, stone-built temples stood at the head of long flights of stone steps, which were crowded with a motley throng of natives, bathing and filling their earthenware *chattis* with water, which the women, in colorful saris, bore away on their heads. All paused to stare at the ship, and a few waved in greeting. A little later, while passing beneath the gun batteries and green slopes of Fort William, the *Galah* was loudly and excitedly cheered by the fortress's red-coated guardians.

At five o'clock, she dropped anchor off the Esplanade after firing a nineteen-gun salute, and scarcely had she done so than a resplendently uniformed aide-de-camp came on board, with a summons for Red to repair at once to Government House, where Colonel Birch, the military secretary, was anxious to speak with him.

"His Excellency Lord Canning is at Barrackpore, sir," the young officer explained. "But we are expecting him back this evening for dinner—to which, of course, you and the officer commanding your military detachment will, I am sure, be invited."

A carriage was waiting—a much more luxurious equipage

than the one furnished by the governor at Singapore—drawn by two fine matching bays, with a coachman and a scarlet-uniformed footman, in addition to an escort of two splendidly mounted troopers of the governor general's bodyguard. In its cushioned interior, Red, accompanied by Captain Maclaren and the young aide, took in with interest the colorful scene about them as they left the dockside, with Fort William's castellated heights above, and drove across the green, tree-shaded expanse of the park called the Maidan. At this hour, it was thronged with the evening parade of Calcutta's wealthy society, seated in their stylish conveyances or astride well-groomed hacks, with a military band playing lively airs in a wrought-iron bandstand bedecked with flowers, about which were grouped white-painted tables and chairs, beneath the shade of brilliantly striped awnings.

It looked quite unlike a city threatened by anarchy and rebellion, the Europeans going about their pleasurable business seemingly without a care in the world. But, the young aide asserted gravely, Lord Canning was deeply concerned, for the news reaching him from upriver was almost daily more alarming. He did not dwell on this, however, leaving the harrowing details to his military superior, and when the carriage drew up outside the imposing entrance of Government House, he hurried them through the great, marble-paved hallway and up a side staircase to the military secretary's office on the first floor.

Colonel Birch, thin, gray-haired, and bewhiskered, received both Red and his passenger warmly.

"You are the answer to prayer," he stated, with evident sincerity, when Fergus Maclaren introduced himself. "And your men worth their weight in gold at this critical time, believe me! I will arrange for you to go up-country first thing tomorrow, to place yourself under Colonel Neill's command at Allahabad. The colonel is leading a relief force of his regiment to Cawnpore, which is under siege by an estimated seven thousand mutinied sepoys under the treacherous Nana Sahib of Bithur."

Maclaren exchanged a swift glance with Red, as the military secretary went into details of the siege. Just as the engineer captain had prophesied, the last of the Mahrattas had betrayed the trust reposed in him by the commander of the Cawnpore garrison, General Sir Hugh Wheeler.

"Sir Hugh is one of our most esteemed general officers," Colonel Birch added, with tight-lipped restraint. "But at Cawnpore he has, I fear, made two disastrous errors. Firstly, of course, he depended on the Nana's loyalty and seeming friendship. Then, instead of occupying the magazine—which would have been impregnable—he chose to set up his defenses at a site close to the Allahabad road, behind a mud wall, with only two substantial buildings on it, in the belief that reinforcements would be sent to him from here." He sighed heavily. "Well, we endeavored to send him reinforcements, but I gravely fear that Colonel Neill will be unable to reach Cawnpore in time. Close on a thousand of our people—almost half women and children—have been under siege for almost three weeks, and with every hour that passes, our fears for their continued safety increase."

Observing the look of stunned dismay on Maclaren's face, the colonel broke off, to eye him from beneath frowning gray brows.

"You know Cawnpore, Captain Maclaren? You have friends there?"

Fergus Maclaren nodded wretchedly. "Indeed I have, sir—a great many. I was stationed in Cawnpore before I went on furlough." He and the military secretary went into lengthy discussion, to which Red listened in appalled silence, as the desperate situation in which the Cawnpore garrison had been placed slowly became clear to him. By comparison with that of Lucknow—where, it appeared, Sir Henry Lawrence, the commissioner for Oudh, had made careful preparations to withstand attack by rebel forces—Cawnpore's fate seemed virtually sealed, the garrison's only course a humiliating surrender unless relief could reach them very soon.

"Brigadier General Havelock was sent for posthaste from Persia," Birch went on, "but he was delayed by a shipwreck—fortunately without serious loss—and arrived here only three weeks ago. He left for Allahabad on the twenty-fifth of June. Since then we have been informed by the electric telegraph that Lucknow is under siege . . . and Havelock has but two European regiments—less than two thousand men—with which to relieve both Cawnpore and Lucknow. And, as I said, Colonel Neill's advance force has not yet reached Cawnpore."

The catalogue of woe continued, Birch holding out little hope. Red was shocked to hear that General Anson, the commander in chief, had died of cholera while on his way to Delhi with the hurriedly formed field force from Ambala.

"Frankly, gentlemen," Birch admitted with a sigh, "until Delhi is once more in our hands, I fear that this insurrection will spread throughout the length and breadth of the province. Even Calcutta may come under attack, unless we can obtain substantial reinforcements in very short order."

He talked on, with unconcealed despair, as much to himself as to his two silent listeners, and then, with a sudden, unexpected change of tone, he turned to Red with a crisply voiced question as to his orders.

"I was under orders from Their Lordships to proceed to China, sir, to join Admiral Seymour's flag in Hong Kong," Red told him flatly. "My orders have not been changed, but—"

"But Governor Blundell took it on his own authority to send you here with Captain Maclaren's detachment?" Colonel Birch put in.

"His Excellency based his decision on the recent consultation he had with Lord Elgin, sir, who left for China on board the *Shannon* just before I made port in Singapore. He informed me, sir, that in view of Lord Elgin's parting instructions, he believed himself justified in ordering me to convey Captain Maclaren's detachment to your aid."

Colonel Birch nodded vigorously in approval. "The governor general has been in touch with Lord Elgin, Captain Broome. The latest information we have had is that he is to come here in person, on board the *Shannon,* and accompanied by two other naval vessels with a contingent of royal marines to reinforce the defenses of this city. We anticipate his most welcome arrival within the next three weeks—sooner, God willing, if that is possible. The war with China would seem to be in a state of stalemate, and for that praise be to heaven, since it will mean that some of our reinforcements will be troops diverted here from that theater. In view of which—" Birch paused, eyeing Red pensively. "It is not improbable that, when His Excellency the governor general returns, he may follow Governor Blundell's example and decide to commandeer your vessel. A fast frigate, Captain Broome, would be of inestimable value to us at this crucial time, particularly as a means of conveying troops here from Madras. I take it, Captain, that your frigate is fit to put to sea if required?"

Red inclined his head. "I shall need water, sir, and some fresh provisions. Once these are loaded and Captain Maclaren's detachment has disembarked—"

He was interrupted by a staff officer in infantry uniform, who burst into the office, white of face and clearly agitated. "Colonel," he announced without preamble, "a message has just come through on the telegraph from Allahabad. It's from General Havelock, sir, and I'm afraid it's very bad news." He thrust a sheet of paper into the military secretary's hand, and Colonel Birch, after studying it for a moment, read the message aloud, his voice harsh with strain.

" 'A report of the fall of Cawnpore received from Lawrence but is not believed by the authorities here. A steamer with a hundred Europeans armed with Minié rifles and two six-pounders starts tomorrow to endeavor to relieve Wheeler.' That is the first message, gentlemen. But the second, sent at dawn this morning, is indeed the most tragic news." He swallowed hard, and, Red saw, his hand was trembling visibly as he held up the sheet of paper to the light from the shuttered window at his back. " 'The news of the entire destruction of the Cawnpore garrison confirmed by messenger, who, carrying letters from Lucknow to Allahabad, witnessed an act of treachery, resulting in a massacre of . . . all defenders.' This—God in heaven, this is appalling! I—I—" Birch recovered his composure and turned to the officer who had brought him the telegraph. "John, this must be given to His Excellency without delay."

"They've not returned yet, sir. I thought—"

"Don't think, man—send a mounted orderly to meet him. No, better still, go yourself. They must be nearing the city— H.E. has a dinner party tonight. He said he would not be late. He—" The clatter of hooves from the driveway below sent Birch and his staff officer rushing to the window. Drawing back the shutter, the military secretary exclaimed in relief, "His Excellency is here! Excuse me, gentlemen, I must go to him at once."

Both officers vanished, and Red, left standing there, looked at Fergus Maclaren. He noticed, without surprise, that the engineer captain's eyes were filled with tears.

"What did the colonel say?" Maclaren managed wretchedly. "A thousand of our countrymen—our countrymen and *women*, Broome—massacred by that treacherous swine the Nana of Bithur! When I think of them, when I see their faces, I—God, I am sickened. Poor, bloody old Wheeler and his daughters! I used to dance with Amelia. . . ."

Red put an arm about the younger man's shoulder, moved by his grief. What, he wondered dully, was the situation now in Ranpur? Were Jenny and Will even now in the same danger of betrayal and mutiny as those poor souls who had died so hideously in Cawnpore? Or had they, perhaps, reached Lucknow, where Sir Henry Lawrence had made preparations to resist a siege? But Lucknow was under siege, Colonel Birch had said. Under siege but still able to send messengers to Allahabad, and with a British regiment, the Queen's 32nd, to fight in its defense.

"Merciful God," Red prayed silently, *"spare my beloved little sister and her husband. I beseech Thee to keep them safe from harm. In—in Lucknow, if it be Thy will."*

Fergus Maclaren got heavily to his feet, and Red said decisively, "We'll go back to the ship, Maclaren, and arrange to disembark your men. And I'll have to break the bad news to my first lieutenant. In any case, we won't be wanted here while this crisis is on. If the governor general bids us to dine, we can come back."

"Yes," the engineer officer agreed. "Sitting here and just thinking about it would be more than I could stomach! By heaven, though, I hope we can be on our way up-country without delay! I have a burning desire to hit back at the treacherous devils who turned on those poor, unhappy souls in General Wheeler's entrenchment. Death is what a soldier faces, but to make war on women and children puts the Nana and his mutinous sepoys beyond the pale! I'll gladly give my life to avenge their martyrdom, and count it well spent."

"I envy you," Red confessed wryly. "Since all I can do is command a troop transport. But—let's be on our way, shall we?"

They were met in the great, echoing hall by the young aide who had summoned them to Government House.

"I'm to escort you back to your ship, sir," he told Red. "And to tell you that His Excellency cordially invites you to dine here this evening, when he will receive you in private after the meal. The invitation does not include Captain Maclaren—Colonel Birch, sir, is putting your orders in hand," he added, addressing Maclaren. "You may expect transport to the railhead for yourself and your detachment within a matter of hours. You will be given the first priority, the colonel says, sir, to carry you to your destination with all possible expedition."

Maclaren's expression relaxed. "And what is my destination, sir?" he asked quietly.

"Lahonda, sir," the young aide answered readily, and Red saw that his companion was smiling.

"I could ask for no more," he exclaimed. "By God I could not!" With sudden impatience he grasped Red's arm and hurried him to the waiting carriage.

Dinner, that evening, was in the nature of a banquet, and Red was faintly shocked by the pomp and ceremony of the occasion, which far outshone any similar occasion he had experienced in Sydney's Government House. The guests numbered close on a hundred—wealthy, elegantly attired civilians, the women bedecked with jewels, the men in white ties and tailcoats, and the military in a variety of uniforms, from the scarlet of the Queen's regiments to the magnificent gold-and-silver-laced blues, greens, and grays of the East India Company's colonial levies, almost outlandish in their splendor and the seeming arrogance of their bearing. Red felt comparatively sober in his naval full dress, and saw only two others like him, both junior officers of the Company's marine.

The governor general and his handsome, vivacious wife received their guests in the ballroom, responding courteously to the bows and low curtsies as the long line progressed slowly in front of them, each guest announced by name and in stentorian tones by a majordomo in a splendid livery of scarlet and gold. Beside them on the low dais was a tall, bewhiskered figure in the blue and silver of the Madras Presidency Army, his tunic ablaze with stars and orders. Red identified him as General Sir Patrick Grant, lately summoned to the capital of Bengal from his own command to act as commander in chief.

To the music of a military string orchestra, the guests passed beneath glittering chandeliers into a vast banqueting hall, its tables set with gold and silver plate, and an army of liveried Indian servants lined up against the picture-hung walls, waiting to serve the meal.

For Red, despite the excellence and variety of the food and wine set before him, the dinner was a strain on his nerves and patience. His neighbors were civilians, two married couples of the wealthy merchant class, who, after one or two probing questions aimed at ascertaining his rank and social standing, talked among themselves of matters so far from his ken that he found himself virtually excluded from their conversation. They wasted few words on the events following the sepoy mutiny—clearly the news of the fall of Cawnpore and the massacre of its defenders had not yet been made public—and the siege of Lucknow seemed not to concern them. The rebels' seizure of Delhi was dismissed in a brief condemnation of the evident unpreparedness of the Meerut command and the admission that the disaster could have far-reaching effects unless the governor general took firm action and the military bestirred themselves.

To Red's shocked surprise, they did not appear aware of any threat to Calcutta, the younger of the two gentlemen declaring, with some annoyance, that he had offered his services to the recently formed militia and been refused a commission.

"For the Lord's sweet sake, Henry," he informed his older counterpart, "the idiots made one of my clerks a damned lieutenant, on the strength of his having served for six months in some yeomanry regiment in Yorkshire! I couldn't put myself in a position where I'd have to take orders from *him,* could I? So I let them have a brace of my polo ponies and bowed out. I just hope I get the ponies back undamaged, when the scare's over."

"Do you think it *will* soon be over, Charlie?" one of the elegantly dressed ladies asked, a note of displeasure in her voice.

"It's disrupting things so. I've even heard that H.E. wants to cancel the evening band concerts, so that he can send the bandsmen to swell the garrison in Benares! As if fiddlers and horn players would be of the smallest use as fighting men!"

"It will all fizzle out," the man she had addressed as Charlie declared assertively, "if Sir Patrick Grant takes decisive action and demands that the European troops we need are sent here. They're not required in Burma or Persia anymore, or in China either, come to that. And the Punjab's quiet, with the Sikhs ready to fight for us. But for God's sake, what use is a commander in chief who skulks here, in Lord Canning's pocket? He should be off up-country, commanding the damned troops!"

"We should send the navy," his wife put in, glancing archly at Red. "A naval brigade, with ship's guns and brave bluejackets to fire them. They could be sent up by river, couldn't they? I'm sure, Captain—er—I'm afraid I did not catch your name—I'm sure that you and your splendid sailors would be willing to volunteer, would you not?"

Lost for words with which to reply, Red inclined his head stiffly, his hackles rising.

But at last the dinner came to an end; the guests rose and were ushered back into the ballroom, whence came the muted sounds of music, as the band struck up a lively waltz and a flock of dancers took the floor.

"Captain Broome—" Attired in mess kit, with an impressive row of medals pinned to his tunic, Colonel Birch was at his side, and Red turned to him in relief. "His Excellency will see you now," the older man said, smiling. "If you'll come with me. His lordship will only be able to spare you a few minutes—he's expected in the ballroom, you understand, and his absence would cause comment. At all costs, we have to keep up the appearance of calm, because the last thing we want here is a panic. And when the newspapers publish the terrible news about Cawnpore, it could well cause a panic. Certainly it will bring the dangers of the present situation home to a great many people who hitherto have had little inkling of its gravity."

Like his dinner partners, Red thought cynically, visualizing the effect such appalling news would have on the woman who had bemoaned the cessation of the nightly band concerts on

Calcutta's Maidan. He followed Birch without comment and found himself in a small anteroom, where the governor general was waiting, General Grant at his side. He was struck, as the colonel made the necessary introductions, by the strained expressions on both men's faces. Lord Canning was, as nearly as he could judge, comparatively young for the position he held—in his mid-forties, perhaps . . . certainly little older—although his dark hair was receding and the neat black beard he wore was flecked with gray. His eyes, as they met Red's, held an infinite weariness, but his voice, in contradiction, was brisk and incisive.

"You have heard the terrible news from Cawnpore, Captain Broome, so you will understand my anxiety. The situation in Oudh is extremely precarious. I have the greatest confidence in Sir Henry Lawrence, but with Lucknow now besieged by thousands of mutineers and Cawnpore taken, there is little even Sir Henry can do to restore peace in the province. At all hazards, we must send relief to him. General Havelock has set out from Allahabad, as probably you have heard, but he has barely a thousand European troops under his command. And Colonel Neill's advance force—led by a Major Renaud, I believe—is now in grave danger of being cut off and annihilated. It will be a miracle if General Havelock can catch up with them in time." He turned his tired gaze on General Grant, and the Madras commander in chief responded with a gruff-voiced confirmation of what he had said.

"If my ship can be of service," Red began, "I—"

The governor general cut him short. "Colonel Birch has explained your position, Captain, and I fully understand that you are under orders from the Admiralty to join Admiral Seymour's flag in China. I shall countermand those orders, having, of course, informed Admiral Seymour that I have done so. You have already been of service by conveying the detachment of Royal Engineers to us from Singapore, for which I am immensely grateful." He paused, glancing again at Sir Patrick Grant.

The general said crisply, "Colonel Birch says you've been supplied with all your needs and are ready to put to sea—that's right, I take it? And the Royal Engineer detachment has disembarked?" Receiving Red's confirmation, he went on. "Then Colonel Birch will prepare your orders, Captain. As soon as you receive them, you will sail for Madras, take on board units of the Madras Artillery with their guns, and convey them here with all possible speed. Your orders will be addressed to Brigadier General Carthew, of the Madras Presidency Army, who will also take passage with you. You will need to load your frigate to the limit of her capacity."

"I understand that, sir," Red acknowledged. "Rest assured that I shall do so."

The governor general permitted himself a brief smile and held out his hand. "I am greatly indebted to you, Captain Broome, believe me. Do you have any questions for either General Grant or myself, before we continue to keep up the appearance of unruffled calm for the benefit of our guests?"

Red hesitated and then, encouraged by Lord Canning's smile, asked diffidently, "On a personal matter only, Your Excellency, if I may take up your time."

"Of course, my dear fellow. Ask away—we'll answer you if we can."

"Thank you, sir. I—" Red phrased his question as concisely as he could. "My sister and her husband, Colonel William De Lancey, are in Ranpur, one of the Oudh outstations. William is commanding a native cavalry regiment there, the Fifth Oudh Lancers. And his brother is my first lieutenant. I wondered if— that is to say, if your lordship had any news from that station? I —needless to tell you, I am anxious, sir."

It was the military secretary who answered him. He said gravely, "The only news we have had from any of the outstations is three weeks to a fortnight old, Captain Broome. I recall that we received a telegraphic message from the district commissioner in Ranpur, via Lucknow. It was to the effect that the garrison had mutinied, but . . . it was one of many, alas, and I do not remember the details. However, if you would care to accompany me to my office, I will have the duty officer extract the message from the files, so that you may read it for yourself."

The message—when the officer on duty hunted for and finally produced it from a stack of others—sent Red's hopes plummeting. With stark brevity, the district commissoner had informed

Sir Henry Lawrence that with all three native regiments having thrown off their allegiance and, in some cases, murdered their officers, the Europeans, both civil and military, had taken refuge in his Residency, which they were defending against attack by the mutineers.

"We have our women and children with us," the message concluded, "numbering over sixty, and have so far, by the grace of God, kept our attackers at bay. It is our intention to try to make our escape by river, when boats and provisions can be procured. An attempt is to be made by volunteers to blow up the magazine, to prevent it from falling into the hands of the sepoys."

"Since that message was received, I do not think we have heard anything further, Captain Broome," the colonel said regretfully. As Lord Canning had done, he offered his hand. "I'm sorry to be unable to tell you more. One can only pray that your sister and her husband are safe. I recall meeting them two or three months ago, when they arrived here from—from Australia, wasn't it? Colonel De Lancey is a fine soldier and the bearer of a most distinguished name. He—"

The young staff officer, who had continued to search the files, interrupted him with a smothered exclamation and rose, a flimsy sheet of paper in his hand.

"Colonel, there was a second message from Ranpur—I thought I remembered receiving it. It came through four—no, five days ago, sir, at the end of one of Sir Henry Lawrence's reports. It says, Captain Broome, that the survivors of the Ranpur garrison, including the women and children, were preparing to evacuate by river, the Residency being no longer tenable. Look, sir, here it is."

Red scarcely glanced at it, his gaze going to the large-scale map of Bengal that hung from the wall of the office. He found Ranpur and searched for the name of the river by which the survivors of the garrison would seek escape. Fergus Maclaren's sketch map had marked its course, but . . . on the military secretary's wall map it was clearly printed, and he drew in his breath sharply as he read the name. The Ganges—the great waterway that carried much of the trade of India northward from Calcutta, to Benares and Allahabad and . . . Cawnpore!

Ranpur was northwest of Allahabad, he knew, a hundred miles or more, and . . . Red's finger traced the river's curving course.

In a strangled voice, he said, "Dear God, they must have been hoping to make for Cawnpore! They couldn't have known of the—the surrender! They couldn't have known that General Wheeler's people had been betrayed and massacred!"

"No," Birch confirmed. "They could not. My dear fellow—" He laid a hand on Red's arm. "I'm most damnably sorry. But don't lose hope. This message is at least five days old, and we don't know when it was sent. It was probably by *cossid*—by native messenger—which could have taken much longer. The news could have reached them before they left for Cawnpore. And there are many tributaries of the Ganges—look, they are shown clearly on the map. It's possible that their boats could take a different route."

"Yes, sir." Red had himself under iron control.

"I will inform you if any further news comes in before you sail, Captain," the older man promised.

Red thanked him and took his leave, to return, in brooding silence, to his ship. With a heavy heart, he summoned Francis De Lancey to his cabin and related all he had learned from Lord Canning and his staff.

By the following day, when his orders were delivered and he prepared to receive the pilot, there had been no further news of the fate of the Ranpur garrison.

Chapter XIV

JENNY DE LANCEY crouched on the dusty, littered floor of Commissioner Melgund's drawing room and caught her breath as a round-shot, fired with alarming accuracy from one of the mutineers' nine-pounder guns, struck the window above her head. The glass had long since been shattered, and the shot, meeting no impediment, passed over her to hit the opposite wall. It lodged there, bringing down a shower of plaster but, to her relief, doing no serious damage.

Nevertheless, it set three or four of the older children crying out in fear, and Jenny, anxious that they should not waken the others, propped the heavy musket she had just loaded against a chair and crawled back, on hands and knees, to try to comfort them.

"It will be dark soon, Andy," she told the commissioner's nine-year-old son. "They will have to leave off then."

It was not true; the firing slackened during the hours of darkness, but it never ceased altogether and, indeed, had not let up for more than a few minutes at a time since the first attack had been launched on the Residency building, three days before. Andrew Melgund was an intelligent boy, and Jenny sensed that he was not deceived by her attempt at consolation, but, evidently recognizing it for what it was, he managed a smile and sternly bade his small sister dry her eyes and go back to sleep.

"You don't want to disturb the little ones, Rosie. It'll be bedlam if you start wailing and wake them up!"

Rosie was only five, a delicate little creature with deep blue eyes and a head of golden hair, which, normally done in ringlets by her *ayah*, her native nurse, now hung in dust-caked disheveltment about her pale, tear-wet face. She did not argue, and when Jenny settled her more comfortably on the cushions spread about the floor, she closed her eyes obediently and drifted back into exhausted sleep.

The others—the two Lund girls and Bella Gillespie's son, Tommy—followed her example, as weary and dispirited as she, and Martha Lund, stretched out on a sofa at the far side of the room, smiled her thanks. She was in the seventh month of pregnancy and, Jenny thought pityingly, must be enduring intense discomfort, for the room was hot and airless, and until darkness fell, none of the Residency's hard-pressed defenders dared risk an attempt to draw water from the well, which was a scant twenty yards across the rear compound. The sepoys had posted sharpshooters in a nearby banyan tree to keep it under fire, and what drinking water remained in the stored *chattis* had to be hoarded and given only to slake the thirst of the smaller children and the more seriously wounded.

Already there were over a dozen wounded, and the toll was mounting. There would be more, probably, when William's volunteers fought their way back from the magazine. *If* they were able to fight their way back, and . . . Jenny's throat was tight. If they were even able to reach the magazine without the sepoys divining their intention. Oh, dear God in heaven, she thought despairingly, what chance would they have, five men, armed only with pistols, against the mob of sepoys and townsfolk ranged against them? The fewer the better, William had insisted. Five of them, with faces blackened and native robes draped over their uniforms, would have a slim chance—the only chance—of reaching their objective. And perhaps—

From the window she had left, Jenny heard the crack of Major Lund's rifle, and recalled to her self-imposed task of acting as his loader, she returned to take the Enfield from him and place the Brown Bess musket in his outstretched hand. He did not thank her; the resentment he had displayed so openly, when William had arrived in Ranpur to take over command of his regiment, still lingered in the cold gray eyes. It was not easy, even now, to forget Marcus Lund's hostility, the lukewarm welcome he had offered them at the end of the long, exhausting journey up-country by steamer, horse-drawn cart, and finally by country boat. And Jenny had not forgotten it, although Martha, kindly soul that she was, had tried very hard to make up for her husband's unyielding discourtesy.

And William had made allowances for it; he had attempted to explain to her, Jenny remembered, sought to rationalize it.

"Marcus Lund's whole life has been spent with the Lancers, Jenny, and his father's before him. The regiment is his life, and it's only natural that he should resent a stranger—and a Queen's officer into the bargain—being given the command over his head. He's years older than I am, and he's known most of the men ever since they joined the regiment. He speaks their language as well as they do, whilst I'm still struggling to make myself understood. He'll come round, I feel sure, given time, when he realizes that I'm not trying to supplant him, simply to work with him and learn from him."

But they had not been given time. The mutiny in Ranpur had come too soon, too suddenly. William had sensed the danger; it had been plain for an outsider to see, for the tension had been there, mounting with each day that passed. But Marcus Lund had obstinately refused to believe that his Lancers—his beloved sowars, as they were called—would betray their trust or question the paternal authority he had always exercised over them.

"My sowars will be true to their salt," he had asserted, over and over again. "Whatever Jeremy Roach's Rifles do, or the police. They're blasted Hindus, most of them, and my fellows are Muslims—they'll never form any sort of alliance with unbelievers."

He had been proved wrong, Jenny thought unhappily. He and Colonel Roach, commanding officer of the Oudh Irregular Rifles, who had held similar views concerning his sepoys, had both been proved wrong when news of the outbreak in Meerut and the capture of Delhi had reached the garrison, borne by *fakirs* and itinerant *sadhus*, holy men who had entered the native lines in secret to spread the tidings among their men. And, because of his refusal to believe in the danger, still less to take steps to meet it, Commissioner Melgund had delayed implementing the precautions William had repeatedly urged on him.

"At least fortify the Residency," William had pleaded. "Make arrangements to bring in all European and Eurasian women and children from the cantonments at the first sign of trouble. Bring in provisions and look to your stock of water, sir, so that you're ready to receive them. And hire boats and set a European guard on them."

"But if we do that, Colonel De Lancey," Melgund had answered, "it would suggest that we *expect* the troops to mutiny. It might even provoke them, since they would suppose that we do not trust in their continued loyalty."

He had said it on the last occasion that she and William had dined in the Residency, Jenny recalled with a pang—dined by candlelight, waited on by obedient, well-trained native servants in government livery, and with sentries of the Rifles standing guard at the gates. But Colonel Roach and his gray-haired, forthright wife had been their fellow guests, and it had been to their quite contrary opinions that the commissioner had listened.

With the result— Jenny finished reloading the Enfield rifle and sat back on her heels, feeling suddenly weak and sickened, as the events of the past few terrible days filled her thoughts.

Colonel Roach's trusted Rifles had been the first to break out in open mutiny. The colonel—who, whatever his faults, had not lacked courage—had ridden at once to the regiment's lines, accompanied by his second-in-command and the adjutant, intent on restoring order. But the native troops had shot all three officers down without compunction, following which—Jenny shuddered at the memory—they had induced the other infantry regiment, the Sixteenth, to join them, and together had indulged in an orgy of looting and arson throughout the cantonments, during the course of which Mrs. Roach had been savagely attacked and left to die in her burning bungalow.

Her children had been saved. Four small, terrified little boys and a girl of twelve had been brought to the Residency by their courageous *ayah* and the colonel's orderly, and both servants had remained, refusing to be parted from their charges. Others had followed them. Officers' wives with their families, many in

their night attire, had come in small individual parties to seek
refuge in the Residency, and ill prepared though he was for the
influx, Commissioner Melgund had opened his doors to them.
Most of them were now in the dining room, at the rear of the
building, which was shaded by trees and was a little cooler than
the living room at the front, where Jenny now was. The basement—normally a storeroom—was the coolest of all, and this
had been reserved for the wounded and the mothers with young
babies, of whose number and identity Jenny had lost count—

"Infernal swine! Rifles, of course, devil take them!" Major
Lund's harsh voice again broke into her thoughts, and she
tensed as he fired. "Missed the fellow, damnation! Give me the
Enfield, for God's sake, Mrs. De Lancey—this infernal musket's too old. I couldn't hit a haystack with it."

He grabbed the Enfield and, with scarcely a pause to sight the
weapon, fired again, a high-pitched shriek of agony bearing witness to its accuracy. Her fingers clumsy in their haste, Jenny
began to reload the musket, but the major took it from her.

"The Enfield rifle, damn it—not that useless abomination.
Didn't you hear me, woman? The rifle's what I need."

She obeyed him in silence, giving him, as William had begged
her to, the benefit of the doubt, despite his churlish rudeness.
Marcus Lund had been wounded in the knee by a shot from the
compound outside, a wound that, since early that morning, had
deprived him of mobility, and was clearly causing him considerable pain. The fact that it had prevented him from joining the
small party of volunteers William had called for, for the attempt to reach the magazine, had added to his rancor; and since
the moment he and she had formed their impromptu partnership at the living-room window, the only words he had addressed to her had been critical and even abusive. . . . Jenny
sighed, meeting the sympathetic gaze of young Cornet
Millbank, who was guarding the window beyond. Poor Archie
Millbank had been given the rough side of his superior officer's
tongue more than once in the course of the long, weary day,
and he, too, had been compelled to suffer it in silence.

Jenny smiled at him in mute encouragement, grateful to him
for the manner in which, when the Lancers had decided to join

forces with their Hindu compatriots, he had obeyed William's order to escort her to the Residency.

As their commanding officer, William had seen it as his duty to remain with his men on the parade ground, in a last, vain endeavor to appeal to their loyalty. They had rejected his appeal, just as they had rejected that of Major Lund, who had, of course, remained with them also. But they had done no hurt to any of their officers, and William, when he had finally reached the Residency, had told her, with an odd note of pride in his voice, that half a dozen of the regiment's senior noncommissioned officers had guarded them throughout the mile-long journey from the lines.

"There were some hotheads crying out for our blood, but they would have none of it. They even sabered a mob of sepoys of the Sixteenth, who tried to bar our way here, and drove them off. They will march to Delhi, they told us, to offer their services to the old emperor, who is of their faith. And," he had added, with a catch in his voice, "the *rissaldar* major, Akbar Khan, asked me, quite seriously, if I would go with them as their regimental commander! It was an extraordinary request, wasn't it, Jenny? I suppose I should take it as a compliment, damn it!"

But it would not have pleased Major Marcus Lund, if he had heard it, Jenny thought, since apparently no such request had been made to him. The *rissaldar* major—a rank equivalent to sergeant major of cavalry, William had explained to her—was a fine old soldier, who wore the medals of the Sutlej and Punjab campaigns on the breast of his gold-braided tunic, and no doubt he had heard accounts of the charge of the British Light Cavalry Brigade in the Crimea and was aware that William had taken part in it. That, probably, had prompted the extraordinary request, or—

"Mrs. De Lancey, it's dark now." Andrew Melgund came across the floor to crouch down beside her. "You said they'd stop firing that cannon at us when it was dark."

The two nine-pounder guns had been pounding the Residency's stout walls at intervals throughout the day, but they had done less damage than might have been expected, for the house was solidly built of brick and stone.

"I expect they'll stop, Andy," Jenny answered absently. She raised herself to the height of the windowsill and peered out. There was still a glow from the smoldering cantonment bungalows, some of which had been set on fire by the looters only that afternoon; and from the roof of the church flames leapt high into the night sky, as if that building's destruction by fire had been an afterthought on the part of the mutineers. Or, more likely, of the criminal element from the native city, who had followed in the soldiers' wake, intent on plunder rather than vengeance on their white rulers.

Nearer at hand, small, flickering fires could be seen, and Major Lund grunted in annoyance.

"The rogues are cooking their evening meal," he observed, without looking round. "It might give us a chance to draw some fresh water from the well, while their attention is distracted."

"I could go," Andy Melgund offered eagerly. "I'm small—they might not notice me."

"You're just a bit too small, Andy," Jenny said, putting an arm about him. "You wouldn't have the strength to pull the bucket up, when it was filled." But he had given her an idea, and she gestured to the Brown Bess propped against the table beside her. "Could you load a musket, do you think? If so, you could take my place and load for Major Lund."

The boy nodded. "Oh, yes, I know how—I've watched you doing it. But . . . are *you* going to fetch the water? I must say, I could do with it. I'm parched."

They had spoken in whispers, and Jenny was not sure whether or not Major Lund had heard them, but he raised no objection when she got to her feet, relinquishing her place to Andy Melgund. No one else paid her any heed as she crossed the room in the dim light, picking her way carefully past the sleeping children. Like them, Martha Lund was asleep, as were two other women, curled up on the floor with the children.

In the hallway outside, three empty water *chattis* stood awaiting replenishment, and Jenny bent to pick one up just as a shadowy figure emerged from the basement cellar to join her. It was the chaplain, the Reverend Walters.

"Ah—Mrs. De Lancey," he said. "I see you have the same

notion as myself. The poor wounded souls down there are sorely in need of water, and since men of my cloth must be noncombatants, I thought I would try to alleviate their suffering by going to the well and getting some. But you—you are a lady, Mrs. De Lancey, and this surely is men's work. Please, let me have that *chatti,* won't you?"

"We could go together, Mr. Walters," Jenny answered firmly. "We'd be much quicker, if there were two of us."

He yielded reluctantly, but Jenny met with fresh opposition when she and the chaplain, carrying the empty *chattis* between them, approached the rear door, where four officers were crouching behind a hastily erected barrier of household furniture and sandbags.

All looked weary and disspirited, and two had sustained wounds, but they turned on her with one accord on catching sight of the *chattis.*

"I cannot possibly let you go out into the compound, Mrs. De Lancey," an elderly captain of the Rifles exclaimed indignantly. "Not without the colonel's permission, ma'am. You would be risking your life, and—"

"The colonel isn't here, Captain Sangster," Jenny reminded him. "And like Mr. Walters, I cannot take a musket and man our defenses. But I *do* know how to draw water from the well, and our supplies are dangerously depleted. Besides," she added untruthfully, "Major Lund did not object . . . and it is pitch dark outside. They won't be able to see us."

The four officers held a brief consultation, peering anxiously out into the darkness as they argued, and finally a subaltern of the Sixteenth was deputed to accompany Jenny and the chaplain and to stand guard over them as they drew the water.

Initially they met with no opposition; working as fast as they could, they had filled two of the *chattis* when, evidently alerted by the creaking of the ancient wheel mechanism, the watcher in the banyan tree opened fire. He got off two shots, both poorly aimed, which fell short of their unseen target, and then their escort returned the fire and brought the attacker crashing to the ground. He made off, evidently not seriously hurt, and the Reverend Walters murmured admiringly, "Oh, well done, Mr. Campbell! That was a remarkable shot."

"I spotted the flash of his musket," Lieutenant Campbell whispered back, busily reloading his own weapon. "Are you nearly done, Padre? Because I fear they'll be back in that infernal tree if we stay here much longer."

"One more bucket will do it," the chaplain assured him. "Ready, Mrs. De Lancey?"

The brimming bucket was hauled to the well top, their combined efforts speeding its passage, when, without warning, a tremendous explosion rent the air. It was followed by a second and a third, and half a mile away flames rose in a blood-red cloud to light the night sky to startling brilliance.

"By heaven!" young Campbell yelled, throwing caution to the winds in his excitement. "It's the magazine! They've done it, thank God—they've blown the whole place up!"

Everyone was cheering when, stumbling under the weight of the heavy *chattis,* Jenny and her two companions regained the rear veranda of the beleaguered Residency. David Melgund came from the basement, his wife and a number of other women following eagerly behind. Morale, which had been at a low ebb so short a time before, was miraculously lifted, as they all crowded onto the veranda to watch the pall of black smoke that now rose from the shattered magazine building, as witness of its destruction.

"Oh, isn't it wonderful! Now the sepoys will not be able to bring any more cannon against us!"

"Or take them to Delhi—that's what my husband's men told him they intended to do, using elephants to haul them."

"There were rifles there too—Enfields, the ones they refused, the treacherous fools, because of that scare concerning the grease on the cartridges!"

"The colonel succeeded, Mrs. De Lancey, against all the odds! He is a very brave man. No wonder he was recommended for the Victoria Cross in the Crimea. You must be very proud of him."

Proud, Jenny thought dully—yes, she was proud of William's bravery and his selfless devotion to duty. But anxiety for his safety had superseded pride, and she could not join in the cheers or respond to the plaudits of the Residency's excited defenders, addressed to herself, since William was not there to receive them. If only they had listened to him; if only they had heeded his warnings, instead of waiting until the Rifles had murdered their colonel and it was too late! Not so long ago, some of these officers and their wives had reviled William, asserting scornfully that he was a scaremonger or worse, ignorant of the Company's army and its great traditions, and on that account would have been wiser to hold his tongue.

If they had listened, the Residency might have been adequately prepared to withstand attack. All the British and Eurasian women and children might have been brought in, instead of just a handful, and the magazine might have been placed under European guard, so that there would have been no need for William to take his life in his hands in order to destroy it.

"Look! Isn't that a Verey light, fired from the river?" Captain Sangster was pointing, his voice suddenly harsh with strain. "A red and . . . yes, that's a green! That's the signal—De Lancey's come back by river. And another red—that means he needs help. Campbell, Lauder, Millbank—get down to the wharf as fast as you can! But for God's sake look out—they may be under attack!"

But there was no firing, even when the three subalterns and the commissioner had set off at a run for the wharf at the far end of the Residency garden. Jenny waited, sick with apprehension, her heart beating wildly. She tried to pray, but no words would come, and then Bella Gillespie, the adjutant's young wife, came to stand beside her, white-faced and trembling. Her husband, Arnold, had been one of William's volunteers, and one of the few officers in the Ranpur garrison who had feared, as had William, that the sepoys' disaffection would sooner or later manifest itself in open and bloody confrontation.

"Oh, Mrs. De Lancey," the girl whispered brokenly, "I—I'm so afraid. Oh, please God, grant they've come back safely!"

Jenny's heart echoed her prayer, and they clung together, anxious and afraid, waiting for a glimpse of the returning volunteers. But first to come stumbling across the darkly shadowed garden was a little group of women, with children clinging to their hands or borne in their arms, and Jenny bit back a cry of disappointment, for it was Cornet Millbank, not William, who led the straggling procession, its rear brought up by two olive-skinned men, in Rifles uniform, both of whom appeared to be wounded.

A shocked voice from behind her exclaimed, "They are Eurasians—the Eurasian bandsmen's families! And they've brought them *here!*"

Jenny did not need to turn around to identify the voice as that of Major Lund's autocratic sister, Mrs. Hall. Amelia Hall was the widow of a Company nabob, who had been a member of the Court of Directors and the governor general's Council, but for some inexplicable reason her husband's death had left her in such straitened financial circumstances that she had been compelled to make her home with the Lunds in Ranpur—an expedient of which she constantly complained, to poor Martha Lund's embarrassment.

"Are we expected," she went on, with biting sarcasm, "to share our already overcrowded quarters with such as these, Mr. Melgund? Surely there are limits, even during a . . . a mutiny!"

Her question had been addressed to the commissioner, but it was William who answered her. He strode up the veranda steps, materializing from the darkness, and Jenny's relief at seeing him was tempered by the fear that he might speak his mind too freely, for it was evident that he was angrier than she had ever supposed he could be.

In the hope of preventing an outburst, she went to him, calling his name, but on this occasion William was not to be silenced. He put his arms about her and turned on Mrs. Hall, his voice shaking with rage.

"I would have you know, madam, that these loyal and courageous people barricaded themselves in the magazine, and in spite of suffering many casualities and being deprived of food and water, they prevented the mutinous sepoys from entering it. They held out for forty-eight hours, against constant attack, let me tell you. Had it not been for their selfless action, we would have found nothing to blow up when we reached the magazine! These are the survivors, madam—all that are left of them, apart from six or seven badly wounded men who must be carried here, since they cannot walk."

Without waiting for Mrs. Hall's reply, William turned his

back on her. Catching sight of the Reverend Walters, he said, with a swift change of tone, "I'd be obliged if you would go down to the boat, Padre. We'll organize stretcher parties, but . . . there are some who are in need of your services. They're too badly hurt to be moved."

"Arnold—Colonel De Lancey, is Arnold there? Did you bring him back?" It was Bella Gillespie, Jenny realized; in her own gratitude for William's safe return, she had forgotten that Bella's anxiety had matched her own, only a few minutes before. She slipped from William's embrace to clasp the adjutant's distraught young wife in her arms, sensing what was to come.

"I'm desperately sorry, Mrs. Gillespie," she heard William say regretfully. "Arnold died covering our retreat. It was . . . it was instantaneous; he did not suffer. We brought his body back, so that it may be given Christian burial."

The rest of his words, uttered in a vain attempt at consolation, were drowned by Bella's heartbroken sobs, until, with unexpected gentleness, Mrs. Hall led her away.

Chapter XV

SUDDENLY ALL WAS feverish activity, in which Jenny was caught up, so that the hours passed so swiftly she had no pause to think or grieve. The wounded were brought up from the boat in which William's party had made their escape, and she and the other women did what they could to ease their suffering, under the direction of the two surviving regimental surgeons and old Dr. Arbuthnot, the white-haired civil surgeon, who, himself wounded in the arm and head, gave instructions and advice from a chair.

All too soon, the basement became so overcrowded that there was scarcely space to move, and the heat was stifling. Jenny pillowed on her lap the dark head of a dying Eurasian, one of the members of the regimental band, and at his request recited the Lord's Prayer as he died, before tearing her petticoat into strips to stanch the bleeding from an ugly wound in the chest of a pitifully wailing child.

The water *chattis,* which she and the Reverend Walters had filled so short a time before, were rapidly emptied, supplies of laudanum and spirits ran out, and from the upper part of the house the sobs of frightened children and a renewal of the cannon fire and musketry heralded another day of torment for the besieged.

Bella Gillespie came bravely to offer her help. Dry-eyed and controlled, she told Jenny that she had seen her husband to his shallow, unmarked grave, with five others.

"Mr. Walters conducted the burial service," she said quietly. "And—Colonel De Lancey was right. I don't think Arnold suffered. It—it was a clean shot, between his poor eyes." Bitterly she added, "And now they are attacking us again, our sowars among them. It's hard to believe that they can hate us so much, isn't it, Mrs. De Lancey? Only a week ago Arnold's *rissaldar,* Mohammed Azziz, was teaching Tommy to ride. Now he is out there, trying to kill us."

A thunderous crash, from somewhere above their heads, brought showers of plaster down, to be followed almost instantly by a second and a third, so that the whole building shook.

"They got some more damned guns from somewhere," a subaltern, whose shattered arm had just been dressed, swore under his breath and then apologized, realizing that Jenny had heard him. "But at least we've got a supply of rifles—Colonel De Lancey's party brought them from the magazine, before they blew it up. We'll hold our own, so long as the walls aren't knocked down!"

But the walls, it seemed to Jenny, as the bombardment continued relentlessly throughout the day, could hardly last much longer; and unless their supply of water could be replenished, the suffering of the wounded would become unendurable, and then the fit defenders would lack the strength to hold their attackers at bay. As for the children . . . She shivered. She had not seen William since early morning, although she had heard his voice; and as she held a cup, containing a few precious drops of water, to the lips of one of the Eurasian drummers, she found herself returning in memory to the early days of their marriage.

Such happy, carefree days they now seemed—days spent on their honeymoon when they had visited Henry Osborne and his family at Marshall Mount. The rolling acres of lush grassland, the quiet beauty of the Australian bush, the heady scent of the ubiquitous gum trees, the birds, bright and varied in their colorful plumage, and . . . the little stone-built church, to which they had driven in the Osbornes' wagon, passing—what had Sarah Osborne called it? Pumpkin Cottage, with its lovely garden, the roses imported from Ireland, the jacaranda from South

America or the Cape, and the wattle, golden-yellow in the sunlight . . . Oh, why had William been so adamant in his determination to leave all that behind and come to India—to *this*? To
the guns and the dark-faced Indian soldiers, who were now
their enemies.

Yet, Jenny thought, biting back the tears that ached in her
throat, she loved William, and given the choice again, she knew
that she would still have married him, wherever he had taken
her, whatever he had asked of her. As poor, heartbroken little
Bella Gillespie had reminded her, a week ago Ranpur had been
at peace. She had lain in her husband's embrace, happy and
fulfilled after their lovemaking, and she had wanted to tell him
that they would have a child. But she had not been sure, so she
had said nothing. It had been too soon to be sure, and she had
also been afraid to tell him, aware that he feared the outbreak of
mutiny was imminent and, because of it, would not welcome
the news.

Jenny put down the empty cup and brushed the limp hair
from her damp and sweat-streaked face before rising wearily to
her feet. Perhaps, when darkness fell at last, she could again
seek out the Reverend Walters and fill the empty *chattis* from
the well. The sepoys took their evening meal at sunset, and
usually then the firing let up, if it did not cease. She picked up
one of the *chattis* and was on her way to the stone steps leading
from the basement when she again heard William's voice.

"As fast as you know how, Lund," she heard him say. "Once
we start the evacuation, there must be no delay."

Evacuation, Jenny thought, with tired dismay. Were they to
abandon the Residency, then, in order to seek safety elsewhere?
By river, she could only suppose, since the boats were there,
tied up to the wharf where William and his party had landed
the previous night. Since the Residency had suffered its first
attack, a guard of officers and civilian volunteers had been
posted in the stone gatehouse overlooking the wharf, and—

William came down the steps, peering about him in the dim
light of the improvised hospital's oil lamps. Seeing her, he came
toward her, his good arm outheld. Jenny went to him, seeking
strength and resolution from his presence, holding up her face

to his and feeling the burning heat of his body against her own
so intensely that, for a moment, she feared that he had a fever.

"No," he said, answering her unvoiced question. "I'm all
right, my love. Just weary, as I'm sure you must be. Darling—"
His arm tightened about her. "This place has become untenable. The front walls will collapse before long, and—worst of all
—the swine have scored a direct hit on our well with one of
their nine-pounders. It's just a mass of brick rubble now, so
we'll have to abandon the Residency—evacuate the children
and the wounded right away, whilst it's dark, and try to make
our escape by river. We've three country boats, equipped with
sails and oars. You'll have to be very brave, Jenny my dearest,
because—" He hesitated.

"Because you're not coming with us?" Jenny put in, guessing
what he was trying to tell her.

"I have to command the rear guard," William said flatly.
"Melgund and Lund will command the boats, but we'll follow,
just as soon as we're certain there is no danger of pursuit." He
managed a smile. "You must not worry about me, sweetheart—
we have the oared boat we returned from the magazine in last
night. We shall catch up to you long before you reach Cawnpore."

"Cawnpore, Will? But—" Cold fingers of fear clutched at
Jenny's heart. "Are they not under siege, too? Mr. Melgund
said that the Nana of Bithur had betrayed them."

"General Wheeler has some European troops, Jenny, and the
last information we had was that reinforcements of the Queen's
Eighty-fourth had reached them and that a relief force was on
the way from Allahabad—a regiment of Madras Fusiliers."
William gave vent to a tired sigh. "It's Melgund's decision, not
mine, but Lund and Sangster agreed with it. I'd have made an
attempt to reach Lucknow and Sir Henry Lawrence, but it
would have taken very much longer, of course, and involved
traveling overland, which could be very dangerous." He bent to
kiss her. "Jenny, my sweet love, granted no pursuit and a bit of
luck, we could all be in Cawnpore within twenty-four hours. I
couldn't argue with Melgund—he knows the country better
than I do; and so do the others. And with so many wounded,
the boats offer the best chance—the poor devils you've been

caring for could not walk, could they? And we've no other transport."

Jenny inclined her head wordlessly, and William added, with an assumption of confidence that she felt sure he had put on for her benefit, "Melgund has sent a *cossid* to Lucknow—a reliable man who was one of his house servants. At least Sir Henry will be apprised of our intentions."

"Yes," she echoed, but her heart was heavy with foreboding. She wanted to beg William to allow her to stay with him, but knew that he would refuse any such request. Numbly she listened while he told her the plans they had made for the evacuation. The wounded were to be taken out first—carried, if they were unable to walk—then the children and their mothers, each party with a guard of armed men, who would accompany them in the boats.

"As soon as the first boat is loaded, it will put off, then the second. You'll be in the third, Jenny, with the older children and the rest of the women, with those who have been guarding the gatehouse. They have a small brass cannon, which I hope they'll contrive to load into the boat. And I'll be after you, darling, don't worry." He kissed her again, with such lingering tenderness that Jenny wondered whether, like herself, her husband feared that this might be the last kiss they would ever exchange, and she clung to him in a vain attempt to put off their parting.

Regretfully but with gentle firmness he let her go. "My love, I'll have to leave you. They'll be waiting for me, and we don't have too much time. Jenny, this has to be done silently. Go with the children, the older ones, and impress on them that they must not make a sound on the way down to the wharf. Keep the Melgunds' boy, Andrew, with you. He's an intelligent lad, and he'll help to ensure that they're quiet. And . . . God bless you, my darling, and keep you safe! I love you, Jenny, now and always. I love you with all my heart."

He was gone, taking the stone steps two at a time, before Jenny could answer him, and a few minutes later the evacuation of the Residency began.

It went remarkably smoothly. Jenny found Andy Melgund and, as William had suggested, invoked his aid when the time came for the older children to steal silently across the pitch-dark Residency garden. Between them, they ushered the little crowd of seven- and eight-year-olds down to the wharf and on board the waiting boat. The first two boats had already shoved off, and as Martha Lund climbed the rickety gangplank, assisted by Bella Gillespie, the men on guard at the gatehouse began the awkward task of dismantling their small brass muzzle-loading gun, in order to mount it in the bow of the boat.

Inevitably this caused delay, and by the time the gun had been transferred and reassembled, the other two boats had vanished into the darkness. Major Lund, in a fever of impatience, ordered the mooring lines to be cast off, and two of the men—both British NCOs—who had been working on the gun had to jump on board as the cumbersome boat was caught by the current and started to move away from the wharf. But they gained the crowded deck unhurt, and with its single heavy lateen sail set, the boat was on its way, heading for midstream, one of the Rifles captains manipulating the steering oar at the stern.

As they drew away, Jenny heard a prolonged burst of rifle fire, coming from the abandoned Residency, and with a sinking heart glimpsed shadowy figures moving across the garden to its rear. Bent low, they were running toward the gatehouse and the wharf, clearly with the intention of cutting off the rear guard's retreat. William had said that he and his companions had an oared boat tied up at the wharf, she remembered—the craft they had used to reach the magazine and in which they were planning to follow the larger, country boats. If the sepoys managed to cut them off from it . . . She bit back a sob. But then her attention was distracted by a violent jarring, which knocked her off her feet. When she picked herself up, she heard Major Lund cursing wrathfully and another voice, which reduced him to impotent silence, announcing ruefully that they had run aground on a sandbank.

It took the combined efforts of a dozen men, waist-deep in the water, to free the boat and set it once more in sluggish motion. Throughout the night, the same impediments slowed their progress. Without the influx of monsoon rain, even the mighty Ganges River was low, and the sandbanks gave no indication of their presence, so that it was impossible to steer clear of them. When the moon came out, to cast a faint, silvery radiance over the scene, the other boats, although some distance ahead, were observed to be in a predicament similar to their own.

Daylight brought a slight improvement, or else Captain Mayhew had gained more proficiency with the sweep oar, and they came within hailing distance of Captain Sangster's boat, only to be warned of a fresh peril.

"Don't let your people drink the river water, Lund!" he shouted across the intervening space. "It's dangerously polluted."

The warning came too late, Jenny thought bitterly, since virtually all those in Major Lund's command had slaked their thirst with river water; and because the children had been so distressed, the adults had helped them to drink, leaning over the side of the boat to fill their cupped hands or soak kerchiefs and even their skirts with it. So far no one had shown any sign of ill effects, although Martha Lund had, it was true, complained of nausea after little Bella Gillespie had gone to great pains to assuage the older woman's burning thirst by lowering her bonnet by its ribbons and bringing it up, in triumph, filled to the brim.

Bella exchanged a rueful glance with her, but neither she nor Jenny ventured to dispute the major's contention; and as the sun rose and its blazing heat added to the general discomfort, more and more people had recourse to the river without a second thought, intent only on gaining relief from their torment.

By evening, the three boats had made some progress, but two wounded men and a Eurasian baby had died, and to Jenny's distress, William and the rear guard had failed to join up with them. The night passed with still more delays caused by the sandbanks, and the children, fractious at first, had sunk into dulled apathy, huddling beside their mothers on the deck and refusing to respond to Mrs. Hall's attempts to lead them in hymn singing. They roused themselves, however, shrieking with terror when the inhabitants of a riverside village opened fire on the boats with ancient matchlocks. Major Lund's boat grounded within point-blank range, adding to the panic that seized them all, but the major endeavored to reason with the attackers, shouting out something in fluent Hindustani. Eventually the firing ceased, and the headman came sullenly to the water's edge to confer in shrill, hostile tones, his long-barreled weapon held menacingly in front of him.

Major Lund asked for food, promising to pay highly for it, but his offer was curtly rejected, and the old man refused to aid in refloating the boat. Jenny understood very little of the shouted exchange, but when they had once more hauled the cumbersome craft into midstream and the sail filled, Lund gathered the officers about him, evidently with the intention of discussing the intelligence he had gathered from his confrontation with the headman. The women were excluded, but Andy Melgund—whose Hindustani was also fluent—explained in a whisper what the old man had said.

"He claimed that the Company's rule has ended, just as the omens predicted, one hundred years after the Battle of Plassey. He said that the *shaitan ka hawa*—that means the devil's wind—had blown throughout Hindustan and all had answered its call to defend the faith. And—" The boy hesitated, his young face adult in its disillusionment. "Mrs. De Lancey, he said that the Nana Sahib will be crowned as Peishwa of the Mahrattas and that . . . that the Cawnpore garrison had been defeated and none are left alive, except a few women and children, who are now being held captive in the city."

Jenny stared at him in stunned bewilderment.

"Oh, Andy, surely that cannot be true?"

"It was what he told Major Lund, Mrs. De Lancey," Andy said. "But—" His sharp ears had picked up an angry expostulation from the group of officers, and his expression relaxed. "Major Lund doesn't believe a word of it, and Captain Sangster doesn't either. They are going to consult with my father in the other boat, but they are agreed that we should go on. And I'm sure they are right, Mrs. De Lancey," he added earnestly. "General Wheeler has British troops in the Cawnpore garrison—they'd never surrender to a fat old pig like the Nana. I saw him, you know, when I was in Lucknow with Papa, and that's just what he is—a fat, pampered old pig! He fawned on General Outram, who was chief commissioner then, and kept paying him compliments . . . he even paid my father a few, for good measure." Andy's tone was scornful. "He'd never defeat a British garrison, if he lived to be a hundred!"

Jenny hoped fervently that he was right. She glanced at Bella Gillespie, who had heard the boy's denunciation of the Nana of Bithur, and saw that she, too, found the headman's claim hard to believe.

"Andy's correct, Mrs. De Lancey," she said. "General Wheeler has a company of the Queen's Thirty-second and some of the Eighty-fourth—the Cawnpore garrison wasn't entirely native, like ours. And the last news we had from Sir Henry Lawrence was that a relief force was on the way from Allahabad—a whole regiment! They'd never surrender. Poor dear Arnold used to say that he wished *we* had been in Cawnpore."

The consultation with Commissioner Melgund was brief and the decision to go on swiftly reached, but darkness fell shortly afterward, and as a precaution the three boats came to anchor, to enable them to defer their arrival in Cawnpore until daylight.

In common with the rest, Jenny lapsed into an exhausted sleep, her last thought the hope that, while they were halted, William and the men who had stayed with him might be able to catch up. But, with the dawn of the new day, they suffered a rude awakening. On the bank, a squadron of native cavalry sat their horses in silent, threatening array, while off to one side a pair of light field guns were trained on the anchored boats. Scarcely had the startled fugitives taken this in when a small flotilla of oared boats and canoes, packed with scarlet-coated sepoys, converged on them from all sides.

Resistance was futile, the danger to the women and children and the wounded crowding the decks too great to permit any attempt to ward off attack; and—effectively to discourage resistance—one of the field guns sent a round-shot across the bow of Major Lund's boat.

Horror piled on horror, humiliation on humiliation as the sepoys swarmed on board, thrusting the women roughly aside, driving the men into line against the bulwarks with their hands raised, and scattering the frightened children with harsh words and blows from their musket butts. One of the cavalrymen, a bearded native officer with an evil, pockmarked face, was rowed out to Major Lund's boat to demand his formal surrender.

"I am Teeka Singh," he announced, tapping a gold-headed cane on the leg of his boot, in a manner intended to parody a British officer addressing an underling. "Lately *rissaldar* major in the Second Light Cavalry and now general of cavalry in the service of His Supreme Highness, the Peishwa of the Mahrattas and Maharajah of Bithur, the great and mighty Dundoo Punth." He recited the string of titles with conscious pride, his expression contemptuous as he took in Marcus Lund's filthy clothing and his unshaven cheeks. "You are from Ranpur, are you not?"

Major Lund controlled his bitter anger and, with what dignity he could muster, inclined his head.

"Yes, we are from Ranpur, and we are armed. We—"

"Armed?" Teeka Singh challenged mockingly, gesturing to the line of officers, from whom the sepoys had now taken both rifles and pistols.

The major blustered. "You are in rebellion against the government and the Company, Teeka Singh, for which you may expect retribution. Her Majesty the Queen will not countenance treachery and rebellion, by the Nana or the King of Delhi or any other of her Indian subjects. British soldiers will be sent here swiftly, in their thousands, to exact vengeance for what you and others like you have dared to do—rest assured of that. Now call off your men and conduct us to General Wheeler Sahib at once!"

His tone was peremptory, his anger barely kept within bounds, and Jenny thought, watching him, that he had more courage even than she had earlier given him credit for. But Teeka Singh was unmoved by the threats. He threw back his turbaned head and laughed, then spat his contempt in Major Lund's face.

"You talk with a loud mouth, Major, but you are but a windbag!" the onetime *rissaldar* major accused. "The Company's rule is overthrown—all Hindustan is restored to the people. Our king rules in Delhi, and here it is the Peishwa to whom we give allegiance. Muslim and Hindu speak with one voice! As to conducting you to General Wheeler, that is impossible—the garrison of General Wheeler perished at our hands two days ago, save for some females with their children, whom we hold captive. The old white-beard general is dead, Major. His bones lie by the riverside, picked clean by the vultures, and yours will shortly join them there!"

Every vestige of color drained from Marcus Lund's stubble-darkened cheeks as his worst fears were confirmed. Many of the women were sobbing; the men were as shocked and stunned as he, as the fact of their utter helplessness was borne home to them. Unarmed though they were, most of them, Jenny sensed, would gladly have turned on their captors, ready to sell their lives as dearly as they could rather than accept the humiliation of surrender and, it seemed from Teeka Singh's last words, death at the hands of rebel soldiers whom they had once commanded.

One of the Rifles' subalterns, who had manned the brass gun in the boat's bow, took a pace toward the abandoned weapon, his intention plain, but Lund's harsh voice halted him before he could reach it.

"What of our memsahibs and children, Teeka Singh?" Lund asked. "Do you intend to murder them also?"

"We do not make war on women and babies," the cavalry commander answered. "They will be held captive with the females from the garrison, to await the Peishwa's pleasure." Tiring of baiting the unhappy Lund, he shouted an order to the sepoys who had first boarded the boat, at which they grinned broadly and started to strip their captives of everything of apparent value, handling roughly any who attempted to resist them.

Jenny stood dry-eyed but inwardly bitterly distressed as her wedding ring and a pretty ruby-and-diamond brooch William had given her vanished into the rapacious hands of a sepoy with the number fifty-three on his cap. The 53rd Native Infantry, she recalled, was the regiment commanded by Martha Lund's brother, Colonel Wiggins, who had visited Ranpur with his wife and two pretty little daughters only a few weeks ago. Were they too, she wondered, also dead, or were the children and their mother among those held captive, to await the Peishwa's pleasure? She found herself praying silently once again, but this time her plea to her Maker was that William and the men who had stayed behind with him should on no account follow the boats in which she and the other fugitives had made their disastrous escape.

"Please God, of Thy infinite mercy and compassion, grant that they are given warning of what has happened here. Send them, O God, to Allahabad or Lucknow—anywhere but here!"

The looting over, Teeka Singh was rowed back to his cavalry bodyguard, and the boats again got under way, their sails hoisted and a sepoy manning each of the steering oars. Without warning, there was a brief commotion on board the leading boat, and a fusillade of shots rang out, coming from both boat and shore.

Beside her, Andy Melgund seized Jenny's arm in small, fever-hot fingers, and he said, his voice shrill with mingled fear and excitement, "It's Papa's boat, Mrs. De Lancey! I—I think they're trying to get away!"

It was a brave but hopeless attempt. Commissioner Melgund's boat had contained the wounded men from the Residency, with a small armed guard, but no women. The commissioner, Jenny thought with a pang, and those who had accompanied him had decided to take the only alternative to ignominious capture left open to them—to escape or die in the attempt.

They did manage to turn their boat and head in the direction from which they had come, but their defiance was short-lived. Both field guns opened fire on them, grapeshot raking the deck, mowing them down. Then the gunners loaded with round-shot, and the boat's thin wooden hull was mercilessly pounded until, listing heavily, it filled with water and sank into the deep, midstream channel, only the tip of its mast marking the spot where it had gone down.

Andy Melgund hid his face against Jenny's breast.

"I—I suppose," he managed at last, his voice choked with sobs, "Mrs. De Lancey, I suppose my papa w-was a hero. He—he must've known that they didn't have a chance. B-but he wouldn't give in. Perhaps he was trying to set us an example—do you think that was it?"

"I think it was, Andy," Jenny agreed, her own throat tight. She lifted the boy to his feet. "Your mama will need you now. You'd better go to her and try to comfort her."

He did as she bade him, walking across the deck to his mother's side, his head held high, a thin little nine-year-old in torn trousers and a filthy shirt who had suddenly and hearteningly become a man.

Bella Gillespie stumbled over to Jenny's side, her face swollen and blotched with tears. She did not speak, and Jenny, finding no words, put an arm about her shoulders, and they stood together in silence, as the two remaining boats made their slow way, under sail, to the city of Cawnpore.

Soon there was terrible, heartbreaking evidence that Teeka Singh had told the truth concerning the fate of the British garrison. Passing a landing place on the city side of the river, they saw the charred shells of some score of country boats, similar to but somewhat smaller than their own. They floated in the muddy water or were held fast, as theirs had so often been, on a sandbank, the oars broken, the straw awnings and sails all but reduced to ashes.

But worse, by far, were the ghastly bloated bodies lying at the water's edge—hundreds of them, it seemed, abandoned to the vultures and prowling jackals and to the human predators, who had evidently stripped them of everything of value—including their clothing. On the slope above the landing place and in front of a small stone temple at its summit, guns had been mounted, trained on the boats below; but now, like the boats and the bodies of the victims, they, too, were abandoned—mute and damning proof of the manner and purpose for which they had been used.

Major Lund buried his face in his hands and wept. He was the first to take in and understand the implications of what they were seeing, and the bitter pain and disillusionment, which came with understanding, were in his voice as he shouted in accusation, "This was betrayal—this was treachery of the basest kind! Don't you see—" He appealed to those about him. "God in heaven, General Wheeler was defending an entrenchment over a mile from here, near the Allahabad Road! The garrison *must* have surrendered, when they ran out of ammunition or food or when their casualties became too high. They must have accepted terms and come here, believing they were to be given safe conduct to Allahabad. That is what the boats were

for. But instead—" His voice faltered and broke, and a sepoy
said something to him in his own tongue that was clearly deri-
sory and calculated to invoke anger.

Marcus Lund's control snapped. With a strangled cry, he
flung himself upon the man, hands reaching for his throat, but
the sepoy stepped back, eluding his rush, and brought the butt
of his musket down with sickening force on the Englishman's
unprotected head. Lund fell, and two other sepoys joined the
first, hacking and stabbing at him with their bayonets. After a
brief scuffle, they picked up the limp and lifeless body between
them and hurled it into the water, to add one more to the
number already floating in the shallows, among the burnt-out
boats. Martha Lund screamed in grief-stricken protest, but the
sepoys ignored her, barring the way when Captain Mayhew and
one of the other officers tried to go to her.

A short time afterward, still numb with shock, Jenny found
herself herded with the rest of the women and children into a
bullock cart, which jolted its way through congested streets and
jeering crowds, finally coming to a halt outside a small, yellow-
painted building with a flat roof and shuttered windows, with a
sepoy guard detachment in the walled courtyard surrounding it.

"Ar' jao—jeldi!" one of the cavalry sowars who had escorted
them through the town shouted at them impatiently. "Inside—
go, go! All *mems,* all *baba log* inside!"

They obeyed him, too exhausted and demoralized to resist
the harsh commands and the jabbing sabers. Amelia Hall
tripped and would have fallen had not Jenny grasped her arm,
and they stumbled inside, to halt in stunned dismay at the sight
of what awaited them.

A small, dark, airless room, which might have held a dozen
women in some discomfort, now accommodated five times that
number. Mothers huddled with their children on a few wisps of
filthy straw spread over a stone floor. Others crouched in cor-
ners or lay, with closed eyes, indifferent to what went on about
them. Many were wounded, their wounds uncovered and sup-
purating, hideous beyond belief.

One woman, in a torn and bloodstained white dress, who had
been reading to a group of older children from a prayer book,

paused in her reading to study the new arrivals with unhappy eyes.

"We are the survivors of the Cawnpore garrison," she said, in an expressionless voice. "All who are left out of almost a thousand souls. And this place is known as the Bibigarh—the House of Women. I cannot say welcome to it, for it is unsanitary and desperately overcrowded; but at least it is a slight improvement on the Savada Koti, where we were first imprisoned, and they have at last given us the services of a doctor. Of which," she added, a sudden bitter edge to her voice, "as you can see, we have been most sorely in need. Are you also victims of the Nana's treachery?"

"We are from Ranpur," Amelia Hall told her. "The mutineers intercepted our boats and took us captive early this morning. I am Amelia Hall, widow of the late Mr. Swinton Hall, who was a member of the Honorable Company's Court of Directors." She paused, clearly expecting some response; but receiving none, she went on, her voice shrill with indignation, "They murdered my brother, Major Lund of the Fifth Oudh Lancers, on the way here. His poor wife, who is shortly to be delivered of a child, is now a widow, and—"

"We are all widows here, Mrs. Hall," the woman in the white dress told her, quite gently. "I am Caroline Moore, widow of Captain John Moore, of Her Majesty's Thirty-second Regiment. Please—" She waved a limp hand to the dim recesses of the crowded, darkly shadowed room. "Please—find what comfort you can." Picking up her prayer book, she went on reading as if there had been no interruption. " 'Our fathers trusted in Thee; they trusted and Thou didst deliver them. They cried unto Thee and were delivered; they trusted in Thee and were not confounded. . . .' "

A child broke into sobs, but the quiet, level voice read on.

Was she, too, a widow now? Jenny wondered despairingly. She bent her head, and the prayer she whispered came from her heart.

"Dear merciful Father, keep William safe, whatever fate may befall me. I count not my life beside his and would gladly die that he might live."

Andy Meldrum tugged at her hand.

"I've found a place where you and Rosie can lie down," he said. "There's some straw there, and I'll guard you and my mama, Mrs. De Lancey."

Chapter XVI

WILLIAM FIRST BECAME conscious of a pungent smell of rotting vegetation and then of the jarring motion of whatever vehicle was carrying him—a bullock cart, he decided, judging by its slow, plodding progress and lack of springs. His head was aching severely, and his whole body felt as if it were on fire, while his right leg seemed to be paralyzed, refusing to respond to his attempts to move himself into a more comfortable position.

It took all his flagging strength to raise himself on his good elbow; and when at last, with infinite effort, he managed to sit up, it was to find himself in semidarkness, with an inert body lying full length on the floor of the cart beside him, its weight imprisoning his leg. The body appeared to be in military uniform; he could feel the rough texture of the braid on the coat . . . and a sword belt, lacking the weapon it normally held, girt about the man's waist.

Whoever it was, he was unconscious, as William himself had been a few minutes before, and both of them were covered by a thick layer of the vegetation, whose strong odor had been the first thing he had noticed on his return to consciousness. William identified it, after a cursory examination, as damp straw, tied into bundles to serve as protection for a load of overripe melons, some of which had burst out of their skins. Faintly sickened by the stench, he managed to free his leg and peer out from beneath the top layer of straw, to discern two shadowy forms, in native robes, huddled together at the front of the cart.

Both were dozing, in the time-honored fashion of bullock cart drivers throughout India, leaving their animals to pick their own way along the rutted road.

Puzzled, William studied their hunched backs for a few moments and then let himself fall back. What, he asked himself, was he—he and the unknown soldier beside him—doing in the cart? Search his memory as he might, he had no recollection of how he had got there or for how long he had lain beneath the malodorous covering in the jolting wagon . . . and still less idea of where it might be bound. He was tempted to call out to the two natives, to ask them for an explanation, but then thought better of it, instinct warning him that he might alarm them. They—or possibly others—had gone to some trouble to conceal the presence of the cart's human cargo, which suggested danger or an attempt to remove him and his companion from a dangerous situation, and . . . Oh, dear God, of course there had been a hideously dangerous situation! The native garrison of Ranpur had broken out in mutiny—*his* regiment, the Fifth Lancers, had joined the Rifles and the Sixteenth Infantry in anarchy and rebellion, and the Rifles had murdered their commanding officer, Jeremy Roach, when he had sought to hold them to their allegiance!

Slowly, painfully, memory returned, and with it the recollection of the officers' bungalows in the Ranpur cantonments going up in flames, of lawless crowds from the native city looting and killing, while the Lancers had roared their war cry, *"Din, Din!"* and chanted the message the holy men had spread so assiduously: *"Sub lal hojega!"*—everything will be red with blood. . . .

William put a hand to his throbbing head, realizing that it was roughly bandaged. He shuddered, as incidents he had wanted to forget now came flooding back into his mind. He and the other officers, abruptly aroused from sleep, had done all in their power to stem the ghastly tide of slaughter, but it had been hopeless from the outset. They had managed to get most of the British women and children into the dubious safety of the ill-prepared Residency, but that was all. Jenny—thanks be to God, Jenny had been saved from the terrible scenes he had been compelled to witness; at least he had managed to spare her that, although conditions in the Residency had been terrible enough. He had sent her there with young Millbank at first light, before the outbreak had properly begun, since—like poor old Roach— he had seen it as his duty to try to keep his men in hand for as long as he could.

And then— William drew in his breath sharply. Then the *rissaldar* major, Akbar Khan, had invited him to lead the regiment to Delhi, as its colonel—an offer made with dignified gravity and intended to merit his serious consideration.

"This is the end of the Company's *raj.* Colonel sahib," he had said. "The end of the Army of Bengal after a hundred years of loyal service to John Company. But my regiment was greatly honored by the appointment of such an officer as you as its commander—an officer who took part in the immortal charge at Balaclava, to whom the great Queen over the sea awarded the highest decoration for gallantry, the Victoria Cross. We will serve you faithfully, sahib, if you will continue to command us. It is the wish of all ranks that I, as their spokesman, beg that you will accept."

Such a strange speech the fine old Indian officer had made, in perfect, almost pedantic English, which he must have practiced for hours and learned by heart, since his English was poor. Of course he had had to refuse, William reflected; but nonetheless he had been at once moved and humbled by the request. And even after his refusal, Akbar Khan and a heartening number of the other NCOs had done their best to ensure that none of their officers were harmed. True, some of the younger rank and file had not concurred with their *rissaldar* major's action; they had shouted in protest when the escort had formed up to take the British officers to the Residency, but they had offered no violence and had not attempted to stop them. Only Marcus Lund had been subjected to verbal abuse, when he had tried to harangue them and remind them of their duty, accusing them bitterly of betrayal. But . . .

Drops of rain touched his face, and in minutes it became a downpour. William gratefully accepted the chance to cool his fever-hot body and slake his thirst. The bullock cart drivers gathered their thin white *chuddars* about them but did not seek shelter or look round.

Apparently roused by the lashing rain, the man who had lain unconscious beside him stirred uneasily and murmured something unintelligible. Fearing that he might be too badly wounded to be able to move, William put a restraining arm about his shoulders and whispered to him to lie still. In the all-prevailing darkness and the obscuring rain, he could not see his companion's face clearly, but he recognized the voice as that of the Lancers' senior subaltern, Harry Cook. Cook had been with him when they had blown up the stored ammunition in the magazine, and he had also volunteered to join the rear guard, William recalled. And he had been there when, the boats safely away, they had made their last stand in the gatehouse, their own way of escape to the wharf cut off by . . . oh, God, by some of their own men, some of the Lancers!

"It's all right, Harry," he said softly. "Don't try to move." Holding out his cap, he managed to gather sufficient rainwater to enable Cook to drink, and the younger man gulped it down gratefully.

"Colonel—is it you, sir? Colonel De Lancey?" His voice was weak, but his eyes, William saw, were open, peering up at him uncertainly.

"Yes, it's me. How badly are you hurt, Harry? Can you sit up?"

"I think so, I—Lord, I'm as weak as a kitten! If you could just give me a hand, sir, I . . . That's better." Cook sat up, to look about him in bewilderment. "Where the devil are we?"

William motioned for him to keep his voice down. "In a bullock cart," he said. "With a load of rotting melons. But I've no idea how we got here or where we're being taken. There are two men driving us—natives, I presume—but I haven't spoken to them. To tell you the truth, Harry, I'm as much in the dark as you are. I don't remember anything after we saw the boats go and were in the gatehouse, trying to hold off pursuit by our sowars. They came into the garden on their horses and . . . yes, I can remember thinking that at all costs we had to stop them from going after the boats."

"We stopped them all right," Cook stated grimly. "But then some of the Sixteenth brought up one of those infernal nine-pounders and opened up on us. *I* remember thinking it was all up, that they'd blow us sky-high at that range. And they did, I suppose, because I have a vague recollection of being buried under showers of rubble." He was feeling his legs and body, attempting to assess how badly he was wounded. "I fancy I've been lucky, sir. Plenty of bruises, but I don't think any bones are broken—though it's hard to tell, cooped up under this straw and . . . what did you say they were? Melons?"

"Rotting melons, I'm afraid, Harry."

"But at least we're alive, Colonel. And the boats got away, all three of them, praise be! They should be well on their way to Cawnpore by now—though the river's pretty low. I hope they were able to keep clear of sandbanks and did not meet with any opposition on the way."

William echoed his hope, thinking of Jenny. But the promised reinforcements must surely have reached Cawnpore by this time. The Madras Fusiliers, Sir Henry Lawrence's latest message had stated, were making forced marches from Allahabad, determined to effect the garrison's relief. He glanced at his companion. Cook was unmarried, so at least he was spared some anxiety on that account—although he had a younger brother, serving in a native infantry regiment in Benares. Or was it Allahabad?

Cook said, attempting to sound cheerful, "They'll get through, Colonel—I'm confident they will. They have that very useful brass gun and the Enfields we were able to salvage from the magazine. And talking of the magazine—I don't think I ever felt more satisfaction than when I listened to the explosions and saw the whole damned place go up in flames! Devil take them, I thought, the bastards won't be able to make a present of our guns to their blasted old king in Delhi! Or take them to the Nana either, will they, sir?"

"No." William sighed. "No, they won't." But the destruction of the magazine had cost poor young Arnold Gillespie's life and — His single hand clenched into a fist at his side. What of the rear guard? Were he and Harry Cook the sole survivors? Were all the others dead?

"Sir!" Cook's voice was tense. "I believe we're approaching a village. I can see lights and—shall I ask our drivers where we are?"

The rain had slackened to a steady drizzle, and William saw that there were, indeed, lights flickering through a screen of trees, some distance ahead. Instinctively he felt for his pistol, but the holster was empty, and his saber, too, was gone.

"Yes, ask them, Harry," he agreed. Like most of his other officers, Cook was a qualified interpreter, able to converse freely in both Hindustani and Punjabi. But although he voiced his questions with fluent clarity, the only response he elicited was a nervous plea for silence from one of the bullock drivers and, from the other, the advice to keep themselves hidden.

"Better do as they say, sir," Cook said, when he had translated the men's request. "God knows where they're taking us!"

The wagon creaked on, through a small cluster of primitive mud houses bordering the road, occasioning no interest on the part of the inhabitants—few of whom appeared, in any case, to be stirring, although there were lamps in some of the glassless windows. Beyond the last house, the bullock cart turned to the left, to jolt along a rutted track and then climb a low hill, at the summit of which was a second village—more typical of most villages in Oudh, for it was surrounded by a loopholed wall, with a deep ditch in front of it.

The cart passed unchallenged through a wooden gateway, to come eventually to a halt outside an extensive, well-built house, on whose veranda three men were standing, clad in the colorful robes of irregular cavalry sowars, each with a rifle slung from his shoulder and a curved saber in his belt. Together the three approached the bullock cart and, thrusting aside the straw and melons, assisted its occupants to their feet.

"Welcome, Colonel sahib—and to you also, Cook sahib." The bearded face of *Rissaldar* Major Akbar Khan was instantly recognizable, despite his change of uniform and the lack of medals on his chest. He spoke in English and then, apologetically, lapsed into his own tongue. Harry Cook translated.

"The *rissaldar* major says, sir, that when the moment came for decision, he could not betray his allegiance. This is his village, and we were brought here by two of his sons." Cook was smiling his relief and pleasure. "The two men with him are both *daffadars* of the regiment, who share his feelings—Mohammed Bux and Ghulam Rasul." The two sergeants saluted, drawing themselves to attention, their smiles echoing his, and Cook's voice faltered, as if suddenly emotion had overcome him. "Colonel, they came to the gatehouse, after the Sixteenth destroyed it, and we—we were the only ones left alive."

So they had all died, William thought with infinite sadness— the brave men who had volunteered to form the rear guard and cover the boats' departure from the Residency wharf. He saw their faces—the begrimed, unshaven white faces of the officers and the brown faces of the Rifles' Eurasian band sergeant and two of his drummers, who had held the magazine against repeated attack. Young Millbank had been one of them, a boy, fresh from Addiscombe and not yet nineteen; and Lieutenant Campbell of the Sixteenth, as well as the quartermaster sergeant of the same regiment, whose name was—had been—Mackay. And an Irish ensign, Rory O'Reilly, who had joined the Rifles less than six months ago.

"Colonel—" Cook broke into his thoughts, and William turned to face him.

"Yes, Harry?"

"The *rissaldar* major invites us to enter his house, where food will be prepared for us and attention given to our wounds. Your head, sir, has bled a good deal."

"Has it?" William echoed, conscious of no pain. But when he started to climb the veranda steps, he stumbled and would have fallen, had not *Daffadar* Ghulam Rasul put out a hand to steady him. Ghulam Rasul had been his orderly room clerk, he recalled—a quiet, self-effacing man and, like the *rissaldar* major, a veteran of the Sikh wars. Such men did not easily betray their allegiance; there was a strong bond always between those who had fought and faced death in battle together.

Inside Akbar Khan's commodious living room, two veiled women were waiting. Neither spoke as, with skilled and gentle hands, they cleansed and covered his head wound with a fresh bandage. William realized, when they discarded the cloth that had previously been wound about his head, that Harry Cook was right—he had indeed bled copiously, from what he supposed was a saber cut, which had laid open his scalp and the upper part of his right cheekbone.

The promised meal was appetizing—a strongly flavored

goat's-meat curry, with fresh, unleavened *chapattis* and rice—
and both men ate hungrily, to the obvious satisfaction of their
host, who watched them from his seat at the head of the table
but did not himself partake of the meal. When they had finished, he spoke at some length to Cook, who was frowning
when, at last, the discourse came to an end.

"Akbar Khan wants us to rest, Colonel," Cook explained.
"He says they will take us on tomorrow evening, after dark."
He managed a wry smile. "He has assured me that although,
for our safety, he wants us to travel again by bullock *gharry,*
they will remove the melons—which will be a relief!"

"Are they to take us to Cawnpore, then, Harry?" William
asked. His heart sank when he saw Cook's headshake. "For
God's sake, why not?"

"He says that the Nana has patrols on all the approaches to
Cawnpore, sir. We would never get through. He's proposing to
take us across country to a place called Arrahpore—that's
south of Futtehpore, on the Grand Trunk Road—where he says
an advance party of Colonel Neill's Fusiliers is encamped.
They're heading for Cawnpore, and—"

"But what of Cawnpore itself?" William interrupted. "Has
there been any word from there?"

"Just rumors, sir—but ugly ones."

"What the devil do you mean, Harry? Wheeler hasn't surrendered, has he?"

Akbar Khan, who had been following their conversation with
a grave expression on his dark, bearded face, answered before
Cook could do so. He said, in English, "Colonel sahib, it is very
bad, if true. All *lal-kotes,* all soldiers, dead. Nana Sahib give
order kill them." Once again he lapsed into his own language,
speaking with an edge to his deep voice, and Cook sounded
shocked when he translated.

"It is still only a rumor, sir. But it seems they accepted terms
of surrender and the Nana betrayed them. If—if it's true,
there's been a massacre."

"And we sent our boats there!" Sick with dismay, William
looked from one to the other of them, his stomach churning.
"We sent our women and children, our wounded there for
safety!" He had sent Jenny, he thought, God forgive him—he

had sent his beloved wife to Cawnpore, in the hope that her life would be preserved, believing that General Wheeler's garrison was still holding out. He swallowed the bile that welled up into his throat.

"They may not have got there, sir," Harry Cook suggested, but without conviction. "They may have been warned and—" He broke off, tight-lipped, as Akbar Khan spoke again. "The *rissaldar* major says that he understands our—our distress. Even so, we cannot go to Cawnpore, for it would be suicide. In his considered opinion, sir, the best course for us is the one he has planned . . . to make for Arrahpore and join the Fusiliers' relief force. We would be risking his life and the *daffadars',* as well as our own, if we attempted to reach Cawnpore. And he's right, sir—we would."

It was the truth, William was forced to concede, however unpalatable. He tried to erase the thought of Jenny from his mind, instead attempting to concentrate on remembered details of the map that had hung on the wall of his orderly room in Ranpur.

Where the devil was Arrahpore? South of Futtehpore, on the Grand Trunk Road, Cook had said; about forty or fifty miles from Cawnpore and approximately the same distance from Allahabad . . . no, Cook had not said that, but he himself remembered it from the map, although his estimate of the distances might well be inaccurate. They were probably greater, and . . . where were they now? Where had Akbar Khan's sons driven them, in the foul-smelling bullock cart?

Harry Cook, after another exchange with the three native cavalrymen, answered his unvoiced question. "They took us across country, Colonel, west of the river. We circled round Cawnpore during the night—last night, that is. Believe this or not, sir, we were in that cart for over thirty-six hours! Akbar Khan says they gave us opiates, to make sure we stayed quiet. He and the other two came here direct—they rode here. This is a village called Kalabad—the *rissaldar* major's father was made landowner here for his gallantry at the Battle of Delhi and the capture of Deig, when he was serving in the Bengal Light Cavalry. He says, sir, that it is also for this reason that he could not bring himself to desert from the Company's service."

"We are in your debt, *Rissaldar* sahib," William said. "And it shall not be forgotten."

The old Indian officer bowed his turbaned head in grave acknowledgment and then, rising, gestured to the two beds on the far side of the room.

"Sleep, Colonel sahib," he invited. "At nightfall we will go on. We take you and Cook sahib to *lal-kote* camp, then return here to till the land."

William had not expected that he would sleep, but to his own surprise he slept deeply and dreamlessly, until *Daffadar* Ghulam Rasul roused him by shaking his shoulder. They ate hurriedly and left the village as darkness fell, he and Cook traveling, as before, in the back of the bullock cart; but instead of the *rissaldar* major's two sons, the two *daffadars* acted as drivers, with Akbar Khan, in peasant robes, riding ahead of them, his mount a thin, jaded animal unlikely to attract unwelcome attention from the Nana's patrols.

The journey, over cultivated land and on rough tracks, seemed endless to both William and his companion. They were concealed beneath tightly strung canvas, buried in bales of straw, and although this had the advantage of keeping them dry, it was appallingly hot; and when they ran into a heavy rainstorm, the pools of water trapped on top of the canvas covering pressed down on them and added to their discomfort.

To their considerable relief, at sunrise the cart halted, and under the shelter of a thick belt of trees, they were able to alight from their airless prison and stretch their cramped limbs. Akbar Khan rode off alone to a nearby village, while the two *daffadars* prepared a frugal meal of *chapattis* and dried fish and fed and watered the weary bullocks.

Below them, distant by perhaps two or three miles, the dusty white ribbon that was the Grand Trunk Road could be seen, with a camel train and numerous bullock-drawn carts proceeding along it in both directions at their usual unhurried pace. It looked peaceful enough, until Akbar Khan rejoined them and pointed to a swiftly moving dust cloud, which resolved itself into a band of horsemen, spurring southward along the road, the rays of the rising sun glinting on their lance tips. In their wake, but proceeding at a snail's pace, came two heavy guns, drawn by teams of elephants and escorted by cavalry. Cook had a spyglass in his pocket, and with its aid he and William identified the troops as those of the rebels, coming apparently from Cawnpore.

"They go to do battle with the *lal-kotes* who move forward from Arrahpore, it is said," Akbar Khan announced grimly, adding in his own tongue, "We must make a further detour, lest we encounter them. Even so, I believe that, if Allah wills it, we shall reach our destination by first light tomorrow. But we must travel all this day, Cook sahib. Tell the colonel sahib what I have said. It will be hot, but it is not safe to linger here."

His estimate proved accurate. Dawn was breaking when the bullock cart came abruptly to a halt, and, hearing English voices, William thankfully thrust the canvas covering aside, to find himself confronted by an officer, with a patrol of the Madras Fusiliers at his back. The men, in shirtsleeve order, with blue linen covers and sun curtains over their caps, were almost all bearded and deeply tanned, their clothes dust-caked and filthy. They looked like men who had gone for a long time without sleep, William thought, but their rifles were leveled at the cart in menacing fashion, and two NCOs had seized Akbar Khan and dragged him forcibly from his horse.

William lost no time in identifying himself, and when Harry Cook joined him, picking wisps of straw from his person, the young Fusilier officer grinned broadly and waved to his men to release their prisoner.

"Forgive me, gentlemen," he apologized, his grin fading, "for according you so rough a reception; but we have to be careful. The Nana of Bithur is reported to be bearing down on us with some four thousand rebel troops and the Lord knows how many guns—and spies have been plaguing the life out of us for the past couple of days, in every guise you can imagine. We've been ordered to halt here, to await the arrival of General Havelock's force from Allahabad. I can only say that they cannot come too soon, as far as we're concerned . . . although we had hoped to take Futtehpore before they got here. Er—my name is Cleland, gentlemen—Lieutenant Cleland, Madras Fusiliers." He gestured to the road behind him. "I'll take you to our com-

manding officer, Major Renaud, if you'll be good enough to
come with me."

"Permit us to take leave of the noble fellows who brought us
here," William responded. "All three are Indian officers of our
regiment, and we owe our lives to them."

"Oudh Lancers, sir? Men who have remained loyal?" Cleland
questioned, eyes narrowed as he studied the three tall men in
their peasant garb. "By heaven, Colonel, we could put them to
good use, if they were willing to stay with us. The only cavalry
we have are two squadrons of irregulars, of doubtful loyalty,
under Lieutenant Palliser. I'm sure Charlie Palliser would jump
at them, given the chance."

But when both William and Harry Cook tried to prevail
upon them to take service with the British force, Akbar Khan,
speaking for all three, rejected their overtures.

"Cook sahib, I beg you, tell the colonel sahib that we will not
betray our salt. We will not take up arms against the Company's
soldiers, but we will not fight against our brothers, either. We
ask the colonel sahib's leave to depart from here and return to
our homes."

It went against the grain to give his consent, but William
gave it nonetheless, respecting the old *rissaldar* major's princi-
ples and his transparent honesty in stating them as he had. All
three men refused money.

"We ask no reward, Colonel sahib. Only that you will remember that three of the Lancers did their duty and were not
guilty of mutinous conduct."

They left as they had come, the *daffadars* driving the bullock
cart and Akbar Khan riding ahead of them on his swaybacked
country-bred horse, his turbaned head held high.

William watched them go and then wearily followed Lieutenant Cleland in search of his commanding officer.

Major Sydenham Renaud was seated cross-legged at the
roadside, drinking tea from a battered tin mug, with two other
officers similarly engaged beside him. He was a good-looking
man, with a heavy, dark mustache and chin whiskers, and clad,
like his soldiers, in a grimy, sweat-stained shirt, with the blue
linen sun curtain attached to his pith helmet.

"They're calling us Neill's blue-caps, Colonel," he volunteered, patting his head covering. "But, by heaven, these inventions of Colonel Neill's have been a godsend on the march, I can tell you." Hospitably he poured two more cups of strong, black tea and introduced his companions. "Captain Spurgin, who joined us yesterday at Arrahpore, having come up by river steamer with a company of our men and two light guns. And Lieutenant Arnold, both of my corps. Cleland says you are from Ranpur?"

William supplied details of the outbreak of mutiny in Ranpur and of his and Cook's escape as briefly as he could. When he described the evacuation of the Residency and the decision to send the three boatloads of survivors to Cawnpore, he saw Renaud's dark eyes widen.

"Colonel De Lancey, have you not heard the terrible news from Cawnpore?"

"Rumors only, Major," William answered, his throat tight. "We were hoping and praying they were not true."

"I fear they are true," Renaud told him regretfully. "By the basest act of treachery, after General Wheeler's garrison had held out heroically for three weeks, the accursed Nana of Bithur offered honorable terms of surrender, which he had no intention of abiding by. The poor people in the entrenchment had lost over half their number during the siege; they had exhausted their food and ammunition and their medical supplies —they could resist no longer. They accepted the terms and the infernal Nana's promise of safe conduct and boats to convey them to Allahabad by river. But when they were embarking in the boats, at a place called the Suttee Chowra Ghat, they were ambushed and massacred." Renaud's voice shook with bitter anger. "There is, alas, no possibility of error, Colonel. We received an eyewitness account of the ghastly affair. I sent one of my officers back to Allahabad with the news, which, I understand, has been sent by telegraph to Lord Canning and Sir Patrick Grant in Calcutta. Hence my orders to halt here and await the arrival of General Havelock's force—the main body of our relief force—which left Allahabad five days ago. We expect and hope to rendezvous with them this evening or early tomorrow morning. It's a fervent hope, Colonel De Lancey, because, as probably Cleland told you, the archtraitor, the Nana, is reliably reported to be heading this way with an estimated force of four thousand rebels, bent on annihilating us!"

William was silent as the terrible truth sank in, and Harry Cook put in flatly, "We saw some of them on our way here, sir. Cavalry and two heavy guns, drawn by elephants."

Renaud grunted. "We meted out justice to every rebel we caught between here and Allahabad," he said, his tone still angry. "After the news from Cawnpore reached us. They are hanging by their treacherous necks from trees along the roadside, as a warning of the retribution to come. But I confess I'd give my immortal soul to put a rope round the Nana's fat neck, by God I would! He showed no pity for the defenseless women and children, De Lancey—our witness told us that they were shot down and sabered with the men. And the boats that were purportedly to take them to safety were set on fire!"

And he had sent Jenny to the place where so many innocents had been savagely slaughtered, William thought, in an agony of self-reproach. God forgive him, he had risked her precious life at the hands of the foul swine who had shown no pity for other defenseless mortals, when they had been at his mercy. . . . He put down his mug, so nauseated that he could not drink the strong black brew.

With wordless sympathy, Captain Spurgin took a flask from the pocket of his stained white shirt and passed it to him, as Renaud added vehemently, "We'll retake Cawnpore, never fear, De Lancey. If any of your people from Ranpur are being held captive there, we'll free them, if it's the last thing we do, the very last!" As if to emphasize his promise, he added, "We're preparing to break camp. As soon as General Havelock catches up with us, we shall move out to meet the Nana, with Futtehpore our immediate objective. Take heart, Colonel—we truly do mean business!"

And so, it became apparent, did General Havelock. The white-whiskered little general's arrival was signaled by the skirl of Highland pipes as the long, hot day drew to a close. With Major Renaud's small force lining both sides of the road, the 78th Highlanders marched up, brave in their tartan, with kilts swinging and their pipers playing the regimental march, "Pibroch o'Donuil Dhu." Behind them, rank on rank, came the

Queen's 64th, followed by a regiment of Sikhs, two companies of the Queen's 84th, a six-gun field artillery battery, and—Havelock's only cavalry—twenty mounted volunteers, including officers from mutinied native regiments, civil officials, and planters, led by a big, broad-shouldered captain with a black beard.

Behind them, strung out over several miles, came their baggage wagons, ammunition tumbrils, and camp followers, in a seemingly endless line.

Havelock's men had marched sixty miles in five days, through torrential rain and pitiless sun; they were exhausted and suffering badly from exposure, having snatched what sleep they could on the bare ground, for the wagons carrying their tents had failed to keep pace with them. But despite their fatigue, after brief greetings were exchanged the combined force immediately moved on, coming finally to a halt some four or five miles from Futtehpore.

Here the order came to take ground on the open plain, pile arms, and break their fast, and the weary men flung themselves down to rest at last.

Their rest was short-lived. William—who, instead of joining Lieutenant Palliser's irregulars, had gone with Harry Cook to offer their services to the volunteer cavalry—had scarcely had time to exchange a dozen words with his commander, Captain Lousada Barrow, when a mounted reconnaissance patrol came galloping back, under fire from guns somewhere out of sight.

"This is it, my friends!" Barrow exclaimed exultantly. "Our first chance to get back at the damned rebels! We've a few spare horses, Colonel De Lancey—pick which you fancy and join us, by all means, both of you. Come on—there's no time to be lost!"

Bugles sounded the call to arms, men rushed to their lines, and General Havelock was on his horse, his aides galloping this way and that with his orders. The Enfield riflemen of the 64th took up the position in a copse ahead of and to the left of the main body and returned the rebels' fire, holding their attempted advance with steady, accurate volleys, as the British field guns were rushed up and swiftly brought into action.

The rest of the infantry was deployed into columns, and William found himself galloping at Captain Barrow's heels to guard the right flank, his ears ringing with the thunder of the guns.

The battle was soon over. The eight field guns were handled with such verve and speed by their veteran gunners that the rebels' own artillery was quickly disabled and abandoned; and when the range closed to almost point-blank and the British infantry charged with the bayonet, the rebels broke into headlong flight, making no attempt to save their guns.

The order came for the cavalry to pursue the fleeing enemy, but only Captain Barrow's handful of mounted volunteers responded—despite the urging of Lieutenant Palliser and his Sikh *rissaldar,* the irregulars hung back, refusing to charge, and the volunteers were recalled.

"Devil take the swine!" Barrow exclaimed wrathfully, as they trotted disconsolately back to their own lines. "What an opportunity lost, thanks to their cowardice! They've been disaffected for some time, I fancy, and only Charlie Palliser's pleas persuaded Renaud to keep the irregulars with us. Well, I don't doubt the general will send them back to Allahabad, and we'll be the only cavalry in his command—just twenty of us!" He snorted indignantly and then added, with a laugh, "But we'll take over the best of their horses—the bastards can march sixty miles back, and be damned to them!"

The town of Futtehpore was taken without resistance. General Havelock permitted his sorely tried troops twenty-four hours rest, and then they marched on, meeting and defeating elements of the rebel forces at a fortified village called Aong— where the gallant Renaud was among the casualties—and again at a bridge over the Panda Nudi River, which the rebels had attempted but failed to blow up.

William took part in both battles, his actions those of an automaton, his mind filled only with the desire to reach Cawnpore. The evening after they had crossed the swollen Panda Nudi and were halted in a fresh downpour of monsoon rain, attempting to light bivouac fires to cook their long-awaited meal, two native spies were brought in by one of the volunteer cavalry patrols.

William did not see or speak to them, but word went round, in whispers, passed from man to man, that the spies had told the general that more than two hundred British women and children were alive and being held in captivity in the city of Cawnpore.

"Survivors of the massacre of General Wheeler's garrison, it seems," Captain Barrow told him, with gruff sympathy, when he returned from an officers' conference with General Havelock. "And others, who sought refuge there after Wheeler's surrender. Your wife could be among them, De Lancey, and your friends from Ranpur. At least two hundred, General Havelock told us. As you will expect, the general has ordered us to assemble at once—we are going on to Cawnpore, my friend, and we shall not stop until we've taken the place!"

Once again the bugles shrilled, and the now-depleted force assembled, their untasted rations thrust into their haversacks, their faces grimly set as they formed up in their ranks.

General Havelock, his white head bared, strode out to address them. He confirmed the rumor concerning the two hundred women and children held captive by the Nana, and then, raising his drawn sword above his head, he cried in ringing tones, "By God's help we shall save them, or every man of us die in the attempt! I am trying you sorely, men, but I know the stuff you are made of. Think of our women and tender infants in the power of those devils incarnate who have already massacred the soldiers of the garrison, in base betrayal of their promise to free them!"

The rest of his words were drowned by the wild cheering of the men. Then, led by the pipers of the 78th Highlanders, they wheeled into line and set off to cover the last sixteen miles that separated them from Cawnpore.

Chapter XVII

IN THE MALODOROUS prison of the Bibigarh, in which they had been confined for so long, the distant sound of gunfire rekindled hopes most of the unhappy captives had long since abandoned. Death, in its most hideous and degrading guises, was no stranger to them now. Already it had robbed the married women of their husbands, the children of their parents, and to many of the sickly, broken-hearted women its advent was a welcome end to unendurable torment.

But although some of the bolder spirits, hearing the gunfire, had cried out that a relief column was at last on its way to rescue them, the *jemadar,* a lieutenant in command of their sepoy guard, had stoutly denied any such possibility, and the prisoners had sunk again into the state of apathy, induced by near-starvation and the appalling heat that had for so long held them in its thrall.

Jenny had fought against it for as long as she could find strength to do so. She had tried to keep up her spirits, for young Andy Melgund's sake, rather than her own. She was all he had now. His father had died before they had even reached Cawnpore, and his mother and his frail little sister, Rosie, had fallen victim to the dysentery that had affected many of them during the past days. Andy clung to her, afraid to leave her side, his courage no longer proof against the endless days and nights of suffering and the humiliation inflicted on them by those in whose charge they had been placed.

The worst of these was, by far, the woman known as Hosainee Khanum, a coarse, loud-voiced harridan who had been servant to one of the Nana's courtesans and who derived a sadistic pleasure from the threats that, from time to time, she delivered, claiming that they came from the Nana himself. It was ironic, Jenny thought wretchedly, hearing the unpleasant creature's voice from the courtyard outside, haranguing the guard—indeed, it was more than ironic that Hosainee had been sent to the Bibigarh in response to the prisoners' plea that something should be done to cleanse the two cramped rooms they were compelled to occupy.

Sweepers had been given the task, and Hosainee had been entrusted with their supervision. . . . Jenny breathed an unhappy sigh. Their conditions had, it was true, been improved, in that the floors had been scoured and the bodies of the poor souls who had perished from disease or the wounds they had suffered were removed each day, while previously they had been left where they lay. But in return for this favor, the prisoners were compelled to endure Hosainee's presence, her insolent taunts and the mental torture she devised in order to provoke them.

On her first appearance among them, she had informed the Ranpur fugitives, with conscious cruelty, that the men who had accompanied them in the boats had been condemned to death by the Nana.

"On the orders of His Highness the Peishwa, all were executed," she had said, pleased when some of the bereaved had wept and cried out. "The sowars under the command of General Teeka Singh carried out the execution, and no one was spared, not even those who begged for their lives!"

But the grief of the Ranpur survivors paled into insignificance when compared with what the poor souls who had survived the massacre of General Wheeler's garrison had suffered. . . . Jenny sighed again, wishing that she could forget what some of the women had told her. They had been full of hope when they had gone down to the Suttee Chowra Ghat, Caroline Moore had said. The Nana had offered them honorable surrender, after their brave resistance; he had sworn a solemn oath that they should be permitted to leave the entrenchment under arms, and had promised that boats and boatmen would be provided, to convey them to Allahabad. And the boats had been there, but . . . so, also, had been the hidden guns on the heights above and the sepoys waiting in ambush. The rifles and pistols the men of the garrison had carried had been of scant use.

The Nana had been seated in a small temple overlooking the landing stage, and he had given the signal for the guns to open fire. The boatmen had flung burning torches onto the straw awnings covering the boats and then swum to safety, and the sowars of the Light Cavalry, who had escorted their former officers and the women and children from the entrenchment with every appearance of pleasure and respect, had ridden their horses into the water and sabered those struggling there, when they had attempted to escape the flames.

They had seen their husbands slaughtered in front of their eyes, the poor, unhappy women . . . then, when the ghastly massacre was over, they had been driven at musket point into a building known as the Savada Koti. There they had been left, without food or water or medical aid, for twenty-four hours, before being brought, in bullock carts, to the Bibigarh. And— Tears welled into Jenny's eyes. They had been here for eighteen days, and only recently had their captors permitted a native doctor to visit them and dress their wounds; only during the past few days had fresh water been brought, to replace that which had long since been used up or gone stale and putrid, so that they dared not drink it.

She had been spared much, Jenny thought, looking down at Andy Melgund's sleeping face, so thin and pale now as almost to be unrecognizable. She had not had to watch her husband die, and perhaps, if God were merciful, William might still be alive. She prayed often that he was, and yet, recalling Caroline Moore's words, when she had first entered this place of suffering, she did not really believe that he could be.

"We are all widows here," Caroline had said, and had then gone on reading from her prayer book to the children clustered about her. Poor, sweet Caroline had grown weaker as the days passed; she could no longer read to the children or lead them in the hymns they had sung each evening, and . . . Jenny's tears fell unchecked. She had tried to take Caroline's place, but the children had not listened, after a while, and only a few of them had summoned the strength and the will to sing.

But, after Caroline had died in her sleep, they had made the effort to give voice to her favorite hymn before her body had been taken away, and now a group of the women who had been her friends greeted the dawning of each new day with a tuneless rendering of "All Things Bright and Beautiful" in her memory.

They were frail and sick, all of them, but few had lost their courage, and all, even the weakest, had resisted Hosainee's cruel attempts to shatter their morale. Amelia Hall constantly defied her; she gave orders to their unpleasant warders over Hosainee's head, and when Martha Lund had been brought to bed for a premature delivery, a few days after their incarceration, the nabob's widow had, by the sheer strength of her personality, obtained clothing for the babe and the native physician's aid for the mother.

The gunfire thundered again, more prolonged this time, and Jenny sat up. Surely the sound was nearer than it had been before. Could there be a force of British soldiers coming to their rescue, in spite of the *jemadar*'s denial? There had been time, surely, for the news of Cawnpore's fate to reach the governor general in Calcutta; time for troops to be dispatched up-country in substantial numbers—

"Listen!" Elizabeth Vibart, widow of a major of the Light Cavalry and the mother of two small, fair-haired girls, gently set down her younger child and got unsteadily to her feet. "Those *are* guns, and they are close at hand. And listen to the sepoys of our guard—they can hear them, and they know what gunfire as close as this must mean!" She tottered across to the barred window that looked out into the courtyard, straining to listen to the subdued voices of the guard outside. After a few minutes, she turned back, the last vestige of color draining from her pale cheeks. "Hosainee Khanum is there. She is—she has ordered the guard to shoot us!"

But the sepoy guard seemingly ignored the order, and in response to the cries of several of the women, the *jemadar* came to the window. At first he denied all knowledge of Hosainee's order but then, reluctantly, admitted that the woman had brought verbal instructions from the Nana that the hostages were to be shot if the British column attacked Cawnpore.

"You have nothing to fear at our hands," he assured his anxious questioners. "Without a written order."

"There *is* a British column!" Amelia Hall exclaimed. "He has admitted it!" She dropped to her knees, offering her thanks aloud in inarticulate prayer, and several of the other women followed her example.

Elizabeth Vibart, her hands trembling as they grasped the bars of the window, called out to the *jemadar,* in brave defiance, "Our soldiers will attack, rest assured of that, *Jemadar-ji!*"

"And if they do, memsahib, they will be defeated," the native officer returned. "They are few and we are many, and the Nana Sahib has placed great guns on the road to bar their way." But he sounded uneasy, and they heard him respond angrily to Hosainee's shrill-voiced reproaches.

The native doctor, coming to pay his daily visit, confirmed the *jemadar*'s admission. He—the only one of their jailers who had shown them pity or kindness—now raised their flagging spirits. "A British force is nearing the city," he told them. "It is not large, but it is led by a resolute general, whose name they say is Havelock. Since leaving Allahabad just over a week ago, they have marched a hundred and twenty miles and have three times defeated the Nana Sahib's army. Now I have heard they have fought their way across the Panda Nudi River. The Nana's brother, Bala Bhat, was wounded in the battle, and it is said that his general of cavalry, Teeka Singh, had his elephant killed under him. Their troops flee the field like jackals as soon as General Havelock's red-coat soldiers are sighted. Soon, ladies, your countrymen will be here to set you free, and your terrible ordeal will be over!"

They hung on his words, repeating them to each other again and again as the day wore on, their hopes bolstered by the now almost ceaseless thunder of the guns, some of which, by their proximity to the city, they recognized as being the Nana's. Soon, Jenny told the suddenly wakeful Andy, soon they would be free, guarded by British soldiers, their suffering at an end. The little boy hugged her, and together they went to join those by the door of their prison, eager to be among the first to greet their rescuers.

They prayed, weeping, and sang hymns, their voices choked with tears, the sick, the wounded, and many of the children roused from their apathy to add their voices to the rest.

It fell to Hosainee to shatter their brief hour of ecstasy. She had been absent for most of the day; when she came back to the house, one of the Eurasian captives abused her, whereupon the former nurse rounded on her savagely, saying with conscious malice that the Nana had ordered their execution.

"A written order will be sent here," she screamed. "Pray that the *lal-kote* soldiers never reach Cawnpore. For you will die before one of them sets foot in the city!"

A stunned silence greeted her threatening words, and Hosainee went out, refusing to retract them, and again the anxious prisoners heard her arguing fiercely with their guards. After a long and heated exchange, the *jemadar* came to the window, indicating that he wished to speak with them.

"Memsahibs, do not fear," he said, when they gathered on their side of the window. "True, the accursed serving woman claims she will bring an order, under the Nana's sign and seal, commanding us to execute you. But we will not harm you."

"If you preserve our lives, General Havelock will reward you," Amelia Hall promised recklessly, and half a dozen others reiterated this promise. Mrs. Hall added, "If you take our lives, *Jemadar,* and General Havelock learns of it, he and his soldiers will not rest until retribution has been meted out to you. They may be few, but they have been victorious whenever they have met the Nana's army in battle—and there will be more, many thousands more, following after them from Calcutta and from England itself!"

She spoke with conviction, and the *jemadar* smiled at her. "Memsahib, I have said that you have nothing to fear at our hands. But so as not to incur the Nana's wrath, should the serving woman spy on us, we will fire through the windows into the walls and ceiling. If you lie down, our musket balls will not touch you. I, *Jemadar* Yusef Khan, swear it!"

They thanked him tearfully, but Hosainee had again vanished, and, still apprehensive, they followed the suggestion of a white-haired Eurasian woman and started to tear strips from their dresses and petticoats, with which they attempted to secure the door into the courtyard.

Exhausted by their efforts, the women sank down to the floor to join once again in prayer, mothers holding their children to them in nameless fear. Andy Melgund clasped Jenny's hand and urged her to lie down, seeking to place his small, puny body between her and the courtyard window. Suddenly, from somewhere close at hand, they heard the crackle of musketry, and fear became panic when Yusef Khan shouted through the window that their kindly little doctor and the sweepers who had served them had been shot, on Hosainee Khanum's instructions.

"The woman comes back, memsahibs!" he warned. "The time has come . . . lie very still, that we may fire over your heads!"

They did so, and, true to his promise, the sepoys' volley passed harmlessly over their heads. But now they again heard Hosainee's hated, strident voice, and in the gathering dusk the terrified prisoners watched her approach. With her, Jenny saw, were five men, one wearing the scarlet uniform of the Nana's bodyguard, the other four peasants of low caste—two, by their stained robes, appeared to be butchers from the bazaar. All were armed with hatchets and knives, the bodyguard with a saber, and they strode arrogantly past the sepoy guards, who, not having reloaded their muskets, stood helplessly by as Hosainee waved a paper at the *jemadar*.

"The order!" she screeched at him. "I bring the Nana Sahib's sealed order, Yusef Khan! March your men from the compound if they fear to carry it out!"

Crouched behind the door, with Andy and little Bella Gillespie, Jenny heard its timbers crack, as the men outside put their shoulders to it. Within the dirty, littered room that had been their prison, the poor hostages waited petrified, the children wailing as, one by one, the pathetic wisps of cloth that held the door shut burst from the handle and a hatchet split the timber panel in two.

The door broke open. Two of the men stumbled into the room, the suddenness of the door's collapse bringing them to their knees. For an instant the aperture was clear, and, blind instinct guiding her, Jenny exerted the last of her flagging strength to push Andy through it.

"Run!" she bade him breathlessly. "Seek out the *jemadar!* He will help you—run!"

The boy had no choice but to obey her. She saw him start to run unsteadily across the courtyard, and then the door was slammed shut and the butchers Hosainee had summoned were among the helpless captives, wielding their knives and hatchets with pitiless effect.

Aware that her last hour had come, Jenny dropped to her knees. Caroline Moore's prayer book was in her hands. Trembling uncontrollably, her voice a whisper of sound that was inaudible above the shrieks and sobs filling the room, she knelt in front of two cowering children and began to read from one of the open pages.

The print blurred before her eyes, and it was her husband's face she saw as death came, with merciful swiftness, at the practiced hands of one of the Muslim butchers.

Two days later, on the morning of July 17, General Havelock's relief force entered Cawnpore. They had fought like tigers every foot of the way, opposed by eight thousand rebel troops who had fiercely contested each village and whose great guns had wrought terrible havoc before a gallant bayonet charge had silenced first one and then another.

Spurred on by the thought of the women and children held hostage by the treacherous Nana—those poor innocents who had endured so much and whose lives must, at all costs, be saved—Havelock's soldiers had not counted the cost, although it had been high.

William had neither eaten nor slept. With Lousada Barrow's handful of gentlemen volunteers, he had ridden until he was close to falling from his saddle from exhaustion. He had charged with them, and—in a manner he remembered from the charge of the Heavy Brigade on the Russian cavalry division at Balaclava—Barrow's twenty-strong troop had galloped straight at the white-robed ranks of the Nana's massed thousand—in-

credibly, for the loss of only three men wounded and one killed
—had driven through them and put them to craven flight.

He had seen the 78th Highlanders, led by their pipers, take
the Nana's giant twenty-four-pounder cannon at the point of
bayonet, when it blocked the road to Cawnpore, and had
cheered the Enfield riflemen of the Queen's 64th as they hurled
themselves at the enemy's entrenched positions, firing as they
went. Like the Sikhs, and like the men of the 84th—with memories of comrades who had defended the entrenchment at
Cawnpore—they asked for and gave no quarter; and the Fusiliers, in the blue linen caps their commander had devised for
them, had the gallant Renaud to avenge, and savagely they
bought that revenge in blood.

But despite the speed of their advance, despite the heroism
and the sacrifices, it had been in vain. Native spies, sent forward
to reconnoiter the approaches to the city, had finally brought
them to a halt. The women and children were dead. They had
been massacred by the Nana's orders, the spies told Havelock,
and the Nana himself was in flight—there was no longer any
need for haste.

The advance guard of the Highlanders and the 64th marched
through the empty, ravaged streets of Cawnpore's native city
and, after entering the yellow-painted house known as the Bibigarh, emerged sickened and appalled, to confirm the truth of
the spies' report.

William went to the house of death, some hours later, his last
hope that Jenny might miraculously have survived bitterly fading as he looked about him. He had gone with Harry Cook, and
both of them wept unashamedly at the ghastly scene before
them.

The bodies had been removed, yet for all that the place was a
charnal house, steeped in blood, with here and there a woman's
bonnet, the frilled muslin of a child's torn frock, books, a bloodstained Bible, and, still hanging from the door, the flimsy rags
that had been tied there in a vain attempt to bar the way to the
murderers. The walls were scarred with sword slashes and the
marks of bullets, with some of the sword-cuts low down, where
some poor crouching woman or a tiny child had tried to ward
off the blows aimed at them by their pitiless assassins.

William could not bring himself to cross the fifty feet between the door of the house and the well, into which the pathetic bodies of the victims had been thrown. Others had done so, but none more than once. A tough, hardened sergeant of the 64th had said, in his hearing, "I've faced death in every form, but never anything like this. If they shot me for it, I could not look down that well again."

Harry Cook grasped his arm, and they started to move away, when suddenly William heard a high-pitched, childish voice calling his name. He turned, half expecting to see a ghost, and a little boy, in torn and filthy clothing, flung himself from the arms of the tall Highlander who had been holding him and came limping forward on legs so spindle-thin that they could barely sustain his weight.

"C-Colonel De Lancey, it's me, Andy Melgund," the poor little apparition whispered. "They—they killed them all, sir, every one of them. M-Mrs. De Lancey made me run, when the door was broken open, and the *jemadar* hid me. He—he saved my life, but the—the soldiers shot him, before I could tell them what he had done."

The boy was sobbing, his words almost unintelligible, and William bent to gather him into his arms, his heart breaking as he listened.

Jenny was dead, he knew now, beyond all shadow of doubt; his beloved wife was dead because he had taken her from her homeland to . . . to *this*. He caught his breath, the knowledge almost beyond bearing as he remembered the horrors of the dark prison he had just left.

But this thin, tortured little boy was alive, and he held him close, having to summon all the control he possessed to answer him.

"I'll send you to Australia, Andy," he promised. "Where you'll be safe. I shall have some more fighting to do, but when, please God, it is over, I'll follow you home."

Andy's arms were around his neck, and after a while his sobs ceased, and William saw that he slept.

Chapter XVIII

SEATED IN FRONT of a blazing log fire in the big, comfortable living room of the Bundilly homestead, Michael, for the first time since he had made his escape from the Port Arthur Penitentiary, was conscious of a sense of well-being that transcended fear.

Outside, the torrential rainstorm, which had led Luke and him to beg for shelter, continued unabated, and despite his earlier misgivings, he was thankful now that Luke had convinced him that he would be running no risk if he were to throw himself on the station owner's mercy.

"It's a tradition in this country," Luke had asserted. "Food and shelter is always given to passing wayfarers, if they're in need. Not in the towns, maybe; but out here in the bush you can count on it. And folk don't ask questions, Michael. I know—I worked on a sheep station in New South Wales for a good while, and no traveler was ever turned away."

Michael sipped the brandy he had been given and let his weary body relax, smiling across at Luke, who was warming his chilled hands at the fire while carrying on a lively conversation with their absent host's two young sons. It seemed the boys had been at the Ballarat diggings at the same time as Luke, and from what Michael could make of the exchange, both had been caught up in some trouble with officialdom, which had resulted in the arrest of the elder, Angus, who had since been freed under a general amnesty. They were talking of the pitched battle at the Eureka field, and Michael heard Luke say wryly that he knew a little about it, having served at the time as a police trooper.

Luke, Michael thought, was constantly surprising him with tidbits of information concerning his past; but these had to be wrung from him, for he was not one to talk about himself, and he never boasted. A fine fellow, Luke Murphy, and he had proved a good friend. Indeed, Michael decided, the best thing he had ever done was to agree to team up with the *Mercedes'* second mate and go prospecting with him after they left the ship. Luke knew the truth about him—or most of it, anyway— and had had no qualms about entering into partnership with an absconder. And for himself . . . Michael took another sip of his brandy.

It had been a shock to read about Price's death—his *murder* —in the local Geelong newspaper. He had felt at once angry and—yes, deprived of purpose when the fact of Price's death sank in. For so long he had been sustained by the determination to avenge himself on the late commandant of Norfolk Island. It had been to that end that he had planned his escape. But suddenly, without any warning, the reason for his escape, the reason he was in the state of Victoria, had ceased to exist. Others, convicts like himself, motivated as he had been, had set on Price and killed him, and now Michael was left with a terrible emptiness in his very soul. In consequence, Luke's suggestion that they become prospectors and head north to the most recently discovered goldfields in the Murray Valley had seemed like a lifeline, held out and ready for him to grasp. And Silas Deacon, the *Mercedes'* master, had accepted the story Luke had concocted—though whether the old man had believed that the Port Arthur stowaway was a newly arrived immigrant was another matter. Certainly he had not questioned the tale, and had permitted Luke and Michael to quit the ship in Geelong without objection—the *Mercedes* had a full crew, and there were always disillusioned diggers ready to sign on as seamen in order to work their passage to New South Wales.

He and Luke had lacked money when they finally went ashore—Luke had only his pay, while Michael had had nothing to contribute toward their mining equipment—so they had hired themselves out as laborers, and that had delayed them for almost a month. Winter was setting in when they had started on the trek north with little more than the basic tools, a packhorse that had seen better days, and an old canvas tent, which let in the rain but had been going cheap.

Michael leaned back in his chair, enjoying the almost forgotten pleasure of being dry and warm. Idly he listened to Luke's conversation with William Broome's two boys, unable to make sense of it but realizing, as he listened, that the three young men had more in common than he had supposed.

"That foul rogue Brownlow is in these parts," Lachlan was saying. "He recovered from the wounds he sustained at the Eureka Stockade—more's the pity—and has become a rich man. He retired from the police service and set up our nearest township—Urquhart Falls, which is about forty miles from here —and he owns most of it. A couple of taverns, the hotel, a gaming den, and if you can believe it, the bank. Lord knows where he got his money from. Extortion, probably." Lachlan shrugged. "Anyway, he's the mayor, and folk reckon they'll change the name of the town soon to Brownlow Falls."

Angus Broome laughed at that. "But at least Captain Humphrey got his just deserts at the stockade. They say a police trooper shot him, and—"

"No!" Luke's interruption was vehement, and both the young Broomes turned to look at him in surprise when he went on. "No—one of the diggers shot him, Angus. A red-haired fellow whose name, I believe, was Carboni—Rafaello Carboni. He shot him from behind the stockade, when the soldiers were going in."

"How the devil do you know that?" Angus demanded. "Were you there, for God's sake, Murphy?"

His interest awakened, Michael sat up. Beyond saying that he had been, for a short time, a police trooper in Ballarat, Luke had not hinted at the part he had played in suppressing the diggers' brief revolt, but now he nodded, in answer to Angus Broome's question.

"I was with the police, under Captain Brownlow's command. And I went after the fellow who called himself Humphrey with the intention of killing him—but Carboni's shot got him before I could. I watched him die."

The two young brothers continued to stare at him in evident surprise, and Luke said, his voice suddenly harsh and strained, "I followed him from California, and his name wasn't Humphrey. When I first knew him he was calling himself Morgan—Captain Jasper Morgan. My brother Dan and I and two Australians, Tom and Frankie Gardener, were in partnership with him in the California fields. We made a big strike, a really big strike, and Morgan stole it and blew up our mine shaft, with Dan and the other two inside." His voice lost its harsh note, and he sighed. "It's a long story, and I don't suppose you'll want to hear it all."

The brothers exchanged glances and then protested in unison. "For crying out loud, Murphy, of course we want to hear it!"

"*We* were in partnership with Humphrey in the Eureka field," Angus exclaimed excitedly. "And I swear he conspired with that policeman Brownlow to have me arrested. The night a mob of diggers burned down the Eureka Hotel, that was. I was there, but I'd nothing to do with setting Bentley's hotel on fire —yet the troopers picked on me and hauled me off to jail. That's right, isn't it, Lachie?"

Lachlan confirmed his brother's claim. "It's God's truth, Mr. Murphy. Angus and I were together the whole time. He didn't do a thing, yet the troopers swore he was one of the ringleaders!"

"It's all water under the bridge now," Angus put in. "All the leaders of the Eureka Stockade revolt were either brought to trial and acquitted or pardoned, as I was, under a general amnesty—including Rafaello Carboni. But let us hear your story— it promises to be very interesting, Mr. Murphy." He grinned. "I guess we'll have to forget you were one of the 'Joes' we used to do battle with!"

"We could start by you two calling me Luke."

"Very good—Luke it is, then. I'm Angus and my brother's Lachlan—Lachie for short."

Luke embarked on his story, and Michael listened in astonished silence as his partner told of the trial that had taken place at the diggers' camp in the Sacramento Valley some seven years ago. On the strength of irrefutable evidence, the man who had called himself Jasper Morgan had been tried in his absence on a charge of murder and condemned to death.

"I came out here in search of him," Luke told them quietly. "And it was quite a dance he led me, always one step ahead of me, changing his name when it suited him. He was in Sydney, then in the New South Wales goldfields, and finally he came here, to Victoria. . . ." He talked on, but Michael, lulled by the heat of the fire and his own weariness, drifted to sleep, hearing only snatches of what the other three were saying. But it was an odd coincidence, he reflected, that both he and Luke Murphy should have come to the state of Victoria on a man-hunt, only to find the object of their search taken from them at the hands of others. Jasper Morgan had been shot by one of the rebel diggers from the Eureka Stockade, and John Price had died, in the prison of which he was in charge, when a gang of the convicts he had mistreated had turned on him and hacked him to death, in what the Geelong *Gazette* had described as "an attack of dreadful savagery."

Rafaello Carboni had been pardoned, according to Angus Broome, but the seven wretched convicts who had taken Price's life were—if the *Gazette* were to be believed—to pay for their crime with their lives . . . as he would have been called upon to do, Michael thought somberly, had his quest been successful.

He was aroused by the sound of a woman's voice and opened sleep-dimmed eyes to see that the station owner and his wife had joined them. They were a pleasant, kindly couple. Mrs. Broome, whom her husband addressed as Dodie, was slim and dark-eyed, with a ready smile and a quick, alert manner, which belied the evidence of her graying hair and the lines on her still-attractive face.

William Broome, whom he judged to be in his late fifties, was short—only an inch or two taller than his wife—and of sturdy build, with a luxuriant white beard and a pair of shrewd gray eyes. A man, Michael had decided, who would not be easily deceived and who might be expected to resent any attempt to pull the wool over his eyes. But—impelled by an instinct he had supposed long forgotten, Michael got to his feet—he wondered whether William Broome had already seen through the guise he had adopted. An Irish immigrant, lured by gold fever and newly arrived in the country—would his story for long hold water? Perhaps it would, if their stay were short and he and Luke resumed their journey when the weather moderated. But . . . Glimpsing his reflection in a mirror that hung on the wall opposite, Michael was conscious of a nagging doubt.

The face that looked back at him was so deeply tanned, the big body so muscular from the years of stone-breaking and heavy toil, that no one could have supposed him to be a gentleman, that was certain. But a "new chum," fresh from the Irish bogs, who claimed to have been a peasant farmer—perhaps that was stretching credulity too far. And there was his voice. He had never tried to disguise his voice or pretend that he was uneducated; on Norfolk Island, because it had provoked Price's ire, he had deliberately retained the voice and manners bred in him from childhood, and Price's floggings had not eradicated them. He would keep a still tongue in his head, Michael thought; he would listen but say little, and perhaps, God willing, it would not occur to his hosts that they were offering hospitality to a convict on the run.

It did not appear to have occurred to Mrs. Broome, at all events, for, turning from one to the other of them, she said graciously, "Our evening meal is ready, if you would both care to partake of it with us. And there is a member of the family whom you haven't met—our adopted daughter, Jane. Sadly, she is deaf and dumb, but she is able to read lips, provided she can see them clearly. So if you talk to her, be so good as to turn to her when you speak."

She beckoned and a small, slight girl of about seventeen or eighteen emerged shyly from the passageway at her back and came to stand beside her, smiling uncertainly. She was startlingly lovely, Michael saw, a blue-eyed vision with delicate features and softly curling ash-blond hair. For some reason, she reminded him of little Prudence Meldrum, although there was no physical resemblance, beyond an impression of vulnerability, perhaps. Without thinking, he bowed when Mrs. Broome introduced him and then, seeing the girl's eyes widen in bewilderment, cursed himself for a witless idiot.

However, no one else had noticed the bow. Luke shook her hand, and the two Broome boys were eagerly telling their father of Luke's acquaintance with their erstwhile partner, which effectively distracted his attention.

"It is the most extraordinary coincidence, Dad," Angus said. "We knew that Humphrey was a strange fellow, but until Luke told us what he had done in America before he came out here, I'd no idea he was such a deep-dyed villain. Mind, I did not like him or trust him, when he got me arrested after the Eureka Hotel was burnt down, but . . ."

Over dinner—a substantial and well-cooked meal—talk continued about the Eureka Stockade affair, and in the course of conversation it emerged that both Mr. and Mrs. Broome had known the parents of the wife Luke had so tragically lost.

"Rick Tempest and Katie—why, of course I knew them well," William Broome declared. He traced the relationship, with his wife's aid, and Michael, to whom all those they spoke of so nostalgically were unknown, was enabled to maintain a discreet silence without seeming in any way discourteous. Mrs. Broome made one or two attempts to draw him into their conversation; Michael answered briefly, and when he again fell silent, his hostess abandoned her efforts on his behalf and contented herself with an occasional vague smile in his direction.

Luke, clearly, was enjoying himself. Prompted by their interest, he was talking more than he usually did, able to give the Broomes news of friends and relatives in New South Wales with whom, over the years, they had lost touch. He even spoke of his wife—a topic he had hitherto carefully avoided—and of the year he had spent working on his father-in-law's land beyond the Blue Mountains.

William questioned him minutely as to wool yields and his father-in-law's breeding policies and, finding Luke unexpectedly knowledgeable, eyed him for a moment or two from beneath thoughtfully lowered brows and then said, "Damme, Luke boy, what do you want with gold digging? It's a chancy business, and for every prospector who strikes it rich there are hundreds who never make enough out of their labor to eat."

"I know that, Mr. Broome," Luke assured him.

"Well, then?" Broome challenged. "Angus and Lachie suffered from gold fever a few years back, as they've told you. But the pair of them learned their lesson, did you not, lads? Now they're putting their faith and their toil into the land, just as I did. I brought a small flock of sheep of my own breeding from our family farm in New South Wales, started up near Launceston, and then came across here, when land was going for the taking and no questions asked." He smiled. "As my flocks grew, I drove 'em onto unclaimed land. Government tried to dispute possession, when it realized what was going on, but I and a good few others who'd done the same thing, why, we claimed squatters' rights, just as they did in New South Wales. Finally the authorities left us be. We were permitted to keep our land, as leaseholds initially, but eventually we bought it for a nominal sum. Now, without boasting, I can truthfully claim to own one of the largest sheep stations in the state of Victoria . . . and that without finding even an ounce of gold dust!"

"It's different now, though, isn't it, sir?" Luke questioned. "I mean, land has to be purchased, and the prices aren't nominal anymore."

"True," Broome conceded. He pushed his empty plate away. "I've more land than I can develop and stock these days, Luke. Skilled labor is simply not to be had, because this infernal gold fever continues to lure men to the diggings. I cannot get the experienced shepherds and cattlemen I need, no matter what wages I offer. I've tried employing the Chinese, but they're no use with sheep—and anyway, Chinese or white, sooner or later they drift off to start panning for gold, leaving me shorthanded. Australia's future's in the land, in wool, not in this crazy quest for instant riches, which damned few ever find. And when they do, most of them waste it."

He was eyeing Luke keenly, Michael saw, and both his sons, guessing what was to come, were looking equally expectant.

"Stay here, Luke," William Broome urged. "I need a first-rate manager, a man I can rely on to relieve me of some of the responsibilities of this holding. If I had a manager, Angus and Lachie would not have to give me so much of their time. They've each got their own land—Lachie wants to breed cattle, don't you, lad? But they're run off their feet, the pair of them, working for *me*. And my eldest son, Tim, is in the navy, at

present serving in the Mediterranean. *He'll* never settle down
on the land." He noticed Luke's embarrassed hesitation and,
sensing its cause, turned to Michael. "I'd gladly give you employment if you want it, Cadogan. An extra pair of hands,
whether or not they're experienced, are always welcome."

Michael looked down at his big, callused hands and bit back
a sigh. He had labored in chains at Longridge Farm on Norfolk
Island, under the superintendent of agriculture, Gilbert Robertson, and, he recalled, he had even derived a measure of satisfaction when Robertson had ordered his chains struck off and employed him as a shepherd. But Price, soon after his arrival on
the island, had dispensed with Robertson's services, and not
long after that the erstwhile shepherd was once more in chains,
toiling in the quarry, where there was no satisfaction to be derived from work well done.

He could not tell William Broome all this, of course, and if he
stayed at Bundilly, sooner or later the fact that he was an escaped convict would emerge—he would give himself away, or
he would be recognized, perhaps, by a ticket-of-leave man in the
township or a constable who had served on Norfolk Island or at
Port Arthur. The anonymity of the gold diggings, the sheer
number of men working there, offered a better chance of avoiding discovery, and Michael knew that he dared not stay here,
however tempting Broome's offer. In any case, it was Luke who
was wanted, and if Luke wished to stay, then that would have
to be the end of their partnership.

He said, hiding the momentary regret he felt, "Thank you, sir
—it's good of you. But I've come a long way to try my luck at
the diggings, and I'm not about to turn back. If Luke has a
mind to take up your offer, I'll not stand in his way. Our partnership was one of convenience, wasn't it, Luke? You are under
no obligation to me."

Luke studied his face uncertainly, and William Broome rose
to his feet. "Sleep on it, Luke. Tomorrow, if the weather mends,
we'll take you out to look at the place, and you can decide when
you've seen what Bundilly can offer. There's no hurry. I don't
mind waiting for a good man, believe me."

Broome had not, Michael thought wryly, made any attempt
to dissuade *him* from leaving; possibly the seeds of suspicion

had already been sown in his mind, or else his guest's unusual silence had contributed to the station owner's suspicions.

Mrs. Broome, as if seeking in her kindly way to make up for her husband's attitude, made a point of engaging him in conversation when they again repaired to the big, fire-lit living room. Michael answered her briefly and evasively, and after a while she abandoned her attempt to draw him out and suggested that they were all tired and might care to make an early night of it.

In the room they shared, Luke did not speak until they had both undressed. Then, seating himself on the end of Michael's bed, he said awkwardly, "We *could* both stay here, Michael. Bundilly is in the gold-bearing area. I know the lads said that they've panned the river for miles without finding anything but dust . . . still, that often happens. Whole gangs work an area and turn up nothing, and then a new bunch comes along and makes a strike. Mr. Broome's told me I can prospect in my spare time, and that would apply equally to you, if you wanted to stay."

"You know I dare not stay, Luke," Michael reminded him.

"I don't see why not. William Broome is a fair-minded man and—"

"There is a law against giving shelter to absconders or employing them. Mr. Broome is a magistrate, his wife told me. I can't stay—it would be an abuse of their hospitality, and that's the last thing I'd do."

"Yes, but—"

"There aren't any buts. Besides—" Michael smiled. "I came all this way to search for gold, and if Angus and Lachie have failed to find it here, then I'll press on. But you—oh, for God's sake, Luke, I meant it when I said you were under no obligation to me! You're not—and I'm heavily indebted to you in any case. You could have earned a reward if you had turned me in to the Geelong police when we landed, but you did not. And you bought our equipment and the horse. You owe me nothing—my contribution was only half of yours. Besides, you want to stay here, don't you? It's what you truly want?"

Luke eyed him gravely. "Yes, it is. Farming is my life, it always has been—I was born to it. I ran away from Pengallon because it had too many memories of Elizabeth and I couldn't bear to stay there without her. I only signed on with the *Merce-des* to get away, Michael—I'm not cut out for the sea, and already I'm tired of wandering. I want to put down roots, get back to the life and the work I know. I could do that here, if you don't mind going on to the fields alone."

"Of course I don't mind," Michael assured him.

"And there is another reason why I'd like to stay here," Luke volunteered. "That poor little girl, Jane. No one talked to her all through supper, did you notice?"

"She is deaf and dumb, Luke."

"Yes, I know. But she can lip-read—she followed everything that was said." Luke's brow furrowed. "I have a friend who's deaf and dumb, Dickon O'Shea, and he's one of the people I like best in the whole damned world. We worked the sheep and cattle together at Pengallon. Often we were away, just the two of us, for days on end, and we got so we could understand each other perfectly. I thought—well, maybe I could help that little girl to communicate the way Dickon and I used to. Because she must be a mite lonely, just listening and never talking." His expression relaxed. "Dickon used to draw pictures, with char-coal, to illustrate what he wanted to say. I might be able to teach Jane to do the same."

Another lame dog, Michael thought. Luke might be sending one on his way, but he had found another.

"You bide here, Luke," he urged, smiling. "I'll go on in the morning, if the rain lets up."

The rain had let up the next morning. Michael loaded the packhorse, and having thanked the Broomes for their hospital-ity, he was about to go on his way when Angus called out to him to wait. He came from the stockyard leading a country-bred bay, saddled and ready for use.

"Take him, Mr. Cadogan," he invited. "Dad says you're to have him for as long as you want. Go on," he urged, thrusting the bay's reins into Michael's hand. "He's getting a trifle too old for stock work, but he'll carry you well enough. And riding's better than walking, in this country." He grinned, when Mi-chael continued to hesitate. "If it bothers you, why, you can bring him back when you've made your strike! Good hunting!"

There was a bulging corn sack hung round the bay's neck, and swinging himself into the saddle, Michael echoed the young man's grin.

"Thanks," he said simply. "I'll pay you for him in gold—you see if I don't." He raised a hand in a farewell salute and, leading the packhorse, trotted off down the rutted road.

Michael did not hurry unduly. He slept in an old, deserted farmhouse the first night after leaving Bundilly, set up his tent ten miles from the township of Urquhart Falls on the second, and rode in on the morning of his third day on the road. The little township was pleasantly situated against a background of rolling, tree-clad hills, with the river—swollen from the recent heavy rain—a stone's throw from the point where the main street came abruptly to an end. The dwelling houses were mostly weatherboard, the shops and stores, with a single exception, constructed of the same material. The exception was a pretentious stone building, standing in the center of town and housing, besides a well-stocked emporium, a tavern and gaming rooms. This bore the name Brownlow carved across its front, and the same name appeared over a new, half-finished building, which proclaimed itself a bank, with a large, handwritten notice in the window announcing that it was open for business.

Horses, laden with packs like his own, were tied to hitching rails outside the tavern and several small eating houses, and most of the men visible in the street were, Michael saw, miners on their way to the diggings. Recalling what William Broome's sons had told him about Brownlow, he decided to give both tavern and emporium a wide berth, but with the appetizing smell of roasting meat assailing his nostrils, he yielded to temptation and dismounted outside a small, shingle-roofed eating house, which offered "Travellers' fare at fair prices."

Inside, the place was scrupulously clean. Half a dozen well-scrubbed wooden tables, set with cutlery, invited customers, but only two of the tables were occupied, and when Michael entered, a buxom, gray-haired woman bustled up to greet him with a beaming smile and invited him to seat himself at a table by the window.

The meal was plain, but it was well cooked and more than ample. The pangs of hunger satisfied, Michael sat back, to enjoy the pot of strong black tea placed in front of him and idly watch the comings and goings in the street outside. The other customers had settled their dues and gone, and the buxom proprietress, seemingly with nothing to do that necessitated her immediate attention, drew up a chair opposite his and sought to engage Michael in conversation.

"You stayin' here, mister, or just passin' through?" she inquired.

"Passing through," Michael told her.

"On your way to the diggin's? I see you got a packhorse out there at my rail."

"Yes, I'm going to try my luck, ma'am."

"At Cutler's Ford or them new diggin's at River Fork?"

Michael drained his mug, a trifle worried by the woman's persistence. But probably she was only trying to be friendly, he told himself, and he answered her question with a shrug.

"I don't know. I intended to look around before deciding. I expect I'll follow the crowd."

"They say River Fork's promisin', but of course they're all headed there now. It'll be cold, this time o' year—the diggings are high up." The woman studied him thoughtfully. "You're new to it, ain't you? Just come out here, have you?"

Best stick to his story, Michael thought; the Broomes had not doubted it, so this woman probably would not. But she was looking at his callused hands, as he poured himself a second cup of tea, and instead he said evasively, "I'm new to gold digging, but I've been out here a while."

Her shrewd eyes were raised to his face again, and she said, with a quick change of tone, half pitying, half derisive, "I get it, mister—you come out at 'er gracious Majesty's expense! Well, good luck to yer, so did I. The name's Martha Higgins. What's yours?"

"Michael—" He could not give her his real name, he decided, and he could not use Wexford. "Michael Mayo."

Martha Higgins appeared satisfied; at all events, she did not pour scorn on his choice of a name, and once again her tone changed, becoming persuasive.

"You set on goin' to the diggin's? With winter comin' on, it ain't the best time. An' I could use a good man, Mr. Mayo. I got a little spread, out of town a ways—a few sheep an' some store cattle. It needs a man, an' since my husband died, it's not bin easy to work it an' run this place as well. Labor ain't easy to come by here, neither. What there is, Mr. Brownlow grabs."

"Mr. Brownlow? Doesn't he own that new bank?" He knew the answer, of course, but Mrs. Higgins's outburst took Michael by surprise.

"Not only the bank, mister! He owns just about everythin' worth ownin' in this town! He was made o' money when he came here, an' he's bin coinin' it ever since. Used to be a p'lice officer, they say, down at Ballarat, an' made it by bribery an' corruption—that's what the folk here reckon. He got hisself shot at the Eureka Stockade, and—why, talk o' the devil! That's him, walkin' across to his bank, see?"

Martha Higgins broke off from her tirade to point to a stout, red-faced man in a black frock coat and stovepipe hat who was crossing from the opposite side of the street. He was too far away for Michael to see his features clearly, but his air of self-importance was evident, and so, too, was the fact that he walked with a pronounced limp—a legacy, no doubt, of the battle at the Eureka Stockade.

"You wouldn't fancy workin' for him, would you, Mr. Mayo?" Mrs. Higgins suggested. "Not too many folk do—he's a skinflint an' a hard man to please. But _I_ ain't hard to please. All I'd ask is a fair day's work for a fair day's pay, an' your grub thrown in. What do you say?"

It was the second offer of employment he had received in twenty-four hours, Michael thought, with a certain wry amusement. But at least Martha Higgins's offer had been made in the awareness that he—how had she put it?—had come out to Australia "at Her gracious Majesty's expense," and it had been coupled with the admission that she herself had come out the same way.

He smiled, liking the garrulous woman and appreciating her honest forthrightness.

"I hadn't planned on staying, ma'am."

"Give it some thought," she urged. " 'Cause there's storms brewin', an' I wouldn't fancy tryin' to keep dry in a flimsy tent —not when it's chuckin' it down with hailstones as big as your fist. An' likely it'll be snowin' at River Fork afore long, take my word for it."

Michael hesitated, looking through the window once again to follow the limping figure of the onetime police officer as it reached the door of the bank and then disappeared inside. Must he always be on the run, he asked himself—was that all that freedom meant? Freedom to hide from ex-police officers, to remain silent at dinner tables such as the Broomes', and . . . yes, to fear to use his own name, lest it lead to recognition and arrest?

"Where is your farm, ma'am?" he asked cautiously. "You said it was out of town?"

Martha Higgins, sensing his indecision, reached across to grasp his hand. "Three miles out, mister, an' set right back off the road the diggers take. It's a tidy little place, with a good cabin on it—an' you'd have it to yourself, 'cept for my son Tommy. He's sixteen an' he does what he can, which ain't much—but he tries. I'm here all day; I just go out to sleep there, an' I put in a day's work with the sheep on a Sunday. Tell you what—" Her eyes were on his face, pleading with him. "Try it for a week—just one week. Clean the place up for me, get in wood for the fires, do the jobs that are cryin' out to be done. If you don't want to stay after a week, you can go, an' no hard feelings. Eh—will you?"

Michael gave in, and she hugged him. They went out to her small farm then and there, and he found it precisely as she had described it, the lad Tommy a good-natured youth, with the gangling gait and vacant smile of a mental defective. There was, as its owner had said, much to be done, and within a few minutes of his arrival Michael hobbled his horses, unpacked his mining gear, and went to work.

In a week, he had achieved a good deal, with Tommy his willing and happy assistant. They were hampered to a certain extent by the rain and hailstorms Martha had predicted, but even in the downpours there was work awaiting him in the cabin and sheep pens, and he tackled it with enthusiasm. True to her promise, on the seventh day Martha paid him his wage and offered to free him, but he grinned and shook his head.

"I'll quit when the place is in proper order—and when the

sun comes out again. I cannot leave it like this, Martha." He listed what still needed to be done, and the woman turned away, not wanting him to see that she was crying. But she was not the kind to weep for long. Suddenly giggling, she started to hum a tune that Michael did not recognize until she put words to it.

> *"We're factory girls,*
> *Refractory girls,*
> *We're frail girls, pale girls—*
> *Keep nit and skip the bail girls!*

"Ain't you never heard that old bit o' doggerel, Michael? Someone taught it to us on the convict ship comin' out. I was only a kid, eleven years old, but I ain't never forgotten it." Martha raised her voice and sang lustily:

> *"We're tried an' true Old Bailey girls,*
> *The strip an' rob you gaily girls,*
> *The true blue gin an' tatter girls—*
> *The assault an' batter Parramatta Factory girls!*

"We sang it to a hymn tune, which made it seem better somehow, an' it used to make the overseers mad. Didn't you ever hear it?"

"No, I don't think so," Michael answered. "The only ditty we ever sang on Norfolk Island began 'True patriots we, who left our country for our country's good' . . . I don't recall any more of it, but I fancy it must date from the early days."

"You was on—Norfolk Island?" Martha exclaimed. "Oh, Gawd, you poor devil! Didn't they uster say that was punishment short o' death?"

"Yes, that was what they called it," Michael confirmed, and he could not prevent some of the remembered bitterness from sounding in his voice. "And that's what it was, when John Price was commandant!"

They did not speak of the past again, but three days later Martha brought a copy of an old Melbourne newspaper with her, when she came from town. In silence she laid it down, opened, in front of Michael, on the table where he and Tommy were finishing their evening meal. There was an advertisement in the center of the opened page, and she pointed to it with a blunt forefinger.

"I reckon you'd better read this, Michael." Her voice was strained. "It's more'n a week old. A customer brought the paper in, an' I just happened to see it."

Michael did as she had asked. The advertisement was headed, in heavy black print, MICHAEL WEXFORD, and his heart sank as he read on:

A reward of £150 is offered to anyone who can supply information as to the present whereabouts of the man known as Michael Wexford, lately a prisoner in the Port Arthur Penitentiary. This information should be lodged at the office of the Hobart *Chronicle* or at this office. It should be made clear that if Michael Wexford himself makes contact with the *Chronicle* in person or by letter, he will learn certain facts which will be to his advantage.

"That's you, ain't it, Michael?" Martha challenged. "You're not called Mayo?"

Michael nodded. But what, he wondered in bewilderment, could the Hobart *Chronicle* tell him that would be to his advantage? And why post a reward?

"A hundred an' fifty quid's a lot o' money," Martha observed, tight-lipped. "An' this dratted newspaper finds its way here! This ain't goin' to be the only copy in Urquhart Falls."

It would not be, of course. . . . Michael rose slowly to his feet, filled with a cold anger he found hard to hide. Martha was watching him, an odd expression on her lined face as she asked, "I s'pose you'll be movin' on?"

"Yes," he agreed. "I'll have to, won't I?"

"It'll be safer," she conceded. "But maybe you could—what does it say?—learn certain facts that'll be to your advantage. A relative might've died an' left you some money."

"That's not likely, Martha."

"I could find out for you," Martha offered. "*I* could write to the Hobart *Chronicle.* I wouldn't need to give nothin' away, only—"

"Only claim the reward?" Michael finished for her, and was shamed by the vehemence of her denial.

"It don't say nothin' about apprehendin' you, does it?" she pointed out coldly. "An' it don't say as you're an absconder."

"No—but I am, Martha. Between you and me, that's what I am, and that's why I'll have to move on. I'd get you into trouble if I stayed and they found me here."

Tommy had listened to their conversation with his usual blank imcomprehension, but the words "move on" penetrated the mists that shrouded his brain, and with a cry like some young animal in pain, he hurled his small, ungainly body into Michael's arms.

"No! Don't move on, Michael! I want you should stay."

Touched by the boy's unexpected display of emotion, Michael held him, rocking him to and fro as he would have rocked a baby. "I cannot stay, Tommy lad," he said gently. "I wish I could, but it's not possible."

"Then take me with you," Tommy pleaded. "I'd be no trouble. I'd work for you, like we worked here."

"Your mother needs you here, Tom. And she will need you all the more when I'm gone. This farm has to have a man to work it, you know."

"I ain't a man," the boy protested sullenly. "An' Ma says I never will be. Let me come with you—you're goin' to the gold diggin's, ain't you?"

It took all Michael's powers of persuasion to convince the boy, but finally and reluctantly he shambled off to his bed, and Martha said, her tone resentful, "Taken to you, hasn't he? I'd have boxed his ears for him, if he'd played up like that with me." Then she smiled, the resentment vanishing. "We'll miss you, Michael—the pair of us'll miss you, an' no mistake. But . . . when will you go? In the mornin'?"

"Yes, in the morning. And I'll be sorry to go."

"Maybe you'll come back?" Martha suggested.

"Maybe." But he would not, Michael knew. Not with an erstwhile police inspector in Urquhart Falls. He added, conscious of how much the reward would mean to her, "Give me a

good head start and then write to the *Chronicle*. You can tell
them I was here, but not where I've gone. And . . ." He hesitated. "And you can tell them my real name, because that will
be proof enough for you to claim the reward. It's Cadogan. I
don't doubt they will have found that out by now."

He left the farm before either Tommy or his mother was up
and, conscious of a genuine feeling of sadness, set off again
northward. The weather, although cold, held for the first two
days, but as he climbed higher into the hills, dark clouds gathered with the promise of rain or, he thought, looking skyward,
possibly snow. The promise was fulfilled an hour before nightfall, and a blizzard descended, blotting out the landscape and
chilling him to the bone. The horses were tired, and Michael
was considering halting to make camp when a distant glimmer
of light decided him to press on.

An isolated inn came into view a short while later, and
thankfully he put both horses under cover in the inn stable,
surprised to find that seven or eight other animals were occupying the stalls and boxes. A youthful hostler was at work, bedding them down, and leaving his own two in the lad's charge,
Michael strode across the yard to the inn. The taproom was
crowded; a group of bearded men, dressed in the rough moleskins of gold diggers, were gathered round the bar, clearly in
high spirits, drinking fairly heavily and toasting each other up-
roariously.

They were paying in gold dust, tipping it out on the bar
counter with lavish hands, and the landlord and his wife, busily
serving them, were beaming their pleasure at what they both
evidently regarded as a windfall.

Diggers who must have made a big strike, Michael decided,
eyeing them curiously. He made no attempt to join them but
took a seat at a table on the far side of the room and waited,
without impatience, for the arrival of the modest meal for
which he had asked.

It came, after some delay, served by a lad in an apron that
was several sizes too large for him, and proved to be tough
mutton that had been greatly overcooked. Hardly up to Martha
Higgins's standard, Michael thought regretfully, but he was
hungry and the potatoes served with the scraggy meat were

plentiful, and the gravy was thick and rich. He ate slowly, washing the food down with a glass of home-brewed ale, and listened idly to the diggers' chatter, hoping to pick up a hint as to the locality in which they had made their strike. But for all their seemingly careless merriment, the men gave no hint. They were well into their cups, staggering unsteadily about the dimly lit taproom, laughing and joking among themselves, and paying the landlord's wife extravagant compliments—which her appearance scarcely merited, but which she accepted with arch enjoyment, while keeping her distance behind the bar.

And then, without warning, the door opened and two police troopers came in, shaking the snow from their outer garments and cursing freely at the weather. The diggers lapsed into silence, eyeing them askance, and in the sudden hush the newcomers' voices carried across the room.

"Rum, Davie, for the Lord's sake!" Michael heard one of them demand. "It's as black as pitch outside, and the bloody snow's coming down so thick you can't see your hand in front of your face! We damned near rode past here without seeing your lights."

"It's no night to be out," the landlord observed sympathetically. "What brings you out, anyway?" Michael noticed that he was nervous, glancing anxiously across at the oddly subdued group of diggers as he poured the troopers' rum.

"A bloody holdup, of course," the trooper returned bitterly. "The shipment from River Fork. The whole flaming lot's gone and two of our boys gunned down." He gulped his drink and went into graphic detail. "Joe Hardy was hit in the stomach, and I don't reckon he'll last the night, the poor old sod. And young Lomax took two slugs in the leg. They were too many for 'em—eight or ten, Lomax said—skulking in ambush at the bottom of Snake Gully, and they opened up with rifles. Hit the team leaders and brought the wheel horses down, upsetting the wagon. It was a bleeding shambles. Old Joe never had a chance, and the goddamned diggers, who should have backed him up, why, they lit out and left 'em to it, Lomax said."

He turned to glare at the moleskin-clad men on the far side of the room. "It's *their* flaming gold! Up to them to defend the

blasted shipment, wasn't it? Hey, you over there!" He addressed
the diggers. "You from River Fork, eh?"

"River Fork?" There had been a perceptible pause before one
of the men answered the aggressively phrased question. "Naw,
we ain't from there, trooper."

"Is that so?" The trooper had drawn his pistol from its holster, and now he advanced into the center of the room, coming
under the beam of an oil lamp hanging from the ceiling. In its
light, his face was clearly revealed, and Michael stared at him in
shocked disbelief, recognizing him instantly as one of Commandant Price's overseers. A savage brute of a man, he had been
known to the Norfolk Island convicts as "Flogger" Smith, an
informer and a toady of Price's who was universally hated and
feared.

Recognition was mutual. Smith turned from the group of
diggers to level his pistol at Michael's chest, a slow smile
spreading across his leathery face.

"Ho, ho! Who have we here, for Christ's sake? Big Michael—
Big bloody Michael, who wouldn't bow the knee to Commandant Price! And serving life, too—which makes him an absconder in my book! Aye, and a scurvy gold robber to boot!
Lend me a hand, Tom Mullan, and we'll take the rogue in!"

His summons brought his comrade to his feet, startled. But
Trooper Mullan moved too slowly; one of the diggers put out a
foot and sent him sprawling headlong, and another grabbed
Michael's arm and hustled him to the door. A shot rang out as
they reached it, and the other men came spilling out after them,
shouting to one another in slurred, excited voices.

Michael heard one of them yell to the landlord that he had
better keep his mouth shut if he knew what was good for him,
and then he found himself propelled roughly onto the back of a
tethered horse. He seized its reins and galloped off in their
midst, into the driving snow. The cold was intense, and apart
from a few remarks concerning the route they wanted to take,
no one spoke. They rode hard for what Michael estimated to be
about an hour and then pulled up outside another isolated tavern. Here they dismounted, and as one of them took the horse
he had been riding, he realized with a faint shock that the ani-

mal was a troop horse—no doubt the property of one of the policemen.

"Come on in, Big Michael," one of his rescuers invited. "We'll be safe an' warm here, an' we can do the honors. My name's Billy, and—" His bearded face split into a grin. "I know who *you* are well enough. There ain't many as served time under that foul swine Price on Norfolk Island that don't remember your name. *An'* what you did!"

He ushered Michael inside a primitive building—a long, low hut constructed of split logs and with a shingle roof—and, over the drinks that a man in a nightshirt sleepily served them, formally introduced himself and his companions.

"I'm known as Billy Lawless, which ain't my real name, an' these are my boys." He pointed to them, grinning as he explained the nicknames they went under. "Tich Knight, the little feller . . . Marty Low, who gets called Slow most of the time, 'cos he's anything but. And Ginger Masters—you can see why, can't you? Chalky White . . . Boomer O'Malley, the loudest voice you'll ever hear . . . and Slugger McFee, who used to be a fist fighter. And this here's Big Michael Wexford, boys. I had the privilege of doing time with him on Norfolk Island, and take my word for it, he's all right." He raised his glass. "May John bloody Price rot in hell! 'Cause that's where he's gone, I'd stake my oath! They did for him at Pentridge Gaol, did you know that, Big Michael?"

"Yes, I saw it in the newspaper." Michael drained his glass, feeling the liquor course through his chilled body. "I'm grateful to you, Lawless—to all of you, for getting me out of a tight corner. It was odd, though—I supposed you were diggers who had made a rich strike."

The man known as Boomer roared with laughter.

"And so we had! A very rich strike. But there's easier ways than digging gold out of the ground, mister—take my word for it. F'instance, holding up a shipment from the mines." The others joined in his laughter.

Lawless waited until the merriment died down and then said to Michael, "You would be welcome to join us, Big Michael, if you've nothing else in mind. You're on the run, ain't you?"

"Yes," Michael admitted, "that's so." A spirit of bravado

filled him; what, he asked himself, had he to lose? These were holdup men, bushrangers, it was true, but what was he? A convict, a lifer, and a fugitive from justice, for whom it would be the rope if he were caught. As an alternative to toiling in the goldfields at the worst time of the year, joining these cheerful, happy-go-lucky men had considerable appeal.

He hesitated for a moment and then held out his hand. "I'll come along."

"Good man!" Billy Lawless grinned, wringing Michael's proffered hand. "We're going south for a spell—it's become a mite too hot for us hereabouts. But we've a prospect about fifty miles or so from here that we intend to look into. I'll tell you about it when we're on our way. Right now, I reckon we could all do with a few hours' sleep. We'll make tracks around noon tomorrow, if the coast's clear. And—we share and share alike, Michael. The risks and the profits. That suit you?"

"Yes, that will suit me well." Somewhat to his own surprise, Michael realized that he felt relaxed and even strangely at ease. With these men, he told himself, he would not have to pretend or keep a guard on his tongue. And they were not vicious killers like Haines and Josh; they were his kind, the kind he had become. Even with Luke Murphy he had had to exercise caution, take care what he said, for Luke's sake as much as for his own. At Bundilly, with the Broomes, he had been ill at ease, and at Martha Higgins's small farm there had been underlying anxiety, despite the trust she and the boy Tommy had shown in him. True, Billy Lawless's gang would have the police hot on their trail after the holdup of the gold convoy, but—

"We only aimed to wing those troopers," Lawless volunteered, as if he had read Michael's thoughts. "But the old feller came at us, set on shooting it out, and it was him or us. But mostly we ain't in favor of violence, and I reckon we should keep it that way . . . you agree?"

"I agree, Billy."

"We'll drink to that," Billy Lawless said. "And then get our heads down. Fill up, boys!"

For what remained of the night, Michael slept dreamlessly and well. Just before noon, they set off on their way south, Lawless riding at Michael's side to explain, at some length, the prospect they intended to look into.

Chapter XIX

KITTY WAS IN Launceston—one of half a dozen false trails she and Johnny had followed—when the letter she had been waiting and praying for finally arrived from Patrick, and she broke the seal on it with trembling fingers.

Johnny, who had collected it from the *Chronicle*'s local office, to which Dominic Hayes had forwarded it, watched her with concern as she read, the color draining from her cheeks.

When she did not speak, he asked anxiously, "Well, is there definite news at last? Has Pat found your brother Michael?"

For answer, Kitty passed him the letter and a printed cutting that had been enclosed with it.

"See for yourself," she invited tonelessly. "But read Pat's letter first. The item from the Melbourne *Herald* is . . . is speculation. It may not be Michael they are referring to, I—please God it is not!"

Johnny spread out the two closely written sheets on the table in front of him. Patrick's letter began with inquiries as to his sister's health and well-being and then continued

I am deeply sorry to learn that your search and John's has led you to so many dead ends, but the advertisement Dominic published in his newspaper and which he caused to be copied in the Melbourne and Geelong papers has at last borne fruit. There was a reply from a woman signing herself

Martha Higgins, from the township of Urquhart Falls on the Goulburn River.

It was badly spelt and, alas, not as informative as I would have wished, Kit, but I believe that the woman's claim to have seen Michael is true. She described him accurately and stated that he had told her that his real name was Michael Cadogan and that he had escaped from the Port Arthur Penitentiary.

It seems he told her that he had passed a night with a station owner named William Broome—a relative, perhaps, of Johnny's—whose place is situated forty miles distant, near the mouth of the Campaspe River, and is called Bundilly. If this Mrs. Higgins is to be believed, Michael stayed there on his way to Urquhart Falls and worked on her smallholding outside the township for about a week. He saw the advertisement in a Melbourne newspaper and gave her permission to reply to it, telling her to claim the reward.

But, she said in her letter, the next day he packed up and left, telling her that he intended to go to the new gold diggings, which I understand are at either River Fork or Cutler's Ford, in the Ovens area—a considerable distance to the east of Urquhart Falls. I am finding out all I can about these fields and how best to get to them, and I have written a cautious note of inquiry to Mr. Broome of Bundilly.

What worries me most is the inevitable delay between the arrival of Mrs. Higgins's letter at the office of the Melbourne *Herald*—to which it was addressed—and the time when you will receive mine. As I am not sure whether you are still in Hobart, I am sending this in care of Dominic Hayes and hope he will know an address to which he can forward it. I did receive the last letter you wrote from Sydney, saying that you had drawn blank there and were going back to Tasmania, but I have heard nothing since.

I promised I would wait for you and Johnny to join forces with me, but clearly, if I do, there will be still more delay and the scent will be cold. Also I am told that this is the worst possible time of year in the northern goldfields, with heavy snowfalls in the mountains. I propose therefore to leave Melbourne within the next few days and visit the

Bundilly station and Urquhart Falls and then go on to the
fields. Cobb & Co. run regular coaches to the fields, from
Melbourne and Geelong, and I am making inquiries concerning their schedules, although I think it likely that I shall
hire some form of horse transport, so as to be independent.

I will leave word for you at the *Herald* office in Melbourne.

Johnny folded the letter and returned it to Kitty, puzzled by
the tense, unhappy expression on her lovely face.

"What is worrying you, Kitty?" he asked her gently. "Surely
this is good news? William Broome *is* my uncle, and surely he
can tell us something about your brother. At least we know
where Michael was staying until a few weeks ago—we know
he's alive and still free. And, my dearest, Pat is setting off after
him. He may even have caught up with him by now!"

"Yes, Johnny, I know, and it is good news," Kitty admitted.
"But you haven't read the cutting from the newspaper."

Johnny picked it up, frowning. It hurt him deeply to see
Kitty worried and unhappy, and he wished, not for the first
time, that she would confide in him and allow him to help and
comfort her. He was, he recognized ruefully, more passionately
in love with her than ever—hopelessly, helplessly under the
spell of her beauty and charm—yet despite their close associa-
tion, she still continued to hold him at arm's length, keeping her
own counsel, instead of permitting him to share her anxieties
and shoulder the full responsibility for their long search. On
their return to Hobart, two weeks ago, she had seemed more at
ease with Dominic Hayes than with himself. Certainly she had
talked more freely to Dominic, and he, taking advantage of this,
had teased and made her laugh over some reference to a horse
named Snowgoose and the Master's Cup. Johnny smothered a
frustrated sigh and started to read the newspaper cutting. There
was a note from Dominic attached to it.

This report, published in the Goulburn Valley *Gazette &
Advertiser,* was sent to me by a colleague in Melbourne, and
it filled me with alarm. I do not know if Pat will have seen it,
but I felt it a matter of urgency that you should.

Johnny's frown deepened as he studied the report, conscious, as he read it, of being filled with alarm, as Dominic had been.

"Daring Robbery at Snake Gully," the headline proclaimed. "Two Troopers Wounded."

A gang of eight or ten bushrangers, armed with rifles and pistols, held up the gold shipments from the new field at River Fork, on the afternoon of August 10th.

The ambush was well planned, the robbers firing from concealment in the narrow gully just before dusk. Troopers Hardy and Lomax were wounded, the former severely, although he is reported to be recovering. The miscreants next turned their fire on the horse team, bringing the two leaders down and causing the wagon to overturn. The driver, Amos Flood, who escaped serious injury, was held at gunpoint whilst the gold from the heavy boxes was unloaded into sacks. The amount is believed to have exceeded 2,000 ounces.

The robbers then made off with their spoils into the bush. Later the following evening, two troopers, William Smith and Thomas Mullan, making a search in the vicinity, came upon a party they suspected of being members of the gang in a tavern called The Travellers' Rest, kept by David McMunn. Trooper Smith, who had previously served as an overseer of convicts on Norfolk Island, believed that he recognized a convict known as Big Michael Wexford—transferred to the Port Arthur Penitentiary, from where he recently absconded—but, on challenging him, the gang set upon him and his companion, and all made their escape, in a heavy snowstorm, taking the troopers' horses with them.

Mr. Commissioner Brackenbury, with a large posse of troopers and volunteers from the mining community, is conducting the search for the bushrangers, and we understand that a reward of £150 has been posted for Michael Wexford's capture.

"Do you wonder," Kitty challenged miserably, when Johnny finished reading the newspaper clipping, "oh, Johnny, do you wonder that I'm sick with anxiety?"

"No, dearest girl, I don't." Johnny rose and went to kneel
beside her chair, putting his arms about her waist. Kitty let her
head drop onto his shoulder, and he heard her muffled sobs as
he held her to him, his lips caressing her bent head. She did not
pull away from him, as she so often did, and after a while she
whispered wretchedly, "He doesn't know—Michael doesn't
know about the pardon."

"No, alas, he does not," Johnny agreed.

"The wording of that advertisement was at fault, Johnny.
Dominic should have stated that a pardon had been granted,
instead of saying that Michael would learn something 'to his
advantage' if he applied to the *Chronicle* office. If I'd known he
intended to publish it, I'd have insisted on his announcing that
Michael had been pardoned . . . then he might have contacted
the *Chronicle,* instead of—"

She broke off, unwilling even to suggest that her much-loved
elder brother could have engaged in the robbery of a gold shipment. But, Johnny thought, she was fully justified in blaming
Dominic Hayes for the wording of his advertisement. Devil take
him, Dominic should have known better. Or perhaps he did—
perhaps the fact that Kitty's abortive search had brought her
back to Tasmania had had some bearing on Dominic's cautious
choice of words.

"We *must* find him, Johnny," Kitty said. She raised her beautiful, tear-wet face to his, and Johnny was hard put to it not to
crush her to him, raining kisses on her parted lips. But he controlled the impulse, reaching into his coat pocket for a handker-
chief with which to dry her tears, reluctant to do or say anything that might reerect the barrier she was wont to set between
them if he attempted to go too far.

"Patrick will find him," he offered, thinking to console her.
"He knows where to look, at least, and we—"

"We must go to Melbourne. We just join him as soon as we
possibly can," Kitty exclaimed vehemently. "It should be easy
enough to find a vessel—any vessel at all, Johnny. I don't mind
how primitive it is, so long as it will give us passage. Can you
make inquiries?"

"Certainly," Johnny promised. "But—"

Kitty cut him short. "Then please, don't delay."

Johnny rose, his reluctance unconcealed. "Very well, Kit. But, my dearest, it will not be safe for you to venture into the gold diggings as matters stand. The diggers are rough men. Women—respectable women—have no place amongst them. You read the report. Robbery is rife, and bushrangers haunt the neighborhood of the diggings. I could not guarantee your safety, unless—"

Again she cut him short, her tone angry and scornful. "I'm not concerned with *my* safety—it's Michael's safety that concerns me, don't you understand? Pat and I came here to find him and we *must,* before it's too late. A reward has been offered for his . . . his apprehension, and I can only suppose that means dead or alive, doesn't it?"

If Michael had been one of the gang responsible for the robbery of the gold shipment and the wounding of two police troopers, then it seemed highly likely, Johnny thought grimly, but he tried to prevaricate, only to have his arguments brushed contemptuously aside.

"I'll try to arrange for our passage to Geelong or Port Phillip," he said stiffly. "It will probably have to be on board a sealer or a fishing vessel."

"I've said I don't mind, Johnny—just so long as you can find a vessel that will sail right away. You have your commission to find Michael and write his story, don't you? And I can pay my own, so . . . oh, please, let's not stay here arguing! We've wasted enough time, been led astray too often by false information. We—" Kitty hesitated, sensing Johnny's lack of response. "Johnny, you *are* coming with me—you are going to take me to Urquhart Falls and the new gold diggings, aren't you?"

Her voice was suddenly pleading, her brief anger fading, and aware that whatever Kitty Cadogan might demand of him, he could not bring himself to refuse, Johnny reddened.

"I accepted a commission from Mr. Hayes to go in search of your brother, Kitty—you do not have to remind me of that obligation. There's no question but that I shall honor it. And I will escort you to Melbourne, to Bundilly to visit my uncle, if you wish, and to Urquhart Falls, to question this Martha Higgins. But I will only take you with me to the diggings on one condition, let that be clearly understood, my dear. If you won't accept it, I'll go alone."

He had, Johnny realized suddenly, adopted a stronger tone than he had ever previously dared to use with Kitty, and for a moment he regretted having done so, fearing her reaction and knowing, all too well by this time, her spirit and her swiftly roused temper. But, to his heartfelt relief, he saw that—far from resenting his high-handedness—she was smiling at him.

"And what condition do you wish to impose on me, John Broome?" she asked him sweetly. "I will agree to almost anything. I—oh, for pity's sake, I *need* you! I cannot go alone. I'm fully aware of the limitations imposed on what you call respectable women in this country. I know that very few of the diggers take their wives with them to the fields, and that those who do go are women of easy virtue—they call them 'cats,' I believe. Well, I have no wish to be mistaken for any sort of feline." Kitty managed an odd little laugh, reddening in her turn. "So what do you wish me to do? What condition have you in mind? Shall I adopt a male disguise? Pretend that I'm Pat?"

The die was cast, Johnny told himself—he must risk losing her, if he were ever to win her for his own. Heaven knew he had been on the point of proposing to her more than a score of times in the past; but always Kitty had contrived to evade him, to brush aside the preliminary words leading up to an offer of marriage, as if their implication had escaped her. And he had allowed his hurt feelings to keep him silent. Even now she was seeking lighthearted excuses to avoid his proposal, for what else could her question concerning a male disguise possibly imply? No man with red blood in his veins would mistake Lady Kitty Cadogan for her brother Patrick, despite the fact that they were twins and bore a strong resemblance to each other. That slim, graceful, utterly feminine body in breeches or a pair of digger's moleskins and a cabbage plant hat would deceive no one who was not blind!

Johnny drew himself up to his full, impressive height and answered, with all the dignified firmness he could muster, "You could marry me, Kit. As your husband, I should have the right to protect you, and I—oh, my beautiful darling, I'm madly in love with you! From the moment when I first set eyes on you,

there's been no other woman in my heart or my life. Only you
—always and only you! You must know how I feel about you,
Kit."

"Yes, I know," Kitty conceded. Her gaze was on his face, the
wide, intelligent eyes submitting him to a searching scrutiny,
which took him momentarily aback. "Johnny, I have to be honest with you. I . . . I respect you too much to lie or pretend to
you. And I'm deeply grateful to you for all you've done to help
in the search for Michael. I owe you a debt which daily be-
comes greater and which I know I shall never be able to repay.
But I—I'm not in love with you. I'll marry you if that is what
you truly want, but *do* you want a wife who cannot give you the
love you deserve?"

Did he, Johnny wondered, did he want her as his wife, knowing that his love for her was not reciprocated? He drew in his
breath sharply, knowing suddenly and with certainty that he
wanted Kitty on any terms. Love could well come with marriage, with the intimacy of married life. He would overcome her
defenses, win her love by the intensity of his own. Unless there
was someone else . . .

He asked the question, dreading her answer, and then saw
her shake her head.

"Not Dominic Hayes?" he persisted.

Kitty's headshake was even more emphatic. "Oh, good heavens no! There was never anything between Dominic and me,
except for his horses. I loved riding them, Johnny. I—" She was
smiling, her eyes bright, lit by some memory he did not share.
Her smile faded, and she added gravely, "There was . . .
someone at home, in Kilclare. But it was just a boy-and-girl
attachment—it would not have lasted. He could not bear comparison with Pat or Michael, you see."

"No one can bear that comparison, I suppose," Johnny suggested, his earlier affronted stiffness returning. To his surprise,
Kitty put out both hands to him, her small, strong fingers closing tightly about his.

"You, nearest of all, Johnny," she told him quietly.

"Then marry me, Kit," he urged, the heady prospect of making her his wife overcoming the last vestige of his doubts.

"Even though you know that I'm not in love with you?"

"Even then," Johnny promised recklessly. "If you are my wife, I'll take you to the goldfields. I'll take you anywhere, my love, and I won't give up the hunt until we have found Michael. You have my word on it."

Kitty's head drooped. Avoiding his gaze, she said, her voice oddly expressionless, "Very well, Johnny, I will marry you whenever it can be arranged. Here in Melbourne, or even in—what is the place called? Urquhart Falls. And I'll try to make you happy, even if I—that is, even if, for me, it has to be a . . . marriage of convenience."

In his delight, Johnny would have taken her in his arms, but, as she had so often in the past, Kitty managed to elude him. He bore each of her hands in turn to his lips, and then she broke away, to beg him, in a brisk, businesslike tone, to lose no more time in securing their passage to the Victoria mainland.

He obeyed her and was able to arrange both their passage and their marriage, thanks to what seemed to him an unexpected stroke of luck. The mail steam packet *Gloria* was due to sail for Port Phillip the following morning, and among her passengers, Johnny learned, was Father Tobias O'Flynn, a Roman Catholic priest, who was leaving his curacy in Launceston on appointment to a Christian Brothers' school in Melbourne. Elated by this discovery, Johnny made a call at the presbytery as soon as he had attended to the passage reservations, and the young father enthusiastically agreed to perform the marriage ceremony on board the mail steamer.

"This is most romantic—a wedding on the high seas! And to a compatriot of mine, indeed. I shall be delighted to oblige you, Mr. Broome. Delighted and privileged."

Kitty's agreement was, to Johnny's chagrin, less enthusiastic than Father O'Flynn's had been, but she gave it without demur, stipulating only that the ceremony be delayed until the ship was in sight of their destination.

"Understand, Johnny, I beg you—ours cannot be a full and . . . proper marriage. Not yet—not until we've found my brother Michael. I must give everything to the search, without distraction. Bear with me, please."

He could bide his time, Johnny told himself, concealing his disappointment. He could wait to claim his bride; and a bride like Kitty Cadogan was infinitely worth waiting for. She would be his wife, in the eyes of the world, when they stepped ashore together in the Victoria capital, and no one—not even her brothers—could come between them.

Their wedding ceremony, performed in the *Gloria*'s cramped and smoke-filled cuddy, in the presence of strangers, was a long way from what he would have desired. Kitty, in her traveling dress, her bonnet held in place by a trailing scarf, did not look bridal; and throughout the service—curtailed because he was not a Catholic—she seemed impatient and distracted, almost as if she wished it over, so that she might give her attention to more important matters.

She made her responses in a low, barely audible voice, and her small hand, when he held it in order to place his ring on her finger, felt cold to his touch. Nonetheless, she looked so beautiful and so desirable that Johnny's heart beat faster when Father O'Flynn pronounced them man and wife and Kitty lifted her face for his formal kiss.

The strangers, including the master, drank their health, the men wringing Johnny's hand, their congratulations envious of his good fortune in winning so beautiful a bride. The few women on board, wives of working men, took in Kitty's elegant velvet, fur-trimmed gown and bobbed curtsies to her, addressing her politely as "ma'am."

But then it was over; the *Gloria*, assisted by a steam tug, nosed her way into the jetty, tied up, and prepared to receive the gangways by means of which her passengers would disembark. There were porters on the dockside, hackney carriages and a horse-drawn bus plying for hire, and a short distance away a notice proclaimed that the Melbourne and Hobson's Bay Railway Company ran a regular steam train service to Flinders Street.

Kitty, looking about her with bright-eyed interest, clapped her hands excitedly when she caught sight of this notice.

"Oh, Johnny," she begged him, "let us go by the steam train! The *Herald* office is in Flinders Street, isn't it?"

The short journey was swiftly and comfortably accomplished, the passengers seated in well-equipped, imported carriages painted in the company's colorful livery and pulled by a magnificent locomotive, which rattled over the rails at a speed, a knowledgeable passenger assured them, well in excess of fifteen miles an hour.

Kitty took an almost childish interest in everything she saw, but when they left the train at the Flinders Street terminus, she became once again impatient and distracted, paying little heed to Johnny's attempts to draw her attention to the fine new buildings and the well-ordered, lamp-lit streets, with their profusion of shops, restaurants, and hostelries. Having visited the town during the early days of the gold rush, he was impressed by the transition from what had been virtually a hodgepodge of weatherboard buildings, acres of tents, and streets that, all too often after rain, had been ankle- or even knee-deep in glutinous mud.

Kitty, however, was ill disposed to linger; she took his arm, urging him to inquire of a passerby as to the location of the *Herald* office. They found it without difficulty, and Kitty's smile returned when the expected letter from Patrick was taken from the rack and given to her. She ripped it open and read it quickly, then handed it to Johnny.

Dated almost three weeks earlier, it was brief and concerned only with Patrick's movements.

I am leaving Melbourne tomorrow morning, having decided to take the Cobb & Co. coach to Bendigo. I have been told there is an excellent livery stable there, from which horses and various types of traps and buggies can be hired. From Bendigo, I propose to make my way to Bundilly to talk to Mr. William Broome—is he, do you know, any relation to Red and Johnny?

These Cobb coaches carry the mail and run through the night, with frequent stops at changing stations for fresh horses, and they are said to average a speed of ten miles an hour. They are American-built Concord coaches, designed for the comfort of passengers, and I would strongly advise you, Kit, to follow my example and travel by this means. But do not travel alone—take Johnny with you.

If I am able to obtain reliable information as to Michael's whereabouts—from Mr. Broome or Martha Higgins in Ur-

quhart Falls—I shall endeavor to find him. I will leave word
for you with Mr. Broome, but I think it unwise, if the trail
should lead to the new gold diggings, for you to venture
there, Kit. Stay at Bundilly or Urquhart Falls and leave it to
Johnny to catch up with me.

In a postscript, Patrick had given the address of the coach
booking office as "23 Bourke Street East—the Telegraph Stage
Office."

"Let's go and book seats on the coach," Kitty said, when
Johnny finished reading the letter. She did not wait for his as-
sent but was out on the street, obtaining directions to Bourke
Street, by the time Johnny rejoined her.

There was a coach leaving that night, and at a cost of eight
pounds each they were issued the last two inside tickets.

"It's one hundred an' twelve miles from here to Bendigo,"
the booking clerk told them, as he scribbled their names on his
list. "The coach carries thirty-two passengers, inside an' out, it's
drawn by six horses, and the journey time is twelve an' an 'arf
hours." He grinned at them proudly. "Ain't nobody goin' to
beat that for a long while, not even if they build a railroad. The
new plank road through the Black Forest 'as made all the difference—that used to turn into a swamp after 'eavy rain, see?"

He added the gratuitous advice that Johnny would be wise to
take his lady for dinner at the Criterion Hotel before departure.

"We leave from outside the 'otel, sir, punctual, an' you'll get
a good meal there. On the way there ain't more'n two changin'
stops where you can count on time to eat, an' the Buckeye
Hotel's the best—that's the last stop afore Bendigo. An' you
can leave your baggage with me, sir—I'll see as it's loaded on
the coach."

Kitty relaxed at last, to Johnny's relief. In their now-frequent
journeyings, she had learned to travel light, for one of her sex,
to eat when it was convenient, and often to go without sleep.
But the strain was beginning to tell, and he found himself wishing that, for her sake, this journey might be the last. Surely her
brother Michael could not elude them forever.

More than a little to his surprise, Kitty acceded to his suggestion that he take a room for her in the hotel, to enable her to

rest for the few hours that remained before the departure of the coach. Johnny left her in a clean and comfortable room and, having time on his hands, returned to the *Herald* office to make a search of the paper's most recent files. He found a fuller report of the robbery of the gold shipment at Snake Gully than the one Dominic had sent them, plus a more recent article, culled from the Urquhart Falls *Weekly Advertiser,* detailing Trooper Smith's claim that he had identified one of the robbers as "the absconder known as Michael Wexford":

> I would know him anywhere. Big Michael, we used to call him at Norfolk Island, because he was a real big man, standing six foot five or six in his bare feet. And he defied the commandant's authority all the time he was there. I don't think I knew a convict who took more lashings than that man did, all of them for breaches of discipline and insolence.
>
> It was Big Michael I saw in the taproom of The Travellers' Rest—I would be willing to swear to it in a court of law.

The *Herald* had added a graphic description of the escape from the Port Arthur Penitentiary, during which a prison officer and a soldier of the military guard had been murdered and the government steamer *Hastings* seized "in an act of piracy":

> For this crime and the murder, subsequently, of the master of the *Hastings,* Wexford's three companions in crime have been tried and hanged in Hobart, following their recapture there. But Wexford has, to date, evaded capture, and it seems more than likely that Trooper Smith did see him, with members of the gang of bushrangers who perpetrated the daring robbery of the gold shipment from River Fork.
>
> A substantial reward has been offered for Wexford's apprehension, and Commissioner Brackenbury is continuing the search for the gang, which local people are now calling the Lawless Gang.

Johnny sighed deeply as he replaced the report in its file. Michael, he thought grimly—his wife's beloved brother—could

with us for at least another week." She did not wait for either his reply or her husband's, but excused herself quietly and made for the door. Reaching it, she paused, smiling at Johnny. "The boys will be in soon—Angus and Lachie and Luke. But save your Sydney news for supper, John, because I'm longing to hear it all. And—you are a journalist, aren't you? I'm sure your father told Will that you were."

"Yes, Aunt Dodie, I am," Johnny confirmed. "I'm with the Sydney *Morning Herald* but on a special assignment for a Hobart paper at present. Why? Was there any particular reason?"

"Yes, as a matter of fact there was," his aunt confessed. "I'm anxious for news from India. My sister Julia—you probably will not remember her—is married to an Indian army officer, Colonel Dermot Macintyre. And as you will know better than I do, there's serious trouble in India—a mutiny of the native troops in Bengal. That is where they are stationed—in Lucknow, which according to the last newspaper I saw is under siege. I wondered if you had any recent news?"

There had been news, Johnny recalled, in the last edition of the Melbourne *Herald* he had seen; but his mind had been on other matters, and beyond registering the fact that the news had not been good, he had not really taken much of it in. There had been something about troops being recalled from China and sent to India, and a telegraphic message from Sir Henry Lawrence to the effect that Lucknow's defenses were in good order, but . . . Johnny sighed. He could recall little else. There had been no mention of Ranpur, where Will De Lancey and Jenny were stationed, and so, presuming that all must still be well there, he had gone back to the task he had set himself—searching back numbers for reports of the activities of the Lawless Gang.

He remembered Julia, however—Julia Dawson, she had been, the elder of Abigail Tempest's stepdaughters—an acid-tongued, unattractive woman, very different from the charming person who was his aunt Dodie. As boys, he and Red had disliked Julia intensely, but he could hardly say so now, of course. He started to quote what he could remember of the telegraphic message from Lucknow, in the hope that his aunt might find it of comfort, but she cut him short.

"The last mention of poor Sir Henry Lawrence that *I* have seen stated that he was killed by a cannon shell," she said sadly. "It was an unconfirmed report, in one of the newspapers Angus brought back from Urquhart Falls. I had hoped that you might have seen a more recent edition before you left Melbourne. News filters through and takes so long to reach us here."

"Yes," Johnny agreed, feeling foolish. "Yes, Aunt Dodie, it does. But let us hope the report about Sir Henry Lawrence was wrong. I . . . my sister Jenny and her husband are in Bengal, too, at a place called Ranpur. It is what they call an outstation, I understand, not far from Cawnpore. I've seen no mention of it in the papers, so I was hoping they have had no trouble there. But—"

Again his aunt interrupted him. "I think," she said, her voice oddly strained, "that I had better show you *my* paper, John. There has been a terrible massacre at Cawnpore, after the garrison surrendered, and . . . I'm afraid that this report cannot be wrong. It names names, and it . . . Oh, dear, perhaps you should read it for yourself. I'll bring you the paper."

She was gone for only a few minutes, leaving Johnny sick with apprehension. On her return, she waved him to an armchair and laid the opened sheet of newsprint on his knee. He read the report with mounting horror, wondering how he had come to miss it. It occupied the front page, and appalling though the whole story was, it appeared to be substantiated by a statement from Lord Canning himself, in which he expressed his anger and repugnance at the base treachery of the rebel leader, the Nana of Bithur.

Stunned, Johnny put down the paper, meeting his aunt's tear-filled gaze when he did so.

"It is terrible, isn't it, John?" she said regretfully and expelled her breath in a long, unhappy sigh. "I had always thought of India as a land of milk and honey and safer than it is here. I used to envy Julia, when she wrote of the luxury she enjoyed, the hosts of servants, the balls and parties she attended. But—" She shivered. "I do not envy her now, or your sister Jenny. They were so brave, those men and women in Cawnpore, and they held out so heroically. Let us pray that Lucknow will be able to withstand the siege, even if Sir Henry Lawrence has been killed. And that Jenny and Will are safe."

Johnny echoed her prayer. The boys came in shortly afterward, and over the evening meal, for which Patrick insisted on leaving his bed, the conversation was general, the subject of India avoided. From Luke, Johnny learned the details of Michael's arrival on board the *Mercedes,* and he saw Kitty's eyes widen as she realized how close they had come to making contact with the fugitive.

"We were on the wharf, Pat and Johnny and I," she said. "I had Michael's pardon, endorsed by the governor, in my purse, ready to hand to him! If only we had *known.* It's heartbreaking to realize now that he was probably hiding a few yards from where we were standing."

"We could not have known, Kit," Patrick said, his tone faintly reproachful. "And even if he had seen us, Michael might not have recognized us. It's been so long."

He sounded tired and discouraged. His illness, Johnny realized, had taken its toll, both of his strength and his spirits. And he raised no objection when it was broken to him that he must remain at Bundilly, leaving his sister and brother-in-law to continue the hunt without him.

"I'm as weak as a kitten," he confessed, when turning to Johnny to offer him congratulations on his marriage—the congratulations, although warmly expressed, somewhat lacking in conviction. "I hope you'll be happy, truly I do." He glanced at Kitty, who was deep in conversation with their hosts. "But Kit is—well, she's a law unto herself, Johnny. You will have to ride her on a very light rein, for a while, anyway. But perhaps, if we find Michael—if we ever find him and are able to get him back to Ireland—perhaps then Kit will have time for marriage. She hasn't now, you know."

He knew, Johnny thought despondently. Kitty had made her feelings abundantly clear. Seated at the long, candle-lit table, as the others talked, he watched her lovely, glowing face, heard her laughter, and observed how the Broome family fell, in turn, victims to her charm. Even his hard-headed uncle William was not immune to it, and the two boys, Angus and Lachlan, were frankly enchanted, vying with each other for her attention, ea-

ger to serve her. Only Luke, seated beside the little deaf and
dumb girl, Jane, had no eyes for anyone else. They communi-
cated in a strange, close-knit silence, with just their lips moving,
but they seemed, to Johnny's surprise, to understand each other
without any need for words. Luke, he reflected almost envi-
ously, had found the cure for his heartbreak, although probably
it would be a while before he became fully aware of it.

After the meal, Kitty went upstairs to see her brother back to
bed, and she stayed with him—to the evident disappointment of
her newest conquests, who eventually, despairing of her return,
sought their own beds.

With his aunt playing a soft accompaniment on the piano,
Johnny stayed talking to Luke and his uncle, exchanging news,
William plying him with questions concerning the rest of the
family in Sydney, and Luke anxious to hear all that Johnny
could tell him of the doings of the Tempests at Pengallon.

"I hated leaving them, you know," Luke asserted. "But
somehow I could not stay at Pengallon, after Elizabeth died.
And I suppose it's odd that I've been able to settle here, but—"
He glanced, smiling, at William Broome and then across to the
piano, where Jane was turning the pages of music as Dorothea
played. "Once I had the gold fever and all I dreamed of was
making a big strike. Then I thought I had the sea in my blood
and found I hadn't. I was born a farm boy, and that's all I want
now—to work with sheep and cattle and end my wandering.
But when you go back to Sydney, Johnny, tell Rick and Katie
Tempest, and Edmund and Dickon, next time you see them,
that they are always in my thoughts—and my prayers, too,
come to that—even if I don't come back."

"I'll tell them," Johnny promised. "If and when I'm able to
go back, Luke."

Luke did not pretend to misunderstand him. He asked, lowering his voice, "You're still going on with the hunt?"

"Yes. I gave my word. I'll see it through." He would lose
Kitty if he did not, Johnny reflected wryly. And there was Michael. He thought suddenly of the diary he had found, in the
empty prison on Norfolk Island, and the emotions it had
aroused in him, the pity and . . . yes, the admiration. After all
this time, he wanted to meet Big Michael face to face. Quite

apart from his obligation to Kitty, he knew that he wanted to see Michael Cadogan set free.

"He is a very fine man, Michael," Luke said unexpectedly. "Whatever they may say about him now, Johnny, he's no killer. He's a very gallant gentleman. I spent quite a bit of time with him, and I *know*, without a shadow of a doubt, that's what he is." Luke hesitated, glancing across at William Broome, who had fallen asleep in his armchair, lulled by his wife's soft playing and the pleasant heat of the big log fire. "Mr. Broome can't help, not in his position, but maybe I can. There's a lot to do here, and we're short of labor . . . all the same, I'm sure he'll let me take time off, if I ask him."

"Time off, Luke? Do you mean—"

Luke nodded. "I mean I'll come with you to Urquhart Falls tomorrow. I don't think Mrs. Higgins can tell you much, but I'm acquainted with a few folk in the town now who just might know more. And besides—" He smiled. "You need me, don't you? I know Big Michael by sight, Johnny, and he'd recognize me. You might need a go-between, if he *is* with the Lawless Gang."

His suggestion was a practical one, and Johnny thanked him.

Luke brushed the thanks aside. "If you do catch up with him, how do you plan to organize his escape? New South Wales first, I take it, and then a ship from Sydney, back to Ireland? It's not safe for him to stay here, in this area."

"Yes, I realize that. A coach from Bendigo, probably, to Albury for a start. We might have to backtrack or take a roundabout route, but depending on circumstances, I think a coach is the best idea. But that's not a hard and fast decision, and I haven't discussed it fully with Kitty or, of course, with Pat." Johnny shrugged. "It depends to a large extent *where* we find Michael. A dash on horseback might be necessary."

Luke nodded his understanding. "What puzzles and, to be honest, what worries me is why Michael didn't do what he told me he intended to do. He said he was going to the new goldfields north of here, and though I know it wasn't the best time of year to start prospecting in the high country, quite a few diggers do stick it out. And Michael is tough—cold and snow wouldn't have put him off, I'm sure of it. And he would have been safe enough in a diggers' camp. But instead he joined up with this gang of bushrangers and started robbing banks, risking his neck and his freedom. It's out of character. And it means that the royal pardon your wife and Pat managed to obtain for him isn't worth the paper it's written on. If he's caught, he'll be tried for robbery under arms."

"He didn't know about the pardon," Johnny defended. "He ran from Port Arthur before we could tell him it had been granted. Come to that, Kitty and Pat did not know until some time after they came out here. They set the wheels in motion, left the lawyers to lodge an appeal, but they had no way of knowing that the appeal would be successful. In fact, I don't think they expected it to succeed."

Luke studied his face thoughtfully. "What was Michael deported for—what crime was he charged with, I mean? He was a political prisoner, wasn't he?"

"He was charged with high treason."

"But he wasn't guilty?"

"No," Johnny said. "The charges, according to the information I have, were brought maliciously by an English military officer who owed him money for gaming debts." He gave the details Kitty had supplied and saw that Luke's eyes were bright with anger.

"And for that the poor fellow has endured years of torture! Years on Norfolk Island under John Price, and then Port Arthur, where they never let him out of the chain gang—except when the overseers arranged an illegal prizefight, with Michael as their champion!"

Johnny stared at him. "God, did he tell you that?"

"Yes, he did."

"Then a small wonder he absconded," Johnny said.

"I don't think that was why," Luke answered. "He had another reason—a very strong one, Johnny. He never told me what it was, but when we went ashore together in Geelong, he seemed suddenly to change. He bought a newspaper, I remember, and something he read in it seemed—well, to take the wind out of his sails completely. I'd suggested he should go up north to the goldfields with me, but he had refused, at first. Said he had urgent business to attend to, something he'd promised himself for years that he'd do, if he were free. But after reading whatever it was in the newspaper, he changed his mind and said he would join me after all. I remember his words. He said, 'I've nothing better to do now—I got here too late. So if you want me to partner you, I will.' Do *you* have any idea what he was talking about, Johnny?"

Johnny considered the question and then shook his head. "No, I've no idea at all, Luke." His host, he saw, had awakened, and the piano had fallen silent. His aunt smiled across at him.

"Bed, John? I've put you and your wife in our guest room at the head of the stairs. If you would like to come with me, I'll show you the way."

The room, when he entered it, was empty, the big double bed unoccupied. Kitty, he thought bitterly, preferred her brother's company to his.

At pains to conceal his resentment, Johnny bade his aunt good night and lost no time in undressing and climbing into the warm, comfortable bed. But, physically tired though he was, he slept fitfully, his peace of mind disturbed by a nightmare in which he had a confused vision of his sister Jenny running barefooted through the streets of an Indian city, with a howling mob at her heels. She was crying out to him to save her, but before he could set his seemingly leaden limbs in motion, the mob caught up with her. In his dream, he lost sight of her in the melee, and when the crowd of turbaned natives parted, it was not her lifeless body he saw but that of a big, dark-haired man, with a gunshot wound in his chest, whom he realized was Michael Cadogan.

The dream was so vivid that, when he wakened from it, his whole body was bathed in perspiration and he was calling Jenny's name aloud. Later, when he had again drifted into sleep, he became vaguely conscious of a movement beside him. It held no significance until, with the coming of daylight, he roused himself wearily and saw that Kitty was asleep on the other side of the bed. She was fully clothed and had her back to him with—absurdly—a pillow erected as a barrier between them.

Johnny swore softly and sat up. If his wife heard him, she gave no indication of having done so, and after a minute or two he left the bed they had so briefly shared and, donning shirt and breeches, went in search of water with which to wash and shave. Kitty was gone when he returned to the bedroom; and on his way downstairs in response to a call from his uncle to join the family for breakfast, he heard her voice and Pat's, coming from her brother's sickroom.

An hour later, Luke brought their saddled horses to the yard at the rear of the house, and, farewells and thanks duly offered, the three of them set off for Urquhart Falls, Kitty riding alongside Luke, and himself behind them, leading the packhorse.

Chapter XXII

LILY WAS IN the kitchen, preparing vegetables for the evening meal, when she learned of Dingo's duplicity. Nelly came storming in and harshly bade her abandon her task and go and pack her bags.

"You c'n get to hell out of here," Nelly added. "You an' the other tarts. You won't be wanted no more."

"But . . ." Lily gestured to the bowl of freshly peeled potatoes, unable to understand the reason for the old woman's sudden outburst. "The boys will be hungry when they come back. I thought—"

"It don't matter a tinker's cuss what you thought, lass. The boys won't be comin' back—they'll be on their way to gaol, an' good riddance! This tavern belongs to me and *Mister* Carter now, an' we'll be runnin' it as a respectable house from now on, not a hidey-hole for a bunch of soddin' bushrangers an' their fancy women! You c'n tell them other cats to be on their way. I want 'em out by noon."

Lily stared at her, scarcely believing the evidence of her own ears. Nelly had always been so servile, so eager to please, the respect she had shown to Billy Lawless transferred to Michael after Billy's death. And Dingo, for all his sullen grumbling, had been the same, touching his forelock and doing what any of them told him to do. But . . . She drew a swift, startled breath, remembering his previous absence with the horse and buggy and the limp excuse he had made for it. Slugger McFee did not really care what he drank, so long as it was liquor—he only demanded whiskey to prove that he was of Scottish ancestry. Yet Dingo had insisted he had gone to replenish the Magpie's stock of whiskey because Slugger had complained!

"You got your money, ain' you?" Nelly pursued unpleasantly. "Poor Billy's share, an' that was a tidy sum. A whole lot more'n he saw fit to leave to us. An' we didn't get the Magpie neither—by rights, Billy should've left *us* the Magpie. If he had, maybe me an' Mr. Carter wouldn't have felt so bad about things."

"Did he, did Ding—Mr. Carter inform on them?" Lily managed, in a choked voice. "Did he inform on Michael for the reward?"

"Use your head, girl—o' course he did. An 'undred an' fifty quid—you don't come by that very often these days. An' there's another fifty to add to that, if Michael's caught in Urquhart Falls. That feller Brownlow give his word it'd be paid." Nelly gave vent to a chuckle. "They'll be waitin' for 'em at the bank—police an' townsfolk, the lot of 'em. Michael won't have a chance in hell, so you'd best forget him an' find yourself another bloke."

Lily's heart sank. She believed it now; Nelly had made no bones about what Dingo had done. She must be sure of the outcome to boast of it openly. Michael and the others were riding into a trap, and . . . oh, God help them, if they entered the bank and found armed men awaiting them! Mr. Brownlow had been a police inspector—he would be well versed in the ways in which traps were set and sprung, and Dingo would have given him all the information he needed to spring this one.

And there was no time now, alas, to warn Michael. He and the others had left almost twelve hours ago, aiming to enter Urquhart Falls just after noon, to reconnoiter, as Michael had put it, and hold up the bank once they were satisfied that the coast was clear. Ideally, Michael had told her, they would wait until dusk, since this would make their escape easier and discourage pursuit, but it might not be possible to wait that long.

If they did, though—Lily looked at Nelly Carter, hate burning in her eyes—she *might* get there in time. It was about thirty-five miles from the Magpie to Urquhart Falls, following the road—a cart track, in reality, scarred by the wheels of the diggers' wagons and deep in mud this time of year—so they would not have been able to make much speed. There was another, more direct route, which Billy had once shown her, across country. He had described it as "the way the crow flies" and said that it cut a good twelve miles off the distance to the township. It offered a chance, if only a slight one, to a rider on a good horse, who was prepared to risk his neck by covering it at full gallop.

She was by no means an expert horsewoman, but she could ride and . . . Lily tensed. There was the half-wild stallion Billy had bought, in one of his few legitimate dealings, from a farmer in the locality, intending it for his own use. But it had turned out to be a vicious animal, and he had never used it. Tich Knight, who had a way with horses, had been trying to tame it—Lily was not sure with what result—and she shuddered apprehensively as a desperate plan took shape in her mind. The stallion was fast—faster than any of the other horses they kept in the Magpie's stables—and if all she had to do were mount it and set its head in the direction of Urquhart Falls, then it would be her best, perhaps her only chance of catching up with Michael before the raid on Brownlow's bank took place.

She owed it to Michael to try, Lily told herself. Even if she came to grief, at least she would have tried. . . .

"What you got in mind?" Nelly demanded suspiciously, irritated by her sudden silence. "Ain't thinkin' of goin' after 'em, are you? 'Cos you'd never catch 'em, that's for sure!"

"We'll see about that," Lily flung back at her defiantly and, leaving the old woman staring after her, tore out of the kitchen. In Tich's bedroom, where his girl Meg was still asleep, she found breeches and a shirt and struggled into them as she gave the drowsy Meg a brief and bitter account of what she had learned from Nelly.

"Why, the filthy old bitch!" Meg exclaimed. "And that Dingo—Gawd, wasn't Billy right when he called the old swine that? Are you really goin' to go after them, Lily? You'll never catch up with them—just get yourself arrested for no reason."

"I'm going," Lily retorted, fumbling with the buttons on the borrowed shirt. "I need boots, Meg—find some for me, will you? And a hat."

Meg bestirred herself and, on Lily's urging, came with her, still in her nightclothes, to the stables. Between them they saddled the big black stallion, thrust bit and bridle onto his struggling head, and Meg held him as Lily gingerly scrambled onto his back.

Dingo made his appearance then, with Nelly screaming furious abuse in his wake. He made a half hearted attempt to stand in her way, but the stallion put his head down and, with the bit between his teeth and Lily clinging to the saddle, bolted forward, forcing the old man to jump aside to avoid being trampled. And then they were away, heading for the open country, the direction they took more the stallion's choice than that of his rider.

By chance, it was the right one, to Lily's fervent relief, for she could exert little control and, indeed, was finding it all she could do to keep her seat on his plunging back. Her mount, intoxicated by his newfound freedom, scarcely felt her light weight and, after a tentative effort to fling her off by bucking, contented himself with a presence that inconvenienced him not at all, as he settled down to a steady gallop. The country was rough, untamed bush, broken by hillocks and gullies, the gums growing thickly in places, sparsely in others, and, where the ground was flat, changing to mulga scrub and saltbush. The stallion picked his way without faltering, seldom slackening speed, a surefooted wild creature at home in the land where he had once roamed free and at will, with a mob of fillies and mares whose owner, a poor settler, had paid them scant regard.

Lily, when she had got her breath, settled down too. The sun, she knew, must be kept on her left hand; Billy had told her that.

"You'll never get bushed if you let the sun guide you," he had said and grinned as he said it. "Many's the time I've lost the fellers who were chasing me, just by taking off into the bush and knowing, better than they did, where I was."

She did not know where she was, Lily thought resignedly, but her mount quite evidently did, and she could only hope that if it became necessary to change direction in order to keep the sun to her left, the big stallion would respond to a tug on his rein.

She dared not part company with him in this desolate country, miles from the road—certainly not before the river came into sight and she was able to get her bearings. She ventured a pat on the horse's sweat-streaked neck and let him have his head. The stallion galloped on, seemingly untiring, and Lily, almost for the first time since she had embarked on her despairing mission, began to hope that it might, against all the odds, succeed.

On the outskirts of Urquhart Falls, Michael drew rein, and from the brow of the low hill on which he had halted he studied the huddle of houses, shops, and public buildings that constituted the town.

He had paid little attention to the town, as such, when he had worked on Martha Higgins's smallholding, but now he subjected it to a prolonged and careful scrutiny, his earlier doubts still unresolved.

In the pale, watery sunlight that had followed the rain, it looked a prosperous place; and it was growing, with business premises, stores, and shops spreading out from the main street, some still in the course of construction. The residential section extended along the riverbank, and below the falls from which the town took its name were a number of brick houses, each with a neatly fenced garden, which spoke of prosperity and increasing settlement.

Where before it had been a market town for the sheep and cattle breeders in the area, Urquhart Falls owed its present expansion to the diggers, on their north-bound pilgrimage to the new goldfields . . . and, Michael reminded himself, to the products of their toil, flowing in the opposite direction.

A shrewd, farsighted man, Leonard Arthur Brownlow, he reflected cynically, to have foreseen the town's potential and to have invested in it when land was comparatively cheap and the return virtually assured. Even if the diggers moved on, as was their wont, the squatters remained; and Brownlow, according to Slugger McFee, had recently purchased a new ferryboat, capable of carrying sheep and cattle, to serve those landowners whose properties lay on the far side of the river. And the whole town would profit from the added trade, particularly now, when the river was in flood tide and the crossings above and below the town were impassable for flocks and herds.

Indeed a farsighted man, Mr. Brownlow, with his new bank likely to prove the best investment of all.

"That's Brownlow's house," Marty Low said, pointing. "Pretty plush place, wouldn't you say?"

And it was, Michael saw, following the direction of Marty's pointing finger. A two-story house, stone built, with an extensive garden and a unique view of the falls, which, augmented by the recent rains, hurtled down forty or fifty feet in a cascade of sparkling foam, to find level ground just above Brownlow's immaculate lawn.

"Aye, he chose his site well," Michael agreed. "He chose it uncommonly well!"

McFee laughed. "Seeing he owns most of the land, Michael, he could pick an' choose, couldn't he? Lord, it will be a pleasure to relieve the swine of some of the profit he's made! And there'll be quite a few in the town who will not hold it against us if we do."

Reminded of the reason for their presence here, Michael became brisk and businesslike.

"Right, boys," he said. "We'll split up here. Slugger and Marty will go in first and we'll follow, as soon as they give us the all clear. Tich will stay with the horses outside Martha Higgins's place, across the street from the bank, and Chalky will hold the spare animals a hundred yards back down the street. I'll go into the bank first, on my own, acting like a customer. When I signal from the door or fire a shot, the rest of you come in after me, with Ginger covering the street from the door."

They all nodded, their faces grave. They had discussed their tactics a dozen times, and each of them, Michael was confident, knew what he had to do; but he added, with heavy emphasis, "No shooting, if it can be avoided—just a quiet, orderly holdup, with maybe a warning shot into the ceiling, to show we mean business. And if Mr. Brownlow chances to be in his bank, we take him as a hostage when we make a run for it. But we release him as soon as we're safely away."

Slugger grinned. "That's the part I like best! I hope the bastard *is* in his bank. I'd enjoy getting my hands on him, by God I would." He touched his horse with his heels. "Come on, Marty old son, let's be on our way."

The two trotted off and the rest dismounted, loosened their horses' girths, and let the animals browse at the roadside. They had not pushed them on the way there, Michael thought, but even so, it had been a fair ride and it was essential that their mounts were rested, for their getaway might have to be a hurried one. Tich, without being asked, pulled up some handfuls of grass and started to rub his own horse down.

"I'll tend to yours, Michael," he offered. "Don't want to get yourself mussed up, if you're to pass muster as a wealthy customer in the bank, do you?"

"No," Michael said. But he was feeling tense and ill at ease, and taking advantage of Tich's offer, he lit his pipe and went to sit down on the tree-shaded bank at the roadside, a few yards away. There were no houses in the immediate vicinity, and apart from a small flock of sheep being driven in the direction from which they had come, the road was deserted. He watched Tich water the horses sparingly from a small stream nearby, and then, his pipe finished, he lay back, resting his head on the trunk of a gnarled bluegum, willing himself to sleep.

But sleep would not come. Why, he wondered irritably, was he so worried about this raid? They had planned it meticulously, allowed for every possible complication or setback, and . . . devil take it, they had all agreed that they would call it off if Slugger and Marty came back to report adversely on the situation in the town! So what could go wrong?

It was a pity that he could not have a word with Martha Higgins before they committed themselves; but he had been reluctant to involve her, and Slugger, who had met and formed a high opinion of the hardworking widow, had been against that notion, too. Besides, Michael reflected wryly, he had ignored her warning to stay away from Urquhart Falls, and to have turned up unheralded in her restaurant would certainly have invited her ire.

The time passed slowly. The other men were dozing, seemingly without misgivings, and the horses were contentedly cropping grass under Tich's sleepy supervision. Michael checked his

Colt revolver—yet another legacy from Billy Lawless—and lit a second pipe, satisfied that the weapon was in perfect order. Only two cashiers and a roustabout, Slugger had said, constituted the bank staff. Pray God they were sensible men, who would put up no resistance. He did not want to have to use the Colt—even to fire shots in the air to intimidate them. And he certainly did not want any of his own men to be driven to use theirs, as they had when they had held up the gold shipment in Snake Gully. The escorting troopers had been armed, of course; and as Billy had said, when the police had opened fire, he had been left with no choice.

"They're comin' back, Michael." Tich's voice broke into Michael's thoughts, and he jumped to his feet, his pulses racing.

"Quiet as a tomb," Slugger announced, when he reined in and slid from his saddle. "Just the two pen-pushers an' the boy in the bank, an' it ain't been busy." He shifted the quid of tobacco he had been chewing from one cheek to the other and spat expertly in the dust at his feet.

"What about Brownlow?" Michael asked.

"We seen him go into the bank about a half hour ago," Marty supplied. "And he hadn't come out when we left town. Before that, he was round at the back where the new buildings are, chucking his weight about with the fellers workin' there. Three fellers an' the foreman," he added, replying to Michael's unspoken question. "They'll be knockin' off soon—" He gestured skyward. "The sun'll be down in a 'arf hour."

The others, swiftly roused from their earlier apathy, were on their feet, crowding round and eyeing him expectantly.

"What about it, Michael?" Boomer's deep voice demanded. "Ain't goin' to chicken out, are you, after we come all this way?"

"No, of course I'm not," Michael retorted angrily. "Let's get mounted."

They obeyed him, murmuring excitedly among themselves, and for the first time since he had joined them, Michael was conscious of an odd, unwelcome feeling of isolation. It vanished as they rode into the town, each man taking the place allotted to him, without the need for words. And the town was quiet—quieter even than Slugger had claimed, the main street virtually deserted. But there could be no going back now. Michael dismounted, Tich took his horse, and he crossed the street to the door of the bank.

Lily reached Urquhart Falls as the sun was setting behind the distant hills, but, spent and saddlesore, she had no eyes for the charm of the little town or the magnificent scenery by which it was surrounded.

The stallion was even more exhausted than she. He had become docile and had permitted her to guide him for the last part of their nightmare journey, so that she was able to take the most direct route the wild, trackless country allowed, always keeping the sun on her left hand. And she had ridden her mount hard, exercising a tenacity she had never realized that she possessed. But keeping the big black animal to a canter—and at times, when she could induce him to quicken his pace, covering long stretches at a gallop—had taken the heart out of him. Now, bathed in sweat, he was lame in the right foreleg, and, his head down, his breathing labored, it was all she could do to kick him into a trot when they reached the town's main street.

She saw Chalky White first, standing with the reins of three horses in his hand outside a draper's shop and looking anxiously down the street; but it was not until she called his name that he turned, clearly puzzled and not immediately recognizing the small, boyish figure on the big stallion's back. Then, when she slithered stiffly and painfully to the ground, he realized who she was and said gruffly, "Gawd, Lily, what're you doin' here? This ain't no place for you, not now it ain't."

There was no time to waste in explanations. Lily gasped out her warning of Dingo's betrayal and saw Chalky's leathery cheeks drain of color.

"You mean they're expectin' us? They know we're aimin' to hold up the bloody bank?"

"Yes, they know. Dingo's claiming the reward for Michael. They'll be waiting in the bank. Chalky—" Lily clutched at his arm, her voice shrill with pent-up fear. "You've got to stop him! Tell him not to go in!"

"It's too bloody late to stop him," Chalky grated. "And I

ain't riskin' my neck tryin'—I'm gettin' out." His foot was already in the stirrup of one of the horses he had been holding, and he jerked his white head in the direction of one of the others. "Leave your horse an' get up on that one, girl. You c'n come with me. No one'll know who we are, an' I'll look after you. Come on, for Gawd's sake—we'll make for the ferry!"

Lily ignored him. She left the horses, including her own—she was too exhausted and stiff to make the effort to mount—and as Chalky set off on the animal he had chosen, she started to stumble on foot toward the bank, pausing only to fling over her shoulder the single word, "Coward!"

But it was too late. She was still seventy yards from her objective when she recognized Michael's tall, unmistakable figure crossing the road, and her strangled cry was muffled by the thudding of hooves, as the horses Chalky had abandoned tore after him. Michael did not hear her, and she saw the door of the bank open and then swing shut behind him.

Martha Higgins had put the "CLOSED" notice in the window of her restaurant as soon as she had realized the identity of the three who had come in, so unexpectedly, half an hour earlier. And Kitty had been frank, somewhat to Johnny's dismay; she had taken an instant liking to the small, buxom woman in the spotless white apron, and even before the meal they had ordered had been served, she had asked about Michael, admitting without hesitation that he was her brother.

The admission had opened the floodgates. Martha was standing in the window, with young Tommy, gauche and awkward, at her side, and she had given free rein to her tongue, extolling Michael's virtues, telling of his kindness to the boy, and insisting that the wanted circulars were the result of a grave error on the part of the police.

"Oh, I know he was on the run; I know he absconded from the Port Arthur prison—he told me as much," she asserted. "But your brother ain't no bushranger, ma'am—leastways not from choice he ain't. He was here, at my farm, the day the gold shipment was held up over at Snake Gully. He only left here that mornin', an' Snake Gully's more'n two days' journey from here. But the police are sayin' he took part in it! Sayin' he shot

not continue to evade capture for much longer. And the royal pardon, on which Kitty set so much store, would be revoked if he were brought to trial—it would hold no water, if Michael should be found guilty of murder and bushranging and God knew what else. Even if Oscar Meldrum's sworn affidavit cleared him of complicity in the killings on board the *Hastings,* he could scarcely plead innocence of the gold shipment robbery and the wounding of the two troopers—Trooper Smith's evidence would certainly preclude that. And the death sentence was mandatory for robbery under arms.

Johnny was about to return the file to the clerk who had produced it for him when another report caught his eye.

It was headed "The Lawless Gang," and his heart sank as he read it.

A gang of bushrangers, believed to be the one known as the Lawless Gang, which perpetrated the gold shipment holdup at Snake Gully, raided the Bank of Victoria branch at the township of Snowdon six days ago. They stole some £700 in cash, and gold from the bank vault of as yet unknown value, but in attempting to make their escape following the robbery, one member of the gang was shot and is thought to be seriously injured.

Hero of the occasion was the manager of the bank, Mr. George Lucas, who opened fire on the raiders from the premises opposite—a barber's shop—where he had gone during his lunch hour for a haircut. In the commotion, however, the robbers succeeded in getting away, taking their wounded accomplice with them.

Mr. Lucas explained that although he does not normally carry a weapon when on duty at the bank, he had engaged to take part in a kangaroo hunt later in the day and had his sporting rifle with him in the barber's shop.

Mr. Edward Jenkins, chief cashier at the bank, described one of the raiders as being "exceptionally tall and powerfully built, with the speech and manner of a gentleman." This would seem to bear out earlier claims that he is Michael Wexford, who escaped from the Port Arthur Penitentiary with three others—since recaptured and executed—earlier this year, when they seized possession of the government steamer *Hastings* and murdered her master and two prison guards.

A substantial reward is offered for Wexford's apprehension or for information leading to his capture.

There could remain no doubt, Johnny told himself. Michael Cadogan—the Honorable Michael Cadogan, heir to one of Ireland's oldest peerages, and deported for life for high treason—had thrown in his lot with a vicious gang of bushrangers and bank robbers, and now, with a price on his head, every man's hand would be against him. It was unlikely that he would elude capture for very much longer . . . but how to make Kitty believe it?

It was in a grimly sober mood that he returned to the hotel to waken Kitty in time for them to dine before the departure of the Bendigo coach.

The room was in semidarkness when he entered, and his bride, he saw with a quickening of the pulses, was sleeping soundly and had not heard his approach. She looked so lovely lying there, her long, dark hair loose and spread out across the pillow, one perfectly formed breast uncovered and her lips curved into a smile, as if her dream—whatever it was—were a happy one. Of home, perhaps, or even of him. Johnny drew in his breath, feeling desire well up inside him. She was his wife and he loved her. . . .

Without conscious thought, he divested himself of coat and shirt, the impulse to take her so strong and all-demanding that he was unable to resist it. His arms were about her, one hand cupping the small, exposed breast, his mouth hungrily seeking hers, and his strong body pressed against her when, to his dismay, Kitty wakened with a cry of alarm and fought to free herself.

"No, no!" Her fingers tore at his face, the nails biting deep, her body stiff and unyielding. "I'll scream for help, I—" As if suddenly realizing that it was he, she bade him, with icy bitterness in eyes and voice, to leave her. "Ours isn't a marriage, Johnny—I told you it was not! I told you I was not in love with you, and you agreed. You knew, when you married me, that there could be nothing between us until Michael is found—you *knew!*"

"Yes, I knew." Johnny was on his feet, angry and humiliated, grabbing for shirt and jacket, his hands shaking as he struggled to tie his cravat, the shirt still unbuttoned. Dressed, after a fashion, he strode to the door and said, without turning round, but flinging the words at her over his shoulder, "I'll be in the dining room. You can join me when you're ready, if you wish to. Otherwise we'll meet on the coach."

Kitty did not answer him, and he ate his meal alone.

When the big Cobb's coach drew up outside the hotel, they boarded it together and seated themselves side by side in its padded interior. It was as if they were strangers, Johnny thought resentfully, or at best casual acquaintances.

He took off his hat and, leaning his head against the cushions, closed his eyes and feigned sleep. Kitty, after a covert glance at him, opened a desultory conversation with her other neighbor as the driver whipped up his horses and the coach gathered speed.

Chapter XX

MICHAEL LAY BACK on the sweet-smelling hay, hands clasped behind his head, enjoying the pleasant feeling of lassitude that came after lovemaking. It had been a long time—longer, almost, than he could remember—since he had lain with a woman and given himself to physical pleasure, if not fulfillment.

The girl, now drowsily relaxing by his side in the hayloft, had been Billy Lawless's girl, and Michael had, so to speak, inherited her, together with leadership of the Lawless Gang, when Billy had died of the wounds inflicted on him after they had staged their successful bank holdup in Snowdon. Michael sighed, with genuine regret. He had liked Billy Lawless a great deal, and, God knew, he and the others had done all in their power to save his life.

The shots that had brought him crashing from his horse had come, without warning, from an infernal barber's shop across the road from the bank. They had been fired by a stout, gray-haired man who had come running out, the barber's towel still wrapped round his neck, to let off two rounds of buckshot from close range.

Poor Billy had been hit in the back, and the buckshot had torn his lungs apart. He had known he was done for, Michael recalled, and had gasped at the others to leave him and save themselves. They had not done so, of course. While Boomer O'Malley had fired back at the apparition in the door of the barber's shop, Michael had lifted Billy onto his horse's withers and jumped up behind him, and then, with two of the others giving them cover, they had galloped out of Snowdon Town as if the devil himself were hard on their heels.

And they had got clean away—although, sadly for Billy, it had meant three hours' hard riding before they could do more for him than stanch the blood from his wounds—the external blood. It was the internal bleeding that had killed him, and without skilled medical help it had been impossible to control that—although the old veterinary at Broken River Crossing, where they had halted, had done his best.

Finally, on an improvised stretcher hitched behind their horses, and with Billy well primed with the veterinary's liquor to dull his pain, they had brought him here, to the Magpie Inn. The others had said the Magpie was a safe haven, an isolated tavern Billy had bought a few months ago, ready for his retirement. It was high in the hill country, where few travelers ever ventured until the new goldfields had started to attract them. For the time being it was safe enough, Michael thought, and Billy had breathed his last free from any fear of pursuit, the old couple he had put in to run the tavern the only mourners, besides the gang and their women, when they had buried him.

He had put his affairs in order with meticulous care and in spite of the pain he was enduring. Michael glanced down at the girl beside him, now fast asleep, and reached for his pipe and tobacco pouch, also inherited from Billy Lawless. The girl's name was Lily—he had never heard her surname and had not asked what it was. She was a gentle, pretty little creature, affectionate as a puppy, and in some ways she reminded him of Prudence Meldrum. To his own surprise—despite her previous history and the fact that she had been Billy's mistress—Michael found that this resemblance had done much to endear her to him. Indeed, he reflected, tamping tobacco into the bowl of the pipe, he was already halfway to falling in love with her . . . and in admitting this to himself, he was conscious of no regrets.

"I found the poor kid in a fancy cathouse in Bendigo six months ago," Billy had said. "She was treated worse than any kid has a right to be by the foul old harridan who employed her, and she came with me willingly. Told me once she was an orphan, an' that the woman in charge of the orphanage made a

tidy bit on the side by sending the girls out as domestic slaves to
whoever would take them, when the supply of convicts ran out.
Lily ran away and ended up in the cathouse. But she's a good
lass, Michael, an' I'd appreciate it if you'd take her over an'
look after her. See she gets my share of our funds, will you,
after you've put me under? The boys can do as they like, but I
reckon you could keep 'em together, if you're so inclined. They
respect you an' they're all on the run, like you are yourself. So
there's no place to go 'cept the bush, is there? Not for any of
you, so you might as well stick together. And there's always
this place to hide out in, if things get too hot. Talk to the boys,
will you, Michael? I'd do it meself, only it hurts too much,
talking does."

He had done as Billy had asked, Michael thought. Poor devil,
it *had* hurt him a great deal to say as much as he had about Lily
and how the gold and money they had amassed should be split;
all the while he had coughed up blood, breaking off, at increasingly frequent intervals, so as to get his breath. But at least he
had died peacefully in his sleep—there was that to be thankful
for, and a lot else besides. He had been a good man, Billy Lawless, according to his lights—another of the "true patriots," of
course, whom the English convict system had spewed out when
he was barely twelve years old, for the trifling crime of robbing
a Newgate pieman during a hanging.

His pipe was going and Michael inhaled smoke contentedly,
leaning back again and staring up at the slatted roof of the
hayloft, against which the rain descended in a steady, relentless
stream. But the weather was improving; there had been no
snow for several weeks, and spring could not be far away. He
was happy enough staying at the Magpie, and none of the others was in any more of a hurry to move on than he was. He had
divided what Billy had called their funds in strictly equal
shares, proportional to the length of time each man had been a
member of the gang. Lily had been over the moon at the size of
the payment he had made to her. . . . He smiled, remembering her excited cries and her stammered thanks as she had
counted her unexpected reward. Low and McFee had gone off
to spend their shares in Urquhart Falls, where, both men had
insisted, they were not known and could safely mingle with the

diggers, seeking drink and distraction and paying for both commodities in dust. They had promised to return within the month, and, staring up at the blue cloud of smoke from his pipe, Michael wondered if they would, or whether some fellow from the gold escort would recognize them and give the game away. It was always in the cards, and, he thought grimly, in his own case it was an ever-present danger, in view of the size of the reward the authorities had placed on his head and the descriptions of him they had issued.

As Billy had reminded him, there was no place for him to go now, except the bush and—for a while, at least—the Magpie Inn. He did not entirely trust the old couple Billy had installed at the Magpie; they ran the inn well enough, but there was little profit for them in it, and if they should get wind of the reward offered for his apprehension, it was by no means certain that they would not be tempted to betray him. Their loyalty had been to Billy Lawless, and Billy, alas, was no longer there to ensure that they kept still tongues in their heads. The old woman, Nelly, was avaricious and mean besides; she paid him lip service and addressed him as "mister," but . . . Michael knocked out his pipe, careful to avoid catching the hay alight from the still-warm shreds of tobacco, and turned again to the sleeping girl beside him, drawing her closer.

Lily wakened at once, lovingly compliant, as she had been since he had first taken her to his bed, her china-blue eyes bright and welcoming as she looked up at him.

"I love you, Big Michael," she whispered softly. Her small, experienced hands caressed him, rousing him—a child with a woman's knowledge, eager and willing to give him the pleasure he sought and to share it with him as their two naked bodies met and moved in now-familiar unison, each a part of the other. "Ah, God, how I love you!"

There had been so many years, Michael remembered, his mouth on hers—lost years, when there had been no woman in his life, no tenderness, only endless toil and the lash to fill his days, and bitter emptiness in the long night hours. His feelings for this waif were, he knew, induced by those years, yet they were as true as any he had ever experienced. Truer, perhaps, since he had been little more than a boy when the redcoats had seized him and dragged him off to jail, fettered and helpless, with only a boy's memories of womankind to look back on . . . and even those had been hazy and incomplete. His sister Kitty had held more of his heart than any of the Kilclare girls he had known—certainly more than any young ladies of the hunting set with whom he had mixed socially or squired to long-forgotten dinners and balls, in the days when he had been a gentleman and Kilclare's heir.

That life was over—just as his life as a convict was over, praise be to God! He heard Lily cry out in ecstasy and, joining his own, deeper cry to hers, gave her the answer to the question she had never put into words:

"And I love you, Lily my sweet. I'll love you till the day I die!"

"Oh, Michael!" She clung to him, and he felt the dampness of her tears on his cheek. "Oh, Michael, I've longed for you to tell me that! Only I never dared to ask you, and I—I was afraid, you see. Because of Billy, and of what I was, and because you—oh, because you are what you are."

Michael kissed the tear-wet eyes, holding her to him. "I'd marry you, sweet, if I were anything but what I am," he assured her gently. "But I'm an escaped felon, a damned bushranger with a price on my head. Not the kind to make a good husband, Lily my little love."

"I don't mind that," Lily answered. "It's enough that you love me, Michael. That's all I've ever wanted."

"Then I'll say it again—I'll love you till the day I die." Michael jumped up, smiling at her. "That's a promise, as good as any wedding vows. Remember it, in case someone takes a pot-shot at me, like they did at poor old Billy. Now dress yourself, child, and let's go and see what old Nelly's cooking for supper. I don't know about you, but I'm powerfully hungry."

"It's love," Lily told him, giggling, her tears gone. "Love gives you an appetite, Michael. You—"

The clatter of hooves in the yard below cut her short. Michael, half dressed, was at the unglazed window, his rifle muzzle poking through the aperture. The loft was their watchtower; as Billy had stipulated, one of them always stood guard in it, which was why Michael was there this afternoon—but because he had been giving Lily all his attention, he had missed seeing the horsemen's approach five minutes earlier. Now they were in the yard, two of them, and . . . Michael exclaimed in relief, "It's Slugger and Marty, praise be! They're back. Come on."

The two men, cold and saddlesore, thankfully handed over their horses to Tich Knight to be bedded down, then followed Michael into the taproom of the inn.

"We've got news, Big Michael," McFee announced. "Soon as we've got a drink inside us an' Tich gets through with them nags, we'll tell you about it. I reckon you'll be interested—it's a job after Billy's heart, that's for sure." He grinned, stretching his cramped limbs, as Nelly's husband, known to them as Dingo—the nickname Billy had bestowed on him—came shuffling in, yawning and clearly just waking from an afternoon spent in his bed.

"What's it to be?" he inquired sullenly. "There ain't no whiskey. Will you take a slug o' rum, McFee, or beer?"

McFee cursed him, but without venom, and he and Marty Low took their tankards of rum over to a table on the far side of the room, where a glowing fire was evidence of Nelly's industry, if not that of her husband. His back to the blaze, Slugger stood steaming in his damp clothes. "Bloody rain!" he said. "Never let up all day. I'm soaked to the skin. Bring the bottle over here, Dingo—one slug ain't going to save me from gettin' pneumonia. Certainly not one slug o' bleedin' rum. What did you do with the whiskey, you old rogue? Drink the lot, while I wasn't here?"

"It ran out," Dingo told him uncompromisingly. "I'll go into town an' get some more when the weather's better. Never known a wet season like it, an' that's a fact." He brought the rum bottle over and lingered, wiping the table with a stained cloth. Glancing from one to the other of the newly returned men with inquisitive dark eyes, he asked in a more ingratiating tone, "You have a good time in Urquhart Falls, the two of you?"

"It was all right," McFee answered shortly. He poured himself a lavish tot and swallowed it at a gulp. He waited until Dingo was on his way back to the bar and then said, lowering his voice, "We ran into a friend o' yours, Michael. Woman that keeps a good eatin' house—Martha Higgins. Your name cropped up, 'cause there's wanted posters about you plastered all round town. They must want you bad. How much was they offerin', Marty?"

"One 'undred an' fifty pounds," Marty Low supplied. He sounded awed. "I reckon they want you real bad, Michael. They—"

Lily came in bearing a tray, and as she set plates of cold meat and cheese in front of the newly returned men, Michael motioned to both of them to say no more. When the girl had gone, he asked, an edge to his voice, "You didn't tell Martha Higgins where I was, did you?"

They shook their heads. "We ain't daft, Michael," McFee protested. "Anyways, we was actin' like we was diggers, an' all we did was hint as we'd run across you at the diggings. But Mrs. Higgins give us a note for you, just in case we was to see you again. You got that note, Marty?"

Marty, his mouth full, nodded and, after some fumbling in the pockets of his moleskins, produced a crumpled sheet of coarse paper and passed it across the table. "Here it is, Michael."

Michael thanked him. The note was misspelled and written in an oddly childish hand:

Dear Michael, me and Tommy hope your alrite and that yuoll soon make a good strike. I done like you said and written to claim the reward for seeing you. I sent it to the Melbourne Herald asking them to send it on cos I weren't sure ow to get it to Hobart. They ain't paid me no reward yet but that don't matter, so long as they tell you what it is to your advantage, Michael.

I think these diggers are alrite. I didn't tell them nothing you can trust me. But they said as they might run into you, so I thought I'd risk given them this.

You better stay away from Urquhart Falls. Theres a big reward posted for you an Mr. Brownlow—him that uster be a policeman an owns the gaming rooms and the bank—he says as he'll give an extra fifty pounds to it and he's bin calling on folks to form a posse, case you and this Lawless Gang come inter town.

Tommy sends his love and so do I. Don't act rekless, Michael. We will be glad to see you but not till its safe. Martha Higgins, Mrs.

"What's she said?" McFee inquired, putting down his knife and fork with a satisfied sigh. "We didn't read her note, o' course."

"She says Urquhart Falls is a place to stay away from, Slugger," Michael answered dryly. "But you've got a different idea about that, haven't you?"

Slugger McFee bared his very white teeth in a pleased grin. "You cotton on fast, don't you? Billy said you had brains." He poured himself another tot of rum and passed the bottle hospitably across the table to Michael. "Have a drink an' I'll tell you what we found out in Urquhart Falls. They got whiskey there, plenty of it, in the gamin' rooms an' the taverns. An' girls. An actin' troupe, dancin' an' singin' an' spoutin' poetry. It was good, but the games are crooked. The same feller owns the lot —feller called Brownlow. Used to be a police inspector till he got hisself shot up at the Eureka. Owns the bank, too, Michael." He paused, eyeing Michael expectantly over the rim of his tankard.

Michael's expression did not change. "Are you suggesting we should hold up the bank?"

Tich Knight came in, accompanied by the white-haired man known as Chalky White, and for their benefit McFee repeated what he had just said. Then, his gaze once more on Michael, he added, "It'd be a pushover, that bank. Easy as takin' the milk out o' a blind man's cup o' tea—honest. For a start, there's no vault—that's not been built yet. Just a safe I could crack with me eyes shut an' some piled-up metal deed boxes. They're kept at the back, in full view from the counter."

He explained the bank's layout, calling on Marty Low to confirm what he was saying.

"And," he finished triumphantly, "the town's stuffed with diggers. They've come in out o' the wet, an' they're waitin' till the weather lets up an' the escorts start again. Meantime they've lodged their gold in the bank. And Brownlow's mean—

he only employs two cashiers an' a roustabout. Does the managin' hisself."

"What about troopers?" White asked.

"There ain't above half a dozen, are there, Marty?"

"No," Marty confirmed. "That's all there is. Brownlow was tryin' to get a posse together when we was in town—to search for you, Michael!" He smiled. "The folks weren't keen. Too wet an' cold, they reckoned. I doubt if he gathered more'n ten—mostly layabouts and diggers that hadn't done no good. They just went along for the reward, and they didn't find anything. I heard they paid a call on poor old Davie McMunn at the Travellers' Rest and beat him up, trying to get him to describe us." He laughed, pushing his plate away and reaching for the rum bottle. "Accordin' to what one of the diggers told me, all Davie could tell 'em was that we was all ten feet tall! Even Tich! An' we looked like diggers to him."

"See, Michael?" Slugger McFee challenged.

"I see," Michael returned. "Well, let's talk it over. Go and find Ginger and Boomer, will you, Tich? If we do what Slugger suggests, they'll have to be in on it."

They talked far into the night. With Martha Higgins's warning in mind, Michael was at best lukewarm concerning the proposed raid, but the others liked the idea and were impressed by McFee's detailed description of the bank premises. The loud-voiced Boomer O'Malley in particular was enthusiastic.

"Sure an' why not?" he asserted, grinning hugely. "The feller Brownlow, by all accounts, is a rogue. And a bloody trooper officer before he lit on Urquhart Falls, wasn't he? Chased poor honest diggers for their license fees at Ballarat, so he did, and now he's cheating them in his crooked gaming house! I say we relieve the swine of his ill-gotten gains. Soon as the rain stops, let's be on our way."

"Why wait for the rain to stop?" the redheaded Ginger Masters demanded. "They'll start the escorts again when it stops, and they're hard to hold up—harder than a bank with two cashiers and no vault. If we're going, let's go! I've had my fill of soft living."

"We'll take a vote on it, boys," Michael said. "First—shall we go for the bank at Urquhart Falls?" The vote, he saw, was unanimous. "All right, that's agreed. Now, do we wait for the weather to let up or set off right away?"

The shouts of "Right away!" came from all except Tich, and he, seeing that the vote was against him, finally nodded his head.

"All right, I'm in. And you, Michael?"

Michael gave his assent, hiding his reluctance.

"We'll sleep on it and get down to planning it tomorrow morning. And we'll leave tomorrow night."

Lily came to his bed and they slept, locked in each other's arms, to make love once again when the coming of dawn awakened them. Theirs was an oddly tender lovemaking, and when it was over and they lay back, side by side, Michael realized that Lily was weeping, harsh sobs wracking her slender body and her face hidden from him, buried in the pillows. But, plead with her as he might, she would give him no reason for her distress, her sobs redoubling when he attempted to press her for an explanation.

"I'm afraid, that's all," she whispered.

"Afraid, my sweet? Afraid for me or for yourself?"

"For you, Michael." Her muffled voice was choked with sobs. "I—I wish you wouldn't go to Urquhart Falls. I can't tell you why. I—I'm just so afraid for you."

"I have to go," Michael told her gently. He threw off the bedclothes and crossed to the window, to see that the rain had ceased. A good omen or a bad one? he wondered. Not that it mattered; not that it could change the decision the others had taken. He dressed quickly and went to the stables, leaving Lily, still sobbing, in the bedroom.

Tich came out of one of the stalls at the sound of his footsteps, his thin face puckered in a frown.

"The hoss an' buggy's gone," he said, "if you was thinkin' of usin' it. Dingo took 'em. Gone to get whiskey, Nelly says. D'you reckon he has?"

Dingo had made an early start, Michael thought. But McFee had given him a hard time the previous evening because the whiskey had run out, and . . . in any event, he had not planned on using the buggy on their raid. He shrugged.

"I suppose he has, Tich. Well, let's get on with choosing the horses, shall we? The gray gelding needs a couple of shoes . . . let's hope Dingo gets back in time to see to it. And we'll need two packhorses—quiet animals that we can leave tethered on the edge of town. And a spare, in case any of ours is injured."

"Aye," Tich agreed, chewing at a straw in the corner of his mouth. "I got 'em picked out. But the ones Slugger an' Marty come in on yesterday won't be no good—tuckered out, they are, the pair of 'em, and the bay's lame. Must have ridden 'em hard, the stupid clowns. That'll leave us short, Michael."

Tich Knight had once been a hunt whipper-in with a famous English pack, Michael recalled, and horses, rather than people, were the love of his life. He laid a hand consolingly on the little man's shoulder.

"Do the best you can," he advised. "And then come in to help with the planning. It will have to be a fast raid, and I want to make sure our timing's right."

"I'll leave that to you," Tich answered. "My job's the hosses, like it always is. I'll put the shoes on the gray, Michael. But—" He hesitated, his frown returning. "I wish we wasn't goin' right away. I got a feelin' in my guts 'bout this—didn't sleep much last night for thinkin' what could go wrong. Still—" He shrugged. "I expect it's just my foolishness, or I'm gettin' old. Forget it, Michael."

But he could not quite forget it, Michael realized, as the day wore on. Lily and Tich had both shared the same doubts, it seemed, and he began to experience them himself. The planning, however, went well enough; Slugger and Marty made a sketch of the bank and the streets to the front and rear, and they all discussed and agreed on their tactics with little dissent, eating as they talked. Dingo had not returned by the time they were ready to leave the Magpie, but Nelly, who had plied them with food all day, took his accustomed place behind the bar and made an acid joke of his continued absence, as she served drinks with a lavish hand.

"Can't keep sober for long, Dingo can't, if I ain't around to keep the old reprobate in check. I'll wager he's sleepin' it off somewhere along the road—you'll likely see 'im on the way. But don't worry, 'e'll get a piece o' my mind when 'e shows up back 'ere, you can be sure o' that! An' there is a couple o' tots o' whiskey left in the bottle, Mr. McFee, so you might as well 'ave 'em, to speed you on your way. An' what for you, Mr. Wexford? Must 'ave one for the road, sir."

Michael shook his head. Despite Nelly's blandishments, they were all reasonably sober, he thought, though only he and Tich were completely so. He had made his farewell to Lily in the privacy of their bedroom, and she had stayed there, still in a mood of black depression, still vainly begging him not to go on the raid.

Poor little Lily! Conscious of a regret he could not voice, he thrust the thought of her from his mind and gestured to the door.

"It's time, boys—let's get mounted."

They trooped out after him, their earlier laughter fading. The rain had held off all day, and a three-quarter moon gave them fitful light as they set off down the steep hill road, a well-mounted cavalcade, each man with a pistol in his belt and a rifle holstered behind his saddle.

Unexpectedly, Tich broke the silence with a resounding "Tally-ho!" The sound echoed back to them from the rocky peak behind the inn, and they grinned at each other and spurred their horses recklessly down the hill, laughing and joking again like schoolboys out on some boyish spree.

Was this, Michael asked himself, the freedom he had longed for and risked so much to attain? Well, perhaps it was. It was futile and foolish to think of Kilclare or to wonder what might have been, had fate not dealt him so cruel a blow so many wasted years before.

From the lighted upper window of the inn, a small, dark figure that was Lily waved him on his way, but Michael did not turn his head and did not see the wave. By the time the small cavalcade reached level ground, he was laughing with the rest, the imminent, heady prospect of danger setting his pulses racing and obliterating his doubts.

Boomer O'Malley started to sing, his deep baritone voice waking the echoes as Tich's tally-ho had done. It was an Irish rebel song, Michael recognized, and he took it up, memory stirring again.

> *"We trust in God above us,*
> *And we dearly love the green.*
> *Oh, to die it is far better*
> *Than be cursed as we have been!"*

"Damned, benighted Irishmen!" McFee accused them mockingly. "Always complaining of your lot. You should learn a good Scots song. Stow your gab, the two of you, and I'll give you 'The Road to the Isles.' "

A quarter of a mile down the road, the man Billy Lawless had nicknamed Dingo heard the singing and, in frantic haste, drove his buggy off the road. Safely hidden behind a screen of trees, his hand over his horse's nostrils, he waited anxiously until the riders had gone past. Only when both hoofbeats and singing were out of earshot did he venture back onto the road, dragging the unwilling horse after him with angry curses.

It had been a near-run thing, he reflected sourly. He had almost run slap into them. But, praise be, he had heard their caterwauling in time, and they had had no idea he was there. Climbing back into the buggy, he whipped up the weary horse and hummed a little tune of his own.

Nelly would be pleased, he told himself gleefully. They would get the reward for Michael Wexford and maybe a bit more, if the others were taken as well. And the Magpie would be theirs into the bargain, with the Lawless Gang behind bars, unable to lay claim to it.

He was still humming when he drew up outside the inn and, jumping stiffly down, hammered on the door for admission.

Chapter XXI

THERE WAS A note from Patrick at the Cobb & Company booking office in Bendigo, addressed to Kitty and marked "To Await Arrival."

She seized upon it eagerly but gleaned little from it, save the fact that he intended to visit the Bundilly station and that he had been able to hire a horse from the coach company's livery stable, at what he described as "a very reasonable rate."

In a postscript, he had added:

There are wanted posters displayed here for the apprehension of Michael—under the name Wexford—with a reward of £150 offered. I have just come across one and have opened this letter in order to warn you and John of it. We must make haste, Kit, or it will be too late.

The date on the letter, Johnny noticed, indicated that Patrick was still almost three weeks ahead of them. He did not draw Kitty's attention to this, hoping thereby to curb her impatience, but—whether or not she had noticed the date—the sight of one of the wanted posters her brother had warned of had precisely the effect Johnny had been dreading. Since the episode in the Criterion Hotel in Melbourne, his wife had maintained a coolly polite attitude toward him, which, though he tried to hide it, he was finding at once hurtful and irritating. And, he told himself a trifle sourly, as she hurried him, hungry and unshaven, to the livery stables, it was also unjust. Throughout the long, twelve-hour drive in the swaying coach, Kitty had scarcely addressed two words to him, while conversing at length with several of their fellow passengers.

One couple—the husband a sheep farmer—had talked of William Broome with envy and admiration.

"The best fellow in the world" had been the farmer's opinion, expressed with evident sincerity. "Came here at the right time, Will Broome did, when the land was there for the taking—and Will took it. I'd hesitate to hazard a guess as to what he's worth now, or how much land he owns. Hundreds of thousands of acres, anyway, like most of the early squatters. When I got here, there wasn't a great deal left, and the government upped the price to three or four times what the squatters paid for their grazing. Some of the diggers, when they struck it rich, were willing to meet the official price, but me—why, like I said, I came too late, and I never found an ounce of gold dust, still less any of those big nuggets you hear them tell of. But I've built up my herd with purebred stock from Will Broome's flocks—he's the biggest breeder in these parts—and one of these days, ma'am, maybe I'll have a success story to tell. Or my grandchildren will."

Johnny had not been in any mood to reveal his relationship to William Broome, and Kitty, asked her name by the farmer's wife, had—whether inadvertently or intentionally—replied that it was Cadogan.

Johnny scowled as, entering the livery stables, she forestalled with a shake of the head the request he was about to make for the hire of a horse and buggy.

"No, no, Johnny, please! Ask for saddle horses and a pack animal. The roads are rough, aren't they? We will make better time if we ride. I can't rest until we catch up with Pat." Then, sensing his disapproval, she added in a more placatory tone, "Those posters and the amount of the reward—truly, we *must* lose no time!"

And they did not. It was two o'clock in the afternoon when they left Bendigo, and Kitty set a punishing pace. She was a superb horsewoman, and Johnny was forced to concede that, even on the hired hack, his wife looked more beautiful than any woman he had ever known. Indeed, under her light and skillful hands, the jaded animal she bestrode carried its head high and moved proudly.

A brief but heavy rainstorm and the coming of dusk compelled her to agree to halt for the night at a roadside inn. But, as the embarrassed landlord explained, the establishment was set up for the convenience of men on their way to the northern goldfields, and it offered little in the way of comfort—certainly nothing that could be considered suitable accommodation for a lady. But his wife gave up her bed, in a recess off the kitchen, and also contrived to produce a most appetizing meal; and Johnny, bedding down in the big, empty men's dormitory, had no complaint concerning the hospitality they were offered.

Breakfast, too, was sustaining and plentiful, with tender lamb chops added to the normal fare of eggs and smoke-cured ham. But Kitty's appetite and her enjoyment of the ample meal were abruptly curtailed by the arrival of a small party of police troopers, whose sergeant announced, in loudly blustering tones, that they were on the track of bushrangers.

"Could be the Lawless lot," he told the landlord, as he and his men gathered round the bar counter, quaffing ale while they waited for their breakfast to be cooked. "Went to ground for a while, they did, but we've had word that they're likely to be on the move again, now the weather's improving. And there's a mighty fine reward offered for their capture—leastways for the Port Arthur absconder they call Michael Wexford. A hundred and fifty quid, dead or alive! I could do with a hundred and fifty quid, and no mistake."

He glanced idly over to where Kitty and Johnny were seated, and, the color draining from her cheeks, Kitty clutched at Johnny's arm and begged him, in a choked voice, to settle their bill so they could leave. Misunderstanding her sudden alarm, the sergeant came over to their table, smiling and with the evident intention of offering reassurance.

"Don't you worry, ma'am," he said pleasantly. "We'll catch the rogues before they're much older. Have you far to go?"

Johnny answered him. "We're on our way to Bundilly, Sergeant." He spoke quietly, feeling Kitty's fingers biting into his arm and praying that she would remain silent. "It's not above fifteen or twenty miles from here, is it?"

"Mr. Broome's station? Nearer twenty, sir. But you should make it before dark. The road's good, apart from a few places where the creeks have overflowed. But if your lady is nervous, why, we'll ride along with you as far as the Stanhope turnoff. Just give my lads time to break their fast, and we'll ride out together."

Kitty's small hand was trembling violently, and Johnny placed his own over it, holding it tightly.

"No need for you to trouble, Sergeant," he said, with well-simulated nonchalance. "These fellows you are after are bank robbers, aren't they—the ones who held up a gold shipment not long ago? I read about them in the papers. I shouldn't think my wife and I would offer inducement enough to a gang of their caliber. But it's good of you to offer. Stay and take your time—the food here is worth waiting for."

"If you say so, sir," the sergeant agreed readily enough, and returned to join his men at the bar.

Tucking Kitty's arm under his, Johnny led her outside. "Wait here," he bade her. "I'll pay our score and get the horses. I'll be as quick as I can."

Kitty did not speak until they were on the road again, and then she said, with a flash of anger, "They talk of hunting Michael as if he were an animal! And for the reward! That's all they think of, the reward. I wish Dominic had never published that stupid advertisement. He started the hunt. But *we* should have announced that Michael was granted a royal pardon. He might have seen it and not—not gone off and held up gold shipments and robbed banks!"

But it would have been too late, even if they had, Johnny thought. An escaped convict on the run had little choice save to take to the bush, just as Michael had. And in these parts neither he nor the police troopers would often see any but a local newspaper.

They had discussed, long ago and many times, how—if they finally found Michael—they would smuggle him out of the country and back to Ireland. He would use Patrick's name, Kitty had said, if that were necessary, and a passage to Ireland or London would be booked for him in that name. In their company, hers and Pat's, dressed and behaving as a gentleman, Michael would be above any suspicion. They had both been so sure of that, and . . . Johnny vented his disquiet in a long-drawn sigh. The plan might well have succeeded, if they could have found him in Hobart, or even if they had found him before he had taken to the bush.

But he *had* taken to the bush, and as Kitty had said so bitterly, they were hunting him now like an animal.

As if she had read his thoughts, Kitty declared defiantly, "Johnny, it's *not* too late, even now, if we can only find Michael, talk to him, tell him how we have planned his escape. The police are searching for a bushranger, a gang of bushrangers—that was what the sergeant said, wasn't it?"

"Yes," Johnny confirmed, tight-lipped. "He did say that." He hesitated, reluctant to dash her hopes. "And they have Michael's description, Kit. His size, his height, even the color of his hair—it's all on those wanted posters. And there was that trooper who claimed to recognize him, the fellow who was an overseer on Norfolk Island in Price's time."

"But if Michael was with us—with Pat and me, going by his real name—he would be safe, Johnny. No one would recognize him, not even that prison guard, however closely he might resemble an escaped convict known as Michael Wexford." Kitty spoke with conviction. "They would not *dare!*"

"Why wouldn't they?"

"Because no one would connect the Earl of Kilclare with a common criminal," Kitty asserted. "And that's who he is, Johnny. I never told you before—Pat said we should keep it to ourselves. But Papa died over two years ago, and Michael's the elder son. He probably won't know of Papa's death or that he inherited the title, but he did, and there are documents to prove it. Johnny, I do truly believe that we can save him, even now, if we can find him before the police do."

There was, Johnny conceded, a chance—a slim chance, perhaps—that they might succeed with the deception Kitty had envisaged. Certainly it would be better than using Pat's name. In Australia there was respect for the aristocracy; colonial society was impressed by titles, and Kitty was right—the onetime

Norfolk Island overseer might well be ridiculed if he attempted to claim that the Earl of Kilclare was in reality an escaped convict. The records of his trial were in Ireland. It would take a long time for any sort of check to be made, and if they could spirit Michael out of the state of Victoria to Sydney, where no one knew or had previously set eyes on him, then . . . He met Kitty's gaze.

There *was* a chance. They could go overland to New South Wales. Cobb coaches ran to Beechworth and from there on to Albury, carrying mail, three days a week, and who would look for a fugitive traveling openly by a scheduled coach service, if he were respectably dressed and accompanied by members of his family and figured on the passenger list as Lord Kilclare? And—Johnny frowned, trying to remember the coach routes displayed at the booking office in Melbourne. There was a service direct from Bendigo to Echuca and Deniliquin and Hay and, if his memory was not at fault, from there to Bathurst. Certainly there was a road . . . better still, surely Cobb & Company carried mail from Albury to Yass and Goulburn?

Fired as he was with Kitty's optimism, his frown lifted. "Perhaps," he told her, "perhaps Pat has found Michael by this time, Kit. He's had three weeks' start on us. That woman in Urquhart Falls might have been able to tell him where Michael was heading."

But when they reached Bundilly and thankfully drew rein outside the homestead, it was to find all their hopes unexpectedly dashed. William Broome and his wife, Dorothea, greeted them warmly but with the news that Patrick was still there.

"The poor young man went down with pneumonia," William said. "Indeed, he only just managed to get here before collapsing. But don't worry, Lady Kitty, he's on the mend now. It was touch and go for a while, but my wife is an expert nurse, and we called a doctor from Urquhart Falls, who worked wonders. Your brother is still very weak, and we're keeping him in his bed, but he'll be overjoyed to see you, I know. He's talked of nothing but your coming since he regained his senses. Dorothea will take you to him now, while John and I have a drink together."

Over the welcome drink, William became expansive.

"It's not often I have a visit from a nephew I've never seen. It's good to meet you, John, and I shall have a host of questions to ask about the rest of the family in due course. In the meantime, though, I should perhaps tell you that the man you are seeking, Michael Wexford, as I believe he is known, spent a night here—what? Nine weeks ago. He came with a young fellow I think you'll remember—Luke Murphy. Luke is—*was* Rick Tempest's son-in-law."

"Yes, of course, I remember Luke, sir," Johnny exclaimed. "He married little Elizabeth Tempest and lost her tragically in childbirth. Her parents were heartbroken and Luke even more so. He shipped out of Sydney in one of Claus Van Buren's trading vessels."

"And ended up here at Bundilly," William Broome supplied, smiling. "He's working for me now and seems to have settled down quite happily. And he's given our little Jane a new lease on life. We took the child in a few years ago—you see, she's deaf and dumb and has always found it hard to communicate, even with us. But Luke has managed to get through to her, the Lord knows how, and . . . well, she really is a new person. And of course—" William refilled both their glasses. "It was Luke who brought Michael Wexford here. You knew that, I suppose?"

Johnny shook his head. "No, sir, we did not. We've been hunting him blind, coming up against one dead end after another. Didn't Pat tell you?"

William gave him a rueful smile. "He told us quite a lot when he was delirious, John, but it was all jumbled up, in no proper sequence. And, frankly, it might be wiser to pretend he didn't tell us about that crazy plan to aid Wexford's escape from Port Arthur! In any event, it was never put into operation, was it? Michael Wexford—Michael Cadogan escaped on his own, according to what he told Luke—and then he contrived to smuggle himself aboard Luke's ship, the *Mercedes*. They left her together in Geelong, when she docked."

Michael must have boarded the *Mercedes* right under their noses, Johnny thought. They had been on the jetty at the Hobart anchorage, he and Kitty and Pat, with Michael's pardon ready to hand to him, legal freedom within his grasp. He released a sigh of frustration. "I'd like to hear how he managed that."

"And so you shall," his uncle assured him. "But it would be better if you hear it from Luke—he'll be in soon, with my two boys. Luke convinced me, he convinced all of us that Michael Cadogan was no ordinary convict. To be honest, I was a mite annoyed when I found out that I'd been harboring a Port Arthur absconder unawares. The penalty for that is still a costly one, and I'm a magistrate!"

"What made Luke bring him here?" Johnny asked.

"Oh, that was pure chance. They were on their way north to the new diggings and were caught in a severe storm." William sipped his drink thoughtfully. "I have to say that there was no abuse of my hospitality. Michael stayed for only one night. I offered him work—in fact I offered both of them work, and Luke took my offer up, but Michael did not. Out of consideration for my position, I fancy—another reason for saying he's no ordinary convict on the run. In spite of what was done to him on Norfolk Island and in the Port Arthur Penitentiary, he must have retained the instincts of a gentleman."

Yet, gentleman or not, Johnny thought, Michael—Michael Cadogan, Earl of Kilclare—had allied himself with a gang of bushrangers, and there was a price on his head. He wondered whether or not his uncle knew this, and William answered his unvoiced question.

"Luke told us nothing, until Pat wrote to me. Even then, he simply said that Michael was an absconder. When Pat arrived here in person—in a state of collapse, as I mentioned, poor young fellow—we learned the rest of the story. Partly from what Pat raved about, when he was semiconscious, and Luke finally told us the rest. After that, my elder boy, Angus, went to Urquhart Falls for provisions and brought back some newspapers and a wanted poster. You realize, don't you, John, that the pardon granted to Michael will be next to useless if he has committed other crimes in the colony? And it would seem he has, if he's with this so-called Lawless Gang. They held up a gold shipment in which two police troopers were shot and severely wounded. And since then they've robbed a bank in Snowdon, I believe."

"I read the reports when I was in Melbourne, sir," Johnny admitted.

"But you are still trying to find him?"

"My wife is. I—"

"Your *wife?*" William stared at him in openmouthed astonishment. "D'you mean you are married to Lady Kitty? Pat never said you were."

Johnny reddened. "I . . . that is, sir, I persuaded Kit to marry me on the way here. Pat does not know. We—that is, we haven't had a chance to tell him yet."

His uncle's eyes were bright. "Well, good God! My congratulations. She is a beautiful young woman, and you are a damned fortunate fellow." He refilled their glasses, raising his own in amused and tolerant salute, and as his wife came into the room he turned to her, smiling. "Dodie my dear, our newly acquainted nephew has just informed me that he's married to the Lady Kitty!"

Dorothea displayed no surprise. "Yes, she has just broken the news to her brother Pat, who appears to be delighted." She came to Johnny's side, her smile warm as she offered him her hand. "I am pleased for your sake, John. You have chosen well. But—" Her smile faded. "I am concerned about the situation in which the three of you are placed. Has my husband told you that Michael Wexford is wanted for bushranging and, if the newspaper reports are true, also for murder?"

"I told John, Dodie," her husband asserted gruffly. "In fact, I was breaking that piece of bad news to him when you joined us." His eyes, shrewd and kindly, searched Johnny's face, a question in them. "But he hasn't told me as yet what he intends to do—have you, John?"

Johnny's color deepened and spread, as he sought to gather his scattered wits. But what, he wondered despairingly, could he say? The truth would be unpalatable to a magistrate—of that there could be no doubt—and to remain there, under his uncle's roof, while engaged in an attempt to aid a fugitive from justice was clearly a gross abuse of hospitality. *And* of trust . . . He lowered his gaze, avoiding his uncle's, and said reluctantly, "I'm committed to a course of action that would not meet with your approval, Uncle Will. Or yours, Aunt Dodie. I'm sorry.

We—in the circumstances, I think we ought to leave Bundilly first thing in the morning, all three of us."

"Pat is not well enough to leave, John," he heard his aunt protest. "He—" William held up a hand and she broke off, catching her breath on a sigh.

"Where do you propose to go, if you leave here?" William asked quietly.

"I—well, to Urquhart Falls," Johnny managed. "That was our original intention, sir. To go there after we had seen you. There is a woman there, a woman by the name of Martha Higgins, who keeps an eating house in the town. We know that Michael lodged with her after he left Bundilly—she replied to an advertisement we had published, asking for information as to Michael's whereabouts. We were hoping—that is, we still hope that she can tell us where he is."

"I know Martha Higgins," the older man said pensively. "A widow, with a smallholding outside the town. A decent, hard-working woman and the soul of honesty. If she has information, it will be reliable. You would be well advised to talk to her, John. And Luke may be able to tell you something."

William did not, as Johnny had feared he would, ask what plans the Cadogans had in mind if, at last, they succeeded in coming face to face with the man they sought. But it was evident, from his decision not to ask and from the glance he exchanged with his wife, that—while they could count on his silence—they must expect no practical help from him. It was a wholly reasonable stance to take, Johnny recognized. His uncle was a magistrate; he could not, in all conscience, condone what at best was a flouting of the law.

His aunt Dodie, on the other hand, seemed as if she wanted to question her husband's decision; but although she opened her mouth to speak, she closed it again and, after a momentary pause, repeated her earlier assertion that Patrick was not well enough to leave.

"He has been very seriously ill, John," she added. "The poor boy met with the worst of our winter weather when he rode here from Bendigo. He lost his way and spent two nights in the open, when it was snowing and blizzarding. Whatever you and —and your wife decide to do, you will have to leave Patrick

an' wounded one o' the troopers. But when he left my place, he was goin' to the new diggings at River Fork."

"*Did* he go there, Mrs. Higgins?" Johnny asked, interrupting her flow.

Martha Higgins sighed. "He meant to, but I ain't sure if he got there," she conceded. She lowered her voice. "There was a couple o' diggers come in here a day or so back, an' they was talkin' about Michael and them wanted posters that Mr. Brownlow's put up all over town. I kept my ears pealed, an' it sounded to me like they knew Michael an' was expectin' to see him fairly soon. They seemed decent enough fellers—one was a Scotchman, he said, though he didn't talk like one."

Kitty was unable to contain her excitement. "Mrs. Higgins," she exclaimed, "did you think they were working with my brother, with Michael? At the diggings, perhaps?"

"Not at River Fork," Martha Higgins said, with conviction. "That's too far away. But they told me for sure they'd be seein' him, though they wouldn't say when or where. But anyway, I gave 'em a note for Michael, an' they promised they'd pass it on."

"A note?" Kitty echoed. "Were you asking him to come back?"

"Oh, *no!*" The denial was vehement. "I was tryin' to warn him to keep away from this town, on account o' Mr. Brownlow an' those posters. With a big reward like that, some folk might be tempted. An' Mr. Brownlow's added fifty pounds to it."

"Why should Mr. Brownlow want him caught?" Luke questioned.

Martha shrugged her plump shoulders. "No reason, 'cept he uster be a police inspector at the Eureka. And for all they're useful to him, he don't like diggers, an' that's a fact. He don't like bushrangers neither. He—"

A high-pitched cry from the street outside interrupted her, and as she turned to look out, the boy Tommy flung himself against the window. His face pressed against the steamy glass, he grabbed her arm.

"Look—look, Ma! It's Michael! He just got off his horse. Him an' those men, those diggers that was in here before!" He was shrieking at the pitch of his lungs, "Ma, Michael's goin' into the bank! That's where the troopers are!"

In his terror, his words were almost unintelligible, but Kitty caught the gist of them. She was on her feet in an instant, and before either Johnny or Luke could attempt to stop her she had opened the door of the restaurant and was running across the street, her hat flying off as she ran. Three men—the men who had been with Michael—were in the doorway of the bank, and there were guns in their hands, but Kitty paid them no heed, brushing by them as if she did not see them, and they stood back, taken by surprise, and let her go inside.

The interior of the bank was dimly lit, but she saw Michael at once. To her relieved gaze, he looked much as she remembered him—tall, imposing, and respectably dressed, so unlike the men with guns in the doorway that instinctively she decided that he could have no connection with them.

"Michael—Michael, it's Kit! Oh, Michael, we've found you at last!"

Michael halted, thunderstruck, recognizing the voice, but for a moment unable to believe in Kitty's presence there at such a time. He took a step toward her, and then, without warning, another voice shouted, "It's him—it's Wexford! Don't let him get away!"

Two of the men who had been with Michael heard the shout and burst through the door as a pistol spoke, and then another; there was the reverberating crash of a rifle, echoing in the confined space, as men—uniformed troopers—rose from concealment behind the bank counter and from the half-built vault behind it, firing seemingly at random. A small figure in breeches and a man's ill-fitting shirt, lingering uncertainly in the doorway, caught the first blast and collapsed without a sound, to lie there in a steadily spreading pool of blood. One of the men who had been outside had also fallen.

Kitty heard Michael cry out in agony, "Lily! Oh, God, it's Lily!" and then rough hands seized her about the waist and she was being propelled toward the troopers. It was one of the men who had been in the doorway. He was strong, and he had a pistol in his hand, which was pressed against her head. She felt

parted; Andy, it seemed, had never left his adopted father's company since they had come on board. William had left him in Cawnpore, in the care of the Fusiliers' chaplain, when Havelock had led his small, outnumbered force to Lucknow, and the boy had suffered a breakdown and almost died. Reunited, on the march back to Allahabad, the two had saved each other, and now, if William adhered to the plans he had made during their homeward passage, he and Andy were to become sheep farmers.

"I shall buy land in the Illawarra area," William had asserted. "Somewhere near Marshall Mount, the Osbornes' place. That was where Jenny always wanted us to settle when—" He had smiled faintly, Red recalled. "When I was ready to turn my sword into a plowshare. Well, I'm ready now. I've had my fill of war."

The sound of Francis's voice calling the side party to attention interrupted his reverie, and Red went to take his place at the entryport, as the governor's boat came alongside. The bo'sun's mates put their silver calls to their lips, and Governor Denison stepped on board, the military secretary and an aide at his heels. Red saluted and was greeted warmly.

"Good day to you, Captain Broome. I am delighted to see you and your ship back in Port Jackson, but . . . not without damage, I observe. Was that suffered in India or on your passage here?"

"On passage, Your Excellency. We were unfortunate in striking exceedingly bad weather off the New Guinea coast." Red made to stand aside to enable William to take his place, but Governor Denison detained him, a hand on his arm.

"But you were actively engaged in the suppression of the mutiny in Bengal, weren't you? You and your ship?"

"I served as a volunteer in the naval brigade furnished by Captain Peel's steam frigate *Shannon*, sir. My ship's company also supplied volunteers for the *Pearl*'s brigade. . . ." Red offered a brief explanation, sensing Colonel Macintyre's impatience—manifested in a discreet cough, coming from behind him—and out of the corner of his eye he saw that William appeared to be amused. "My ship remained in Calcutta, sir," he ended, "with a maintenance crew. Sir, I—"

"One moment." Governor Denison studied him thoughtfully. "You must have done good work, Captain, indeed you must, for I understand from Commodore Pellew, who arrived here recently, that you have been gazetted to post rank. He tells me also that their lordships of the Admiralty have ordered you to return to England, as soon as your relief arrives, in order that your ship may pay off. My congratulations, Captain Broome—on both counts."

Red thanked him gravely, but as the governor, recognizing William after a momentarily puzzled glance, moved past him with a cordial "Colonel De Lancey, is it not?" his emotions were decidedly mixed.

Promotion to post rank was, of course, deeply gratifying, but the orders to return to England to pay off were far less welcome. After his long absence, he had been looking forward eagerly to his reunion with Magdalen; they had spent so little time together since their marriage. But at least, while he was on the Australian station, such shore time as he could be shared with her. And there was the little daughter he had scarcely seen —Jessica, Jessica Rachel, born just before he had left Sydney. He would be a stranger to her.

Hearing another, less discreet cough, Red was about to respond to it by introducing Colonel Macintyre, but the colonel, without waiting to be introduced, stepped into the governor's path. He had evidently heard the word "Lucknow," for, without apology, he announced loudly, "Colonel Macintyre, Your Excellency, of the Honorable Company's Engineers. I can give you at first hand any information you may wish to have regarding the siege of Lucknow, sir. My wife and I were among the garrison."

"Were you indeed?" Denison exclaimed. The interruption had startled him, but, as always, he was coldly polite, and he waved a hand at his military secretary. "You'd appreciate a firsthand account, wouldn't you, George? We must arrange a meeting at Government House, as soon as you and—er—Mrs. Macintyre are settled in here, Colonel. My aide will see to it. Now, De Lancey, as you were saying . . ."

"Perhaps Your Excellency would care to go below to my cabin?" Red put in quickly, and was rewarded by an approving nod. He led the way below. When his steward had served the visitors with coffee, he excused himself and, leaving William deep in conversation with the governor, returned to the deck.

To his relief, Macintyre had vanished, and Francis observed, with satisfaction, "He went below in a huff, sir. Let's hope he stays away! And look, sir—" He offered his glass. "Our wives and families have realized we're home and have gathered in your garden. But I fear they are not going to be pleased when they learn that we have to go to England to pay off. I confess I'm not too pleased myself."

"We can't sail until we've had a refit, Francis," Red reminded him. With the aid of the glass he was able to make out the faces of those who, as Francis had put it, had gathered in the garden of the small, white-painted house his father had occupied before him, with its view of the cove. He saw Magdalen and his heart quickened its beat, as he responded to her wave. He would not be permitted to bring her back to England with him, he thought glumly; Their Lordships, who had once allowed the privilege to the commanders of Her Majesty's ships of war, now frowned upon the practice of allocating free passages to wives and families, even on voyages halfway round the world. Females and children, it was held, impaired the efficiency and fighting qualities of the ships' companies—although, when it suited them, the Board of Admiralty relaxed the rule. He sighed. It had suited them to give passage to Colonel Macintyre and his family, as well as to several other Lucknow survivors, sent on convalescent leave to Sydney. But he and Francis would still have to sail alone, when the time came for the *Galah*'s departure.

And, as a newly promoted post captain, he might well be kept for a year or more on the beach, and on half pay, before Their Lordships saw fit to appoint him to a new command. Red glanced a trifle uneasily at his first lieutenant, and Francis said, as if guessing his thoughts, "Dora will seek to keep me here, you know. And damme, sir, I'm tempted. This is my country— I want to stay here, to be honest. It's different for you, of course, now you've made post rank. My warm congratulations, Captain Broome. I couldn't help hearing what H.E. said."

"Thanks." Red smiled at him. "Off you go, Francis—call away the gig and take a run ashore. You can join them in my garden and break the news as tactfully as you know how. Tell Magdalen I'll be with her as soon as my duties permit."

"Aye, aye, sir," Francis acknowledged, with a pleasure he made no attempt to conceal. "Everything's in order, sir. I'll send word to Judge De Lancey—er, my father, sir—to expect William and the boy, shall I? And may I take it that the watch below will be granted shore leave?"

Red nodded his assent. The gig put off for the shore five minutes later, but it was another hour before the governor and his staff finally took their leave, after inspecting the ship, bearing William and Andrew Melgund with them. They were followed by a disgruntled Colonel Macintyre, with his wife and numerous family, and when the last boatload of passengers was on its way to the shore, Red left the officer of the watch to supervise the unloading of their baggage and stepped into his gig.

There was what almost amounted to a reception committee awaiting his arrival in the garden of Cove Cottage: his father, looking spruce and fit; his aunt Rachel, proudly leaning on Francis's arm, with Dora on his other side; Judge De Lancey, who had been joined by William; and Johnny and Kitty Cadogan, who, they told him, were now married . . . news he scarcely took in.

But, the greetings over, Red had eyes only for Magdalen. She came to him, happy and smiling, offering no reproach, although it was evident that Francis must have broken the news to her of the *Galah*'s imminent departure. For now, it seemed, she was content to have him home, and she clung to him, oblivious of those around them, lifting her lips to his.

It was left to Andy Melgund to grasp a pretty little auburn-haired toddler by the hand and lead her to him.

"This is Jessica, Captain Broome," the little boy told him solemnly. "She's your daughter. I've been playing with her a bit because she reminds me of my sister Rosie. Only she's smaller, of course. Rosie was five."

There was a moment's embarrassed silence, and then Red picked up his daughter, holding the small, plump, squirming body high above his head. The little face beamed at him, and he

the rapid beating of his heart and heard him shout defiantly, "Hold your fire! The lady gets it if you don't!"

Abruptly the firing ceased. For Kitty the whole scene took on a nightmare quality; unable to believe that it was really happening, she did not attempt to struggle or to protest, but her frightened eyes sought Michael in mute appeal . . . and he, too, she saw, had a pistol in his hand. Blood was dripping from his left arm.

"Let her go, McFee," he ordered sternly. "Do you hear me— let her go!" The pistol was leveled unwaveringly at her captor, Kitty saw, Michael's finger on the trigger.

"I ain't lettin' her go," the man who held her roared. "I'm gettin' the hell out of here, and I'm taking her with me!"

"Then I'll have to kill you," Michael said.

For an interminable moment they faced each other, the man behind her breathing heavily. Kitty could feel his fear as if it were a living thing, holding him motionless and unsure of what he must do. Then he came to a decision and his arm tightened about her, and the pistol no longer pressed against her head but was turned on Michael as it spoke. She did not see whether the bullet had found its mark, but the next instant Michael was beside her, his big body somehow between her and her erstwhile captor, thrusting her to the floor and out of immediate danger. His pistol butt descended on her assailant's head, and the man fell as if poleaxed, to lie quite still a yard or so from her, breathing stertorously and robbed of all menace.

"You're safe, Kit." It was Michael's voice, his hand grasping hers to help her to her feet. "God knows what you're doing here, but—" Johnny was there, and Kitty went into his arms, as Michael turned away.

He was standing motionless, looking about him, when the nightmare began again. The voice that had identified him as Wexford was raised in accusing fury.

"I tell you, that's Wexford—that's the bloody absconder! *Take him!* There's two hundred quid on his head!"

Several of the troopers moved cautiously forward, their weapons at the ready. Michael ignored them. He walked to the door, to stand for a moment looking down at the small figure in shirt and breeches who had fallen when the first shots were fired. Then he turned back to face them.

"You've killed her," he told them bitterly. "The devil take you, you've killed her!"

No one answered him. Then, to Kitty's stunned horror, one of the troopers, holding his pistol in both hands, stood framed in the doorway. He gave no warning but fired into Michael's back at point-blank range, to send him crashing to the floor.

"I got the other two outside," the trooper yelled. "But this was the one you was wantin', wasn't it, Mr. Brownlow?"

Pandemonium broke out. They clustered round Michael, and Kitty, sobbing, broke from Johnny's embrace and went to kneel beside her brother, pillowing his head on her lap. He was alive but in hideous pain, and she called out despairingly for someone to summon a doctor.

Michael heard her voice and managed a smile.

"What are you doing here, Kit?" he asked faintly. He recognized Luke in the crowd that had gathered about him and gestured to him to come closer. "Are you with Luke?"

"Yes," Kitty confirmed, fighting for control. "And with Pat and—and my husband, John Broome. You were granted a royal pardon, Michael, and we—we were searching for you to tell you that you are free."

Michael closed his eyes, seeming as if he had not heard her; but then, opening them again, he echoed bitterly, "Free? Dear God, I wish I'd known that! I . . . Pat—you said he came with you. Is he here?"

"He's at Bundilly, Michael," Luke put in. "He's been ill, and—"

"Give him my best, will you? Say I'm sorry not to have seen him."

"You will see him," Kitty whispered. "We'll take you back to Bundilly."

"Bundilly? No. They wouldn't let you take me, and anyway—" Michael spoke with an obvious effort, beads of perspiration breaking out on his brow. "I fear I'm done for, Kit. Maybe it's as well. The pardon would not be of any value now, in these—these circumstances, would it?"

The town's doctor, a bespectacled, gray-haired man, appeared, and the crowd parted to let him through. His examination was brief, and as he rose from his knees he met Kitty's beseeching gaze and regretfully shook his head.

"I'll do what I can for him. It's not much, I'm afraid. But I'll try to make him more comfortable."

Kitty yielded her place to him and, once again, found comfort in Johnny's supporting arms. The crowd was growing, the bank filled to overflowing with alarmed townsfolk who had heard the shooting and had come to ascertain the cause of it. The voices carried; she heard one voice that was familiar and realized it was the same voice that had twice shouted out that Michael was the Wexford of the wanted posters.

"I'd swear it was him. Hell's teeth, he was on Norfolk Island when I was an overseer there! And he was the scoundrel who attacked me at The Travellers' Rest!"

"You must be wrong, Smith." It was one of the bank's cashiers. "That young lady's his *sister*, and they reckon she's come from Bundilly. Besides, I saw him come into the bank, and he was by himself. The bushrangers came in afterward and they were masked—he wasn't. And he saved the young lady's life. He *can't* be Wexford. What do you say, Mr. Brownlow? That trooper shouldn't have shot him."

"The trooper acted precipitately," another deeper, more authoritative voice replied. "But all the same, I fancy he's Wexford. Trooper Smith is positive he is. And the trooper who shot him cannot be blamed. He thought Wexford was trying to escape, and . . . he did deal with the two villains who were making their getaway. He winged one and shot the other. That's good work by any standards."

Sickened by the bank owner's cynical assessment, Kitty buried her face in her hands, fighting a losing battle to ward off the scalding tears that threatened to overwhelm her. It was so cruel, so unjust that their long search should end like this, she thought miserably. If only they could have found Michael sooner, or if she had seen and recognized him before he had entered the bank, it might not have been too late. They could have spirited him away, as Johnny had tentatively planned. A Cobb's coach across the border into New South Wales and then a passage by ship, back to his beloved Ireland, in his own proud name, and he would have been free at last.

Johnny held her to him. "Bear up, Kit," he urged her softly. "The doctor's finished, and I think Michael will want you with him."

"Yes, I . . ." Kitty's teeth closed about her lower lip, and somehow she managed to regain her self-control. She saw that Martha Higgins was kneeling at Michael's side now, a flask in her hand, which she was holding to his lips.

"The doc said it wouldn't do him no hurt, ma'am," the woman whispered. "An' it might ease his suffering."

Evidently it had, for Michael's voice was stronger when she slipped to her knees and he saw who she was. "Oh, Kit—dear, sweet little Kit! I'm sorry for the trouble I've caused you. It would have been good if we could have met again anywhere but here."

"Yes, yes it would. But we did not know where to look, Michael."

"I ran too fast for you, eh?" he suggested, with a return to the jocular manner he had, in the past, so often used with her. "You've grown into a beautiful young woman, Kit . . . and now you've a husband, didn't you say? The tall red-haired fellow, is it? And he's a Broome?"

"Yes," Kitty said huskily. "John Broome. He—he's a nephew of Mr. William Broome of Bundilly."

"Then you've chosen well. Be happy, Kit. I'm no loss, you know."

"Oh, Michael . . ." Kitty could no longer hold back her tears. She turned her head away and saw that they had found a priest, an old man, like the doctor, in a faded cassock, with a grave, unsmiling face. He walked unsteadily through the crowd, leaning on Brownlow's arm.

She heard Brownlow say forcefully, "We need a confession, Father. We need him to admit he's Wexford."

"That is not my function, Mr. Brownlow," the old priest demurred. "If, as you say, the man is dying, I will hear his confession and give him absolution. But the secret of the confessional is between this man and his God. I will not disclose one word of it, to you or anyone else. I—"

women and children and the wounded in the van, and later he had marched with them, first to Cawnpore and then to Allahabad, with William among those borne painfully on a litter, praying for a death that had been denied to him.

But there had been many other deaths, between June and the raising of the siege in November. The noble little General Havelock, exhausted by all he had endured, was buried in Lucknow —as was Sir Henry Lawrence, Lucknow's heroic defender—in an unmarked grave, to save it from desecration by the mutineers. William Peel, only slightly wounded in the final attack, had succumbed to cholera in the camp at Cawnpore; Colonel Neill, of the Madras Fusiliers, just promoted to the rank of brigadier general, had been shot down as Havelock's advance guard was making for the Residency. . . . Red sighed, wishing he might erase some of the more terrible memories from his mind.

Others, less exalted, had also died: soldiers and seamen, loyal sepoys, officers whose regiments had mutinied—as had William's in Ranpur—their defenseless women and children, even their servants and their pets. And, on the other side, countless rebels—sepoys and peasants, the Nana's followers—had been killed in battle, hanged, blown from the mouths of cannon, or shot as traitors, in a blind quest for vengeance by those who had seen or subsequently learned of the savage butchery that made the name Cawnpore a British battle cry.

Red saw that a boat was putting out from the shore, and raising his glass to his eye, he recognized the governor in the sternsheets. Signals exchanged earlier between the *Galah* and the South Head station had identified his ship and whence she had come, and he had been ordered to proceed to the anchorage in the cove, instead of the normal naval anchorage in Watson's Bay. The governor, it seemed, was anxious for news from India, and it was best that William De Lancey should give him a full, firsthand account. William was almost recovered now, although he was a gaunt, heartbroken shadow of the fine-looking man he had once been, haunted by Jenny's cruel death. Only his affection for the Melgund boy—the boy Jenny had saved—kept him from sinking into a state of melancholia. From all accounts, he had fought like a demon during General Havelock's brief and bloody engagements with the Nana's forces on the way to Lucknow, and, despite a complete disregard for his own safety, he had come through unscathed, until the last battle of all.

Francis De Lancey, the *Galah*'s first lieutenant, was at Red's side and looked at him inquiringly.

"His Excellency is on his way out to us, sir," Francis informed him. "I've assembled the side party."

He, too, had a wife and young family in Sydney, Red reflected, and clearly was wishing, as he himself was, that Governor Denison had postponed his visit to the ship until a more opportune moment. But he had not, and so . . . "My compliments to Colonel De Lancey, Francis," he said formally. "And ask him to come on deck to receive His Excellency, if you please."

"Aye, aye, sir," Francis acknowledged. He passed the order to the midshipman of the watch and added, lowering his voice, "I fancy my brother will have plenty to tell H.E., don't you? Shall I suggest that their consultation might be conducted at Government House?"

"You can suggest what you wish, Francis," Red returned, suppressing a smile. "Certainly my cabin might become a trifle overcrowded—I see that Colonel Macintyre is also anxious to be on hand to receive His Excellency."

He gestured to where Julia's stout, red-faced husband was standing, a hand shielding his eyes as he peered shortsightedly at the approaching boat in an attempt to identify its occupants. Dermot Macintyre had not enjoyed universal popularity with the *Galah*'s officers, despite their sympathy for all those who had served in the Lucknow garrison during the siege. He was a long-winded, opinionated little man, who expressed his views aggressively, and during the hurricane he had strained tolerance to its limit by his prophecies of doom and his criticism of the manner in which the ship had been handled. And his acid-tongued wife had made few friends among either her fellow passengers or the ship's company. Yet, Red reflected with sudden bitterness, she had survived the horrors of the mutiny, and Jenny, poor little Jenny, had died.

William stepped onto the deck at that moment, moving stiffly, the boy Andy, as always, at his side. They were seldom

"Then be damned to you!" Brownlow retorted angrily. "I'll get his admission myself." He sought to thrust Kitty aside, with a brusque "Make way, madam," but she jumped to her feet, holding up a hand imperiously, her eyes bright with an anger that outmatched his.

"You will not lay a finger on my brother, Mr. Brownlow," she told him with icy contempt. Brownlow halted, taken aback, and behind him the crowd of townsfolk voiced their indignation against him, Martha Higgins in the forefront, holding her sobbing young son by the hand.

"Like Mr. Dorman says, he saved the young lady's life," one of the men argued. "And at the cost of his own, seemingly. You're a brave gentleman," he called out to Michael. "For you'd no part in the raid, had you, sir? I seen you go into the bank minutes before the Lawless rogues went in. Aye, and I'd swear to it in a court of law, Mr. Brownlow!"

Shocked by their concerted hostility, Brownlow glared at them, his puffy, red face suffused with color. He rounded on Kitty. "If he's your brother, ma'am," he demanded thickly, "then tell us who he is. We'll take your word for it."

"His name is Michael Cadogan," Kitty began. She felt an arm go round her and realized that it was Johnny's. "And I have searched for him for—oh, for over a year, to bring him the royal pardon granted to him by Her Majesty the Queen. He is the Earl of—" she began, but Michael himself cut her short.

"No, Kit—no, in God's name!" He raised himself on one elbow, and his voice was suddenly loud and strong. "That title was never mine, and it belongs to Pat now. Let him do honor to it, since I cannot. Good people, you shall hear the truth—I'm Wexford. I absconded from Port Arthur, and I led the Lawless Gang . . . and I'm not ashamed of it," he added defiantly. "Now leave me with the priest, for I must confess to my sins before I go to meet my God. Perhaps, of His mercy, He will forgive me, for I swear to you I took no man's life."

The crowd moved back, Brownlow with them, in an oddly awed and respectful silence, and the old priest fell on his knees at Michael's side, murmuring a prayer.

Michael lived for half an hour after his confession had been heard, but the effort of making it had sapped what little remained of his failing strength, and he did not speak again until the end came. Kitty, with his hand clasped in hers, heard him whisper softly a name she knew was not her own, and then his hand slipped from her grasp and she sensed that he had gone . . . to join, perhaps, the woman whose name he had breathed, which had sounded like Lily.

She rose, stiff and drained of emotion, and Johnny gave her his arm.

"Mrs. Higgins has offered us rooms above her restaurant," Johnny said. "There are only two, but Luke and I can bunk in together. We thought you'd prefer that to staying in Brownlow's hotel."

Kitty thanked him gratefully and let him escort her out, the boy Tommy shambling awkwardly ahead of them to lead the way.

She said, when they reached the street, "I'm your wife, Johnny, and tonight I—I could not bear to be alone."

Johnny did not answer her, but she felt the warm pressure of his hand on her arm and knew that he had understood.

On the other side of the street, Tich Knight stood, the rein of his horse looped over his arm, and watched them cross and enter Martha Higgins's diner. He guessed what had happened from the expression on their faces and the little boy's tears, and he breathed a pent-up sigh, as the tension slowly drained out of him.

He had left the gang's horses tied up to the hitching rail, taking only his own, and no one had given him a second glance. He could have made a safe getaway a long time ago—when the shooting in the bank had first started, in fact—but something had held him back. He had seen Lily shot down and had sworn impotently at the waste of a young life. Poor little lass, she must have come to try to warn them, though heaven knew how she had managed to get to Urquhart Falls, for she was no horse-woman.

But . . . she must have found out that they had been betrayed, that the bloody troopers would be in the bank, waiting for them. And, if she had found out, there could be only one suspect, one person who had had the time and the opportunity . . . Dingo Carter! He had been absent from the Magpie for

said, "I hope Jessica will grow to be just like Rosie when she's five, Andy."

"Yes, I hope so too, sir," Andy agreed. He looked at William. "Rosie was awfully pretty, wasn't she, Uncle Will?"

It was, Red thought sadly, perhaps a fitting epitaph for those who had died in the infamous Bibigarh. Certainly for the one who was missing from this family gathering . . . His sister Jenny had been pretty, God rest her soul.

Magdalen's hand felt for his as he put his daughter down. "Tea," she said softly. "It's all ready. Let's go in, shall we?"

They went inside together.

HER MAJESTY'S STEAM-SCREW frigate *Kestrel* arrived in Port Jackson to relieve H.M.S. *Galah,* and the *Galah*'s commander, Red Broome, swore aloud as he watched the new arrival come to anchor in Watson's Bay.

His own ship had completed her refit only a week ago, and with the damage she had sustained on her passage from Calcutta now repaired, he was unhappily aware that he would have to sail for England as soon as he had handed over his responsibilities on the station to the *Kestrel*'s captain.

But . . . it would be inhospitable in the extreme were he not to make his successor welcome. A dinner party at his house, after the formalities were completed, would best fill the bill, Red decided. His wife, Magdalen, was a skilled hostess; she would be as distressed as he was by the *Kestrel*'s unexpectedly early arrival, yet he knew that he could depend on her to make the meal a memorable one, since it would be his farewell, as much as his relief's welcome.

He had cause, however, to regret his impulsive decision during the ensuing days. The *Kestrel*'s captain, Commander Rupert

Harland, proved to be considerably older than Red himself and several years senior in service, his lack of promotion the result of the findings of a court of inquiry, which had held him to blame for the death of a midshipman serving under his command in the West Indies.

The boy had been the only son of the Second Sea Lord, and because of that, Harland confided sourly, Their Lordships had kept him on half pay for the past five years. His appointment to the *Kestrel* had come only after the death of the vengeful old admiral, and the last station he had wanted was the one he had been ordered to take up.

"A damned convict colony!" he asserted belligerently. "And for two years, God forgive them, for I cannot! I'd give my eye teeth to exchange with you, Captain Broome. I've a wife and family in Dorset, and after skimping and saving on half pay for five long years, I can't afford to bring them out here."

And he, Red thought, as he listened with restraint to the tirade, would gladly have given more than his eye teeth to make the exchange, had that been possible.

His instinctive dislike of his successor came to a head within a week of first making his acquaintance. Claus Van Buren—now one of Sydney's most valued merchant traders—brought his beautiful American-built clipper *Dolphin* into port when Red was with Harland in the commodore's office, overlooking the cove. Harland had watched the schooner with admiring eyes—despite the fact that his command was powered by auxiliary steam, at heart he was a sailing ship man, which was a point in his favor—and, on his expressing interest in the beautifully designed vessel, Red offered to arrange a visit of inspection for him.

The visit went well initially, for Rupert Harland's interest was genuine, his knowledge of clipper design remarkably comprehensive, and his manner toward Claus, if a trifle condescending, was polite. Claus's wife, Mercy, and their two young sons were on board, and when the lengthy inspection was at last completed, Mercy came on deck to issue an invitation to the visitors to take refreshments in the great cabin.

Entering and observing the beautiful paneling and luxurious fittings of the cabin, the hand-carved dining table and chairs, the silver, cut glass, and exquisite bone china on the sideboard, Commander Harland was visibly impressed. He bowed over Mercy's hand and confessed his readiness to take a cup of tea, and as she poured it he continued the discussion he had been engaged in with Claus concerning the *Dolphin*'s rig and cargo-carrying capacity.

"I'm surprised you did not have her ship-rigged. If you want speed—and I presume you do, if you engage in the wool trade —I should have thought you—" He broke off, startled, his jaw dropping in shocked astonishment. "Who in the world—" The curtain covering the cabin doorway had parted, and the young Maori chieftain Tamihana came in, with the easy familiarity of long custom, to accept a teacup from Mercy Van Buren and take his seat at the table.

Red, aware of the chieftain's friendship with Claus, and having been previously introduced, greeted him by name, but Harland continued to stare at him as if he were an apparition from another world. With his heavily tattooed face and lithe, copper-colored body, which was naked save for the woven flax kilt draped about his waist, Tamihana's appearance as he solemnly sipped tea was, perhaps, understandably startling to a new-comer from England. Even so, Red was unprepared for his brother officer's reaction.

Harland leapt to his feet, his teacup falling from his hand, as he exclaimed furiously, "In God's name, Broome, you may have gone native, but I have not! I was prepared to stretch a point where Captain Van Buren was concerned, but I cannot be expected to sit down with a damned aboriginal savage. That's asking too much!"

Tamihana eyed him in mild surprise and then, carefully setting down his own cup, observed in faultless English, "If you will forgive me, Claus, I will go on deck with your boys. We were, as it happens, in the middle of a most entertaining game. Excuse me, please, Mrs. Van Buren."

No one spoke until the curtain had swung back behind him, and then Claus, with a warning shake of the head in Red's direction, said coldly, "The young man you have just insulted, Commander Harland, is not an Australian aboriginal. He is, in fact, a Maori—one of the most influential chieftains in New

Zealand's Bay of Islands, and an honored friend of mine." Harland attempted to interrupt him, but Claus would have none of it. "Hear me out, Commander. I spend a great deal of my time in New Zealand, where I have extensive trading interests. These are based and, indeed, are largely dependent on the friendly relations I have built up, over the years, with the Maori tribes. In all my dealings with them I regard them as equals, and I respect their culture, their standards, and their honesty. Sentiments which they reciprocate, sir."

Rupert Harland recovered himself. Very red of face, he retorted with a sneer, "That, for one of your color, is understandable, Captain Van Buren. Like calls to like, does it not? You—"

Angrily, Red attempted to restrain him, but once again Claus shook his head. "Permit me to explain the current state of affairs in New Zealand to this gentleman, Red, if you please. If he is to replace you on the Australasian station, it is important that he *should* understand."

"Then carry on," Red invited, tight-lipped.

"Certainly." Claus turned to face Harland. "I must tell you, sir, that there could well be war in New Zealand in the imminent future. Settlement has increased tenfold, and everywhere on the North Island it is expanding with alarming rapidity. And the settlers are bringing trouble on themselves. Too many of them are greedy and dishonest, and they pay scant heed to the Maoris' just rights and grievances. They cheat and dispossess them of their land, lull them with false promises, and fail even to make promised reparation for the vast acreages they have seized."

"New Zealand is a British colony," Harland blustered.

"True," Claus conceded. "But the Maoris were there many years before the first white man set foot on New Zealand soil. And, sir, the Maori people cannot be dealt with as the aborigines of Tasmania were—they cannot be banished to some barren island to die of disease and neglect. There are too many of them. They are a proud, strong, and warlike people—they will fight for what is theirs. And, sir, the settlers are in no state to join battle with them—they are farmers and merchant traders, like myself. If the Maori tribes are provoked into war, Commander Harland, it will take a great many of your Royal

Navy's ships and Her Majesty's fighting regiments to prevent a bloodbath. I would ask you to remember that, sir."

He looked across at Red and added regretfully, "I'm distressed to learn that you have been ordered to England, Red. I had hoped, I am bound to tell you, that you and Her Majesty's ship *Galah* would have been permitted to remain on this station, in order to pour oil on troubled waters."

His tone throughout had been conciliatory, but Rupert Harland was in no mood to respond to conciliation. He picked up his cap, jammed it wrathfully onto his head, and prepared to depart, glaring at Red when he remained seated.

"In my view," the *Kestrel*'s commander said spitefully, "the only way to deal with recalcitrant native populations is by force. It is all most of them understand. And if it's left to me, Van Buren, and your Maori friends engage in plotting and rebellion, my ship's guns will not be silent. There may be a bloodbath, but it will be Maori blood that is spilled, not British. I give you good day, sir."

He stormed out of the cabin, ignoring Mercy, and Red said apologetically, "Devil take him! I'm sorry I brought him aboard, Claus . . . Mercy."

"Let him go," Claus responded. "Stay with us for dinner, Red. You could not possibly have known how he was going to react. Besides," he added, smiling, "if you stay, you can at least pour some oil on Te Tamihana's troubled waters . . . and believe me, my friend, it is necessary. Some of the settlers' blood has already been spilled, and it only wants a spark to land us in full-scale war."

Rebels and outcasts, they fled halfway across the earth to settle the harsh Australian wastelands. Decades later— ennobled by love and strengthened by tragedy—they had transformed a wilderness into fertile land. And themselves into...

The Australians

WILLIAM STUART LONG

___THE EXILES, #1	12374-7	$4.95
___THE SETTLERS, #2	17929-7	$4.50
___THE TRAITORS, #3	18131-3	$4.50
___THE EXPLORERS, #4	12391-7	$4.50
___THE ADVENTURERS, #5	10330-4	$4.50
___THE COLONISTS, #6	11342-3	$4.50
___THE GOLD SEEKERS, #7	13169-3	$4.50
___THE GALLANT, #8	12785-8	$3.95
___THE EMPIRE BUILDERS, #9	12304-6	$3.95
___THE SEAFARERS, #10	20112-8	$4.95
___THE NATIONALISTS, #11	20354-6	$4.95

long enough to drive to town in the buggy and get back again, and, the devil roast him, he had been in the taproom, unnoticed and unsuspected, when they had discussed their plans for the robbery.

Well, he would settle with Dingo. The old swine had four deaths on his conscience, Tich reckoned. He had seen Boomer shot in the doorway of the bank and Marty wounded, seen them carry Ginger's lifeless body out, and watched the troopers lead Marty and Slugger away in irons, Slugger barely conscious. And the crowd had told him that the troopers had killed Michael. Of Chalky there had been no sign; but Chalky was a windy old sod and, like himself, had been in a position to make a run for it—the difference being that bloody Chalky *had* run and he hadn't.

Tich shifted his feet uneasily, as he saw the beautiful young woman and the two men who were with her go into Martha Higgins's back premises. He wondered who they were. Connections of Michael's, very probably . . . He frowned. Big Michael was not in the usual run of convicts—certainly not in the usual run of lifers, in his experience. Try to hide it though he had, Michael was a gentleman—that was plain to see—and his life, like poor little Lily's, had been wasted. They had flogged and tortured the poor devil on Norfolk Island, and that had made him what he was. . . . Tich sighed regretfully. A good man, Michael—a gallant gentleman, whom the blasted convict system had never broken or tamed. And he had done the impossible; he had made a successful escape from Port Arthur Penitentiary. Maybe someone, someday, would write his story down so that folk could read it and remember him.

But now— Tich pulled his horse to him and felt for his stirrup iron in the gathering darkness. He would go back to the Magpie and give Dingo what he deserved—he was the only one who could now, that was for sure.

He rode slowly and unchallenged out of town, and whistled softly as he went, a tune Michael had been wont to sing. Tich did not remember all the words, but the song began, "True patriots we, who left our country for our country's good . . ."

Perhaps, he thought, it was a fitting epitaph for Big Michael Wexford, a rebel out of Ireland.

Epilogue

THE FULL HORROR of the events in India during the mutiny of the sepoy Army of Bengal was brought home to the Australian colonists when H.M.S. *Galah* limped into Sydney Harbor, with a jury-rigged foremast and a six-foot-long gash on her starboard bow, just above the waterline.

Red was thankful to have brought his damaged frigate safely to port, for the hurricane that had come close to wrecking her in the Coral Sea had sent several other vessels to their doom, off the inhospitable coast of New Guinea. But she was home at last, and among her passengers were Julia Macintyre and her husband, with their four young children and a stepson. Also on board were William De Lancey—severely wounded in General Havelock's gallant attempt to relieve Lucknow—and a little boy named Andrew Melgund, whom he had adopted.

Red stood on the quarterdeck and looked about him as the signal gun fired the customary salute and he brought the *Galah* slowly to anchor. Sydney, in the early-morning sunlight, looked more beautiful than any city he had ever seen, he thought—more beautiful and infinitely more peaceful. In the thirteen months that he had been away, he had seen war at its most savage. He had seen the House of Women in Cawnpore in which his sister Jenny had met her death, and, attached to the naval brigade of H.M.S. *Shannon,* he had fought his way into Lucknow's beleaguered defenses. On the never-to-be-forgotten night when the *Shannon*'s gunners, under the command of Captain William Peel, had covered their escape route, he had witnessed the successful evacuation of the garrison, with the